THE QUEEN OF DEATH

THE LOST MARK BOOK 3

MATT FORBECK

THE QUEEN OF DEATH

The Lost Mark · Book 3

©2006 Wizards of the Coast, Inc.

Cover art by Adam Rex
Map by Rob Lazzaretti
First Printing: October 2006
Library of Congress Catalog Card Number: 2005935543

9 8 7 6 5 4 3 2 1

ISBN-10: 0-7869-4012-3
ISBN-13: 978-0-7869-4012-7
620-95540740-001-EN

U.S., CANADA,
ASIA, PACIFIC, & LATIN AMERICA
Wizards of the Coast, Inc.
P.O. Box 707
Renton, WA 98057-0707
+1-800-324-6496

EUROPEAN HEADQUARTERS
Hasbro UK Ltd
Caswell Way
Newport, Gwent NP9 0YH
GREAT BRITAIN
Save this address for your records.

Visit our web site at www.wizards.com

Praise for *Marked for Death*, the first book in the Lost Mark trilogy . . .

"A rousing action-packed science-fiction/ fantasy novel, full of unknown and wondrous creatures . . . sword fights, flying ships, magical creatures, and magic that left me wondering what was going to happen next."

— *The Arbiter*

THE LOST MARK
BY MATT FORBECK

Book One
MARKED FOR DEATH

Book Two
THE ROAD TO DEATH

Book Three
THE QUEEN OF DEATH

DEDICATION

For the Beloit Catholic High Class of 1986.
Time and distance cannot keep friends apart.

Special thanks to Mark Sehestedt, Peter Archer,
Christopher Perkins, and Keith Baker.

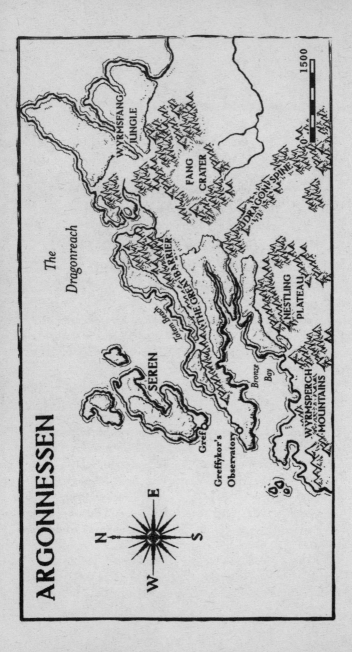

CHAPTER

1

I said we're going to Argonnessen to take on the dragons, and I meant it," said Kandler.

He scowled down at Monja, the halfling shaman who'd joined them when they'd passed through the Wandering Inn. Bringing her along at the time had seemed like a good idea—they'd needed a healer like her, and Burch had vouched for her—but now Kandler wondered if bringing on another passenger had been worth it.

Monja arched an eyebrow at Kandler. She stood on the lower part of the airship's wheel so she could see over the bridge's console as she steered the ship. A natural flyer who'd spent many hours in the air atop the scaly glide-wings the halflings of the Talenta Plains sometimes used as mounts, she'd made quick work of mastering the ship. For that, at least, she'd proved her worth—that and the way she'd brought Kandler and Sallah back from the brink of death just the night before.

"She just asked how wise that was, boss," Burch said. The shifter sat perched on his bare feet atop the back rail of the bridge. The cold winds whistling down off the Ironroot

Mountains to the east ruffled the long, black mane of hair that swept back from his deep-tanned, feral face. "Fair enough?"

Kandler wanted to snarl at his old friend, but he knew he needed as many people on his side as he could. Angering someone who'd always had his back wouldn't help that.

"Look," he said, glancing at each of the others. "It may not be a great plan, but it's the only one we have."

Xalt nodded. Kandler hadn't known the warforged long, but he had proven himself trustworthy over and over. If Xalt saw the logic in Kandler's reasoning, then the justicar could feel confident in his own judgment. As a creature born in the forges of war—or those of House Cannith—his impassive face seemed impossible to read.

Duro, the dwarf who'd led Kandler and the others deep into the heart of the mountains to find the lair of the dragon Nithkorrh, grunted and ran a hand through his long, brown beard. "My people lived under a dragon's shadow for centuries. That was just one. Taking on a whole continent filled with the winged beasts . . ."

Sallah nodded in agreement, the sun glinting off her red curls and her battered armor. When Kandler had first met her only a few weeks back, the steel had glimmered like a mirror. Both it and she had been through much since then.

"We should head straight for Thrane," she said, no hint of doubt in her voice. "The Church will take us in and provide us sanctuary."

A wry grin twisted Te'oma's flat lips like a fold in a seam of fabric. "Can you protect the girl there as well as you did in Mardakine?"

"We were but five knights then," Sallah said, her emerald eyes flashing. The fact that she now stood alone, the other knights—including her father—dead, added to the frustration in her tone. "In Flamekeep, we would have an army to protect her."

"It wouldn't be enough," said Esprë.

The young elf had said little since dawn had broken over the mountains off the port bow. All eyes turned to her now.

Although she looked younger than any of the others, Esprë was at least twice as old as Kandler. Elves took far more time to reach maturity than any of the other races, and with luck she would live many times longer than Kandler had any hope for himself.

Despite this, Kandler couldn't help but think of her as a little girl—his little girl, in fact. She looked just like she had the day he'd married her mother Esprina years before, and he could still see his dead wife every time he looked at her face. She was all he had left of his wife, and he planned to fight for her to his last breath.

"Kandler is right," Esprë said. "Too many people want me dead. I can't hide forever."

Sallah put her hand on the girl's shoulder. Her gauntlet looked massive next to Esprë's face. "You wouldn't have to hide in Flamekeep," she said. "The Silver Flame will protect you."

"Might as well paint a target on her forehead," Burch said as he took his crossbow from across his back and checked its action. "Soon as the world knows where she is, it's over."

"We have to take the fight to her attackers," said Kandler.

"Didn't say that either." Burch pulled the trigger, and the string on his empty weapon twanged.

Duro snorted. "You think you can hide her away, like a treasure under a mountain? My people have tried that time and again, friend. It never works."

"I made a life of it." The shifter leaned back against the rail behind him.

"Vol managed to locate her once before," Te'oma said. "She will do so again."

"Sure," Burch said. Satisfied, he slung his weapon across his back again and slipped off his perch. "If you stay put. A moving target, that's a lot harder to hit."

"It's not just that horrible lich after her," Sallah said, sweeping her hair back from her face. "It's everyone. If I do not return soon, Jaela Daran will send other knights after me. Every nation of power has an interest in the dragonmark that Esprë bears. Karrnath knows about her now, too. Do you think the Captain of Bones has not already sent word of the reappearance of the Mark of Death back to King Kaius?"

Kandler rubbed his eyes. Too many things threatened Esprë at once. He couldn't possibly take on them all—at least not at once.

"One thing at a time," he said. "We can't sit around and wait for someone to come and kidnap Esprë again—or kill her instead. We have to take the fight to them."

"To whom?" Sallah asked. "The dragons of Argonnessen? Or the Blood of Vol? Or the Emerald Claw? Or the elves of Aerenal? They all want her dead."

Kandler bit back a snarl. The start of a romance had blossomed between Sallah and him. After Esprina died, he'd given up on that kind of love ever finding him again. Still, he refused to let his feelings for the lady knight influence his thinking about keeping his step-daughter safe.

He'd hoped that Sallah would side with him, but he should have known better. Sallah had lost so much already on her quest to bring Esprë safely to Thrane. She wouldn't give up hope of accomplishing her own goal. She couldn't.

"We start at the top," Kandler said. "We take down the dragons after her, and we send a signal to the others."

Monja giggled. To Burch, she said, "Is he always so silly? 'Take down the dragons.' Ha!"

"I'm not joking," Kandler said.

Monja lost her smile. "Then you are a bigger fool than you seem," she said. "You cannot expect to destroy all those dragons. We only barely managed to kill one yesterday—one."

"Challenging them all is folly," Duro said, "but we don't have to. Having guarded a dragon's lair for many years, I know a thing or two about those creatures. Fact is if you ask three dragons a question, you get nine different answers. They can't agree on a damned thing."

"Not even destroying the Mark of Death?" Xalt said. "The dragons put a halt to a war against the elves to eradicate that dragonmark once. It seems able to inspire an amazing level of diplomacy among mortal foes."

"That's why we're going to Aerenal first," said Kandler, "to ask for the elves' help."

"The pointy-eared bastards will kill us all," said Duro. He shifted his weight and scratched his neck. "Well, me for sure. They don't much care for dwarves, I hear."

"Didn't you want to go to the Wandering Inn first?" Monja asked Kandler. "My people won't be much help against the dragons, I'm sure, but they can get us well fed before we head off."

"It could take us days to find the place," said Kandler, "and it's not in the right direction. Burch tells me there's an outpost in the Goradra Gap we can hit for supplies."

Sallah frowned. "I say we put this to a vote. That should appeal to your Brelish sense of fair play."

Kandler shook his head. "Breland's no democracy, and this ship isn't either."

"You don't own this ship," Te'oma said. "You stole her from that crazed elf."

"You didn't even do that," Sallah said. "Burch did. She's his ship."

Kandler rolled his eyes. "Burch?" he said, still staring at Sallah.

"I'll back your play, boss, right or wrong." The shifter reached out and put an arm around Esprë. She clung to his side.

"Esprë's my responsibility, and I'm taking her to Argonnessen by way of Aerenal." Kandler looked at each of the others. "If any of you want off the ship, we'll drop you off somewhere on the way."

CHAPTER

2

"Y ou sure know how to win 'em over, boss," Burch said as he padded up behind Kandler, who stood at the ship's prow, staring out at the ice-capped mountains beyond.

"I'm a soldier, not a diplomat."

Burch showed his teeth. "That's clear."

The two stood silent for a moment.

"How long until they mutiny?" Kandler asked.

Burch grunted. "Not sure. Figure we got at least three on our side—you, me, and Esprë. Sallah thinks you're nuts, and Te'oma—well, she's hard to figure, but she probably does too. Monja, she'll follow my lead, at least until we hit the sea. Same for Xalt, though he'll stick around until the ship falls apart."

The shifter leaned out over the railing to inspect the rune-carved restraining arcs that held in place the ring of elemental fire that kept the *Phoenix* aloft. "Which might not be all that long the way she's looking."

"That's five for us and two against. I should have taken a vote."

Burch shook his head. "Wouldn't have changed anything.

7

Thought she liked you better than that though."

Kandler ignored Burch's leer. "How long until we reach the Gap?"

The shifter stared out at the mountains and said, "Another day. Maybe a bit more."

Kandler looked back and saw Duro coming up behind them.

"Don't tell me you're still planning to head to Goradra," the dwarf said. "I know we've not known each other all that long, but please don't tell me that."

"What's wrong with the Gap?" Kandler said.

Duro eyed Burch before responding. "Haven't you told him anything about it?"

"It's a big hole in the ground," Kandler said. "We're in an airship."

"It's not just a big hole," Duro said. "It's the deepest hole in the world. It tumbles down so far that sunlight can't ever reach the bottom, even at high noon. They say it doesn't stop until it hits Khyber itself."

"Who says that?" asked Burch.

"Everyone."

"Everyone?" Burch smiled. "I don't say that."

"You know what I mean." The dwarf scowled. Kandler saw that he'd hoped Burch would help him talk some sense into the justicar, but the shifter had turned against him instead.

"Have you been there?" Burch said. "I have. Looked right down into that pit."

"You say it doesn't reach Khyber?" Duro said, daring the shifter to gainsay him.

"I didn't say that either."

"Stop playing—"

"It doesn't matter. If it does reach Khyber, it's so far down that the demons there would take years to climb up it, and you'd see them coming a mile away."

"What about falling into it?" Duro said with a shiver. "You could tumble through that bottomless shaft for hours."

"Thought you said it bottomed out in Khyber?" Burch smiled. "Either way, it doesn't matter if it's a hundred feet down or a hundred thousand. You fall that far, you're dead when you land. A longer fall just gives you more time to think about it."

Duro's eyelids twitched. "Can't we just resupply someplace else? Why bother with Gaptown?"

"It's right out there in the open," Kandler said. "It's easy to reach by airship. Anything else in this area means a dwarf settlement, and that means crawling deep under the mountains."

"My people will welcome us at any of our homes along the entire range. You would be my honored guests. As the slayers of Nithkorrh, we would be welcomed as heroes and treated like kings."

Kandler shook his head. "It's tempting, but if we stop moving, we become a target. We can't afford to waste that much time."

Duro looked hurt. "Time spent in a dwarf city is never a waste—it's an investment. If you could see the halls of Krona Peak, you would find yourself drawn to spending hour upon hour contemplating their stark beauty. The works of mankind have nothing to compare."

"Time to meditate upon the wonders of dwarf society is exactly what we don't have."

"Krona Peak lies right along our path. If we proceed along the Ironroot Mountains here, we will practically pass over it."

Kandler gazed down at the dwarf for a moment. "If you want us to drop you off there—"

Duro cut him off with a sharp snap of his head. "Not at all. I would only suggest—"

9

"Why not?" said Burch. "Come with us, and the best you can hope for's to choose which kind of dragon tears off your head."

Duro snorted. "I am not some child to be frightened by such talk. If you thought so little of our chances, would you bring the elfling along with you?"

Kandler glared at the dwarf. "There's no safer place for her than with me."

"Even when you fly into the dragons' collective maw? We could leave her with my people. They would care for her as their own. Then we could assault the dragons, free from the fear that she might be killed in the effort."

"You'd still come with us then?" Kandler asked, trying not to sound so surprised.

Duro smiled wide beneath his bushy beard. "I am no coward. I spent years guarding the den of that damned dragon beneath my clan's mountain. Now that job is over, and I find that I have an itch to see the world beyond. I can think of no better calling than to save a youngling by battling even more dragons in open combat."

"You're sunstruck," said Burch. "I've seen it in dwarves before. All that time stuck in those dark caves, you get a taste of fresh air and you go mad."

Duro's grin never slackened. "Think what you will. Some of my clan might agree with you. I might once have too, but if my insanity can serve a greater purpose, then so be it."

"We'll try Goradra first," said Kandler. "If that doesn't pan out for supplies, we'll make a quick stop at Krona Peak." He glanced between the dwarf and the shifter. They both nodded at him, content for now.

❦

"You don't have to listen to him, you know," Sallah said to Esprë.

The girl stared up at the lady knight. Up in the thin, cold air, the warmth of the clear, bright sun only managed to take the edge off the chill, but Sallah never seemed to notice it. Did the knight's Silver Flame burn so warmly in her as to ward off all such discomforts?

As Esprë shuddered in the open breeze swirling around and through her, Xalt came up from behind her and wrapped a blanket around her shoulders. "I found this in the hold," he said. "Some of the workers at Fort Bones must have been sleeping there between shifts."

The elf smiled her thanks at the warforged and reached out to caress his metallic cheek.

"You are older than he," Sallah said. "You are ready to come of age yourself and make your own decisions."

Esprë nodded. She heard the wisdom in Sallah's words, but the knight's clear desire to bring the elf back to Flamekeep made her wary.

"Do you love him?" Esprë asked.

Sallah froze. She wore her defiance on her taut lips and her jutted chin. When she spoke again, though, her face relaxed, and she looked more human in a way that Esprë knew that Xalt could never have managed.

"I believe I do," said Sallah. "My head swirls about as if caught in a whirlwind when I am with him."

"That's just the altitude," Te'oma said as she slipped up behind the others.

Sallah scowled at the changeling. "You are fortunate that we didn't dump you overboard the moment the dragon died. After all you've done—"

"That's gratitude for you," Te'oma said, arching a pale eyebrow. She ran a finger along Xalt's back, right where she had plunged a dagger into him back in the warforged city of Construct. "You'd think saving everyone's lives would change a few minds."

"Burch brought down that dragon," Sallah said. "You only saved his life because he clung so tightly to you that you had no choice."

Te'oma's face blurred for a moment, and Sallah found herself staring into her father's eyes. "Does the Silver Flame not teach us to forgive?"

Esprë stepped between the two as Sallah's sword leaped from its scabbard and burst into flames. She knew that the knight would not harm her, but she didn't know how long she could manage to keep the pair apart.

Sallah held her blazing blade before her. "You desecrate my father's memory," she spat at the changeling, "and you tempt death by mocking me with it."

"Perhaps," Te'oma said, taking Sallah's own form instead, "you'd prefer to look your hypocrisy in the face."

Esprë flung her arms up to protect herself from the enraged knight. As she did, she felt the changeling's presence behind her disappear. Then something heavy thudded against the ground.

Esprë spun about and spied Te'oma lying face down on the deck, Xalt's heavy form atop her. The warforged had the changeling's arm twisted behind her back, and her face—her own face now—contorted in pain.

"You shall cease to take our forms," Xalt said, "or those of people we love. If you do so again, I will be forced to mark you so that we can always tell you apart from those others."

"How will you manage that?" Te'oma said, sneering through the pain as the warforged gave her arm a terrible wrench.

"I do not think your powers allow you to replace a missing limb."

"That's enough," Esprë said. She felt the dragonmark on her back start to itch. "You made your point."

Xalt looked into the elf's eyes and let the changeling go.

He jumped back to his feet and let Te'oma pull herself up on her own.

"We need to work together," Esprë said. "When you hope to take on a force made of dragons, you need all the friends you can get."

Despite this, Esprë refused to lend Te'oma a hand up. She recalled too well how the changeling had kidnapped her and intended to trade her to the Lich Queen in exchange for the resurrection of her own long-dead daughter.

"True," Sallah said, "but we also need to remove every other enemy in our way."

With that, the lady knight stalked off, sheathing her blade as she went.

"Thank you," Te'oma said to Esprë.

"Don't," the elf said. "I don't like you any more than she does. In other circumstances, I'd let her and Xalt toss you overboard."

"Why don't you?" Te'oma asked.

CHAPTER

3

We're here, boss."

Kandler woke at Burch's touch and lowered himself from one of the hammocks hanging in the *Phoenix's* hold. He reached out into the dim light streaming through the open hatch and touched the edge of Esprë's hammock. It swayed light and loose on its anchors.

"She's up top already," Burch said. "Got the wheel."

Kandler grunted, wondering if he'd been the only one to sleep so late. Despite the healing magic Monja had worked on his flesh, his muscles still ached from the battle against Nithkorrh. He felt the new-made scars, marveling at them. He'd felt his lifeblood flowing out through them yesterday, yet here he stood. He'd been given another chance at life, and he intended to make the most of it.

He took Ibrido's fangblade sword from where he'd hung it next to the hammock, and he strapped its belt around his waist. As he pulled on his boots, he saw Duro, Monja, and Sallah rousing themselves.

"Where's the changeling?" Kandler said as he followed Burch up through the hatch.

"Scouting duty," the shifter said, pointing at the sky. "Wanted to stretch her bloodwings."

"You left her out here with Esprë?" Kandler tried to keep the irritation from his voice. Even though he knew he couldn't fool Burch, the shifter would appreciate the effort.

"Xalt's with her."

Kandler squinted as he climbed into the morning sun. The crisp breeze swept away the warmth of the hold that had surrounded him. Mountains loomed to the east, closer now than they had been at sunset. An eagle spun in the sky off the port bow, circling over a wooded plateau, hunting for prey.

"Where is it?" Kandler said.

Burch pointed over at the port rail and hooked his finger down. Kandler waved at Esprë as he followed his friend over to the ship's edge, and she and Xalt waved back. Kandler hadn't seen her smile so freely in months, since before the strange killings had begun in Mardakine. The sight warmed his heart.

Kandler reached the railing and peered over it. All thoughts fled from his head.

The Goradra Gap stretched below them like a gigantic wound in the earth, inflicted during some horrible war among gods. Even at its narrowest point, it had to be a mile across, and it stretched east to west across the mountain range for several leagues, so far that Kandler could not see the end of it, despite how high the *Phoenix* sailed.

Snowcapped mountains surrounded it in all directions, but nearer to the edge of the gap the land turned green and fertile. Then it fell off into nothing, as if the world was hollow underneath and had given into gravity's insistent pull. The land had sheared away here, exposing striated layers of rock stacked on each other forever.

Kandler stared down into the abyss and realized he could not see its bottom. It fell away from him for what seemed like a mile or more before the shadows there swallowed it whole. Just looking into it made Kandler's head spin.

"Quite a drop," Burch said.

Kandler shook his head and looked back at the shifter, aware that he had been leaning over the railing just a bit too far. "Where's the settlement?"

The shifter pointed a clawed finger at the Gap's northern wall. There, about a hundred yards or more down from the Gap's edge, hung a series of scaffolds, ladders, and platforms strung together with rickety stairwells or rope bridges that hung in a perpetual breeze that gusted up from the depths of the gap. From this distance, the buildings looked small and fragile, something that could be brushed from the wall like dust from a window.

"The buildings front a series of tunnels that run through the cliff," said Burch. "Place is like an anthill. Can't see all the activity underneath."

"What do they call it?" Sallah asked as she joined Kandler and Burch at the railing.

"A classic example of reckless idiocy," said Burch, turning to smirk at the knight. "It wouldn't take much to bring that whole thing down."

Duro, who stood next to Sallah scowled. "The dwarves of Clan Nroth are renowned as some of the finest architects of our age. That place has more buttresses flying about it than one of your flimsy cathedrals."

"I'd stay within a quick dash to the *Phoenix* at all times, and don't tie the mooring lines too tight."

"Always on the look for a quick getaway, eh?"

"Rather not see the ship pulled down with the rest of the place."

"I meant, what is its name?" Sallah said.

Kandler noticed the airship had turned so that her prow aimed straight for a prominent terrace that jutted out from the largest of the buildings attached to the gap's north wall.

"Durviska," Duro said, still glaring at Burch.

"That's Dwarven for 'Watch that last step,'" the shifter said.

"It means 'Overlook,' flatlander!"

Burch smiled down at the dwarf, showing all of his fang-like teeth.

"Let's get those mooring lines ready," Kandler said to Burch. He grabbed the shifter by the shoulder and pointed him toward the stern.

Burch winked at the justicar and trotted off. Kandler glanced at Sallah, but she looked away. He shrugged and made for the line near the bow.

Kandler respected Burch's advice. They'd only use two lines to tie off at the side of that terrace, which looked more and more like a dock as they approached it. Ropes this thick would hold the airship in place as she floated there above the Gap, but a few quick hacks with a sword would get the *Phoenix* moving again in a pinch.

Kandler thought of the dragonfang blade riding on his hip, the one with which Ibrido had nearly killed him. A single slice from that blade would sever the rope's fibers like a scythe cutting hay, he guessed. He wondered what dragon had given up a tooth for the weapon or what another dragon might think to see it in a human's hand. If his plans worked out, he'd have the chance to find out.

As the airship neared the dock, which jutted out a dozen yards from the building's face, a squad of dwarves padded out from a wide set of doors in the middle of the place. They fanned out along the wood-railed edge and signaled their readiness to catch a mooring line and tie it fast.

Kandler spotted a sign swinging free over the place's door. It depicted a winged dwarf diving into the open air. The words emblazoned below it in crystal letters set into the dark, weathered wood read THE FLYING LEAP.

The justicar tossed a coil of rope to one of the waiting dwarves, and Burch did the same. Before their fellows had even moored the ship tight, the others dwarves toted out a wide, railed gangplank and tossed it out to hook onto the *Phoenix*'s port rail.

Duro leaped up on to the plank and sauntered down to the open dock. Sallah and Esprë stood at the railing, waiting for Kandler and Burch. Monja peered out over the wheel now, having taken it from Esprë, and Xalt stood next to her, peering down over the ship's aft rail as if he could plumb the abyss with his unblinking ebony eyes.

"Hail and well met!" a deep voice from inside the building boomed. A white-haired dwarf with a loose, bushy beard stomped out after it, grinning up at the newcomers. "Welcome to my hang-out!"

Duro met the dwarf at the bottom of the gangplank, and they grasped each other's arms in greeting.

"Krangel Mrothdalt of Clan Nroth," the elderly dwarf said. Despite his years, he seemed hale enough to take Duro in two falls out of three.

"Duro Darumnakt of Clan Drakyager. These are my friends. Treat them as you would a fellow dwarf."

The snow-haired dwarf raised a craggy eyebrow. "Drakyager, eh? How does the dragon treat you?"

Duro beamed at his host. "Nithkorrh is no more. These folk slew the dragon, blasting his cursed corpse from the sky."

Every dwarf on the platform—and a number more peering out at the newcomers through the windows that lined the building's front—stared at Kandler and the others in disbelief. For a moment, Kandler feared the dwarves might pluck the gangplank from under him, just as he'd started to lead Esprë on to it. Then Krangel tossed back his head and laughed.

"Excellent!" the host said, clapping Duro on the back hard enough to make Kandler wince. "That tale alone might be enough to pay for your cots here tonight—even more if it's true!"

Kandler sighed with relief then took Esprë by the hand and led her down to the dock. Sallah followed close on his heels, with Burch right behind.

Kandler looked back to see Xalt and Monja waving at them as they disembarked. He scanned the sky, but the changeling seemed to have disappeared. Perhaps she'd taken her leave of them, but Kandler couldn't believe she'd go that easily. He wasn't that lucky.

"Come in! Come in!" Krangel said. "I've never seen such a motley crew in such dire need of a cold ale!"

CHAPTER

4

Te'oma spun high above the Goradra Gap, letting her wings carry her higher and higher as she circled on the warm updraft flowing up from the depths. She hadn't felt safe sleeping in the hold with the others, so she'd curled up on the deck, her back to the ship's console and her cloak wrapped tight around her. Although the others hadn't said anything, she could sense their gratitude that she'd chosen to bed down away from them.

Although Te'oma had risked her life to help save Esprë, she'd been the one who put the young elf into such dangerous circumstances in the first place. Never mind the fact that she'd done so in a desperate attempt to convince the Lich Queen to bring her long-dead daughter back from Dolurrh. To these people—and to Kandler and Burch in particular—she was an irredeemable villain who could never be trusted.

In truth, this didn't bother Te'oma much. As a changeling, she'd had few friends throughout her life, and she didn't see the need for them. She preferred to stand on her own at all times, as life had long since taught her that relying on anyone else would only lead to disastrous disappointments.

The only person Te'oma had ever loved had been her daughter, and she'd done a poor job of caring for her. She'd left her to be raised by others, and they hadn't protected the shapeshifting girl from the deadly fury of an angry mob.

Although Te'oma had not spent much time in her daughter's presence, she'd established a telepathic link with the girl from the first possible moment, and she'd kept in contact with the girl every day since. No matter how far apart Te'oma's journeys placed them, she could always reach out and converse with her daughter's mind.

Te'oma was a thousand miles away the day her daughter died. She'd known that trouble had been brewing, but she had no way to reach the girl in time. Her daughter died with her screams echoing in Te'oma's head.

When the first rays of the sun broke over the lowest points of the Ironroot Mountains, Te'oma had been dreaming about her daughter. She woke to find that she'd been weeping in her sleep. This sort of thing happened to her far too often these days, which was yet another reason for her to sleep away from the others.

"Are you hurt?" Esprë had said.

Te'oma had looked up to see the young elf peering at her over the bridge's inside railing. She had known her face probably looked wet and puffy, but in a flash she'd morphed it back into its standard, unreadable state.

"Never better," she'd said. She'd stood and let her cloak unfurl around her, the leathery edges flapping in the breeze as it spread out into wide, batlike wings.

"Wait," Esprë had said before the changeling could flap away.

Te'oma had leaped into the air and turned about, her wings beating fast enough to keep her hovering the air before the bridge. Xalt, the warforged, had stood beside the girl, his hand on a knife tucked into his belt. Esprë had kept her hands on the wheel, keeping the airship on an even keel.

The elf-maid had stared up at the changeling for a moment then opened her mouth and said, "Thanks."

Te'oma had nodded and flung herself high into the air. Whirling her way around the barely restrained elemental ring of fire that encircled the ship, she peeled off into the sky and let the wind carry her away.

The changeling spent more than an hour swirling and soaring through the sky on her own, always keeping the airship within sight. For a long while, she'd considered finding a tailwind and riding it to wherever it might take her, letting fate determine her path. She'd done that for much of her life, wandering wherever her whims led her, using her shapeshifting powers to slip in and out of places nearly unseen.

Te'oma rarely made any sort of impression on those she left behind. She stayed in one place just long enough to grab some rest and steal whatever she needed, then moved on. Most of her victims never even realized they'd been robbed.

After taking part in this strange adventure, in helping the others slay a dragon, she didn't know if she could go back to that. She knew that if she left she'd likely never see the others again, never take part in the end of this amazing tale.

Of course, she still had the telepathic bond she'd forged with Esprë. Through that, she could keep in touch with the girl and discover her ultimate fate. When she thought of that, though, and the likely outcome—the elf-maid's death—she didn't think she could stand to go through feeling a girl die like that again.

She mulled over severing the bond, but that would cut her off from the girl. She didn't know if she could bear that either. She'd been prepared to try, though, right up until Esprë had said that single word to her as she left the ship.

Damn, damn, damn, Te'oma thought as she turned back toward the *Phoenix*, fighting a headwind. A fool never takes the easy way.

Fortunately, the ship had been heading in her direction the entire time. If the changeling hadn't known better, she'd have thought the ship had been chasing her instead of heading straight along the edge of the mountain range.

As the ship reached the Goradra Gap, Te'oma raced ahead of her, spiraling higher into the air whenever she found a thermal she could ride. Her wings tired easily, and only by working with the winds rather than against them could she remain aloft for long.

Te'oma spotted the Flying Leap clutched tight to the canyon's northern wall and knew that this would be the *Phoenix*'s destination. She spied lookouts stationed in blinds high atop the ridge, and she guessed that they would relay news of the airship's arrival to the dwarves below in plenty of time for them to be ready for her arrival.

Hoping the lookouts might think her nothing more than an eagle or hawk, Te'oma flapped off to the east, directly along the seam of the Goradra Gap. This put her on a direct path toward the blinding sun, which soon hid her form from anyone scouring the sky for her from the direction of the Flying Leap.

Te'oma opened her wings there and let them take her in broad, sweeping circles over the gaping, bottomless chasm. When she looked down, it felt like she might be spiraling about over a starless sky. All she had to do to let it take her would be to fold her wings against her, to let them envelope her in their warmth, and allow gravity to establish its hold on her once more.

Instead, she wrenched her gaze back toward the Flying

Leap. She watched as the a number of the people on the *Phoenix* strode down a gangway and stood talking with a clutch of dwarves on a dock that stuck out into the unprotected air like a wooden giant's tongue.

From this distance, she couldn't be sure who had left the ship and who had stayed behind. Esprë stood shorter than most, but so did the dwarf and the halfling. She could distinguish Sallah by the way the sun glinted off her armor as she stood on the dock, but the others were harder to pick out. Soon she gave up trying.

Only two people remained on the ship, while five disappeared inside the inn. Te'oma considered sweeping down to join them, but the thought of having to deal with twitchy dwarves kept her away.

Then a body fell from one of the lookout blinds. It tumbled down into the gap without a sound, its limbs flinging about as it spun helplessly.

Te'oma guessed that whoever it happened to be was already dead. She tore her gaze away from the first body just in time to spy a second one plummeting out of the other blind.

Te'oma hovered in the air, hanging there on her flapping wings, staring at the blinds. A rope spilled out of one and then the other. The ends of each landed atop the slanted roof of the Flying Leap. No one stood on the deck any longer, and the pair of figures on the bridge of the *Phoenix* seemed oblivious to the danger, their backs turned to the inn as they gazed over the airship's other side at the vast, magnificent canyon beyond.

A handful of figures slipped out of each of the blinds and down the ropes. They zipped down the lines and lit on the inn's roof like finches finding fresh perches. Even from her spot hanging in the sky, though, Te'oma could tell these were murderous birds of prey.

CHAPTER

5

Esprë had never been in a dwarf inn before. Ibrido had led her through the abandoned halls under Mount Darumkrak, but that didn't count. The only dwarves she'd seen there had been Duro and his compatriots, the warriors charged with the defense of the dragon's lair. Hospitality had been the least of their concerns.

She looked around, eyes wide, as she strode into the place at Kandler's side. For a moment, she had an urge to hold his hand, but she suppressed it. She'd been through too much lately to think of herself as a child anymore, no matter how much she might yearn for the comforts of childhood.

The floor of the inn commanded Esprë's attention first. The dock outside the inn had been fashioned from wood, as had the roof, face, and every other part of the building that jutted out from the front of the canyon's sheer face. Inside, though, the entire floor seemed to be made from a single, large flat stone cut to a perfectly flat surface.

Esprë couldn't guess at what kind of dwarf architecture had been employed to keep the floor from toppling into the abyss. Perhaps it had been a natural shelf on the cliff face, or maybe the dwarves of Clan Nroth had carted up piece after piece and fitted them together so tight that no eye could find a seam.

The walls of the rear part of the inn's main hall were made of the same stone, and every surface bore some sort of carving, either runes or artistic depictions of the history of the clan or perhaps just Krangel's direct line. A dozen wooden tables squatted about the place, each of them made for customers with the dimension of dwarves. While Esprë could sit at one of these comfortably enough, she had to stifle a giggle at the thought of how Kandler, Burch, or especially Sallah would look perched atop the tiny, sturdy chairs sitting around the tables.

"Come in!" Krangel said. "It's not often we get outsiders around here." The snow-haired dwarf cocked a finger at a young dwarf behind the low, marble-topped bar. "Raumeese! Bring out the big folk's table!"

The dwarf, who'd been staring at the newcomers in stunned silence, leaped to his feet and scurried out of the room. The other patrons in the room—perhaps a dozen dwarves—snorted at Raumeese as he left. A few of them nodded a greeting to Esprë and the others if they happened to catch their eyes, but the others returned to their food and drink.

The smell of food made Esprë's mouth water. She'd not had a proper meal since her last night at Fort Bones, and that seemed like a lifetime ago. It had been far longer since she'd been in an inn of any kind. There never had been one in Mardakine.

"You don't get other airships through here?" Kandler asked. Esprë heard the suspicion in his voice.

Burch scanned the place pointedly. "Awful lot of effort to build a dock like that and not use it." He spied a nervous dwarf woman staring at him and flashed her a toothy grin.

She flinched and looked away.

"We get some," Krangel said, "just not as many as we'd like. Still, lots of clansfolk come up here for the view. When a trader airship comes through, you should see this place. People crushed in here from wall to wall, tighter than a collapsing mineshaft. Now, though"—he waved his hand around—"nothing but room to sprawl."

The door through which Raumeese had disappeared swung open again, and a round tabletop rolled out through it on its edge. Raumeese followed close after it, guiding it to an open spot in the floor near to where Krangel stood.

When the young dwarf pulled the tabletop to a stop, Esprë wondered if Krangel meant for his new guests to sit on the floor. With a slap of Raumeese's hand, four legs sprang from the bottom of the table, and he tipped it up onto them. It stood at a level comfortable for humans, and the young dwarf trotted off again.

He returned a moment later with a stack of wood in his arms. With one hand, he drew a bundle of wood from the top of the stack and snapped his wrist. The wood unfolded into a finely crafted chair made of thin dowels crisscrossed against each other to fashion a sturdy seat. He snapped out five chairs in all, then gave the newcomers a sharp, short bow and dashed back behind the bar.

"Thanks for your trouble," Kandler said. He didn't appear impressed at all, just worried. "We can't stay long, though. We just need some supplies: food, water."

Krangel's face dropped. "We can help you with that, sure, but please impose upon our hospitality." He looked them up and down. "I can't remember the last time I saw a lot as needful of a break as you."

Sallah reached out and took Kandler's hand. Esprë felt a bit strange about seeing that. Since her mother's death, Kandler hadn't shown any interest in women. He'd thrown himself into helping build Mardakine and into taking care of her the best he could.

Esprë had heard some of the girls and the ladies in Mardakine whisper about Kandler. She knew that he could have taken up with many of them. She had to admit she'd been relieved that he hadn't. Now, though, as she watched Kandler pull his hand from Sallah's, she felt a pang of regret for him.

Esprina had been dead for years now, and their marriage vow had always been "until death." Of course, at the time of the wedding everyone had expected Esprina to outlive Kandler by hundreds of years. No one had thought that she wouldn't find love again after his death—not even Kandler, and especially not Esprë.

Sallah's lips drew tight across her face, but she bit back whatever might have been on her tongue. Regret tinged Kandler's eyes when he glanced back at her, but he pushed it aside and addressed Krangel instead.

"We don't have a lot of time," he said, "and we have a long way ahead of us."

Duro arched an eyebrow at the justicar. "It's never a good idea to refuse a dwarf's kindness," he said. "It's not likely to come around again."

Esprë reached for Kandler's other hand before he could reply. Instead of pulling away from her, he grasped her hand tight, her fingers nearly disappearing in his grip. He looked down at her, a question on his lips.

"It seems like such a nice place," she said, flashing Krangel a smile, "and it's been years since we've dined at an inn. Can't we?"

Kandler tried to summon up some resistance to the girl's request, but he gave up almost instantly. He reached out and tousled her golden hair instead. "We'll stay for a bite."

The justicar looked to Burch. The shifter gave him a half grin. "On it, boss." He turned to the dwarf and put a hand on his shoulder. "Let's you and me talk business while they eat."

"Aren't you, er, hungry?" Krangel said, staring wide-eyed at the furry hand on his shoulder.

"Dwarf cooking don't do a thing for me," Burch said as he led the innkeeper off to a low table in the room's back corner.

Raumeese bustled up to the table with a tray of bowls and slapped one of them down in front of Kandler, Sallah, Duro, and Esprë. The young elf leaned over the bowl and sniffed a lungful of the steaming scent. It smelled delicious. She grabbed for her spoon and dug in.

The others set to their food straight away too. Duro inhaled the food as if it might be the last he'd ever see. Given the direction the *Phoenix* was headed, Esprë realized it might well be the last bit of dwarf cooking he'd have for a good, long time.

The girl put down her spoon for a moment. "Shouldn't we invite the others in to join us?" she asked.

Duro's mouth bulged with so much food that Esprë wondered if he might get stuck that way. Sallah, who'd barely touched her soup, started to speak, but Kandler interrupted her.

"Xalt doesn't eat. You can call Monja in if you like."

Esprë smiled and got up from the table. She walked to the open door and the wooden dock that stretched out over the Goradra Gap. Monja and Xalt stood staring over the opposite railing, taking in the majesty of canyon as daylight plumbed farther into its depths. The halfling sat atop the warforged's shoulders and leaned far over the open hole.

Someone screamed from high overhead. At first, Esprë thought it might be a raptor diving down from the skies, trying to flush nervous prey before it, but the scream sounded like it had words.

"Run!" it said. "Run!"

Esprë froze, unsure of which way she was supposed to run—or even if she should. She saw Monja and Xalt turn back to look for the source of the scream. As they did, a handful of arrows zipped through the air over Esprë's head.

One of them caught Xalt in the shoulder. As he slumped to the deck, another shaft went straight through Monja's side and knocked her off Xalt's shoulders.

As she watched the halfling tumble over the side of the *Phoenix*'s rail and into the open air above the Goradra Gap, Esprë heard someone screaming again.

It was her.

CHAPTER

6

Kandler launched himself out of his chair and dashed for the door, but Burch got there before him. The shifter reached out and snatched Esprë back through the doorway by the back of her shirt. He tossed her back to Kandler, who wrapped her in his arms.

"What is it?" the justicar said. As he spoke, he saw Te'oma's winged form plummet past the *Phoenix*'s far railing as if she'd been flung from a catapult pointed straight down. The changeling had turned on them, just as he'd expected her to.

Kandler set Esprë down on one of the chairs, right next to where Duro stood. "Guard her with your life," he told the dwarf.

Duro wiped the soup from his beard with one sleeved arm then hefted his axe with the other. A sharp nod told Kandler he understood. The other dwarves pulled weapons of their own from various stashes located around the room. They hadn't looked armed when Kandler and the others had entered the place, but the justicar had suspected that they wouldn't be so foolish as to leave themselves defenseless.

Kandler drew the dragonfang sword and made for the door, but a signal from Burch held him up short. The shifter had already stopped Sallah as well, despite the fact that the knight's eyes burned at least as hot at the blazing sword now crackling in her fist.

Using the complex set of handsigns they'd employed on the battlefield during the Last War, Burch told Kandler there were people on the roof—at least three, maybe more. In battle, they'd used the signs because the clash and clang of such conflicts made it hard to hear anyone do more than howl. Since then, though, they'd often used the signals to communicate when they didn't want to disturb the surrounding silence.

Kandler pointed to the two, wide unshuttered windows that stood to either side of the doorway. Burch winked then slipped over the sill of the one to the right. Kandler headed for the one on the left. As he went, he gestured for Sallah to walk straight out through the door.

"Of course," she said, understanding. "I'm the one wearing all the armor."

The tension between the two of them had disappeared, rent to pieces by Esprë's scream, the fragments displaced by the current crisis, whatever it might be. Kandler found himself feeling grateful for that and then hating himself just a bit for finding he preferred facing danger alongside Sallah rather than dealing with her head-on.

There was no time for that now. He slipped over the windowsill and peered out at the *Phoenix*. He couldn't see Xalt or Monja, and the realization made him ill. He thought he heard a scream being carried farther away, but he couldn't be sure it wasn't just a trick of the winds rushing through the canyon.

Sallah strode out through the doorway and stood there under the eaves, her armor clanking and scraping as she moved. Even as well built as the armor of the Knights of the Silver Flame might be, it sounded as loud as a military marching band compared to the movements of Kandler and Burch. When Sallah stopped, though, Kandler heard nothing but the soft whispers of the whirling winds and the hungry crackle of the knight's blazing blade.

Burch waved for the other two to freeze. The shifter cracked his neck, the pupils of his yellow eyes squeezing together into slits as he let the animalistic part of his nature take over. He pulled back his lips in a silent snarl and stretched his neck back and up until his nose pointed straight up at the eaves overhead.

The shifter raised his crossbow, moved one step to the right, and pointed it toward the eaves. Then he pulled the trigger.

The bolt slammed through the shingles overhead and stuck there, embedded halfway. From above, someone shouted in pain.

Kandler gripped his sword tighter and watched Burch slap another bolt into his crossbow as he slipped back over the windowsill. Sallah looked at him, a question on her lips. Before she could ask it, though, a figure swung down from the edge of the roof and slammed into her, knocking her back into the inn.

Kandler only got a glimpse at the figure, but what he saw was horrible. It was shaped like a man, but its skin was as pale and drawn as that of a long-dead corpse. Kandler turned to charge after Sallah and her attacker, who'd already gotten closer to Esprë than he would have liked. Before he got three steps, though, two more of the ghost-faced intruders flipped down from the roof and landed in front of him.

Both of the newcomers looked like the one who had just flitted past. They wore identical outfits, loose-fitting clothes the color of wet ash, with a headpiece that wrapped around the skull, exposing faces that looked to have been painted to resemble grotesque skulls.

Ready for battle, Kandler slashed out with the sword he'd taken from Ibrido. The serrated blade passed through the nearest intruder's chest like a scythe through wheat. Kandler expected the creature to ignore the wound and come howling at him, but instead it fell over with a soft gurgle, clutching at the blood pouring from the open wound as if it held some hope of keeping it from spilling from its body.

Kandler brought his sword back up and saw the other creature lying next to its compatriot, a crossbow bolt jammed through the front of its throat and jabbed out of the back of its neck.

Burch was already reloading his weapon. The shifter scowled down at the two cooling corpses as growing pools of blood stained the decking around them. "Bleed better than any undead I've ever—"

Three bodies swung down from the roof. The first hit Burch in the head as he tried to duck away. The momentum knocked them both through the window behind the shifter and into the inn. Then the second and third followed close behind, tumbling after the others.

Kandler started after them as three more of the attackers swept down from the roof at him. His lurch toward the open portal put them behind him, and they landed on the decking like a giant knocking on a door: bam, bam, bam.

Kandler turned and glared at the three assassins as they fanned out to try to surround him. They meant to cut him off from the others inside.

The justicar glared at his attackers—and heard the sounds of battle erupt from within the inn—when he realized that the people facing him were not some Karrnathi nightmares forged in a necromancer's terrible lab. He could see their eyes—blue, brown, and gray—and he could hear their panting breath. While they looked like some sort of undead, they were as alive as he was.

Kandler knew then that Esprë could handle herself in the inn. With Sallah, Duro, and Burch by her side, not to mention the dwarves who ran the place, she had little to fear. Monja and Xalt, however, were another question.

One of the assassins' blades licked out at Kandler. Instead of charging the attacker and being forced into taking on three blades at once, Kandler spun on his heel and raced straight for the *Phoenix*. He smiled as he heard the footsteps of his attackers pursuing.

As Kandler dashed up the gangplank that led to the *Phoenix*'s main deck, however, his grin vanished. Just as his feet left the dock, one of the assassins leaped at the justicar. Long, spindly arms wrapped around Kandler's legs and brought him to the plank. His fangsword spun out of his hands and landed on the ship's deck.

CHAPTER

7

Monja knew she was dead. She'd stopped screaming after the first few seconds. When the shock of having an arrow stuck through her side wore off and the pain started in, she began to scream again.

She'd tumbled forward off of Xalt's shoulders, and now the constant spinning threatened to make her vomit. Despite the pain in her side, she flung out her arms in a desperate attempt to stabilize herself. As she did, the arrow tore free from her shirt and twirled away into the air. The wound burned like fire, and the arrow took a good chunk of her flesh along with it, but this told her that it hadn't gone as deep into her as she'd feared.

The rushing wind whipped her long hair around her and tore at her eyes, making it hard to see. She realized she was facing downward now, and through the tears, she saw nothing straight below her but darkness. There might have been a reddish glow in the center of the gap, but it could just as easily have been her imagination filling her terror-stricken mind with traditional images of Khyber.

Monja fought through the pain for another deep breath

and screamed again. She'd been destined to lead her clan to great things, or so her father had always told her. Now it looked as if destiny had other plans for sealing her fate. She flung her arms out farther, as if she were one of the glide-wings that her people rode in the sky.

When she'd been but a child, she'd seen her uncle knocked from just such a beast during a skirmish with a flight of harpies that had been terrorizing her people. As he'd fallen, he'd thrown out his limbs out like this, forming his body into a large **X**, and had managed to even use the winds to angle himself toward the nearby River Cyre, like a giant bird with shredded wings. Still, in his own way, he'd flown. Perhaps Monja could do the same.

Of course, her uncle had hit the river's surface like a rock, and he had never come up again.

Monja tried to will herself to move about in the winds, but nothing happened. She just kept falling straight down. She moved her left hand up and felt herself tipping to the right. She smiled at the thought of any kind of control returning to what little might be left of her life.

Then she frowned again. Even if she managed to figure out a way to steer herself toward the nearest of the gap's walls, what good would that do her? She had no way to slow her descent, only guide it, and if she hit anything at her current speed, she had no doubt the impact would turn her bones to jelly.

Monja closed her eyes then and prayed to the spirits that watched over her and her people. She couldn't see what they could do for her, but she'd relied on them throughout her life. This didn't seem like the right time to stop.

She had trained to be the shaman of her clan, to take over for old Wodager when he retired or died. Prayer had sustained her in her darkest hours and had made her a leader among her people, despite her tender years. Her father, their clan's lath—now lathun of all the clans of the Talenta Plains—often said that the spirits listened when she whispered. If so, she hoped they would hear her as she shouted for their aid, straining to even hear herself over the wind roaring in her ears.

"Got you!" A voice from above rang out, echoing off the nearest wall of rock, which blurred by, only scores of feet away.

Then slim, white hands reached out and grabbed Monja under her shoulders and brought her up close as a body slammed into her, knocking the wind from her lungs. The halfling wondered if she'd somehow managed to summon the spirit of a great glidewing to her aid. She couldn't believe that the spirits would favor her so, no matter what happy evidence to the contrary, but she wasn't about to refuse their good will.

She craned her neck to look back over her shoulder and saw Te'oma's face twisted with strain as she wrapped her arms around Monja's chest. The changeling's wings were angled tight and near her shoulders.

"Hold on!" Te'oma said. "This is going to hurt!"

Monja drew in a big breath and held it tight. The wound on her side—which had to still be trailing blood behind them as they plummeted toward the canyon's unseen bottom—stabbed her with pain as she fought to expand her lungs, but she ignored it as best she could.

Then Te'oma spread her batlike wings, stretching them out as wide as they would go. The wind filled them like a sail unfurled into a storm, and they whipped open with a crack that sounded like the snapping of bones and enveloped Monja and Te'oma in their shadow.

For a moment, Monja thought the changeling's grip on her might give, and she clung to Te'oma's ghost-pale arms hard enough to draw blood with her nails. The changeling refused to let go, though, despite the fact her wailing told Monja that her weight must nearly have pulled Te'oma's arms from their sockets. The halfling wondered how well the bloodwings attached to the changeling's back would hold up.

It didn't seem like they had slowed at all, despite the deployment of the wings. However, Monja could feel a change of momentum. Instead of heading straight down, they now angled up just a bit.

Te'oma folded her wings back again, and they started to drop as fast as ever. Now, though, they headed closer to the wall.

"Is this helping?" Monja asked, trying to keep the panic from her voice. She knew that Te'oma could have just let her fall to her death—and still could—but she couldn't help but be dismayed at how little the changeling seemed to have been able to do.

"Quiet!" Te'oma snarled, not looking down at the halfling at all. Instead, Monja saw her gaze had locked on the sheer wall nearest to them.

The halfling looked at the wall and noticed how near it was. She followed the changeling's gaze down and spied a wide shelf of rock jutting out from the wall below.

"No!" Monja said, clutching Te'oma's arms in a desperate grip. "We're still going too fast!"

Falling into a bottomless pit now seemed like a far better choice than smashing into that shelf. Monja didn't doubt something just as solid awaited her in the canyon's depths, but at least she wouldn't hit it for a little while longer. In a way, she thought, her fall through the canyon was a metaphor for life. Once you started it, you were going to die either way, but later had to be better than sooner.

"I said, quiet," Te'oma said. "Don't make me regret this."

Monja closed her eyes and began to pray again. If the spirits had sent Te'oma to help her, then she should do her best to accept that aid. She prayed for the serenity to accept her death.

Gravity tugged at her even harder, and Monja squeaked in fear that it might tug her right from the changeling's arms, which had to be getting tired. She clung to Te'oma tighter than ever and opened her eyes.

Then she screamed.

The canyon wall rushed toward her nearly as fast as the shelf below. A startled mountain goat bleated as Te'oma and Monja zipped by.

The shelf zoomed up from the depths as if it wanted to smack the pair of them right back out of the canyon. For an instant, Monja wondered just how high they would bounce. She wanted to close her eyes again but found she couldn't.

Then Te'oma flung her wings wide and flipped her body backward. The wings caught the air hard, and Monja felt the changeling's arms pulling her back up into the sky. Would it be fast enough, hard enough, to keep her from smashing into the rocky shelf?

The changeling's wings not only caught the air this time but rode it. Monja felt the pair of them hook from a plummeting fall into a tight, brief rise, and the air left her lungs.

As they came out of the short hook upward, Monja looked down and saw that they were still a score of feet over the shelf. She screamed as they fell toward it again, and she felt Te'oma's arms and legs wrap around her, protecting her like a mother would an infant.

They hit the shelf hard, but Te'oma's body and wings cushioned the impact for Monja. The halfling heard the changeling's head crack against the rock behind her, and the arms around her went limp.

When Monja could breathe again, she rolled off Te'oma's still form and onto the unforgiving rock. She took care to roll toward the canyon wall. The thought of spilling out into the open canyon again terrified her. She'd never been afraid of heights before, but this experience had given her a healthier respect for them.

Stunned to be alive, Monja got up on her knees and stared down at Te'oma. Blood had started to pool under the changeling's head. She breathed still, but perhaps not for long.

"To think I didn't trust you," Monja said as she began to pray.

CHAPTER

8

Sallah fell back to the floor, the weight of her attacker crushing the air from her. She glared up at his face and saw an ivory-colored skull staring back down at her. Unlike most skeletons she'd seen in her life, though, this one had eyes of the brightest blue.

Sallah gave thanks to the Silver Flame for her well-fitted breastplate and slashed up and out with her flaming blade. The assailant tried to twist out of the blade's path, but it gouged deep into the side of his head instead.

The thin, gray linen wrapped around the attacker's skull burst into flames. He flopped to the ground, still bleeding, and tried to smother the fire consuming his head.

Sallah scrambled to her knees. She saw Burch come tumbling in through the window to the right of the doorway, another of the assassins on top of him. The shifter growled and slashed at his attacker with his claw-tipped fingers, but the gray-clad shape had wrapped his legs around the shifter's throat and then started to squeeze.

Sallah leaped to her feet, ready to force the attacker from Burch's throat. As she did, two more of the assassins swung in through the window, landing on the ground as lightly as cats. Long, bone-handled daggers appeared in their hands, and each crossed their pair of blades before themselves, ready to tear through Sallah's defenses.

Burch gurgled something from his place on the floor as he struggled against the assassin sitting on his chest. He would be strangled in a matter of seconds if Sallah didn't do something, but she couldn't reach him without exposing herself to the killers before her.

Esprë pushed away from Duro and rushed to help Burch. Her hands crackled with a black energy, and Sallah knew that the girl had summoned the power of her dragonmark.

The thought that such a young creature could wield such horrible power chilled the lady knight. When she'd begun her quest to find the bearer of the Mark of Death, she'd thought only of her duty, not of the unknown soul who'd been branded by powers beyond her ken.

Now, though, as her love for Kandler blossomed, she'd come to care for his stepdaughter as well. In many ways, Esprë was barely more than a child, and now she had to bear this horrible burden that had put her life at risk and the lives of anyone near her. Whenever Sallah felt saddened at her own losses, she had only to think of Esprë to put them into perspective.

As Esprë charged, determined to kill once more, the object of her attack flicked his wrists out, and a pair of daggers appeared in his hands too. He drew one of them back to throw, and Sallah saw that the killer would hurl the blade into the girl's chest long before she had any hope of reaching her target.

Esprë skidded to a halt in the face of the assassin's weapons. No matter what the girl's powers might be, they would do her little good if she died before she could use them. But as she slid to a stop, she slipped and fell flat on her back.

The assassin smiled at this, drawing back his teeth to expose another set beneath them. Sallah saw then that the first set of teeth had been tattooed across the killer's lips, part of a mask of death etched upon a living face.

An axe appeared in the center of the grinning killer's chest. Blood seeped from around the wound as the assassin's eyes rolled back up into his head. Somewhere behind Sallah, Duro hollered, "Yes!"

As Burch bucked his attacker's corpse off of him, Sallah moved toward the other two, interposing herself between them and Esprë. The girl scrambled to her feet and stood beside the lady knight as the killers reassessed the situation.

Sallah figured there were more than a dozen dwarves in the room, along with her, Esprë, and Burch. Four of the assassins lay dead, including the one who had failed to extinguish the flames devouring its head in time.

Only two stood in here, although only the Flame knew how many others might be lurking outside. She had to presume that some of them had kept Kandler too busy to join her and the others inside the inn.

The two killers seemed to realize their odds at the same time as Sallah. They spun and fled.

Six more battle-scarred axes spun through the air and struck the killers down before they reached the door. Two of the weapons clanged into each other and off their mark, but the others all hit deep in the assassins' bodies, and they fell without a sound.

Sallah glanced down at Esprë.

"Kandler!" the girl said, already rushing for the dock.

❦

Kandler lashed out with his fist. It smashed into the killer's jaw, and Kandler felt the satisfying crunch of smashed teeth.

Kandler kicked free from the stunned assassin's grasp. He spied his fangsword on the far side of the deck, but the other two killers would be on him before he could do more than gain his feet. Instead of scrambling for the weapon, he reached back and ripped a dagger from the hand of the assassin sharing the floor with him. When the killer offered resistance, Kandler slammed his elbow into the assassin's nose, and the blade came free.

Just in time, Kandler brought the dagger up to parry a thrust from the first of the two other killers racing up the gangplank. As the attacker's blade turned wide, Kandler punched out with his left fist with a blow that cracked the bone around the assailant's eye.

As Kandler shoved the assassin off him, the other flung a dagger at his chest. The justicar threw up his arm to protect himself, and the blade went right through his arm, its point stabbing straight in and out of his muscle. The pain forced him to drop the knife in his hand.

Sensing that Kandler might be ripe for the kill, the assassin leaped atop the justicar, stabbing at his belly with his other knife. Kandler wrenched himself out of the way just in time.

As the killer landed on the deck, Kandler reached back and slashed at the assassin's neck with the blade still embedded in his arm. Pain lanced straight up through his shoulder with the move, but his aim struck true. The tip of the knife punctured the killer's throat, spilling his blood across the deck.

Kandler staggered to his feet, the knife still stuck in the flesh of his dripping, red arm. Two of the killers were still alive and hungry for his death, and they stood now too, their blades flashing as they readied to take the fight to him once more.

Kandler left the knife in his arm. He'd seen too many battles in which men had pulled free a weapon in their body and watched their lifeblood pour out after it like wine from an unstoppered bottle.

He went for his fangblade instead. One of the assassins hurled a dagger at Kandler as he scooped up his sword, but it just grazed his shoulder, laying open his shirt and tracing a shallow, crimson line along the flesh.

Kandler swung around, bringing the fangblade up in a wide, slashing arc. It caught one of the killers in the chest and nearly cleaved the man in two. It sprang free just as smoothly as it had entered the killer's form, its ivory blade now turned crimson.

The last assassin stared at Kandler as his compatriot's corpse slumped to the deck. He cursed then, a single word under his breath in Elven. Then he flung both of his daggers and Kandler at once.

The justicar dodged one of the blades and knocked the other out of the air with his sword. The assassin hadn't even bothered to see if the knives would strike their target. Instead, he turned and raced back toward the gangplank. When he reached it, he stutter-stepped once, betraying perhaps an instant's hesitation. Then he leaped out into the open air between the airship and the dock and disappeared.

CHAPTER

9

As Kandler reached the gangplank, Esprë burst from the inn, calling his name. He glanced below, looking for the killer. Seeing no trace of the assassin, he stumbled down to the deck and took his stepdaughter in his good arm.

"You're hurt!" Esprë said, staring at his injured arm.

Kandler nodded as Sallah came up behind Esprë, relief and concern warring on her face. She took the justicar's wounded limb and held it up to inspect it. As she did, Burch emerged from the inn with Duro right behind him. Krangel poked his aged nose out of the door after them, and the other dwarves in the inn peered through the open windows, each of them jostling for the best positions near the sills.

"That all of them?" Burch asked, nodding at the two cooling bodies lying on the airship's deck. He cocked his crossbow as he spoke.

"One of them dove into the gap," Kandler said, pointing to where he'd last seen the suicidal killer.

Kandler could see the shifter was steaming from having been caught unaware by these assassins. He stalked the dock as if he might decide to stomp down through the

47

boards to relieve his temper.

"I can help with that," Sallah said, taking Kandler's arm more tenderly in her hands, "but we'll have to remove the knife first."

Kandler nodded and gritted his teeth, ready for the worst. He focused on the woman's lidded eyes as she gripped the handle of the blade and prepared to pull it free. As he did, he heard Krangel shouting orders to the other dwarves in the inn, and they leaped into action, their feet now padding along the dock.

Sallah yanked the dagger free in one swift move. Kandler hissed through his teeth, and Esprë reached up to hold his free hand to comfort him. As the blood poured from the wound, Sallah wrapped her hands around the injured area, forming a ring with her palms and fingers.

While Kandler's blood seeped through her fingers, Sallah closed her eyes and said a solemn prayer to the Silver Flame. As she spoke, her hands began to glow with a silvery light. The glow spread out from her hands and enveloped Kandler's arm, which seared with heat.

Just before the warmth became painful, Sallah released Kandler's limb. He held the arm out and flexed his fingers. Although his blood still covered it, he felt not a twinge of pain.

Kandler reached with his healed arm around Sallah's waist and pulled her to him for a gentle kiss. "Thanks," he whispered.

Sallah started to say something, but before she could complete even a syllable, Burch called out, "Ha!" Then he loosed his crossbow straight into the deck.

The bolt stuck there, half buried in the wood. From below, a horrible scream sounded and then faded away.

"There's your suicide," Burch said. "With just a bit of help."

Kandler glanced up at the roof that overhung the front of the inn. Whoever Burch had hit with his first bolt no longer stood there. The assassin had probably fled after the shifter had wounded him.

For a moment, Kandler considered hunting the would-be killer down, then he thought better of it. If this was to be a war between his friends and those who would take or kill Esprë, then it was time to begin sending their foes a message. For that, they'd need a courier, and a wounded witness to how they'd massacred these assassins sounded like a fine start.

Kandler heard Esprë gasp. He turned as she dashed past him toward the airship. There stood Xalt at the end of the gangplank, the tip of an arrow jutting out through his shoulder.

"Monja?" the warforged said, his voice unsteady. "What happened to Monja?"

❦

Monja had thought about pushing Te'oma over the edge of the rocky shelf. Hurt as she was, the changeling likely would never have awakened before she slammed into whatever awaited in the depths of the Goradra Gap.

Monja didn't care for the changeling at all. Anyone who would kidnap children—even lethally dangerous children like Esprë—came low on her list of people she wished to help. To now have to pray on Te'oma's behalf galled her.

True, the changeling had risked her life to save the halfling from certain death—and succeeded. Monja owed Te'oma for that, but the shaman could save Esprë, Burch, and the others a great deal of grief, she thought, by removing the changeling from their lives.

Despite Te'oma's insistence that she bore no love for the Lich Queen, Monja suspected that the changeling would turn on the others in an instant if it served her needs. However, even if Te'oma was an amoral beast who could not be trusted, Monja knew the same wasn't true of herself.

She placed her hands on the changeling's head and prayed. She felt the crack in Te'oma's skull knit closed, and warmth returned to the changeling's paler-than-parchment skin.

When Te'oma's eyes fluttered open, Monja smiled down at her. "Welcome back," she said, "and thanks."

"Thank you," Te'oma said as she sat up and took in their surroundings. She craned her neck all the way back and stared up at the strip of blue sky above. It seemed forever away.

"For saving my life, I mean," said Monja. "My thanks. Now, though, I think we are even."

A set of pale eyebrows appeared on Te'oma's face, and she arched one at the halfling. "I suppose so," she said, her mouth twisted in a wry grin, "although you only had the chance to save my life because I nearly died saving yours."

"The spirits balance the scales in strange ways," Monja said with a shrug. She grasped the changeling's shoulder. "Can you still contact Esprë?"

Te'oma nodded. "Doesn't that mean I'll be saving your life again?"

Monja smirked. "Don't fool yourself. You're saving your own skin this time. I'm just along for the ride."

❦

"They're alive!" Esprë said.

Kandler let out a sigh of relief. The girl had been walking around on knives, hoping for some kind of contact from Te'oma. She'd paced the length of the ship countless times, nearly in tears. Only when she'd frozen in her tracks had Kandler held out any hope.

The justicar's cynical side told him that Monja was dead

and that Te'oma had probably run off at the first sign of the assassins—assuming she hadn't brought them here in the first place. If that had been the case, maybe she'd just hovered overhead until she saw the killers get slaughtered and then flown away.

Not a small part of him wished the changeling gone forever. True, she'd helped them track down Esprë and even to defeat the dragon, but she'd also stolen the girl from his home in the first place and just about destroyed Mardakine—a village he'd helped found—in the process. He didn't think he could ever forgive her for that, much less forget.

"Both of them?" Burch asked, rushing up the gangplank. After dispatching the hidden assassin, he'd made a point of sweeping the area for any others who might be hiding, and he'd pressed Krangel and his fellow dwarves into that service.

The white-haired host of the inn had apologized a dozen times over for the failure of his lookouts. When word had come back that those dwarves were missing from their posts, though, no one had any doubt what had happened to them. A few of the dwarves had wailed at the loss, and more than that number had shot murderous looks at their guests, blaming them no doubt for their friends' misfortune.

Esprë nodded at the shifter. "They're on a shelf way down the wall."

"Is it stable?" Kandler asked. "Can they hold on for a while?"

Esprë's eyes unfocused for a moment, then she nodded again. "They're well, although they want us to come for them as soon as we can.

Kandler wrapped an arm around his stepdaughter and gave her a hug. "Just as soon as we're ready," he said. He shouted for Krangel.

The dwarf poked his head out of the inn's front door and scowled at Kandler. "What?"

"How fast can you get us loaded up?"

The dwarf's face split in a tight grin.

CHAPTER

10

"Forget Aerenal," Kandler said. "We're going straight to Argonnessen."

The others stared at him. Sallah, Esprë, and Monja gaped at him. Even Xalt's jaw dropped. Duro grinned as he thumbed the edge of his axe.

Kandler couldn't read Te'oma's face at all, but if changelings were good at anything it was hiding their true selves. Even if he thought he could have picked up on how his words made her feel, he couldn't have trusted his assessment.

Burch didn't say a word. He just spat on the ground. From long experience, Kandler knew that meant the shifter was with him, whether he thought they were heading in the right direction or not.

"That's madness!" Sallah said. "You can't possibly be serious."

"You want to sail straight into an entire continent full of dragons?" Monja said.

"It's the stuff of legends," Duro said. "Bards will sing of our deeds for generations to come!"

"Assuming we don't all get killed," Sallah said, shaking her head. "Who will sing a dirge for us if none survive to tell the tale?"

"Maybe the dragons will make up a song about us," Burch said, smiling.

"It'll be called, 'What I Had for Dinner,' " said Monja, who didn't smile at all.

Xalt stared at Kandler with his unblinking ebony eyes. "Why have you changed your mind?" he asked. "Would we not have a better chance against the dragons if we had the help of the Undying Court?"

Kandler looked down at the body of one of the assassins. Burch had hauled it up on to the bridge so that they could all take part in the discussion, even Esprë who had taken the wheel when they'd left Durviska behind. Kandler had wanted Sallah or Monja at the wheel, but Esprë had pointed out that, since she was in telepathic contact with Te'oma, she was the best choice. He'd had to agree.

As the dwarves toted the new supplies on to the *Phoenix*, they'd also brought the bodies of the assassins along and deposited them on the deck. "Consider it a way to repay the discount I'm giving you," Krangel had said.

Kandler could only agree to that too. The crew of the *Phoenix* didn't have a great deal of gold among them and little else to barter with. Krangel had given them a good deal on enough supplies to take them to the southern shores of Khorvaire, which would have to be enough for now.

Besides, Kandler had wanted to get a better look at the killers. He pointed down at the corpse on the bridge now. The blank eyes of the assassin he'd stabbed in the neck stared up at the open sky. Kandler reached down and removed the body's gray hood.

Under the fabric, the corpse had a shaved head that—like his face—had been tattooed with white inks and darker shadings to resemble a bleached skull. The ears stood up straight and proud and bore fine points on their tops.

"Elves," Sallah said. "Are they one and all?"

Kandler glanced at Esprë and saw that she'd taken one hand from the wheel to feel the tops of her own ears. They bore points just like those on the corpse.

"They're Stillborn," Burch said from where he'd perched on the bridge's rear railing.

"Look like adults to me," Duro said, tugging at the roots of his beard.

"It's a cult," Burch said, "made up of a bunch of young elves who think waiting to die takes too long. They want to take the short path to the most elite club in elf society: the Undying Court."

"They'd rather be dead than alive?" Esprë said.

Monja looked up at Kandler. "Haven't you taught this girl anything about her heritage?"

Blood rose into Kandler's cheeks. "Her mother came with her to Khorvaire when Esprë was just an infant. She knows about elf ways, but . . ." He looked Esprë wistfully.

Should he have taught her the ways of elves? When Esprina had been alive, he hadn't worried about such things, and since then such things hadn't seemed all that important. Carving out a life on the edge of the Mournland had always taken precedent over running through the details of distant land filled with people who hadn't seemed to care about them at all.

"I know about the Undying Court," Esprë said. "It's just, well, why would anyone be in a hurry to die? To me, that's one of the best parts about being an elf: the long life you can expect, unless something horrible happens to you."

Kandler could tell her mother had crossed her mind with those words. These days, so many things weighed so heavily on the girl. She reminded him of those months right after Esprina had died. She'd been so morose he had wondered if she'd die of a broken heart as well.

Caring for Esprë during those dark days had been the one thing that had kept Kandler going. If she hadn't been there, he probably would have fallen into an abyss of despair himself. Her needs, her grief, had burned so much hotter than his own, and he'd used that as the light he'd needed to guide them both out of the darkness. If not for her and the never-shaken support of Burch, he might have lain down and died himself.

"Elves hope to ascend to the Undying Court when they die," Burch said. "That's the ultimate power for them, and they only get it after a lifetime of service to their people." He spat at the corpse, and his spittle landed in the open eyes. "These clowns think the world owes them a shortcut."

The shifter swiveled his head to focus his yellow eyes on Te'oma. "I hear they're in bed with Vol."

The changeling squirmed when she realized everyone was staring at her. "I've heard that too," she said, "but I don't know that it's true. Vol rarely did more than give me orders. I didn't know many of her others servants outside of Tan Du and his crew."

Xalt stepped into Te'oma's face. She flinched away from his stony eyes. "Did you bring them here?" he asked, voicing the question on everyone else's mind.

Te'oma's pale pink tongue licked her thin, white lips. She seemed ready to bolt, and Kandler tensed, hoping he could strike her down before her wings carried her away.

"No," Te'oma said. "I've quit the Lich Queen. I want nothing more than to kill her. Since there's little chance of that, I'll go for the next best thing."

"Which is what?"

The changeling's white-eyed gaze fell on Esprë, who shivered in it.

"Keeping from her the thing she wants most. If I can't be her killer, I'll settle for being her spoiler."

Kandler put a hand on Esprë's shoulder. "This just makes me more sure. We can't go to Aerenal. If Vol can send so many Stillborn assassins to find us in the middle of nowhere, we wouldn't last a moment in the elf homeland."

Burch nodded. "Chances of finding help there weren't much anyhow—even if we got an audience with the Undying Court."

"Now you're against that plan?" Sallah asked, exasperated. "Why did you side with it before?"

Burch bared his teeth in what Kandler hoped was a smile. Sometimes with the shifter it was hard to tell—on purpose. "I stand with my friends."

Sallah's face flushed with anger at this. "Are you implying that I have anything than the best interests of Kandler and Esprë at heart?" Her hand rested on the pommel of her sword. Kandler wondered if it might burst into flames right in its scabbard with her so infuriated.

"Let's just say I'm less conflicted. I don't have a god I answer to."

Kandler winced at the comment, then stepped forward and put his hand on Sallah's. She had her sword halfway out of its scabbard.

"I've gone through too much here—lost *far* too much—for *anyone* to question my loyalties."

Sallah shoved her blade back into its scabbard and tore her hand away from Kandler's. "As much as I care for you and your daughter, I can't watch you do this," she said to him. "I can't just sit here while you sail off through the sky with her toward certain death."

"I'm all she has in the world," Kandler said, angling his head around so he could look into Sallah's eyes. "I have to do what I think is best for her."

Sallah brought her head up and glared at him. "How could you possibly think that taking a young girl into the dragon homeland is what's best for her?"

Kandler started to speak, but then shut his mouth. He'd had doubts of his own about this course of action, but he didn't see any better choice. He knew that Esprë's dragon-mark would only grow stronger as time progressed, and the people who wanted to control her for it would only become more desperate and bold.

"She has to take a stand sometime," he said, struggling to keep his voice even and low.

"Then let it be in Thrane," Sallah said, clasping her hands around Kandler's. "The Silver Flame will protect her. We knights can keep her from harm."

Burch opened his mouth but Kandler shut him up with a stern glance.

"That would only bring the troubles to Flamekeep," Kandler said. "We have to do this. We can't wait for the troubles to come to us, to fight us on their terms. We need to set the conditions of the contest ourselves, not let them do it for us." He looked deep into Sallah's eyes. "Esprë is an elf. She'll outlive me by hundreds of years. I only have a short time in which I can help her. We have to take matters into our own hands, and we have to do it now."

Sallah dropped Kandler's hands and stepped away from him. "Very well," she said. "You go ahead and get yourself and your girl killed on your terms. I won't stay to watch it. When this airship next lands, I'm getting off."

CHAPTER

11

"Battlefield romances never last anyhow," Monja said, clapping Kandler on the butt. He nearly leaped over the railing in surprise.

The justicar had been wrapped in thought, and the others had chosen to give him his space as he watched the sunset, considering everything that had happened since the day the Knights of the Silver Flame had come to Mardakine. It now seemed so long ago. So much had happened since then.

Kandler arched an eyebrow down at the halfling, who winked up at him and patted the decking next to her. "Sit on down here and tell Monja all your problems," she said with a smile.

Kandler searched that look for some hint of sarcasm, but she seemed sincere. He let himself down next to her and grimaced at her. "I thought shamans only dealt with religious matters."

Monja snorted. "Out in the Talenta Plains, we all ride many different mounts. Shamans serve as healers, leaders, counselors, even cooks. You should try my roast beetles."

"I think I'll pass."

Monja patted Kandler on the knee. "She would have left you eventually," she said. "You know that."

Kandler shook his head. "I guess I didn't."

"A Knight of the Silver Flame? Setting up a tent with a Brelish spy?"

"Agent of the Citadel, and I gave all that up years ago."

"Are the knights even allowed? Don't they have some sort of vows of chastity?"

Kandler stared back across the length of the airship at Sallah, who stood behind the wheel. Her crimson hair whipped behind her in the rushing wind as the airship sailed south, toward the sea. Her eyes blazed with the light of the dying sun.

"I hope not," he said.

He hadn't considered the question before, and now, he realized, he might never have a chance to learn the answer. Sallah had kept away from him since storming off, not an easy trick on a craft the size of the *Phoenix*, but she had managed it.

"Not a lot of pretty girls where you come from?"

Kandler laughed, despite his sour mood. "Not many," he said. "I think Esprë's beautiful, of course, but I'm biased." His gaze shifted to where she and Xalt and Duro huddled together near the port rail.

They had nothing on the ship to use for a cookfire, and Esprë had wanted a hot meal. Xalt had managed to rig up a long wooden arm, which he'd stabbed through a hunk of beef they'd gotten from the dwarves in Gaptown. He stood now with his arm extended, holding the steak as close to the airship's elemental ring of fire as he dared, and it had already started to brown.

As Kandler watched, the ring of fire flared angrily at the warforged, engulfing the food. Xalt drew back the flaming food instantly and blew out the flames with a blast of air from his lungs. This set Esprë to nearly hysterical giggling, and for the first time in a long while Kandler saw her happy.

"She reminds me so much of her mother," Kandler said.

"What about Sallah?"

Kandler shook his head. "They're nothing alike. You wouldn't have caught Esprina dead in a temple. She was the most even-tempered person I'd ever met. Sometimes . . ."

He wondered why he felt compelled to tell Monja anything. Had she worked some kind of spell upon him? He hadn't known her all that long, but maybe that was the reason he felt he could unburden himself on her. That, and the fact that she'd asked for it.

"Sometimes she'd look at me, and there was this horrible sadness in her eyes. I just knew it came from the fact that she thought she'd live on for hundreds of years after I died. To her, loving me must have seemed like trying to hold on to summer. Eventually you know autumn has to come, but you ignore it as long as you can and try to enjoy the best days of the year the most you can."

"And that's different from how Sallah looks at you?'

Kandler shook his head. "No. That part's exactly the same."

❧

Her belly full of scorched beef eaten from the tip of a sword, Esprë wandered over to where Kandler sat chatting with Burch. She'd been dreading this for some time, but she didn't see that waiting to take care of it would make it anything but worse.

The sun had long since set, and the night would have been crisp, cool, and filled with stars and moons had it not been for the ring of fire that kept the airship aloft and had cooked her meal so well. As it was, she could make out a few of the constellations out beyond the ship's prow, off toward the southern horizon, and the heat from the ring of fire forced the chill far away.

"Hey," Kandler said as Esprë came closer. "You get enough to eat?"

She nodded and rubbed her belly. "I'm sure I've had better, but I can't remember when."

"Leave any for us?" Burch said, licking his lips.

Esprë felt mortified. "I'm sorry," she said, happy that with the ring of fire to her rear her face was shrouded in shadow. "I didn't think—"

"Relax," Burch grinned. "I'm only joking. I can see from here that Xalt's already got another steak on that stick of his."

"I'm sure it will be even better than the first," Esprë said. "He's a fast learner."

"What's on your mind?" Kandler said.

"Does anything have to be on my mind?"

Kandler smirked. "I know you, Esprë. Don't try to hide who you are, not from me."

The fact that Kandler knew her so well frustrated Esprë, and at the same time, it comforted her. It felt good to realize that there were people in her life who had been around her enough to know how to read her intentions, her moods.

"I—I just wanted to say that I think we're doing the right thing."

Kandler's smile shed as much warmth as the ring of fire. "Thanks," he said. "That means more to me than you could probably know."

"I just . . ." she started. Then she stopped and took a deep breath. She wanted this to come out right.

"Yes?"

"I just don't know if I need everyone to come with me on this—this . . ."

"Quest?" said Kandler.

"Suicide mission?" said Burch.

"Whatever. I just don't see what good having a lot of people with me will serve. I'll be facing down a horde of dragons, right? All together we barely managed to kill one dragon."

"Don't forget that half-dragon he had with him," said Burch, only half serious. "He had to be worth at least," he looked to Kandler, "what would you say?"

"Oh, a half a dragon. At least." Kandler laughed, and it felt contagious. Esprë had to join in.

The next moment, though, Esprë turned serious again. "Even rounding up, call that two dragons. How many are we likely to see in Argonnessen? Two dozen? Two hundred? Two thousand?"

"What's your point?" Kandler said.

"What good are all these people going to do?" she asked. "Why risk everyone's lives? We don't all have to die."

Kandler looked hard into the elf-girl's eyes. "Is this because Sallah wants to leave?"

"She makes more sense than you admit." As the words left her lips, Esprë wished she could take them back, but it was far too late.

Kandler pursed his lips for a moment. "Who would you put off the ship?" he asked. "Duro? Xalt? Monja?"

Esprë nodded.

"Te'oma?"

"Certainly." She stifled a laugh.

"Why stop there?" Burch said.

"What do you mean?" Esprë said. It felt like a stream of ice had shot through her guts.

"Why not get rid of Kandler and me too?" Burch asked.

Esprë couldn't read the shifter at all. She'd never been able to.

"That's what you're suggesting, isn't it?" Kandler asked after Esprë hadn't responded for a long moment. "You want to get rid of all of us and go off on your own."

Panic threatened to choke Esprë. "I can fly the airship better than anyone," she said. "You said so yourself. I don't need anyone else. I can make it on my own."

Kandler stared at Esprë, and now she realized she couldn't read him either. She couldn't tell if he was about to jump up and start yelling at her or if he'd just have Burch handle it for him.

"Thank you," Kandler said, reaching up for Esprë. She fell to her knees next to him and wrapped her arms around his neck. She hadn't realized until then that she'd been trembling.

"What for?" she said. "Because I don't want you to come along with me?"

Kandler stroked her long, blonde hair. "For wanting to save me," he said. "For trying to see if there was a way you could do this on your own."

"I—I just wanted to do the grown-up thing," she said.

Kandler smiled. "Even grown-ups know they need all the help they can get."

CHAPTER

12

"What in the name of the Silver Flame is that?" Sallah asked.

Kandler peered out over the airship's gunwale. They'd been flying south for two days now, and these were the first words Sallah had said to them since she'd declared her intent to leave the *Phoenix* the next time the airship landed.

For that reason, Kandler had decided to avoid Krona Peak, the capitol of the Mror Holds, despite Duro's pleas. Kandler declared that they already had plenty of supplies to make it to the southern coast, and he didn't intend to stop for anything until they could see the sea. The dwarf had sulked for the better part of a day, but he'd perked up when they'd skirted the active volcano that towered over the southern end of the Ironroot Mountains.

"The Fist of Onatar," Duro had said, gaping in astonishment at the reddish lava leaking out of the mountaintop. "It must be. I've heard of it my entire life but never set eyes upon it."

"Onatar?" Xalt had said. "Is that not your god of artifice?" The warforged had managed to patch his arrow wound so well that Kandler might never have known it had been there.

"Aye, and of the forge. He usually appears as a dwarf smith, you know."

"And as a brass dragon," Monja had said.

That had been enough for Kandler to order the ship to give the mountain a wide berth.

From there, they'd steered clear of the mountains and kept over the burning sands of the Blade Desert, which followed the southwestern curve of the Endworld Mountains. This range stretched all the way to the ocean, and Kandler planned to follow it to its end.

As Kandler gazed down at the desert floor below, he spied what had upset Sallah. Below them sat a windswept, sandy valley tucked up next to the mountains, and bones covered it from one end to the other.

Even from as high up as the *Phoenix* scudded through the sky, Kandler could tell that these were bones. Scores of them stood as thick and tall as pine trees gathered as tight as a forest. He could pick out ribs, legs, arms, even wings. He spotted long, flat skulls too, some of which had to be as wide as a wagon and three times as long.

"Those things could have swallowed a threehorn whole," Monja said, as she and the others joined Kandler at the rail.

Te'oma had the wheel, and when Kandler glanced back at her he saw her trying to crane her head high enough to see what all the commotion was about. He thought he saw her neck actually stretch a few inches.

The halfling turned to Burch, her eyes wide with awe. "Is this . . . ? It has to be," she said.

The shifter nodded as he leaned far out over the gunwale. Kandler had to repress an urge to pull his friend back, even though he knew Burch could keep hold of the ship better than anyone. Instead he put an arm around Esprë, who'd put her head and arms over the railing.

"The Boneyard," Burch said. "A dragon graveyard. Some say it's leftover from the Dragon-Elf War, but that's mostly Valenar elves boasting over ale."

"They would peddle such lies," Duro said gruffly. "Warmongers and glory hounds to a one."

Esprë glared at Duro. When the dwarf finally noticed, he blushed and said, "Or so I've heard."

"My people believe that dragons once ruled the entire world," Monja said. "They once flew as thick through the skies of Khorvaire as a cloud of bats." She spoke in hushed, reverent tones. "This is where their eldest came to end their days, to mix their bones among their own kind."

Kandler felt Esprë shudder beside him. Sallah noticed too.

"There are few such creatures in Khorvaire these days," the lady knight said, a comforting hand on the young elf's arm.

"Nithkorrh was enough," Esprë said, her voice barely more than a whisper.

Everyone else nodded.

"Should we go down?" Xalt asked.

Kandler and the others stared at the warforged in horror.

"You never disturb a graveyard," Monja said. "Ever."

"Why not?" Xalt sounded like all of his five years of age. Although he'd been made whole and full-grown, he'd not had nearly the world experiences of Kandler or even Esprë, and he could be ignorant about the strangest things.

Monja held her hands in front of her and spoke slowly, as if to a young child. "Because the living protect the dead. That's especially true with the Boneyard. Those who disturb a dead dragon's bones risk bringing down a living beast's wrath."

"Isn't that what we want?" Xalt asked. "A dragon to fight?"

Burch snorted. "We don't want just any random dragon to show up. We want the ones who want to toast our little girl here."

"Don't they all?"

"Do all warforged think the same?"

Xalt inclined his head. "I see." He looked to Kandler. "Then how will we find the right dragons when we reach Argonnessen?"

Kandler scowled.

"Yes," Sallah said, her hands on her hips. "Tell us."

"I didn't say it was a great plan," he said before he walked away. "Just the best one we have."

❦

Kandler spat over the gunwale. The others had left him alone since they'd passed over the Boneyard. Perhaps the thought of so many dead dragons had sobered them. The thought that there were so many of the creatures to begin with shot ice through his guts. He wondered if he could really conceive how many of them there might be on an entire continent.

He glanced at Esprë. She sat on the deck below the raised bridge, soaking up the sunshine and chatting with Xalt and Duro. It warmed his heart to see her be able to put aside her cares, even if for a short time. All too soon, she wouldn't have time for anything of the sort. None of them would.

Te'oma swooped overhead, and Kandler's hand went to his sword. He left it there as she landed on the deck next to him.

"Spot anything?" he asked.

"Mostly a lot of sand," Te'oma said. Her eyes turned the

exact same shade of green as Sallah's and twinkled at him. "But I did see one thing."

Kandler watched Burch leap down from the bridge, where he'd been talking with Monja. The shifter sauntered over to them as if there wasn't a thing in the world worth rushing for, and that made the justicar suspicious.

"What's that?" he said, resolving to keep his eyes on the changeling.

Te'oma looked down at Kandler's sword and allowed herself a tiny laugh. *You have nothing to fear from me,* the changeling's voice said in his head.

In an instant, Kandler had his fangblade out, creasing the changeling's throat. "I could have taken your head," he said. "You leave mine alone, and I'll leave yours."

Te'oma leaned back, away from the blade, exposing a thin, red cut where the blade had been. "Understood," she said.

"See you two've become good friends," Burch said as he strode up.

Kandler sheathed his sword. With Burch next to him, the changeling wouldn't dare try anything.

"He did the same thing to me when we met," the shifter told Te'oma. "He's not much of a diplomat, but he gets his point across."

"What did you find out there?" Kandler asked the changeling.

Te'oma smiled, exposing teeth whiter than even her skin. "A ruined city," she said.

"Out here in the desert?" Kandler said. He wondered if she could be lying about this and, if so, why.

"It's inhabited," she said. "I saw yuan-ti."

Now Kandler was sure she was lying. At least that settled one issue for him. If she'd lie about this, then she'd lie about anything.

"She's right," said Burch.

Kandler snapped his head around to stare at his friend.

"It's called Krezent. Used to be filled with couatl. Now it's just the snakefolk."

The justicar felt like he'd been slapped. "Anything else about it you want to tell me?"

Burch nodded. "They all worship the Silver Flame."

Kandler groaned.

Burch jerked his head back at Sallah, who stood at the wheel now, talking with Monja. "What do you want to do?"

"Yes," Te'oma said, enjoying herself. She gave a little wave to Sallah, who ignored her. "Are you going to tell your girlfriend where she can get off?"

Kandler fumed for a moment, wondering if anyone would miss Te'oma if he sliced off her wings and dumped her overboard right now. "Don't say a word to her," he said.

"See," Te'oma said, reaching out to caress Kandler's cheek. "It's not so hard is it?"

"What's that?" he asked, his eyes locked on Sallah.

"Doing the wrong thing for the right reasons."

CHAPTER

13

Yes?" Sallah said.

When Kandler stalked on to the bridge, Monja took one look at him and scurried away. He suspected he knew what was on his mind, and he appreciated her giving him the space he wanted.

"I . . ." He looked into Sallah's green eyes, the ones that Te'oma had mimicked so well, and his tongue froze in his mouth.

"Ah," the lady knight said, nodding. "I'd forgotten which one of us wasn't talking to the other. Thank you for making that clear."

"No," said Kandler. "I just wanted to . . ."

He chewed on his bottom lip, not sure what he wanted to do. He just knew that he loved Sallah and wanted her to stay with him. All he had to do to make that happen for at least a few days longer was keep his mouth shut.

Where was the harm in that, he wondered? It would only be a few days more she'd be forced to stay with the *Phoenix*. Of course, she was right. They hadn't been talking at all for the past couple of days, so why drag out the inevitable?

He should have dropped her off at Krona Peak, although he'd known that stopping there would never have been as simple as slowing down the airship enough for Sallah to get off. Duro would have bragged about how they'd killed Nithkorrh, and the dwarves there would have insisted on hearing the story over and over again. There would have been feasts to dine upon and counsels to keep, and all of that would have added up to more wasted days than Kandler cared to think about.

Here, though, they could leave Sallah at Krezent and be gone—just like she'd said she'd wanted. Of course, she hadn't objected to his bypassing Krona Peak. Perhaps she wouldn't mind if he did so here.

If he mentioned the possibility to her, it would only cause trouble. It would be better to keep quiet about it. He was sure about that.

"We're near a place called Krezent," he said. "It's not much more than a ruin, but a group of yuan-ti live there."

He stopped talking and tried to read Sallah's reaction, but he'd seen statues display more emotion.

"They worship the Silver Flame. I'm sure they'd be happy to take you in."

Sallah stared at Kandler for a moment, her face blank. Then she leaned forward and kissed him softly on the lips. This surprised him so much that he barely returned it.

"What was that for?" he asked, afraid he didn't want to hear the answer. The kiss had felt something like good-bye.

"I knew it," she said, a gentle smile parting her full lips. She hadn't looked upon him so kindly in days.

"You knew about Krezent?"

She nodded. "I'm a Knight of the Silver Flame. I've been trained to become one since birth. Of course I know about even the most remote outposts of our faith, but that's not what I was talking about."

Kandler squinted at her smiling face. Here, in the sun, she had a few freckles across the bridge of her nose that he'd never noticed before.

She reached out and caressed his cheek. "I knew you couldn't hide it from me, that you wouldn't. That's not your way."

Kandler smiled back at the lady knight. Then his face fell. Such compliments meant little in the way of consolation if it meant she was going to leave. His eyes fell to where her hands rested on the wheel, then he glanced up to check the position of the sun.

"I noticed you haven't changed course," he said.

Sallah shook her head. "I'll stay with you until we reach the coast."

Kandler sighed in relief, then caught himself. "I knew you wouldn't abandon us." Then, seeing the look on her face, he added, "Yet."

"Do you know anything about Krezent?" she asked.

"Just what Burch told me."

"It's the remotest sort of remote. The reason no one but the yuan-ti live there is that it's not suitable for other sorts. They have little contact with the outside world, just the occasional trading caravan that wanders through—or off course, as happens more often than not.

"If I disembarked there, I wouldn't have any way to go anywhere. I'm sure the priests there would take me in and protect me, but finding passage for me back to Thrane might take weeks or even months. Better that I stick with you until we cross a better-traveled path."

"Ah," Kandler said, his face falling. The spark of hope in his heart that they might be able to work something out faded without catching fire.

"I'm not going to Argonnessen with you," she said, her voice tinged with regret. "It's a fool's journey. The Order has lost enough knights in this quest already. I'll return to Flamekeep to tell your tale."

"Don't you want to know how the story ends?"

"If you go through with your plan to cross the Dragonreach to take your fight to Argonnessen, I'm afraid I already do."

She kissed him. This time, he responded, knowing it might be the last time. When they broke apart, he turned and walked away.

❦

"You see those horses?" Burch asked, pointing down at a trio of riders who had broken off from the main force of cavalry.

Kandler shaded his eyes as he watched them gallop off to the south. They rode faster than the airship, although Esprë wasn't pushing the *Phoenix* hard right now. Kandler had asked her to take the wheel at the first sighting of the army, and the others had joined him at the prow to learn what they could of the tableau below.

"Those are Valenar cavalry, the best in the world," Burch said. "They go out of their way to prove it any chance they get. They're bastards, and they're always spoiling for a fight."

"Then what are they doing out here in the desert?" Duro asked. "There doesn't look like much around here to pick on other than lizards and birds."

"Some of the clans of my people used to roam these lands," Monja said. "They got tired of dealing with these invaders, so they looked for friendlier lands with better neighbors.

Kandler nodded. "The Valenar warclans used to run strikes into southern Cyre every couple of weeks. Ironic when you consider that Cyre brought them into the Last War as an ally in the first place."

"They do not bother the warforged or the Lord of Blades," Xalt said. "The Lord of Blades sometimes sends his best fighters to test their mettle against the warclans, though. Sometimes a warclan will wait for weeks outside of the Mournland, waiting for a warforged force to show itself and enter battle."

"That's madness," Te'oma said. "They fight just to fight?"

"Not everyone does it for money," said Burch. "Some people take pride in their work."

"I never took pleasure in it," the changeling said.

"Can they do anything to harm us up here?" Sallah asked.

She addressed Kandler directly. The two of them were speaking to each other again; although they both treated each other so respectfully, so dispassionately, Kandler felt like they might as well have kept their distance instead. Still, if she wanted to play things that way, he didn't wish to stop her. Being with her, even in such a stilted way, was better than not being with her at all.

"No," he said. "We're too high up now. Sometimes they have a wizard or sorcerer in their retinue though. That's why I had Esprë move us higher as soon as Burch spotted them."

"Where are those riders headed?" Sallah asked.

Kandler looked to Burch. "Probably Taer Shantara," the shifter said. "It's one of the six forts that stretch around the last stable border Valenar had. The warclans always try pressing out farther—into Q'barra and the Talenta Plains these days—but geography and weather always tar up their supply lines. Besides which, none of the Valenar elves want to bother with guarding a supply caravan instead of being in the thick of things, so eventually they run out of food and water and come galloping home."

Te'oma stared at the shifter. He raised a quizzical eyebrow at her. "I think that's the most words I've ever heard you say in one stretch," she said.

"You're not usually worth talking to."

"Are we headed for Taer Shantara?" Sallah said. "It seems it would be a logical place to gather supplies for your journey across the sea."

Kandler noticed that she hadn't included herself in that journey.

Burch shook his shaggy head. "The elves at Shantara are too war-crazy, and those riders are sure to get there before us to warn that we're the vanguard of an invasion from the north." He held up a hand to cut off protest. "True or not, it doesn't matter. Better to pass them by for Aerie instead."

"That sounds like my kind of place," said Duro. "Clear mountain air and filled with eagle-riding dwarves, I'm sure!"

Burch snorted. "It's the westernmost Valenar fort, the favorite launching pad for raids into Q'barra. It sits in the foothills at the very end of the Endworld Mountains, overlooking the sea. It's our last chance to stop."

"Assuming the elves there don't decide that we're the leaders of an invading force too," said Sallah.

Burch smiled, showing his pointed fangs. "Last chances are last chances," he said.

CHAPTER

14

L et me do the talking," Burch signaled as he and Kandler threw the *Phoenix*'s mooring lines out to the elves standing on the cliffside dock.

Kandler nodded. He'd never been to this part of Valenar before, and he trusted the shifter's judgment. He didn't want any trouble here, just to stock up with plenty of supplies and head out over the Dragonreach, which beckoned beyond. His instincts told him that the longer they waited before making the trip the harder it would be.

"This doesn't look much like what I expected," said Esprë. She'd stuck close to him ever since they'd spotted the warclan and its riders.

The thought of exposing her to a society of elves bothered him a bit. Since Esprina had died, they'd had precious little contact with elves. None but Esprë had lived in Mardakine. Esprina had never sought the company of her own kind, instead preferring to surround herself—and by extension her daughter—with all sorts of people, mostly human.

"I love the human perspective," Esprina had once said

to Kandler. "It's so fresh and immediate. There's a touch of innocence to it, which you'd expect in people so young, but that just makes it all the more precious."

She'd never wanted to talk much about why she'd left Aerenal. It had happened decades before Kandler had been born, when Esprë had been just an infant. Whatever the reason, she hadn't tarried in Valenar either, despite landing there when she reached Khorvaire.

"Your mother and you didn't spend long here," Kandler said.

Esprë shook her blond head. "We spent less than a week in the capital, Taer Valaestas. Just long enough to get our bearings. I barely remember it. Then we were off for Cyre."

A gangplank thrust out from the dock and over the airship's gunwale. Burch went down it first, with Kandler and Esprë close behind. Sallah and Monja came after them, leaving Xalt, Duro, and Te'oma on the airship.

Te'oma had morphed herself to look like Shawda, the last woman who'd shown up dead in Mardakine before the changeling had come to town with Tan Du and his vampire spawn. Kandler respected that the changeling didn't want to call any attention to herself—any changeling would have done so in a village like this—but her choice of disguise riled him. He saw tears well up in Esprë's eyes every time her eyes happened to fall on the false Shawda, and that made him want to stomp over to Te'oma and beat her face into another shape.

Kandler feared, though, that the sight of such a conflict might send Esprë right over the edge. It had turned out that Esprë's dragonmark had caused her to kill a number of people in Mardakine while she'd been sleeping. Shawda—the mother of the girl's best friend, Norra—had been the last of these, and Esprë and the rest of the people of Mardakine had seen the woman's body only after the Knights of the Silver Flame had hacked it to pieces. Seeing a copy of the woman standing on the bridge of the *Phoenix*, her hands wrapped around the wheel, turned Kandler's stomach.

Still, if Esprë could manage to ignore it, then so would he. At least with the changeling staying on the ship with Duro and Xalt, they wouldn't have to put up with it much longer.

As Kandler and Esprë reached the dock, he glanced around. The *Phoenix* had come upon Aerie from its northern edge, and the land there sloped up gently to the only gate set in the fort's tall stone walls. A horsed patrol galloped out onto the dusty road there as the airship came in for a landing.

The southern wall of Aerie looked out over a sheer cliff that fell more than a hundred feet to the wide, fertile plains below. Beyond these gentle lands, Kandler could see a long shore of white sand at which the roaring waters of the Thunder Sea began.

As the elves who founded this place came up from that wide beach and crossed the untamed lands, this spot must have seemed like perfect place for a band of warriors to build a nest. From here, they could watch over all the lands around, like hungry birds hunting for prey.

At Burch's instruction, Te'oma swung the airship out around the fort, far out of catapult range from the place's walls. Then she came up slowly and easily to the airship dock that topped a short section of the southern wall, jutting out over the precipitous drop. The elves there flashed a welcoming signal—or so Burch said—and Te'oma brought the ship in to moor.

Kandler spoke fluent Elven, which had come in handy both as an agent of the Citadel and in courting his wife. He and Esprë sometimes used it as a code in front of the ignorant, but it would not serve them well that way here, where everyone would speak the tongue better than they.

As he, Esprë, Sallah, and Monja waited on the dock, Kandler nudged his stepdaughter. Jerking his head toward Burch, who stood talking with a stern elf dressed in full battle regalia, he shot Esprë a questioning look. She shrugged.

Kandler noticed that every one of the elves he'd seen so far wore a suit of armor and some kind of weaponry. The dockworkers favored spears or short swords, but the lookouts further down the wall in each direction carried longbows and stood nearby loaded ballistae and catapults that were ready to loose their loads at anyone so bold as to invade the space around the fort without permission.

Every piece of equipment bore fine filigree run through with images of death and war, and they looked delicate by human standards. Kandler knew, though, that they'd likely been made by the finest smiths and crafters. Valenar elves never made anything cheap or fragile. By comparison, the *Phoenix* seemed like a crude bit of hackwork churned out in a mill staffed by idiotic children.

The buildings of Aerie might have seemed ridiculously ornate to the untrained eye. Kandler knew that they would stand up to an assault better than all but the best fortifications in the Five Kingdoms. He spied few balconies or terraces built to take advantage of the spectacular views to the south. Those he did see were framed with trellises and colonnades that let in vast amounts of sky. They would also, however, protect from any attacks from above, whether by airship or some other means. The people of Aerie took their security seriously, as they should, given their proximity to the frontier nation of Q'barra, the border of which lay scant miles to the east.

"I do not care for this place," Sallah said quietly.

Monja nodded in agreement, her head bobbing like that of a small child. "A fort like this can quickly change from a haven to a trap."

Burch bowed to the elf he'd been talking to then trotted back to the others. Try as he might, Kandler could not read the shifter's face. He'd known Burch long enough to realize that this was not a good thing.

"The dockmaster welcomes us to Aerie," Burch said.

"Just how welcome are we?" Kandler asked.

Burch pointed at the heavy weaponry mounted on the turrets nearest the airship. "Those aren't for show," he said. "I'm told the elves who staff them don't care much for dwarves and have itchy trigger fingers."

Esprë gasped. "Shouldn't we bring Duro with us then?" she said. "We can't just leave him out there to be shot down."

Burch smiled. "He's safer there than he would be in the fort. At least out there an elf would have to work at it to pick a fight with him. Here, he'd find himself in a tangle inside an hour."

"Have you located lodgings for us?" Sallah asked.

Burch cocked his head at her. "We're staying on the ship."

"You may be," Sallah said, "but once you leave, I will need a place to sleep, unless you can help me arrange for passage out of here before the rest of you depart."

Kandler winced inside, but Burch took it all in stride. "I'll see what I can do," the shifter said.

Kandler hoped his friend wouldn't go out of his way to succeed.

"What about supplies?" Kandler asked. "I'd like to get underway as soon as we can." He avoided Sallah's gaze as he spoke.

Burch grimaced. "They don't always sell supplies to outsiders, but they're under orders to deal with us as if we were citizens of Aerenal."

"How's that?" Kandler asked, suspicious.

He glanced around and saw the dockmaster regarding him with an imperious smirk. An awful lot of the weaponry on these battlements seemed like it could be pointed at him as easily as the *Phoenix*.

"There's someone here—someone important—who wants to have a word with us."

"And this elf has enough pull to get us access to the supplies we need?"

Burch nodded. "If we go see him right now."

Kandler narrowed his eyes at the shifter. "Who is it?"

"Name's Ledenstrae."

Kandler felt his head spin, and he heard Esprë gasp in shock.

"My father?" she whispered.

CHAPTER

15

Esprë hadn't objected when Kandler ordered her back onto the *Phoenix*. Whether she thought it was the right idea or was just too stunned to object, he couldn't tell. Either way, she had let Monja lead her back onto the airship without comment.

"Take us to Ledenstrae," Kandler said to the dockmaster in Elven.

The dockmaster stared cold-eyed at Kandler from under his high-crested helm—a crimson feather topping its crest of polished brass—and gave Kandler a thin-lipped sneer. "My orders are to bring you all to him at once."

Kandler's fangsword leaped from its scabbard and parted the air just over the dockmaster's head. The sword returned home before any of the nearby elves could even reach for their blades. The feather from the dockmaster's helmet flipped before his eyes as it floated to the ground.

"We'll be enough," Kandler said.

He'd wanted to take the elf's head off, and he'd had to fight with himself to keep it from happening. Spilling the dockmaster's blood wouldn't get him what he wanted:

supplies and a good northerly wind to send them on their way.

The dockmaster pursed his lips as he tried not to display being impressed. "Very well," he said, using the common tongue. His thick accent betrayed how rarely he saw fit to use the language, and from the sour look on his face it seemed to leave a rancid taste in his mouth. "Your friends will stay here."

Kandler knew they'd be safer on the *Phoenix* than in Aerie. With a little luck, the airship might be able to make a clean getaway in a pinch, especially if the first rounds from the large weapons in the turrets went wide of the craft's restraining arches. Such weapons packed a devastating punch, but they took forever to reload, and the *Phoenix* had proven she could take a devastating amount of punishment and still remain skyworthy.

The justicar gestured for the dockmaster to lead the way. The proud elf with the featherless helmet marched them down off the battlements and into the fortified village.

Unlike most of the wartime cities Kandler had walked through, Aerie had clean, sharp lines. Each street, building, and square had been planned out before the first stone had been laid. Everywhere the justicar looked, the best way in and out of any given area seemed painfully clear.

"Who would build such a place?" Sallah asked. "The moment invaders managed to breach the walls, they would have an easy path to every important building in the town."

The dockmaster scoffed at the lady knight and her companions. "These walls never have been breached, and they never shall. The warriors in this region are dogs scratching at our doors—if they manage to crawl that close."

"Tell you what," Burch said, his eyes constantly scanning the walls and roofs for the best angles for a shot with the crossbow that hung against his back. "How about you just shut your pointy yap until we get where we're going?"

They continued on in silence until they reached the foot of a tall building. Its ivory-colored walls soared high into the air, the top of it invisible from the street. "The ambassador's chambers occupy the upper three floors," the dockmaster said.

The guards standing at the building's entrance swept aside for the dockmaster and his guests, holding open a large brass door on which an elf skeleton in exquisite robes had been carved in bas relief. Inside, a massive foyer with a high, plastered ceiling occupied the entire floor, except for a large basket set off behind a short fence created by a semicircle of ebony ropes. The dockmaster led Kandler, Burch, and Sallah to the basket and removed one of the ropes so they could climb into it.

The elf then replaced the rope, putting it between himself and the visitors. "Please give the ambassador my regards." He glared at Burch then. "I hope we meet again, under less pleasant circumstances."

Then the dockmaster spat out the Elven word for "up," and the basket began to rise into the air toward a wide hole in the alabaster ceiling. The hole became a timber-lined cylinder that encased the basket like a dart in a blowgun as it ascended.

Sallah clutched Kandler's arm as they entered the hole, the only lighting coming from the occasional doorways they passed. Each of these stood closed, though their centers featured panes of stained glass that depicted skulls, bones, and other images of death. Kandler reached out to hold the lady knight's arm, but that seemed to bring her back to her senses. She drew her holy sword and held it aloft, its silver flames illuminating the dark shaft.

The ceiling of the shaft soon came into view, and the

basket stopped shy of it, close enough that Sallah had to lower her sword to prevent scorching the plaster above. The north wall had a door in it, and as soon as the basket came to a halt, the door opened outward.

Sallah stepped out through the door, and Kandler and Burch followed her. They emerged into a magnificent room with high, vaulted ceilings. Weapons and trophies of war decorated the walls: spears, swords, bows, each tainted with blood. Skulls lifted from creatures of all sorts, from pixies on up to a bulette, hung from lacquered panels engraved with their details in a fine, elvish script.

The room let out onto a balcony, and a white-haired elf stood there in its entrance, framed in the streaming sunlight. He wore light robes of black linen that left his arms and legs exposed down to his bare feet. The contrast of the fabric against his snowy skin made him seem paler than a changeling. As he stepped into the room, his eyes seemed to glow a sickly yellow.

Kandler recognized the elf as Ledenstrae. Esprina had described her husband as looking exactly like this, and every time she had, she'd shuddered. Kandler felt a sympathetic shiver run down his spine. He missed his wife more than ever at that moment.

The justicar looked over at Sallah. He knew he would miss her too. These might well be the last few hours he would ever spend with her. Perhaps once everything with Esprë had been resolved one way or the other, he might find a way to get to Thrane. If he could make his way to Flamekeep, he knew he would be able to locate her.

"Welcome," the elf said, raising an open hand in greeting. He addressed the justicar directly and ignored the others. "I've waited a long time to meet you, Kandler. I'm glad to finally have the chance. It is intriguing how destiny plays with our lives, is it not?"

"Destiny didn't bring me here," Kandler said. "Your dockmaster did—on your orders. I'd rather be loading up my airship right now and leaving this place behind."

"*Your* airship?" the elf said with a wry grin.

Kandler ignored the condescending tone. "So you're an ambassador now? I always heard you were an elf of leisure."

Ledenstrae arched his brows, noting the point that Kandler had scored against him. "My family is well-connected within the political spheres in Aerenal. It had finally become time for me to put those connections to use—for the greater good of our society."

Kandler glared at the elf. "What do you want?"

Ledenstrae feigned shock. "Is it so unusual to want to meet someone with whom I have so much in common? After all, I understand we were both married to the same . . . lady—if I can use that term for someone who absconded to this wretched land of yours with my daughter."

"She hated you."

Ledenstrae smiled without a trace of warmth. "Does it matter? Ours was an arranged marriage, a union joined on behalf of our society's interests in building wealth and good breeds. In that, it succeeded admirably—or so I'm told. After all, I haven't seen my daughter since shortly after she was born."

"She hasn't missed you."

"I think we should let her judge that for herself. I want you to bring her to me."

"Why would I want to do that?"

Ledenstrae shrugged. "I care little for what you may want. Esprë is mine, and I intend to reassert my claim as her father and bring her back with me to Aerenal."

"No damned way—"

Ledenstrae cut Kandler off with a wave of his hand. "Do you think your ways matter to me? You forget where you find yourself. Here, the viceroy has shown nothing but the utmost respect for me. My word is as good as law to the elves who call this outpost their home."

Burch started to say something, but the elf cut him off.

"If you can keep your mongrel there on a leash," he said, "I will put this into simple words that your minds can digest: Give me my daughter back, or I will kill you all and pry her hands from your corpses."

CHAPTER

16

Kandler felt his hand on the pommel of his fang-sword, and he wondered how it had gotten there. He glared at Ledenstrae. "Forget it," he said. "Esprina left her to me."

The elf smiled back at him. "You believe you have a choice in the matter. How amusing."

Sallah put her hand atop Kandler's, keeping him from drawing the weapon. He turned to spit something spiteful at her, but when he did he saw the look in her eyes. His voice caught in his throat, and he closed his mouth.

Sallah cleared her throat and spoke to Ledenstrae. "It's not clear that allowing you to take Esprë would be in her best interests. Kandler loves your daughter very much, and he only wants to see her happy and well. He believes that those purposes would best be served by keeping her with him."

Ledenstrae rubbed his chin. "Such a man who would let his mate speak for him is not one whose words I can take seriously."

Kandler started to curse at the elf, but Sallah shut him

up with a finger across his lips. In frustration, he looked to Burch, but the shifter didn't notice. He was too busy staring at the decorative bits of furniture, artwork, and tightly trimmed foliage that screened the room and the balcony beyond off from the outside world.

"I'm surprised that one who speaks with so many invectives would be given a post as an ambassador, unless, of course, the aim of Aerenal is to plunge its offspring nation into war with its neighbors."

Ledenstrae smiled. "The title 'ambassador' is only a ceremonial one, I'm afraid, given to any member of my family who cares to travel beyond the shores of fair Aerenal. I have no direct political duties. I am only here to recover what is rightfully mine."

"Don't you mean 'who'?" Kandler said. " 'Who' is rightfully yours?"

Ledenstrae bared his teeth, which were as even as the edge of a book. "The girl is of my blood. In the absence of her mother, I am her only family. Now that I have found her again, I wish to reassert my claim on her, and splitting definitions in your barbaric tongue will not dissuade me from the rightfulness of my aims."

Kandler stepped toward Ledenstrae now, angling away from Sallah as he spoke. "Where have you been for the past few decades? Have you even been looking for her? Where were you for the past four years while I raised her on my own? Where were you when her mother died?"

Ledenstrae's ivory cheeks flushed pink, although Kandler could not tell if this effect was rooted in anger or shame. "You have your point of view, of course, and you deserve my thanks for taking care of my daughter when I was not available to do so myself. Know, though, that I would have been with her every day since her birth had her mother not stolen her away from me."

"Escaped from you is more like it," said Kandler. "You think Esprina never told me how you treated her?"

Ledenstrae pursed his lips. "Yes, I would like to hear that story someday. I suspect her point of view deviates sharply from reality, but that always was one of her more egregious flaws. I do hope that penchant for exaggeration hasn't been passed down to our daughter. If it has, I suppose I shall have to cure her of it."

"You got any other children?" Burch asked, his eyes still scanning their surroundings.

The elf stared at the shifter as if contemplating whether or not speaking to Burch was beneath him. He followed Burch's eyes around the room, then seemed to decide that in a foreign land he could afford to be more liberal with his words.

"Esprë is my only offspring," Ledenstrae said. "Children are rare in Aerenal. With as long as we live, if we bred like humans or shifters the entire continent would be overrun in no time."

"Children's rarity is what makes them so valuable," Sallah said.

The elf gave her an approving nod. "The Undying Court carefully selects breeding partners to produce the finest possible children. Only the greatest of the great achieve the goal we all wish for ourselves, to ascend to the Undying Court and exist with the other heroes who have gone before us into immortality."

"Does being a father who's lost a daughter harm your chances?" said Kandler.

"There is that," Ledenstrae said. "It is far from the only reason I wish to reunite with my daughter." The elf paused for a moment before continuing. "When I heard of the Day of Mourning, I feared that Esprina and Esprë had been consumed in it. Reports in Aerenal indicated that there were no survivors, and since I knew them both to be living in Cyre at the time, I knew there would be little chance that they had survived.

"I wanted to launch an investigation of my own at the time, in the slim hopes of locating them, but the Last War still raged. Such an undertaking would have been hazardous in the extreme. I would have risked it, but it seemed clear that no one in Cyre had survived.

"I consulted with mystics of all sorts, but none of them were able to find a trace of Esprina or Esprë at the time. Perhaps this was due to some sort of magical disruption emanating from the Mourning, but at the time I believed the results. They merely confirmed my worst fears.

"I mourned for my daughter and yes, even my wife. Despite what she may have told you"—the elf looked at Kandler—"our marriage never ended. In the eyes of the Undying Court, we were matched for all time, and no dalliance with a member of a lesser race could undo that."

Kandler checked his rage himself this time. He could tell the elf meant to provoke him, and he refused to give Ledenstrae the satisfaction. He glanced at Sallah and Burch instead.

Sallah smiled at him in a way that made his heart hurt. Despite the fact that they would part soon and likely forever, he would have preferred to spare her watching him spar with his wife's first husband.

Burch caught his eye with a hand signal. The shifter had spotted at least four guards hiding somewhere in the room or on the balcony, perhaps more.

Kandler gave the signal to sit tight. He should have realized that a noble elf like Ledenstrae would never risk death at his hands by failing to protect himself. The elf probably had been hoping Kandler would attack him, giving the guards an excuse to chop him to pieces. With Kandler dead, that would make his claim as Esprë's father all the stronger.

Kandler wondered why the elf hadn't just killed him straight out. He supposed that Ledenstrae's influence here in Aerie might not be enough to cover up a cold-blooded murder. If so, then getting out of here with Esprë wasn't as hopeless a cause at it had seemed.

"Why now?" Kandler asked, suspicious. "What made you come searching for Esprë now? What are the chances that you'd end up waiting for us here, right in our path?"

The elf nodded sagely. "These are all fine questions. To answer: Now seemed like the right time. Certain information came to me that Esprë was, in fact, alive and well, and I set out to find her. As for how I managed to track you down, I'll admit I had a bit of help with that. An old friend of the family contacted me after running into you recently and alerted me to Esprë's plight. Fortunately, we have a great deal of influence in Shae Cairdal, and I was able to arrange for transport here immediately."

Kandler stared at the elf. Who could have tipped Ledenstrae off to their whereabouts? The Lord of Blades or his lieutenant Bastard? Vol? Ikar the Black? The Captain of Bones?

Even if any of them had, how would Ledenstrae have known that they were headed here? Kandler hadn't made the decision to head south until after they'd survived the battle with Nithkorrh and Ibrido.

There could only be one person.

"That changeling bitch," he said. "She sold us out to you. She went from one mistress to another."

Ledenstrae grinned, pulled back his thin, pale lips to reveal sharp, white teeth. "I'm sure I don't know who you're talking about," he said. "You must feel surrounded by traitors on all sides. Perhaps your lady knight there betrayed you so she could serve her own cause?"

Kandler glanced at Sallah, who stood scowling at the elf.

When she noticed the justicar watching her, she snorted in disgust. "Could you really think such a thing of me?"

The elf giggled. "Perhaps it was your shifter friend there instead. How well do you really know him anyhow? He's barely more than a wild beast, is he not?" He gave Burch a cold look. "I've heard of curs turning on their masters."

Burch stared at Ledenstrae for a moment then barked at him. The elf flinched back in fear, and the shifter chuckled. He stopped when he saw the murderous look on Kandler's face as he glared at the elf.

"Who was it?" Kandler demanded.

A figure sauntered in from the balcony then, one whom Kandler recognized instantly. The emaciated, paper-skinned elf stood there before him and took the arm that Ledenstrae kindly offered to her. Her fine robes of green and blue silk flowed around her, billowing in a gentle breeze. She opened her cut-like mouth and smiled so wide that Kandler feared her knife-sharp cheekbones might slice through her skin. Madness and glee danced in her sunken eyes.

"Majeeda," Kandler said, his voice tight and low with shock.

CHAPTER

17

How wonderful to see you again," Majeeda said to Kandler, Sallah, and Burch. "I feared our paths might never cross again."

Kandler stared at the mad elf as if his eyes might fall from his head. Sallah and Burch remained silent too, just as stunned as he. Ledenstrae struggled to stifle a vicious laugh, enjoying the situation but clearly wanting to avoid insulting his surprise guest.

Then Kandler realized he'd stopped breathing. He took in a deep breath then plastered a pleasant smile on his face. He thought that Ledenstrae would see it for the thin disguise it was, but he didn't care. He knew from experience how dangerous the wizard was. If he treated her with the respect she felt she deserved, she would gobble it up, or so he hoped.

"My Lady Majeeda," Kandler said in Elven, after clearing his throat. "How wonderful to find ourselves in your presence again."

Majeeda arched a desert-dry eyebrow at these words. "Is that correct?" she said, hiding her suspicions under the thinnest veil of civility. "The manner in which you took your leave of my hospitality would seem to indicate otherwise."

Kandler gave the deathless elf a short bow. "My deepest apologies if our actions caused you any distress, my lady. We were called away in an instant and didn't wish to disturb your rest as such a late hour."

Majeeda rasped at this such that Kandler thought she might fall over from lack of breath. The he realized she was laughing. "My foolish soldier," she said, "do you not know that those such as I do not require such things?"

Kandler feigned disappointed shock. To nail home that effect—he hoped—he switched to the common tongue again. "Please allow me to double my apologies over this incident. We must have seemed rude in the extreme to leave so hastily. Please believe that we had only your interests in mind."

The justicar looked to Sallah, who nodded regally. She seemed to see the need to pay Majeeda some respect, whether authentic or not, but she didn't enjoy playing along with the charade.

Kandler felt something somewhere in the room thump against the floor. He'd been in enough fights to recognize it as a body slumping to the ground, and he coughed to clear his throat once more. Before he could say anything, though, Majeeda raised a skeletal hand to silence him.

"May I ask what you have done with the airship?" she asked. Her papery lips shook as she spoke, and Kandler knew everything turned on giving her the right answer here.

"When we discovered her, we realized that she must have belonged to the intruders you had mentioned to use during that wonderful dinner you served us. Since she had sat for so long, unused, we thought . . ."

The skeptical look on Majeeda's face told Kandler he was losing her. He struggled to find the right words and felt himself starting to panic. His hand fell to his sword.

Dealing with Ledenstrae was one thing. That elf had something to lose. Majeeda, on the other hand, was not only crazed but powerful. She could probably kill them all with not much more than a word, and where would that leave Esprë then?

Perhaps if he could unsheath his fangblade quickly enough he could kill Majeeda before she could cast a spell. Killing something already dead was always tricky though, and he would only get one try.

"That's how you found us," Sallah said to the deathless elf. "Isn't it?"

Majeeda stopped staring so coldly at Kandler and smiled at the lady knight. Her lips crinkled like paper around her yellow teeth. "Of course," she said. "I am a seer of many things—especially those that I own. When something has been in my possession as long as that horrid airship, I know where she is. Finding her is as easy as closing my eyes."

She did just that by way of illustration. Her eyelids folded and unfolded like ripe husks, and Kandler realized that he'd never seen her blink before.

"Why?" Kandler said. "If you know so much, then you must understand what Esprë means to Ledenstrae." He meant to speak around Esprë's dragonmark. So far, neither Ledenstrae or Majeeda had said they understood her horrible powers, and he didn't care to tip that hand without some kind of confirmation that they'd already seen it. "Why would you help the people who abandoned you so long ago?"

Majeeda's head wobbled atop her neck, and Kandler feared it might fall off. Instead, she spoke. "Don't you see, my dear soldier? Your stepdaughter is my way back into the good graces of proper elf society. She's my way into the Undying Court."

The deathless elf spoke with such breathless glee at the end that Kandler thought her concave chest might burst from the rare stress of expressing a happy emotion. He nodded at the creature, whose presence turned his stomach more than ever. He didn't want to incur her wrath, but he refused to consider turning Esprë over to Ledenstrae, now more than ever.

Kandler gave Majeeda a half-hearted smile. "I am pleased to hear that you've managed to find your way home. Permit me to take my leave of you once more so that I might go and tell my daughter the good news."

"Please," Ledenstrae said, stepping forward to show Kandler the door. "I'm looking forward to seeing *my* daughter again. It's been far too long."

"Of course," Majeeda said, "we must do something to repay the man for all his trouble of taking care of your darling for so long, mustn't we?"

Ledenstrae cocked his head at the deathless elf, surprised at the turn the conversation had taken. "How do you mean?"

"It is unseemly to not present such a man with a gift to demonstrate your gratitude for all his efforts. Just think what sorts of horrible fates might have met young Esprë, wandering through this cruel land, thinking herself to be an orphan."

Ledenstrae narrowed his eyes at the elf. "What did you have in mind?"

"Why, the airship, of course."

Ledenstrae's suspicious frown evaporated. "What a splendid notion."

"You want to trade me an airship for Esprë?" Kandler couldn't believe the words passing through his own lips.

"If you have no further need of her, I will pay you handsomely," Ledenstrae said, warming to the idea. "I'll even arrange for your passage home—wherever that might be."

Kandler hesitated. He had no intention of letting them take Esprë, no matter the price, but he wasn't ready to declare that to them yet.

"You'll probably be happy to get rid of her," Ledenstrae said. "A ship like that is nothing but a target."

The elf's tone bore just a hint of menace, enough so that Kandler couldn't miss it. Majeeda, on the other hand, showed no sign of detecting it. She smiled blankly at both him and Sallah.

"I'll have to discuss it with my crew," Kandler said. He bowed toward Majeeda. "My thanks for your kindness, my lady." He nodded sharply at their host, then turned and left. Sallah followed close behind.

"Where's Burch?" she whispered as they stepped into the basket.

Kandler kept his mouth closed until the basket began to descend. "Don't worry about him," he said. "He'll let himself out."

"What are you going to do?" Sallah said.

"Just what I told Majeeda. I'm going to discuss it with the crew. Then we're going to sail out of here as if we had a horde of dragons on our tail."

"What about me?"

Kandler looked at her, surprised. "I—I don't know," he said. "I hadn't thought that far ahead."

"You can't leave me here after you race out of town. They'll have my head on a pike."

"You could come with us."

Sallah's nostrils flared as she glared at the justicar. He turned away.

"We'll find someplace safe to drop you off," he said. "Maybe in Q'barra. Wyrmwatch isn't that far from here, I think."

Sallah nodded. "One of our faithful is the lead elder there, a man by the name of Nevillom. That could work."

When the basket reached the ground floor, the guards showed Kandler and Sallah to the door. "The dockmaster returned to his post," one of them said. "You can show yourselves back."

The door to the tower slammed shut behind them. As it did, Burch appeared from where he'd been hiding behind the door.

CHAPTER

18

"Have a nice talk?" the shifter asked as he fell into step with the others.

Sallah craned her neck up to see how far down the shifter must have climbed to get out of Ledenstrae's place. She let out a low whistle.

"We're getting out of here," Kandler said. "They want to trade Esprë for the airship."

"And our lives," said Burch. "This isn't the kind of offer they let you refuse."

Kandler smirked. "Then we'll just let them figure out what our answer is when we're gone."

Burch pursed his lips and nodded. They walked along in silence toward the docks.

"You're too quiet," Kandler said, "both of you. What's on your minds?"

Sallah winced. "I'm wondering if maybe we should run. After all, Ledenstrae's sure to find the body of that guard that Burch took out."

Burch snorted. "All three of them probably," he said. "Can't believe I let that last one slip like that." He cracked his knuckles. "Must be losing my touch."

"How about you?" Kandler said. "That's not what's keeping you quiet."

Burch shrugged. "Don't know if I should say."

"How long have we known each other?"

Burch stared at Kandler for a moment, a sad, wry look on his face. "All right," he said. "How about we give Esprë to her father?"

Kandler stumbled over a paving stone that seemed to have reached up to grab his foot. He righted himself, then glared back at the shifter. "You were right," he said. "You shouldn't have said a thing."

"You asked."

The anger rising in Kandler's throat surprised him. He'd long thought he could trust Burch with his life. Now to hear these words come from the shifter seemed like the worst kind of betrayal.

They walked along, Kandler silently steaming. He wanted to say something, to shout at Burch for even suggesting such a thing, but he didn't want to draw attention to them. He just wanted to get to the airship and leave.

Ledenstrae would have the craft tied down tight, of course, but Kandler figured the fangblade would cut through just about anything the dockworkers could muster. If he worked fast, he might be able to free the ship before the soldiers in the turrets could bring the heavy weapons to bear on them.

"Maybe he's right," Sallah said.

Kandler goggled at the woman. He had worried that she'd torn him from her heart upon announcing her intention to leave, but he'd never thought she'd stoop to sabotaging him like this.

"Think about it for a moment," she said. "You're about to fly across the ocean to challenge a land filled with dragons on behalf of Esprë. Does it make sense to risk her life at the same time?"

"Right," said Burch. "She'd be safer in Aerenal with Ledenstrae. Once we deal with the dragons, we can go get her then."

Kandler stopped and gaped at them. "You're both mad," he said. "Since when have the two of you agreed on anything?"

Sallah frowned. "That should tell you that we're right."

"At least gnaw on it a bit," Burch said.

Kandler stomped ahead. "No time for that," he said. He turned back to focus a murderous glare on each of them. "Not a word about this to Esprë from either of you. It's better if she never knows."

When they reached the airship, Kandler confirmed the worst. The airship had been tied down with thin, elven chains while they'd been gone. While they didn't weigh enough to cause the ship to sag in the air, no steel was stronger.

There would be no quick and easy escape here. Still, Kandler was as determined to leave as much as ever. He scowled at the dockworkers as he approached the deck and stormed up the gangplank.

Esprë greeted him at the gunwale, throwing her arms around him the moment he set foot on the ship. He held her tight, not wanting to ever let go. He knew as soon as he did he would have to look her in the eye and lie to her face, and he wanted to put that off for just a moment longer.

"You're crushing me," Esprë said with a giggle. She pushed herself free, and Kandler lowered her back to the airship's deck. She looked up at him with hope and excitement in her sparkling blue eyes.

"What happened?" she asked. "Did you really see my father? What is he like? I don't remember anything about him really, although I've often wondered."

Her face fell as she looked at Kandler. "What is it?" she asked.

Kandler shook his head. "I'm sorry, Esprë. It wasn't your father. Just someone who used his name to get us off the ship."

"Why would someone do that?" she asked, disappointment marring her face.

Kandler swept his arms wide and tried not to look her in the eye. "They want the airship," he said. "See what they did to her while we were gone?"

"We tried to stop them," Xalt said. "They insisted, with swords."

Kandler shrugged and patted the warforged on the back, glad that someone had interrupted his conversation with Esprë. "I'm sure you did the best you could under the circumstances."

"I was all for splitting their skulls," said Duro, "but Xalt and the ladies here stayed my hand."

"We didn't want to start a fight that would have ended with us sailing away without you three," Monja said. She looked at Sallah. "Is everything well?"

Kandler saw the lady knight scowl. He knew she liked this even less than he did, but he hoped she'd respect his wishes as Esprë's parent. He shot her a pleading look, which she caught with a resigned shrug.

"How would they have known to use my father's name?" Esprë asked without a hint of suspicion in her voice. The thought genuinely confused her.

Kandler hemmed for a moment, then tapped his head with a thick finger. "Psion," he said. "Just like our friend up there at the wheel." He pointed up at the bridge where Te'oma stood, still in Shawda's guise.

"That's funny," Esprë said. "I haven't really thought about him in years."

"He's been on my mind," Kandler muttered.

"Now that they have us tied down, what is our plan?" Xalt said. The warforged looked at him with eyes as innocent as Esprë's.

"Break out of here," Kandler said.

❦

Kandler stood on the bridge of the *Phoenix* and outlined a plan of action. Monja, Te'oma, Duro, Sallah, and Xalt riveted their attention to him as he spoke. At his request, Burch had taken Esprë to the ship's bow. He didn't want her to hear everything he had to say.

"Why can't I help?" Esprë had said.

Kandler's chest tightened as he continued to lie to her. She'd proven herself to be both capable and dangerous. Under other circumstances, he would have find something for her to do, perhaps not vital but important enough to let her discover a bit more about what she could do. Right now, though, he had told himself he couldn't risk even that much.

Kandler's plan was simple enough. It involved Te'oma and Burch sabotaging the nearest ballista and catapult, which the dockmaster had trained on the airship. At the same time, Kandler and Sallah would destroy the posts to which the chains holding down the *Phoenix* were bound. Breaking through the wood would prove easier than hacking away at a chain, even with such amazing swords as theirs.

Monja would take the wheel, with Esprë at her side, while Xalt and Duro provided cover with their crossbows. With luck, they wouldn't have to kill too many elves.

"You worry about harming those who would hold us captive?" Te'oma asked, disbelief marring Shawda's normally stolid face.

Kandler fought the urge to beat the visage from the changeling, all too aware that such commotion would bring the guards running to see what was going on. Then he wondered if he could somehow work that into the plan.

"They're just doing their jobs," he said.

"Is that what you told the people you killed when you worked for Breland?"

Kandler stared at the changeling for a moment. "If you want to pick a fight with me, can you wait until we're back in the air? I'll be happy to dump your body overboard then."

Te'oma smiled back at him. "Whatever you say, *boss.*"

The label brought Burch back to mind. Kandler had his back to the wheel and the rest of the ship. He turned around to look for the shifter, but he could not find him anywhere.

Esprë was gone too.

Kandler lashed out and caught Te'oma around the throat. "Where are they?" he said as he bore down on her. The pressure started to choke her, and it guaranteed that if she tried to lash out or run he'd slam her to the floor.

Sallah put a hand on Kandler's shoulder, but he shrugged it off. Duro and Xalt gaped at the scene unfolding in front of them.

"I've seen this coming for days," Monja said with a sigh.

"Where?" Kandler said louder. He squeezed the changeling's neck harder for emphasis. She began to turn pale, and he wondered if it was from a lack of blood or because she meant to change shape again.

"Don't know," Te'oma said. She tried to shrug, but Kandler, wary of a trick, shook her like a rag doll.

"She's telling the truth," Sallah said.

He glanced at her and saw the pain in her eyes, along with the ugly image of his angry visage reflected there. Disgusted, he shoved Te'oma away. She fell to her knees and coughed and hacked fresh air into her lungs.

"The rest of you stay here," Kandler said, not caring how nasty his snarls might sound. "I'm going after my daughter."

CHAPTER

19

I can't believe that Kandler would keep me from my father," Esprë said as she and Burch entered the basket that would take them to the top of the tower. The shifter shot her a look, and she blushed. "You're right. I can."

She leaned over and panted as the basket began to ascend. They'd run hard to make sure they would get here before Kandler, and she wanted to catch her breath before she met her father.

What would this Ledenstrae look like, she wondered? She had no memory of him at all. Her mother had taken her from Aerenal while Esprë was still an infant, and she'd not been in her father's presence since. Had she ever? Had he held her even once?

She ran a hand through her hair, worried now that she might not measure up to his expectations. The time on the road from Mardakine to here had not been kind to her. She'd not had a bath since shortly after she'd awakened in Fort Bones—unless she counted getting dunked in the frigid underground lake in which the dragon Nithkorrh had lived.

She knew she didn't look much like a princess. Her mother—always practical—had never treated her that way. That was part of the land she'd left behind, and she and Esprë had to carve out their own way in this strange new place.

Kandler had even fewer illusions about proper society and culture, of which there had been none in Mardakine anyhow. He'd been trained as a soldier, an agent, but never as a father. Despite that, she knew he'd done his best.

At first, after her mother had died, Esprë had feared that Kandler would send her away, perhaps back to Aerenal, to live with people she didn't know. Then, after he'd made it clear he would do his best to raise her, she wondered if he'd only offered to do so out of some sort of sense of duty to her mother.

Over the years, though, she'd come to know that Kandler loved her for herself, not just for whose daughter she might be. She admitted to herself that she'd come to love him too.

That's why it hurt so much that he'd decided to keep her from her father this way. Did he think that she would just jump into this stranger's arms and let him steal her away? Did Kandler really think so little of her? Was his faith in her so small?

Burch moved in the basket next to her, and she looked at him. The shifter seemed to be standing on his toes, ready to leap from the confined space as soon as he could. She reached out and grabbed his arm, both to steady him and to gain his attention.

"Isn't he going to kill you?" Esprë asked.

Burch stopped squirming around and stared at the girl with his yellow eyes. "Probably. We've known each other a long while, but it's never good to get between a papa and his cub." He shrugged. "Kill's probably too strong a word."

"I meant figuratively." She shuddered. "He wouldn't

really kill you. Would he?" Her voice sounded far less sure than she wanted it to.

Burch shrugged.

"Why did you tell me when he wouldn't?" she asked.

The basket reached the end of its journey, and Burch escorted her out into the room beyond without a word. She tugged at his shirt. "Burch," she said.

He didn't look at her. "Did I mention Majeeda's here too?"

"What?" Esprë said, her guts filled with ice.

"Hello!" a strange elf said in Elven as he strode into the room from the balcony beyond. His white hair shone in the late-day sunlight, complementing his pale skin and contrasting with his robes of black linen. His golden eyes sparkled with joy.

The elf dashed forward and put his arms on Esprë's shoulders. "How good it is to see you again," he said, marveling, his accent featuring the regal tones of Aerenal. "I would know you anywhere. You are your mother's daughter, to be sure."

Esprë stared up at the elf. He stood much shorter than Kandler, perhaps about Burch's height instead. He seemed thin and frail, like he might not be able to heft a proper sword, but he still radiated a powerful confidence that Esprë found comforting.

"Hello," she said, her voice barely more than a whisper. She cleared her throat. "Hello, Ledenstrae."

The elf reached out and took her chin in his hand. Holding it, he peered into her eyes and smiled. "You may call me Father, young one."

"As you wish," Esprë said, "Father." The word felt strange on her tongue. She'd not had a father for so long that the concept seemed like an invader from a strange but familiar land.

Majeeda strolled into the room behind Ledenstrae, her bones creaking with every move. Esprë couldn't tell if the soft, fragile sounds she heard came from the rustling of the deathless elf's robes or her tissue-thin skin.

"Oh, my little darling," Majeeda said, opening her arms for an embrace. "It's such a relief to see you safe and sound. When you disappeared from my home—"

As Esprë flinched at the old elf's approach, Burch stepped between them with a wicked grin. He spread his arms wide, ready to accept the wizard's affections, but she recoiled, not bothering to hide her disgust.

Ledenstrae had stepped back to permit Majeeda to greet Esprë. Now he reached out and brought Esprë to him, holding an arm around her. She couldn't tell if he meant to protect her from Majeeda or Burch, or if he just wanted to establish his parentage by showing some sort of concern.

The fact that he hadn't shown any such concern over the past decades of her life wasn't lost on Esprë. She would never forget that he'd not been around for her since, well, ever. She wondered, though, if their blood-bond would be enough, something they could build a relationship on now. Perhaps their chance to know each other had been delayed but not destroyed.

"I am glad that Kandler saw the wisdom of returning you to me," Ledenstrae said.

"You didn't give him much of a choice," said Burch. He blew a kiss at Majeeda and grinned as the bony creature shuddered with revulsion.

"He didn't return me to you," Esprë said, finding her voice. "I came of my own accord."

Ledenstrae squeezed her shoulder. "I knew you had my blood in you," he said. "I could see it the moment you walked into the room."

Esprë heard something less than joy in the elf's tone.

Wistfulness? It was hard to say. She didn't know Ledenstrae at all, but she'd spent little time in the company of elves other than her mother. Once she learned their ways, perhaps her father's demeanor wouldn't seem so strange.

"It is as I told you," Majeeda said. She ran her hands down the front of her robes, trying to smooth out the wrinkles there and regain her composure. "My knowledge of such things knows no peer."

Ledenstrae grimaced at this, then gestured toward the balcony beyond the room in which they stood. "Come," he said. "Let us sit in the sun and speak. I would like to get to know my daughter better."

Esprë looked up at the elf and took his hand in hers. "I think I'd like that," she said.

CHAPTER 20

"Open that door," Kandler said, his hand on the hilt of the fangblade hanging from his belt.

The three guards standing in front of the portal that led into the ground floor of the tower refused to budge. They didn't even acknowledge the justicar's presence as he walked up to them. Kandler recognized the tactic, meant to imply that someone like him was so little a threat as to be not worth noticing.

He'd used it himself from time to time, but never when faced with an armed opponent. An idiot with a sword still had a sword, and Kandler had never seen the wisdom in treating any lethal threat casually. He preferred the direct approach.

Kandler drew his sword and pinned one of the guards to the door behind him before any of their blades even cleared their scabbards. The fangblade lanced right through the elf's unarmored shoulder, and the justicar pulled it back in front of himself in time to catch the blades of the wounded guard's two companions along its shaft.

"Open that door," Kandler said.

This time, the guards didn't ignore him. The injured elf slid back along the wall, away from the fight, to give his friends more room to maneuver. It did them little good.

The fangblade licked out and sliced through the forearm of one of the attacking guards. The elf dropped his blade with a pained cry.

Kandler kicked it aside as he parried a counterattack from the third guard. He didn't have the time to mess around with these hired swords. If they called for help, they could have most of the fortress surrounding the tower in no time.

Still, he didn't care to kill them. As he'd told Te'oma, he had no quarrel with these elves. They were but soldiers doing the job they'd been trained for.

As the third guard came at him, Kandler blocked the incoming swing with his fangblade. The enemy sword broke in two on the fangblade's edge. As it fell apart, Kandler smashed out with his fist and caught the startled elf square in the nose. Blood spurted from the guard's face as he sat down hard.

Kandler kicked the last of the guards aside and let himself into the tower. As he did, he heard the guards begin to shout for help.

He slammed the door behind him and barred it. Then he dashed over to the basket, which dropped into place as he reached it. He leaped into it, and it began to ascend.

❦

"We cannot wait here for them to come back," Sallah said. She shaded her eyes as she stared off from the top of the bridge at the tops of the towers that dotted the village. She thought she recognized the one in which they'd met Ledenstrae.

Xalt cocked his head at the lady knight. "Kandler told us

to wait here," he said. "His instructions were clear."

"If you followed instructions to the letter, Kandler, Burch, and I would be dead, and you would still be wandering about the Mournland." Sallah tried to take the edge off her comment with a wry grin, but she found she couldn't summon one.

"She's right," Monja said, her hands wrapped around the top spars of the airship's stationary wheel. She had to stand on a couple of the lower spars to be able to see over the top of the bridge's console, but the position seemed to grant her not only height but authority.

"I saw the look in Kandler's eyes," the halfling said, glancing at Te'oma. "He's spoiling for a fight."

"Then let him find one," the changeling said, still rubbing her throat where Kandler has strangled her.

"Do you blame him for not trusting you?" Sallah asked.

"None of you do." Te'oma spat on the deck, unable to keep the bitterness from her voice. "Why should he?"

The changeling paced the deck for a moment, then stopped and turned on the others. "I could have flown away from here at any point. On the trip from Fort Bones to the Ironroots, I could have just slipped over the ship's railing at any time and been gone, but no, I stayed here, with you, so I could do something to . . . to . . ."

The others waited for a moment.

"To kill a dragon?" Duro asked, his voice high and uncertain.

Te'oma scoffed at him. "You're insane," she said. "Spending your days guarding the lair of a dragon, armed with nothing more than axes, hoping you could do something to stop it when it wanted to get free. If I'd known what was going to happen—I'll be honest. I would have flown away. The last you would have seen of me would have been my wings flapping into the sunset."

Xalt interrupted her rant. "That is not true. As you say, you could have escaped at many points. Even after we discovered Nithkorrh, you had many opportunities."

Te'oma turned away and muttered something to herself.

Sallah raised a hand to reach out to the changeling, then thought better of it. Instead, she spoke. "Your actions earned our respect, if not our unwavering trust. You must recall your actions thrust us along this perilous road."

Te'oma spun back about. "Don't you think I know that?" she said. "If I could change one thing I'd ever done, I'd— Well, I'd have to start a lot farther back than that." She bowed her head. "Now, with nothing left for Vol to dangle before me, I just thought I could do some good for once."

"Especially if that good would thwart the lady who betrayed you," Monja said.

"She's no lady," Te'oma said with a shiver. "She's beyond such things, like royalty is beyond peasantry. If you'd ever seen her sitting on that frigid throne of hers in Illmarrow Castle, you'd know her for what she is: a queen. The queen of death."

Silence fell over the bridge then. Duro shifted uncomfortably. Monja stared out from the wheel as if charting a path toward the ocean that appeared as a strip of grayish blue on the southern horizon. Xalt stared at each of the others in turn, focusing his unblinking eyes on them like a lantern's light.

"I believe in you," Sallah said to Te'oma as Xalt's gaze fell on her. As the words left her, she wondered why she'd bothered to speak them.

"So you said." Te'oma huffed and frowned. "It's easy to believe in someone when your god lets you know if she's telling the truth."

Sallah shook her head. "I didn't use the powers of the Silver Flame for that."

Te'oma stared at Sallah through reddened eyes. "You're lying," she said.

A soft smile crossed Sallah's lips. "If you really want the trust you ask from us, it would help if you could extend it too."

"Why would you tell Kandler to believe me?"

Sallah gave a slight shrug, barely enough to move the shoulders of her shining armor. "Because I did."

Te'oma considered this for a moment. Then a smile slowly spread across her face. "How are we going to break this glorified dinghy free from the dock?" she asked.

Sallah looked to where a pair of thick chains moored the *Phoenix* to the dock. They had no tools that would snap such weighty links. They would have to try another way.

Duro cleared his throat. "I think I have an idea."

CHAPTER

21

Esprë squirmed in the hard chair across from her father. She knew it was an expensive piece of furniture of the finest elf fashion, and it probably was worth a small fortune. Try as she might, though, she could not make herself comfortable in it.

Instead, she longed for the worn, rickety chairs around the table in her home back in Mardakine. She knew that she'd probably never see that town again. Even if the Mark of Death somehow disappeared from her skin, she could never return to the place where her burgeoning powers had unwittingly caused the deaths of so many of the townspeople. Now that she knew that the responsibility for those murders could be laid at her feet, she could never look the survivors in the face again.

The image of Norra, her best friend ever since she had come with Kandler to Mardakine, leaped into her mind. She missed Norra terribly, but should they ever find themselves in the same room again, Esprë knew that she would flee the place rather than confront the fact that her dragon-mark had killed Norra's mother.

With no home to go back to, Esprë wondered if there might be a place for her in her father's life and land. She'd left Aerenal shortly after her birth, but that had been her mother's doing not hers. Now it seemed like Ledenstrae meant to take her back with open arms. She could hardly believe her luck, but she couldn't yet tell if that fortune was good or bad.

"Father?" Esprë said. "Where would we live in Aerenal?"

Ledenstrac beamed down at the elf-maid. "My family—which is yours too, of course—has places all over Aerenal. Our ancestors are wise and powerful, and they comprise one of the most powerful factions within the Undying Court. We would have our pick of places in which to reside."

"Where would you take me?"

Esprë noticed that Ledenstrae had not offered Burch a seat with the others. The shifter had not seemed to notice the affront though. Instead, he stood watching over them, his head cocked to one side from time to time as if he were listening for something.

"We would arrive in Pylas Talaear," Ledenstrae said. "We could stay there for some time, until you feel more comfortable with proper society. She has been gone so long," he said to Majeeda.

The ancient elf clapped her hands with glee. "As have I! We could practice our etiquette together."

While the thought pleased Majeeda, it turned Esprë's stomach. She knew that the elves of Aerenal all aimed to someday become deathless like Majeeda, to take their place within the Undying Court, but it seemed horrible and unnatural to her.

Was that why Esprina had taken her away from Aerenal? To save her daughter from an eternal life as such a horror? Or to save herself from the same?

"Why did my mother leave you?" Esprë asked.

The question slipped from her before she had a chance to consider it. As it did, though, she felt grateful for it. If her mother hadn't trusted Ledenstrae, if she'd been willing to abandon her homeland to get herself and her daughter away from him, Esprë needed to know why.

Ledenstrae coughed hard and reached for a nearby platter on which sat a steaming teapot, a number of small cups and saucers, and a small selection of cookies that seemed as if they'd stood there untouched for decades. As he poured himself a spot of brackish tea into a cup and drank it, Majeeda scowled at Esprë as if she had thrown a soiled diaper into the middle of the floor between them.

"I'd rather not get into the details of the parting between your mother and I," Ledenstrae said. "I don't wish to speak ill of the dead."

When he saw the disappointment on Esprë's face, he continued. "I'd long hoped that your mother and I might reconcile. As elves, our lives are long. Perhaps we might not have reached an accord until we both found ourselves ascended to the Undying Court, but I had faith that it would someday happen.

"Perhaps that's why I never bothered to track you down before now. In my heart, I thought that Esprina would one day come back to Aerenal with you. I never thought that she would be so horribly lost. To not even know where her body is . . ."

"I know where her body is," said Esprë.

Ledenstrae's eyes flew wide. Esprë looked to Burch, who gave her a tiny shrug. She knew he would have preferred for her not to talk with her father about such things, but she'd already opened that door, so she continued through it. As she spoke, she saw Burch turn and leave. She wanted to ask him to stay, but she feared what he might say to her. As it was, neither Ledenstrae nor Majeeda paid him any heed as he went.

"Kandler and Burch found her body in the western part of the Mournland, near where they helped found Mardakine—that's a settlement of Cyrans located in the bottom of a blast crater," she said.

Ledenstrae perched on the edge of his seat, his eyes boring holes through Esprë. "What did they do with her?"

"They buried her by a black river and placed a marker over her grave."

Ledenstrae and Majeeda gasped in horror. The deathless elf clutched at her chest as if her dead heart might start beating again.

"Savages!" Ledenstrae said. "Did your stepfather not know what that meant, to bury an elf rather than recovering her body? It's been years. The worms might have devoured every bit of her flesh by now."

Now Esprë understood Ledenstrae's shock. In Aerenal, she knew, the Undying Court evaluated the lives of dead elves. Those deemed worthwhile were brought into the court itself to sit at the sides of their ancestors. Others, who had not yet had a chance to prove themselves, were usually resurrected by magical means. Only the worst sort were abandoned to the cruelty of Dolurrh, the land of the truly dead.

"Those killed in the Mourning cannot be brought back to life in any way," Esprë said. "Kandler would have moved the moons to bring my mother back to me. It couldn't be done."

"Is this true?" Ledenstrae asked Majeeda.

The deathless elf frowned, and Esprë wondered if her jaw might fall off. "From what I have been told," Majeeda said. "I've never seen anyone actually try to work such magics on the victims of the Mourning. Those are the domain of the gods, and I fear I have ignored such beings now for countless years."

"But Vol said—"

Esprë leaped up from her chair. It crashed backward behind her.

"Vol?" She could not feel the air in her lungs. "You've been in contact with Vol?"

Esprë watched her father's eyes dart back and forth as he struggled to figure out what to say, what he could say to salvage the situation.

"I'm afraid so," he said. "These are desperate times, I'm afraid, and I took desperate measures."

"Do you even know who she is?"

"Of course he does, dear," Majeeda said. "I introduced them."

❦

"Get out of my way," Kandler said as he exited the basket.

Burch stood in front of him, his hands held up before him to keep the justicar from storming past him. "She deserved to know," he said.

"That's not for you to decide," Kandler said. "She's my daughter, not yours."

Burch folded his arms across his chest. "You don't want to try that line. She's with her real father now."

Kandler brought up the fangblade, which he'd never bothered to sheathe. Its tip came within an inch of Burch's neck. At that moment, the justicar wanted to drive it straight through.

The shifter didn't flinch. His eyes didn't even flicker toward the sword.

"I don't have time for this," Kandler said. "Every moment she spends with that cold-hearted bastard, she's in danger of—"

"What? Learning he's a bastard?"

Kandler adjusted his grip on the fangblade. "Don't joke about this."

Burch unfolded his arms, the grim look on his face softening. "She's a good elf, boss. She'll figure this out on her own, and she deserves the chance to do it."

"But what if—"

"You have to have faith in her." Burch closed his mouth for a moment then tried again. "There's a damn good chance we're going to get ourselves killed here, soon. How are you going to protect her then?"

Kandler rubbed his eyes with his open hand. "You'd better be right."

"Have I ever steered you wrong?" Burch grinned. "Don't answer that."

CHAPTER

22

Esprë felt like her head might explode. She'd stormed off the *Phoenix* to go find her real father, despite the fact that she knew that Kandler had lied to her about him being in town. She'd known he'd just been trying to protect her, and that had made her even angrier and more determined to find Ledenstrae.

Thankfully—or so she'd thought at the time—Burch had been willing to show her the way. Otherwise, she knew that she and Kandler would have had a horrible screaming match of a fight. Avoiding him instead had been the better course—or so she'd told herself.

Now, though, sitting alone with two elves who'd been in contact with Vol—the Lich Queen who'd sent Te'oma and a pack of vampires to kidnap her from her home—she had to wonder where it had all gone wrong.

Maybe at her birth.

"Why would you do something like that?" Esprë said to Majeeda, her voice constricted with horror.

"I thought that they would have a lot to say to each other," Majeeda said. "After all, they are related."

The pressure inside Esprë's skull increased. "How?" That was the only word she could squeak out. If Ledenstrae and Vol were related, it meant that she and Vol were somehow bound together too, and by more than just the dragonmark they both shared.

Ledenstrae grimaced at Majeeda's words. "That's not exactly clear," he said. He reached out a hand to Esprë, who was too stunned to pull away. "It's possible, but not certain."

"Of course," Majeeda said with a dismissive wave of her hand. "Many of the records from the days of Vol were destroyed long ago, and it wasn't just the elves working hand-in-claw with the dragons who did that."

"What—what do you mean?" Esprë said.

The feeling seemed to be coming back into her limbs. She needed to understand this, to wrap her head around it. The deathless elf's words meant little to her. She decided to prod Majeeda into jabbering away until all the thoughts whirling about her coalesced into something resembling sense.

"The dragons and elves who joined together to destroy the House of Vol? They wanted to eradicate every last drop of blood that could contain even the barest potential for the Mark of Death, and they made good headway at it too. Every elf who had even the most tenuous claim to being a part of the House of Vol was put to death."

"Except Vol, you mean."

"Oh, she was killed too," Majeeda said, "but as you see, death isn't always permanent—especially for an abomination like a lich."

This didn't agree with what Te'oma had told Esprë about the Lich Queen, but she didn't care to argue the point. She just wanted to keep Majeeda talking.

"They killed an entire house?" she said. "How could

they do that? Didn't anyone stand up for them?"

Majeeda's face parted in a cold, crinkled smile. "This crusade against the House of Vol gave the dragons and the rest of the elves something in common—a foe against which they could rally together. It put an end to the Dragon-Elf War. To many on the Undying Court in those days, that alone was worth the sacrifice of a single house."

"How many elves would share the blood of the House of Vol?" Esprë asked. Her mind balked at trying to come up with a number.

"That is exactly the issue," Majeeda said. "To be absolutely safe, to make sure you got rid of every last drop of that tainted, hateful breed, you'd have to kill every last elf who still drew breath."

❦

"Tell me again why we can't just walk in and kill them," Kandler whispered to Burch. The justicar knew the answer as well as his friend, but he wanted little more than to ignore that wisdom and give in to his anger instead.

"Majeeda would flash-fry us," Burch said, "and probably Esprë. We need some sort of distraction."

Kandler grimaced as he listened down the shaft that led to the ground floor. Someone pounded at the door below, and he heard the sound of splintering wood.

Burch squinted at the justicar. "You let the guards live?"

"They were just doing their jobs."

"Now it's their job to kill us."

"You said you wanted a distraction. There's your distraction."

Kandler reached into the shaft with his fangblade and began to slice the basket into small pieces. The broken bits tumbled back down the shaft to the stone floor dozens of feet below.

"That should slow them down," the justicar said, "but they'll still make enough noise to get Ledenstrae's attention." A thought struck him then, and he narrowed his eyes at the shifter. "What happened to all the guards who were hiding up here?"

Burch gave Kandler a winning grin.

"You didn't think that would cause a problem?"

"Thought we'd be long gone before anyone found out."

Kandler nodded. Since they'd come back before anyone had noticed, it had worked out all right. The fewer problems they had to deal with up here in the top of the tower, the better. He had a feeling that Majeeda would be trouble enough.

"She sounds scared," Kandler said as he crept forward.

"That's because she's smart," said Burch.

🌢

Esprë heard someone pounding on the door of the tower. Ledenstrae glanced in the direction of the room into which the shaft to the lower level opened up. He scowled at the interruption but ignored it for the moment.

"The Undying Court convinced the dragons that the sacrifice of the House of Vol would be enough," Ledenstrae said. "However, the dragons live even longer than elves. Despite the fact that it has been millennia since that house's eradication, the dragons have not forgotten the threat of the Mark of Death. If it were to arise again . . ."

Esprë felt as if her heart had stopped beating. "You know," she said, staring at her father. "That's why you wanted to find me now. You know."

Ledenstrae held up his hands to calm the girl. "When Majeeda first contacted me, I had no idea. She just told me that you were alive. You can't imagine how that news thrilled me."

Esprë just nodded. She didn't know what to think any more.

"Then how did you . . . ?" She stared up at her father, who now seemed more of a stranger than ever.

"The Undying Court became aware of the reemergence of the Mark of Death via its powerful seers," Ledenstrae said. "My ancestors warned me of this. When Majeeda contacted them about you, they recognized you instantly."

"How did they know about my dragonmark?" she said. "Majeeda never saw it."

"True," said Majeeda, "but it didn't take the Undying Court long to connect the two occurrences. Only so many things happen in the Mournland that are strange enough to attract their attention."

"So," Esprë said to her father, "what do you plan to do with me?"

Ledenstrae's face became grave. "If you bear the Mark of Death, my fair child, I'm afraid there is no other choice. For the good of all of Aerenal, you will have to die."

❦

"Do it," Duro said to the changeling. "It's now or never."

"It's not you who's laying herself out as a target," Te'oma said as she sat on the gunwale near the edge of the bridge, her legs dangling out over the open air below. She hefted Sallah's sword in her hands.

"For a heartless killer, you're a bit of a whiner," the dwarf said, rolling his eyes.

He stood next to her on the gunwale and tried to ignore their precarious position. Having lived most of his life underground, he hadn't had too many dealings with the terrors of open heights. He tried to pretend the cliff was just one side of an open mineshaft, but it didn't take the edge off his fears.

"The sword won't be heavy enough to pull you to the ground," he said. As he spoke, he glanced around to make sure that the others had gotten into position. They all seemed ready. They just needed the changeling to start it all off. "It's light as a feather, and you're not even carrying the scabbard."

"Easy for you to—" Te'oma's words turned to a scream in mid-sentence as the bottom of Duro's hobnailed boot smashed into her backside and shoved her off the railing. She failed her arms as she fell.

"Woman overboard!" Duro shouted at the dockworkers. Inside, he said a quick prayer to Olladra, the goddess of luck, that this would work. He had been betting that Te'oma would remember to unfurl her bloodwings before she hit bottom. He winced as he wondered if she might forget in her panic. "Help!"

CHAPTER

23

Kandler and Burch strode into the room. Ledenstrae stood, but he did not offer a hand in friendship. Majeeda sat, her eyes burning with such anger that Kandler feared they might set her dry, crinkly skin on fire.

"Get away from her," Kandler said to Ledenstrae. The fangblade was in his hand.

Burch held his crossbow pointed at the ground. Kandler knew he could put a bolt straight through Majeeda's skull before she could draw another breath. Of course, she didn't need to breathe.

Ledenstrae offered Kandler and Burch a strained smile. "I understand what you feel you must do here, but you don't understand how pointless your objections are."

"You sure know how to sweet talk your friends," Burch said.

Ledenstrae put up his hands in mock surrender. "Permit me to explain," he said. "I only have my daughter's best interests at heart in this matter."

Kandler wondered if he could stab the man through the heart before Majeeda could stop him. As tempting as the idea seemed, when he glanced at Esprë it melted into frustration. He knew he couldn't bring himself to murder her father in front of her—not if there was any way to prevent it.

Ledenstrae chuckled. "I have made no such threats. I explained the situation to Esprë as it is. If she bears the Mark of Death, then she must die—for the good of all."

The elf gazed at his daughter. "Would you put your single life above that of every other elf? Once word spreads that you bear the Mark of Death—if, in fact, you do—legions will hunt you down to kill you. Would you want to condemn your entire race to oblivion along with yourself?"

Esprë sat bolt upright in her chair, her lower lip trembling. "No," she said, her voice softer than a whisper. "No," she said, louder. "I couldn't have that."

Kandler wanted nothing more than to hold her right then, to make everything all right for her, but he feared if he pulled his attention away from the others it would all go bad. As Esprë's eyes began to redden, he raised the tip of the fangblade toward Ledenstrae and put his free arm around his stepdaughter.

Majeeda muttered something cold under her breath, but Ledenstrae cut her off with a sharp snap of his neck. The words caught in the deathless elf's dry throat like leaves in a hollow log.

"There are other ways," Kandler said to Ledenstrae, his arm still around Esprë. "Once we leave here, we're off to Argonnessen to confront this problem head on."

Majeeda's eyes widened so far that Kandler wondered if the desiccated orbs behind her lids might fall out. "I see that you must love my daughter," Ledenstrae said, "to embrace such folly. I'm impressed, although I'm not sure if it's by bravery or stupidity."

"They're not always so far apart," said Burch.

Kandler squinted at Ledenstrae. "What if Esprë doesn't bear the Mark of Death?"

The elf smiled. "Then no one would be happier than me. I would have her accompany me back to Aerenal so that I could prove to the world that she was innocent of the crime of being born of such tainted blood."

"And if she didn't want to go?"

Ledenstrae grimaced. "That would be foolish in the extreme. Already five groups are aware of her growing powers. If we cannot prove her innocent of the charges against her, they will hunt her just to be sure. This is no Brelish court with your pedestrian ideas about innocence. Perception is just as important as reality."

"Five groups?" Kandler said. He did a quick count in his head. First there had been the Blood of Vol and the Knights of the Silver Flame and then the dragons of Argonnessen. Later, there had been the Stillborn elves they'd fought in the Goradra Gap, and now the Undying Court.

He looked down at Esprë. She hadn't been there that long before he showed up again. "How much did you tell them?"

"Very little." She spoke as honestly and openly as ever.

Kandler stared at Ledenstrae, sizing him up. "You're one of the Stillborn."

❦

Te'oma cursed Duro and every one of his ancestors as she tumbled away from the airship. She hadn't cared much for this plan in the first place, and as she fell, spreading her bloodwings out to catch herself in midair, it seemed worse than ever. The wind filled the batlike appendages, and the changeling swooped away from the onrushing ground in an inelegant arc.

After a moment, Te'oma brought her flight under control. As her wings beat, keeping her in the air, she turned to look back at the top of the cliffside. Already the dockworkers there had spotted her and started to point at her and yell for assistance.

She pumped her bloodwings hard, pulling herself higher and higher into the sky. As she went, she heard more voices join in the shouting, then the telltale clack-clack-clack of a siege engine being cranked around on a pivoting base. She looked down just in time to see the ballista being aimed straight at her heart.

Te'oma folded her wings close to her and let gravity resume its pull. As she dropped, the long, thick bolt from the ballista zipped through the air, right where she had just been.

The changeling spun around and saw Xalt, Duro, and Sallah hacking away at the spots on the airship from which the mooring chains hung. Under Monja's guidance, the *Phoenix* pulled away from the airdock hard and fast, stretching those chains taut. It would not take much damage to the mooring cleats for them to spring loose. So far, the plan seemed to be working.

Then Te'oma heard a lever being yanked back hard. She glanced toward the other turret nearest the dock and saw the arm of the catapult there slam forward, launching a blazing ball of fiery pitch in her direction.

❦

Ledenstrae cracked a nervous smile. "It might be more accurate to consider me a silent supporter of their aims."

"You sent them after us?" Esprë said. Kandler squeezed her shoulder.

"They were meant to bring you to me," Ledenstrae said. "I had no guarantee that you would come toward Valenar. If you had decided to head for Q'barra or other parts unknown, our chance to intercept you might have been lost."

"They almost killed us," Esprë said. "They murdered the dwarves' lookouts."

Ledenstrae shrugged. "When compared to the fate of our race, such sacrifices do not budge the scales."

"They were ready to kill me."

Ledenstrae waited to see if Esprë would let her anger carry her farther along. Instead, she sat stone still and stared at him. Then she placed a hand on Kandler's where it rested on her shoulder.

"I do not regret the decisions I've made," said Ledenstrae. "The stakes are too high. Now, if you don't mind, I'd like to see your dragonmark and put any questions about it behind us."

＊

Sallah hacked at the straining mooring cleat with her flaming blade. Her blow removed a chunk of wood near the base of the cleat, and the groan of the stretching chains grew louder.

Duro's axe bit into the gunwale on the other side of the cleat. "Wood is weaker than metal," the dwarf said. "We'll be free faster than a rockslide."

Sallah grunted in response. Toward the aft of the ship, Xalt chopped at the cleat there with an axe he'd found in the hold.

A ballista bolt whizzed overhead, then Sallah felt a blast of heat as a ball of blazing pitch arced through the air above the ship. She glanced up and saw Te'oma try to wriggle out of the way, but the massive missile smacked into one of her bloodwings and sent her spinning out of the sky, that wing already ablaze.

A cheer went up from the guards in the turrets and the dockworkers below. Then one of them spotted what Sallah and the others were trying to do and raised an alarm.

One more blow, Sallah told herself. She put everything she had into the strike.

It would not take long for the guards to reload their heavy weapons. If the *Phoenix* hadn't broken free by then, the guards would pick her apart like a snared bear. A crossbow bolt zinged by the knight's ear to emphasize that point.

Sallah's swing cut into the gunwale at the same time as Duro's next blow. Already under tremendous pressure, the cleat sprang free from the wood to which it had been attached.

The chain jerked back then fell loose like a cut bowstring. The airship's prow swung away from the dock so fast that Sallah lost her footing and tumbled to the deck next to Duro. The dwarf grinned at her from ear to ear.

"That's how I like to see a plan work!" he said.

Sallah noticed that they weren't moving any farther. Toward the aft of the ship, the chain still hung on, and Xalt had crumpled to the deck too. He struggled to stand, but the axe that had been in his hand was nowhere to be seen.

"I think you spoke too soon," she said as she scrambled to her feet and tried to ignore the dwarf's curses.

CHAPTER

24

Esprë removed Kandler's hand from her shoulder and stood up. Far below, he heard the door give way and the guards come streaming into the building's first floor. From the noises below, there had to be far more than the three elves he'd left behind the door. They cried out in dismay when they saw the remains of the basket scattered about the stone floor there, but he knew it wouldn't take them long to find an alternate route upstairs.

Esprë moved toward her father, calm and collected. Kandler knew her better than anyone alive, and he noticed how stiff her gait was. He was sure that Ledenstrae would think it the movements of a proper young elf obeying her father's orders, but the justicar recognized it as the kind of resolve he'd seen her display when forced to face up to a mistake she'd made, unsure of what punishment she might be made to endure.

When she reached Ledenstrae, Esprë turned her back to him. "It's between my shoulders," she said. "I've only seen it once."

Kandler had seen it just once himself. He moved around

to Ledenstrae's side to get a better look at Esprë's back. The fact that this brought him closer to the elf in case he had to start swinging his sword did not escape him.

Majeeda craned her neck over from her chair, and Burch padded over to stand behind her. The ancient elf wrinkled her nose at the shifter's scent, and Burch allowed himself a vicious smile, confident she couldn't see it.

Ledenstrae reached up with a steady finger and pulled the back of Esprë's collar back and down.

The dragonmark stood out against Esprë's ivory skin like a livid wound. The mark itself almost glowed a bluish-black. The edges of its border with the girl's skin shone like an angry, red welt.

To Kandler, the dragonmark seemed like some horrible cancer that threatened to keep growing, taking over Esprë's flesh an inch at a time until it covered her from head to toe. At that point, there would be no more of the young elf he'd come to love so much. Only the dragonmark would remain.

The justicar fought the urge to lash out with his fang-blade and try to cut the dragonmark from Esprë's skin. He wondered if a tool fashioned from a dragon's tooth would have a better chance than one forged from cold iron, but he knew that to even try might kill her.

Kandler had never heard of someone trying to remove a dragonmark. In every other case, their owners cherished them for the amazing powers they bestowed. With the Mark of Death, though, it had become far less of a blessing than a curse. Perhaps some great magic could manage it. Maybe he could persuade Majeeda to try.

"So," Esprë said. "Is it?"

❦

Duro sprinted toward Xalt and the still-chained mooring cleat, Sallah fast on his heels. "It was a good plan," he said. "It should have worked."

He wheeled about, scanning the sky for the changeling. He spotted her off to the south, trailing smoke and fire as she angled toward the deck of the airship like a wounded duck. She'd be lucky to land on the *Phoenix*, and if she did, she'd land hard. Instead of working as a distraction any longer, she'd draw more attention to the airship instead.

The ballista crew had already reloaded, and the catapult team didn't seem to be far behind. They'd gotten the arm reset and were muscling a fresh ball of pitch into the weapon's bowl. One of the elves stood next to the bowl, ready with a burning torch to set the pitch alight as soon as it sat solid in its home.

Duro eyed the straining cleat. Xalt's efforts hadn't done much to the wood around it, and they didn't have much time left to finish the job. Even if they broke free right then, they'd have to deal with the siege weapons from those nearest turrets and possibly from others farther off. To add to their troubles, a patrol of guards had reached the edge of the docks and were leveling their bows at the airship.

They needed another distraction, now.

"Hit that cleat," Duro shouted to Sallah. "Hard!"

Before the lady knight could ask what he planned to do, the dwarf leaped atop the gunwale. A flight of arrows whizzing around him, he launched himself out into the gap between the swaying airship and the dock below. As his feet left the *Phoenix*, he slung out his axe and caught the taut chain under the curved side of the weapon's head.

Hanging from his axe, Duro zipped straight down the chain at a dizzying speed. Just before he reached the dock, he wrenched himself up and forward. His axe came free from the chain, and he tumbled straight into the elf archers arrayed at its base, knocking them over like a stand of loose-stacked rocks.

Kandler brought his sword up behind Ledenstrae, and he saw Burch swing his crossbow up to bear on Majeeda. If the pair of elves said the wrong thing, made the wrong move, Kandler and Burch would attack. They'd probably only get one shot at killing their foes, so they'd have to make it count.

"I—I don't know," Ledenstrae said, frustration marring his ageless face. "I had thought it would be obvious just from looking at it. After all, the Mark of Death is the stuff of legend." He turned to Majeeda. "Can you tell?"

Majeeda pushed her fragile frame up out of her chair and leaned over Esprë's bared back. Her bones creaked as she moved, and Esprë shuddered at her touch when the deathless wizard pulled her collar even lower.

Majeeda cleared her throat as if to speak, and the action coughed a fistful of dust up from her bone-dry lungs. As she waved it away, she said, "I cannot be sure. It resembles the drawings I've seen of Vol's mark, but those were printed by hand on parchment that was already ancient when I saw it. This dragonmark could be the Mark of Death."

"Or?" Ledenstrae asked.

"Or it could just be an aberrant mark, a magical mistake."

"How can we tell for sure?"

"We could bring her to Vol, of course, to compare it with the skin she no longer wears. I understand she keeps it stretched out in a glass case in Illmarrow Castle."

"That would entail entanglements in which I would rather we not become ensnared."

Kandler tried to nod in agreement and readjust the grip on his sword, but his head and hand refused to comply. Panic rising in his heart, he realized he could not move at all.

Majeeda turned to smile at him and Burch, showing a mouth full of teeth attached to their gums by only the tiniest bits of pale, dry flesh. "You don't really think I'd let you kill us, do you?" she asked.

❦

Sallah screamed at Duro to stop, but she couldn't reach him before he plunged over the airship's edge. Determined not to let his sacrifice be in vain, she set to the gunwale fast and hard with her silver-burning sword. As she worked, she heard something thud into the deck behind her, but she was too engrossed with her work to even turn her head to look at it.

Within a handful of strokes, the battered railing creaked and then snapped. The airship zoomed backward, and Sallah tumbled toward the broken railing. She might have fallen through it had Xalt not managed to grab the back of her tunic and haul her back.

"Go back for Duro!" Sallah shouted as she scrambled to her feet and clambered on to the bridge. "We can't just leave him there."

Monja screwed up her face as she brought the airship about in a tight curve and pointed the *Phoenix* toward the fortress. Below, Sallah could see Duro swinging his axe back and forth, cutting a swathe through the elf guards foolish enough to get close to him. As she watched, another patrol of archers streamed onto the docks and leveled their bows at the battling dwarf.

Sallah watched in horror as the airship's prow eclipsed the scene below. "What are you doing?" she said, grabbing Monja by her shoulder.

"What Duro would have wanted," she said as she pulled the *Phoenix* hard to port. "If we go back for him now, his effort will be wasted. We have to let him go."

A flaming ball of pitch spun past the starboard gunwale and arced out into the distance beyond. Then something slammed into the bottom of the ship and shook her hard. Sallah fell to her knees.

"Ballista bolt," Monja said as she leaped down from the spars on the wheel. "Here, take over—and fly for Esprë's father's tower. You know where it is, right?"

Sallah leaped forward and grabbed the wheel before the elemental trapped in the airship's ring of fire could take control and destroy the ship. "I think so," she said.

"You'd better know so," the halfling said as she left the bridge. "Soon we'll have a whole fort full of soldiers out after us."

"Wait!" Sallah said. "Where are you going?"

Monja pointed toward Te'oma's collapsed form, still smoldering in the middle of the ship's main deck. Xalt knelt over the changeling, beating out the flames on her wings with his bare hands.

Sallah reached out with her mind and urged the elemental to swing back to the starboard. As she did, the top of Ledenstrae's tower appeared straight in front of her, and she prodded the *Phoenix* forward at full speed.

CHAPTER

25

Kandler?" Esprë said. "What's wrong?"

When her stepfather didn't answer, the young elf pulled her shirt's collar back up and turned on the wizard and her father. Kandler and Burch stood behind them, but neither of them said a word as she gazed at them. They didn't move an inch. They didn't even blink.

"What have you done to them?" Esprë asked Majeeda.

The deathless wizard gave Esprë a smug look and fanned her fingers, which crackled with the movement. "I've excused them from our little talk," she said. "This is a conversation between elves."

Ledenstrae nodded his approval. "We need to make our decisions about this based on what is best for our race. Peoples like humans and shifters cannot have the perspective our years bring. They cannot comprehend as we do the long-term effects of the choices we must make here today."

Esprë steeled herself as her father reached out to caress her cheek. She had longed for such affection from him for years, but now it only made her want to run screaming into the streets. She'd not known much about him, except from what her mother had told her, and she'd discounted some of Esprina's comments as naturally biased against the husband she'd abandoned back in Aerenal.

Esprë realized now how she'd become infatuated with the idea of her father rather than the real person. It had been easy enough—perhaps too easy, as she hadn't had any new information about him to deal with since shortly after her birth. Once her mother died, her daydreams about her father had grown stronger, helping assuage her terrible loss. With one parent gone for good, she clung to the idea that she and her father would one day be reunited.

Kandler had been much more of a father to her than Ledenstrae, but she'd allowed her fantasies to come between them. When Esprina had been alive, Esprë had known that both she and her mother would outlive Kandler by several of his lifetimes. If they'd somehow had a child, as sometimes happened between humans and elves, she'd live longer that that younger sibling too.

It had been easier to keep Kandler at a distance, but then Esprina died, and Kandler had been all she had in the world.

"Why don't you send me back to my father?" she'd asked the justicar once over a meal. He'd just come back from a mission with Burch and a couple friends, scouting the land that would soon after become the town of Mardakine.

Kandler had put down his fork and knife, then swallowed his half-chewed food. "Do you know your father?" he'd asked.

She'd shaken her head.

"Neither do I," he'd said. "All I have to go on is your mother's word, and from what she tells me he's not a nice man."

"He's not a man at all. He's an elf."

"You know what I mean."

"Wouldn't I be better off with him?"

Kandler had stared at her hard. He'd come back the day before, covered in ash and singed by what he'd described as living fireball spells. His skin had looked like he'd stayed out in the sun far too long, and most of his eyebrows had fallen off after he'd bathed.

"I swore to your mother I'd take care of you if anything ever happened to you."

"She made you do that?"

"She—she didn't *make* me do anything. I made that vow to her, and she accepted it."

"Why would you do something like that?"

Kandler had stuffed another bite of food in his mouth, and he'd finished it before he responded.

"I wanted to. We both lived dangerous lives. I knew something might happen to her."

"Did she vow to take care of me if you died?"

Kandler had grinned at the joke. "I think she thought she already had that covered."

They'd returned to their meal then. After a while longer, Esprë had pushed back her plate and spoke.

"I relieve you of your vow."

"I didn't make the vow to you."

"You made it to my mother about me. I am her heir, and all her assets pass down to me, including the obligations of others. I absolve you of your vow."

"Very well."

Esprë had almost fallen out of her chair, but she'd recovered from her shock before Kandler had noticed—or so she'd hoped.

"I can leave then?"

Kandler had pushed back his own plate then. "You can leave any time you want. I'll even go with you if you like,

escort you back to Aerenal. I bet we could even convince
Burch to come with us."

"But?"

"But my vow still stands. I made it not just to your
mother, but to myself. If you'll allow me the honor, I'll make
it now to you."

Esprë had pursed her lips at that. "Give me a moment to
think about it."

"Take as long as you like."

After dinner, Kandler had taken Esprë for a walk outside the camp to look up at the moons and stars. When they'd
reached the top of a hillock, they'd lain down on the grass
to take it all in.

"Do you really want to go to Aerenal?" Kandler had
asked after a quiet moment.

"No. I—I just wanted to make sure you wanted me
around."

Kandler had sat up. "Have I given you any reason to
think I didn't?"

Guilt had welled up in her for even giving voice to these
thoughts, but she had pressed on. "You married my mother,
not me."

"You were always part of the package. I never thought
otherwise."

"Did you always want the whole package?"

Kandler had hesitated then, and she had waited for the
lies to start. To her relief, though, he had spoken as honestly
with her as ever.

"No," he had said. "When I found out your mother had a
child, it bothered me at first. The kind of work I do, it's not
easy to have a child around, even an elf-child, but . . ."

"But?"

"I don't know when it happened really. I couldn't pin-
point the exact spot, but I came to think of you as my child

too." He had torn his eyes from the sky and gazed back at Esprë where she lay on the ground. She had smiled up at him.

"I'm not going to start calling you 'Father.' "

He had beamed down at her. "I can live with that."

"Then I accept your vow."

What Kandler hadn't known then—and still didn't know now—was that Esprë had made a similar vow to herself that night. She'd sworn to take care of him too, no matter what.

"Let them go," Esprë said.

As she spoke, she felt the dragonmark on her back start to itch. She wondered if Ledenstrae or Majeeda would have been able to see the mark change if she hadn't already covered it back up.

"Once Majeeda and I are done talking," Ledenstrae said. "This is important. In fact, you could say your life depends on it."

Esprë felt the black energy from her dragonmark start to spread across her shoulders and feed down her arms.

"This isn't your decision to make," she said. "It's mine." She narrowed her eyes at her father. "You'd really kill your own daughter?"

The elf arched an eyebrow at Esprë. "If she wasn't mature enough to make such a decision herself." He leaned forward. "If I found myself in your shoes, and the entire fate of my race depended on my death, I'd toss myself into the nearest volcano just to make sure there was no trace of me left to resurrect."

Majeeda eyelids rustled like dry leaves as she batted them at the girl. "Young lady, you are fortunate that we are bothering to having this conversation at all. Many of our ancestors would have simply killed you on the spot rather than risk even a hint of the Mark of Death be found in their blood."

"Maybe I have spent too much time among humans then," said Esprë. "I don't feel that lucky at all."

The black power reached her hands then, and they began to glow. Her fingers felt like she had dipped them in ice, and they hungered for something warm in which they could bathe to relieve the sensation.

"Let them go," she said again.

Majeeda gave Esprë a condescending smile at the threat in her voice. "Or else what?" Then she glanced down at the young elf's glowing hands and burst into a dry, hacking laughter.

"My dear," she said. "Do you think your dragonmark holds any power over me? I am long since dead. Do you mean to threaten to kill me if I do not release your two friends?" She giggled again, and it sounded like rain falling on a mound of brown leaves.

"No," Esprë said. "Not you."

Her hands shot out and grabbed her father's arm. He yelped in pain and surprise and crumpled into his chair like a smacked child. Despite this, he seemed unable to pull himself free, as if all his muscles had knotted up at once, paralyzing him in his contorted state.

"Let them go, or my father dies."

CHAPTER

26

As Ledenstrae's tower loomed larger, Sallah pulled back on the airship's speed. They would be there in a matter of seconds, but then what?

"How is Te'oma?" she shouted out over the rushing winds and the crackling of the *Phoenix*'s ring of elemental fire.

"She will be fine," Xalt called back. "I put out the fire in her wings, and Monja should have her healed up soon."

"Fantastic!" Sallah said. "Hold on to something tight."

"Why is that?" Xalt said, standing up, confused.

Sallah tore a gauntleted hand free from the ship's wheel and pointed at the tower toward which they were headed. She could see the balcony right there, the one from which Ledenstrae had come when she, Burch, and Kandler had visited him. The trellises and arbors that covered the area hid the occupants from view—if there were any.

Sallah wondered if they'd gone to all this trouble for nothing. Perhaps Kandler and Esprë had managed to work things out amicably with Ledenstrae. Maybe Duro had sacrificed himself for nothing. Maybe they weren't coming to the rescue but had made a horrible mistake.

Every instinct in her, though, told her that they had no time to lose. Then she remembered something.

"Bring Te'oma here!" she said.

Without even a nod, Xalt knelt next to the changeling to carry out Sallah's order. He slipped his arms underneath her, ignoring Monja's protests.

"She's not healed yet," the halfling said. "I need more time."

"Sallah needs her now," Xalt said, standing up and hefting Te'oma in his arms. The changeling clutched at him, her back arching in pain.

"I know what she wants," Te'oma said, her voice a weak rasp as Xalt clambered up on to the bridge with the changeling in his arms. "Tell her that we have to go in now. Otherwise, they will all die."

Xalt looked to the knight.

"I heard her," Sallah said. "Grab one of those safety straps on the console or the rail. We're going in!"

❦

Majeeda stared at Esprë, then threw back her wizened head, and laughed.

"Such bravery can only be found in the young," Majeeda said. "Why would you think I would care about your father's fate?"

Esprë nearly let loose her grip on Ledenstrae's arm.

"Do you imagine your powers might work on me, little one?" Majeeda asked. "Perhaps you should give them a try. Perhaps that's not the Mark of Death you carry after all. You might be able to harm me."

Majeeda leered at the girl, and Esprë saw the barely repressed madness dancing in the ancient elf's eyes.

"On the other hand," the deathless wizard said, "you might not."

Esprë paid no attention to that last bit. She had another voice in her head, demanding a different answer from her altogether.

Are you hurt? Te'oma asked.

"Majeeda is here," Esprë said out loud. "She's frozen Kandler and Burch with her magic, and she plans to kill us all. Come help now!"

Majeeda narrowed her eyes at the girl. "To whom are you talking?" She glanced toward the only entrance into the balcony, but no one was there.

Ledenstrae groaned in fear and pain, and Esprë felt his clammy sweat growing beneath her palms. Something had to happen here soon, or she would end up killing him for sure. She feared if she let him go she would lose the last bit of leverage she had against Majeeda.

Threatening her father's life hadn't seemed to shake the wizard much, but it was the only thing that Esprë had. She considered telling Majeeda that she would throw herself off the balcony if she didn't let Kandler and Burch go, but that would only give the wizard what she wanted.

"If Ledenstrae dies," she said to Majeeda, "your dreams of going home die along with him."

Majeeda stiffened at these words, and the mirth fled from her face. Esprë twisted herself around behind her father, putting his tortured form between herself and the wizard. As she did, she allowed herself a vicious grin.

"Who's going to introduce you to the Undying Court if he's gone?" Esprë said. "Who could even bring you back to Aerenal? Without his help, you'll have to go back to the safety of your tower in the Mournland. Isn't that right? You'll have to stay there, trapped again, forever."

"You don't know of what you speak," Majeeda said, her

voice like the hiss of a cornered snake. "I am going back to Aerenal to become a member of the Undying Court. I am!"

Esprë smiled at the desperation she could hear in Majeeda's voice. She knew she had pierced the deathless elf's armor of serenity. Now she just had to drive her point home.

She let loose of her father's arm for a moment. He screamed out in terror and pain.

"Esprë!" he said. "You cannot kill me. I am your father!"

"The fact I'm your daughter didn't mean much to you," Esprë said. Her words bore more bitterness than she had realized she felt. She tightened her grip on him again.

"No! Please!"

Esprë averted her eyes from her father and stared at Majeeda instead. "Let them go," she said.

"I should kill you myself," the wizard said. "I could destroy you where you stand."

"You would have done it already," Esprë said, hoping she was right. "Quit wasting my time. Let them go, or he dies!"

"All right!" Majeeda said, panic filling her voice. She closed her eyes for a moment and muttered something. As she did, Kandler and Burch staggered forward from where they were and took deep, grateful breaths.

"Hear that?" Burch said, jerking his head in the direction of the vertical shaft that let out into the room beyond. "Guards on ropes. Be here in a second."

"The airship is—"

Something large smacked into the building and cut Esprë off. The balcony shook, and the sound of a raging fire filled the air. The screening structures around the outside of the balcony began to collapse, some simply falling to pieces while others went up in flames.

Kandler reached out and grabbed Esprë around the waist. "I think our ride is here," he said as he carried her toward the low wall around the balcony and hefted her into the air.

Esprë saw the broadside of the *Phoenix* appear in a gap in the screens. Xalt stood there, his arms extended toward them, ready to pull them in. "Jump!" he said.

Kandler swung Esprë up and out, and she found herself sailing through the air, across the gap between the airship and the building. Xalt caught her in his strong, hard arms and fell backward to the deck, absorbing her fall.

❦

"Bring her back!" Ledenstrae shouted. "Without her, we're all doomed!"

While Esprë still flew to the *Phoenix*, Kandler brought his sword around and slashed at the elf. Ledenstrae flinched away and cowered on the floor.

Kandler hesitated for a moment. As much as he disliked Ledenstrae, he had no desire to execute an unarmed foe who seemed to think curling up like a baby offered some sort of defense. Then he heard an angry voice start to speak from the far corner of the room.

Majeeda was chanting.

A crossbow twanged to Kandler's right, and a bolt appeared in Majeeda's throat. The feathered end of the missile jutted out from her withered flesh, but no blood flowed from the wound. Still, she clutched at it as if in mortal pain.

Kandler strode to the elf and raised his sword. While Ledenstrae posed little threat at the moment, Majeeda had only been checked for a moment by the bolt. As soon as she could remove it and regain her voice, she would help the elves of Aerie track them down. She had some kind of tie to the airship that only her death could sever, and Kandler meant to solve that problem in the most direct way.

As the justicar charged, he heard a strangled cry behind him. He ignored it for the moment and swung his sword in a flat, level arc that connected with devastating force.

Majeeda's head sprang free from her shoulders, almost as if it had been waiting for a chance to do so. Her body collapsed to the cold, stone floor, her bones rattling loosely in her papery skin.

A trio of elf guards clambered out of the vertical shaft and into the room beyond the balcony. Getting into a fight with them would only cost Kandler time, but he guessed he'd already spent more of it than he had to spare. Rather than challenge the guards, he turned and raced toward the balcony's edge.

As Kandler sprinted for daylight, he had to bound over Ledenstrae. The elf lay in a widening pool of his own blood, a crossbow bolt sticking out of his chest. In one hand, he clutched a throwing dagger by the point.

Ledenstrae swept a feeble hand at Kandler, but his grasp had no strength to it and fell uselessly away. The justicar ignored it and vaulted over the balcony's railing to the deck of the airship beyond.

He rolled with the landing and sprang to his feet, his sword still in his hand. As he rose, he snapped his head toward the bridge and saw Sallah standing at the wheel. He drew a great breath to shout, "Go!"

Before the word left his lips, the *Phoenix* shot forward like a ballista bolt, pulling Kandler from his feet.

CHAPTER

27

Kandler's tumbling came to a stop at the base of the main deck beneath the bridge. As he jumped to his feet, the airship's deck pitched hard, and he had to fight to keep standing.

A fiery ball of pitch soared past the airship. It had come close enough to pierce the ring of fire like a stone thrown through a hoop, but it hadn't hit a thing. Then something smacked into the aft of the ship and Kandler found himself on his knees again.

He dove for the nearest gunwale and stuck his head over the edge. Below, it seemed like the entire fortress had mobilized to attack them. Ballista bolts and balls of burning pitch sailed through the sky toward them from every direction.

"Get us out of here!" he shouted.

Sallah didn't say a word. She just bared her teeth and concentrated on what she had already been doing.

Kandler scanned the deck. Back toward the port rail, Burch stood crouched over Esprë, who huddled beneath him, still holding Xalt by the arms. The shifter had his crossbow out and seemed to be training it on any incoming attacks, as if he thought he could knock them from the sky with a good shot.

Esprë seemed unhurt, which was the most important thing to Kandler. She started to crawl toward the wall under the bridge, which offered just a hair more protection than the middle of the open deck. Xalt crept along with her, ready to throw himself into the path of any attack if need be.

Toward the bow, Monja knelt over a still form that seemed to smolder where it lay. It took Kandler a moment to recognize it as Te'oma. As he watched, the changeling sat up.

The justicar dashed to the aft of the ship and yanked himself up on to the bridge. "Where's Duro?" he asked Sallah.

"He sacrificed himself," she said, not turning to look at him. The ship's nose pitched forward then, and another ballista bolt skipped off the prow.

"What?"

"He dove into the guards on the dock so we could cut the ship free."

Kandler grabbed the wheel. "What happened to him?"

"I don't have time for this now!"

Kandler wanted to object, to pull Sallah's hands from the wheel and make her tell him what had happened, but right then a ball of pitch soared into the *Phoenix*'s ring of fire.

The elemental fire incinerated most of the pitch at once, but what was left exploded out from the ring and spattered down like flaming drops of rain all over the fore section of the main deck.

Esprë screamed. She'd been climbing on to the bridge when the ball of pitch had burst open.

"Take the wheel!" Sallah said to Esprë. "I need to help Monja!"

Esprë nodded and dove for the wheel, wrapping her hands around it and taking control of the willful airship. The instant the girl's fingers touched the wheel, Sallah shoved herself away from it and leaped down to the main deck.

Seeing Burch and Xalt race up after Esprë to protect her, Kandler snapped a salute at them and chased after Sallah. Looking around, he saw that they had just cleared the east wall of the fortress. Within moments, they would be far beyond the reach of even its most powerful weapons. They just had to hold on a few moments longer to escape.

When he jumped down to the main deck, Kandler saw that the burning pitch had clumped into little fires all across the bow. Because of the nature of the source of the airship's power, the *Phoenix* had been magically fortified against flame. The blazes would not spread.

One of them, though, had landed on Monja. As the halfling burned, Te'oma knelt over her, trying to beat out the tongues of fire with her bloodwings. The pitch proved to be a stubborn fuel though, and it kept scorching the young shaman in its sticky grip.

Kandler smelled the horrible stench of burning flesh as he got nearer. By the time he reached Monja, Te'oma had managed to put out all the fires on the halfling, although many splashes of nearby pitch still crackled along.

"Is she dead?" he asked.

Te'oma turned her face up toward him—her own face, not that of Shawda or anyone else—and he saw nothing but desperation there. "I don't know," she said.

Sallah shouldered the changeling aside and knelt down next to the halfling. Monja's skin had blistered all over—at least where it had been exposed—and large, black flakes already peeled off it in the wind from the airship's rapid flight. For a moment, Kandler thought she couldn't possibly be breathing, but then she let loose an agonized scream.

"She's not dead yet," Sallah said. "With the grace of the Silver Flame, I may still be able to save her."

The lady knight put up her hands in supplication and bowed her head. She murmured a soft but sincere prayer to her distant deity, and her hands began to glow with a silvery light. As she spoke, though, Monja cries turned to a horrible, hacking cough, and blood started to spurt from her mouth.

"Hurry!" Te'oma said. "You have to hurry,"

Sallah gave no indication she even heard the changeling's words. Instead, she finished up her prayer and brought her hands down to cradle the halfling's crispy head.

Much of the hair had been burned off it, leaving only blackened scalp behind. Kandler guessed that the burned flesh might still be hot enough to scorch Sallah's fingers, but if the lady knight felt any pain she showed no sign of it.

The silvery glow flowed from Sallah's hands and engulfed Monja's head. As it did, Sallah continued to murmur prayers to the Silver Flame, praising it for its mercy as she petitioned it for yet more aid for her fallen friend.

Burch came up behind Kandler and stood mute as he watched the halfling heal. "Damn," the shifter said. "I'm about ready to thank the Flame myself."

Kandler looked over at his friend. The shifter sighed and said, "Telling a friend his child is dead is one of my least favorite things."

Kandler frowned, then patted Burch on the shoulder. As he turned to go back to the bridge, he said, "Then it's a good thing we don't know Duro's father."

When Kandler reached Esprë, she said, "We have to go back for him."

The justicar squeezed his stepdaughter's shoulder and shook his head.

"We can't just leave him there," she said, her voice rising as she spoke. "They'll kill him."

Kandler put an arm around Esprë shoulders and hunched down next to her. He spoke softly into her ear, to make sure she could hear him. "You see what happened to Monja down there?"

Esprë nodded.

"If we go back, that could happen to any one of us—maybe to all of us—and even if we got through all that, we'd have to fight our way through an entire fortress filled with elf warriors to even get near to Duro. That's assuming we're not already too late."

Esprë looked like she wanted to throw up. "I—I know you're right," she said, "but I just can't stand it. The thought of him lying there dead on the dock, maybe hacked to bits like—like Shawda . . ."

"We don't know he's dead," Kandler said. "Valenar elves are a hard but fair people. If they capture him alive, they'll bind his wounds and nurse him back to health."

He didn't mention that it would likely only be so that the dwarf would be well enough to stand trial. The justicar didn't know much about the Valenar system of justice, but he suspected that Duro might find a death sentence to be getting off easy. A dwarf could live a long time, and even if Kandler had the fortune to die in bed with his boots on, Duro might still be rotting in Aerie's prison when it happened.

He promised himself that once all this was over he'd come back to discover Duro's fate, whatever it might be. He knew the odds against him being able to manage it were staggering, but he tallied it up yet one more mark under the heading "Why I Can't Die Yet."

"Thanks," Esprë said, pressing into Kandler's arm while still keeping her hands on the wheel.

"For what?"

"For trying to come up with a way to make me feel better."

Kandler snorted softly and squeezed Esprë tight. "It wasn't just for you."

CHAPTER

28

"Y̶ou're still determined to sail for Argonnessen?" Sallah said.

Kandler felt like he'd had this conversation with the lady knight a dozen times before. She already knew what his answer to this question would be, and he didn't feel like going through it all again.

He nodded and said, "As soon as we resupply."

The sun had set long ago, and the stars and moons shone bright and clear in the night sky. The chill wind carried the scent of the distant seas on it and swept the stench of the remains of the burnt pitch away. A distant screech from an unseen hunting bird stabbed through the roar of the airship's ring of fire.

Esprë had the wheel now, and Xalt kept her company. The warforged and she had taken a shine to each other, and the justicar had to admit that he couldn't have picked a better bodyguard for the girl. Without the need to eat or sleep, little could distract Xalt from his chosen duties.

Burch and Monja huddled near the hatch that led to the hold. The shifter had built a small fire there, and he and the shaman sat on the edge of its heat, talking in low, friendly tones.

Sallah's healing powers had brought the halfling back from the edge of death, and Monja had called upon her people's spirits to heal herself nearly as good as new. Still, her fresh-knit skin shone red and smooth, like that of a sunburned baby. Despite her smile, Kandler knew she was all too aware of how close she'd come to death that afternoon.

Te'oma knelt near the fire, cooking the remains of a tribex that Burch had felled from the deck of the *Phoenix* just before dusk. He had spotted a herd moving along a stream in the foothills of the Endworld Mountains, and he'd ordered the ship low enough for him to kill it. The shifter had gutted and cleaned the kill before hauling the carcass back up on deck, and Te'oma then set to roasting it bit by bit.

The changeling steered clear of Kandler and Esprë most of the time. He saw her chatting with Burch and Monja every now and then. Te'oma and Burch had formed some sort of a bond during the battle against Nithkorrh, and Monja trusted Burch's judgment completely enough to be friendly with the changeling too.

Kandler wondered if she might feel differently about Te'oma if she'd been around when the changeling had kidnapped the girl. The first time Monja had seen Te'oma had been when she'd been tossed from the captain's quarters of another airship after Ibrido had all but killed her. The changeling couldn't have looked less menacing at the time.

It had been Monja who'd brought Te'oma back from the brink of death. This seemed to have forged a bond between them, despite the fact that Kandler had only wanted the changeling to be healed so she could tell him where his daughter was. Once the furor had died down, Te'oma had expressed true gratitude toward Monja, and the halfling had basked in the appreciation.

Now the seven of them, this motley crew that hadn't so much been assembled as drawn together, were about to set sail for a continent full of dragons, all of them except Sallah, who still seemed determined to leave.

"It's madness," Sallah said.

Her hand fell to the hilt of her sword—the one she'd taken from Brendis's body, actually. Hers had been destroyed in the battle with Bastard back in the warforged town of Construct.

"I should just take her from you," she said. "I could bring her back to Flamekeep myself."

"Can you at least wait until we grab some supplies? I hate to have you lead a mutiny on an empty stomach."

Sallah pointed at the roasting tribex. Kandler shrugged.

"It's only mutiny if you're the captain in the first place," she said.

"I'm not?"

"Didn't Burch find the ship?"

"That I did," the shifter said as he joined the pair at the ship's bow, "so maybe she's mine. Unless you think we should bring her back to Majeeda."

"She's dead," Sallah said as she turned and put her back on the gunwale, leaning on her elbows there.

Burch spat something over the railing. "She was dead before. We left enough of her behind. They can always bring her back."

"That's not the point," Sallah said with a scowl. She glared at Burch, "Why is it? Why do you follow this man? Why is Kandler in charge?"

Kandler raised his eyebrows at his friend in mock surprise. The shifter winked at him.

"Someone has to be," Burch said, "but no one's in charge of me. I am my own."

"You call him 'boss,' and you follow his orders."

Burch seemed to consider this for a moment. "I listen to what he says. Don't you?" Before Sallah could protest, he continued. "As for 'orders,' if what he says makes sense, I go along with it." He shifted his gaze to Kandler now. "If not, I don't."

"Like telling Esprë about her father today," the justicar said. He tried to keep the anger from his tone, but Burch knew him too well for him to hide it that well.

"Like that."

"We lost a good dwarf today."

"A good friend," said Burch.

"He went willingly," said Sallah. "We couldn't have stopped him."

"If you'd kept your mouth shut, that wouldn't have happened," Kandler said to the shifter. "We'd have restocked our supplies and been on our way."

"Maybe." Burch spit on the deck this time. "Maybe not."

"You think Majeeda and Ledenstrae would have just let us go?" Sallah asked Kandler. "Just let us sail off with our hold laden with elf goods?"

"There'd have been a fight either way," Burch said.

Kandler cocked his head at his friend. "Are you telling me you did that to get Esprë out of there before the fight started? How could you think she'd be safer in that tower?"

Burch shook his shaggy head. "Either way held trouble. This way, she got to see her father."

"And that's good?"

The shifter peered back over his shoulder at the girl. Esprë stood at the wheel, framed in the bright light of the ring of fire that encircled the ship. She laughed at something that Xalt said to her. The warforged seemed confused for a moment, then joined in.

When Burch turned back, he glanced at Sallah. "A girl should know her father."

The lady knight nodded at that. "When else would she have ever had a chance?" she said, almost to herself.

"Esprë only knew about her father from what you and Esprina told her," Burch said. "She had to have some doubts."

"We told her the truth," said Kandler.

Burch shrugged. "Some things you got to see for yourself. Stuff like, 'Your father's one bad elf,' No one takes that all on faith."

"You never knew your father," Sallah said. "Did you?"

Burch gave her a wry grin. "It doesn't always work out that neat, does it? He died before I was born."

"Your father was a good man," Kandler said to Sallah.

Grief threatened to fill her eyes, but the lady knight pushed it back. "He was a great man and a great knight." She pursed her lips. "Not always a great father, but a great knight."

"I still think she'd have been better off not knowing him," Kandler said of Esprë. He wanted to deflect the conversation from talk about Deothen, both for Sallah's sake and because he was still mad at Burch. "I'm her guardian. You shouldn't have done that without talking with me."

"She's older than you."

"You know it doesn't work that way. She hasn't even come of age yet."

"Is that ever going to happen? We're a long way from Aerenal here, and we seem to have worn out our welcome in Valenar."

"Elf ceremonies aren't the only way for a girl to grow up."

"You're missing the point, *boss*." Burch shot Sallah a

sarcastic look as he hit the last word. "She's already grown. She's figuring it out. It's time you did too."

Kandler felt his temper rise. He quashed the urge to punch his best friend in the snout. "Her mother just died—"

"Four years ago. That's a lot, even for an elf."

Kandler stopped cold. He knew Burch was right, but he couldn't bring himself to yet admit it—at least not right now.

"Just look at her," the justicar said. "Does she look full-grown to you?"

"She has a dragonmark. Those don't show up in children."

Kandler winced. "Dragons below," he whispered. "You got me there."

He peered past Burch at Esprë again. In the warm, flickering light from the ring of fire, she seemed as young as ever, but Kandler knew that was just an illusion. Despite the fact that she'd barely seemed any different than the day he'd met her—that she might not look much different the day he died—she was growing up.

Esprina had been dead for years. The last Kandler had seen of Ledenstrae, the elf had been lying in a pool of his own blood. Even if the healers of Aerie managed to save or resurrect him, he wouldn't be around to help Esprë through all this. Ever.

It was Kandler's job.

CHAPTER

29

Esprë giggled at Xalt. "You're so terribly innocent," she said with a smile.

The warforged stared at her with her unblinking eyes. "I have seen much of the world in my short time on it," he said, "but I will never be as old as you."

"You might live longer though," Esprë said. She adjusted her hands on the wheel and glanced up at the ring of fire crackling almost overhead. "No warforged has ever died of old age."

"We are a young people," said Xalt. "Time will answer many questions about us—in many ways."

Esprë nodded. "You see the fire," she said, pointing up at the ring. "It's alive, just like you and me. It's been alive for centuries, maybe even eons. It's impossible to tell."

"Does it not remember?"

"Time doesn't pass for elementals as it does for us. It hails from a plane of existence filled with nothing but fire and things to burn. Moons don't spin around planets there. The sky never grows dark. The elementals live forever—or at least until they burn out."

"How do you know these things?"

"My mother told me some of it. She was a battle mage, a sorceress of some power. I never saw her at war though."

"And the rest?"

Esprë smiled. "The elemental tells it to me."

Xalt's mouth froze in confusion for a moment. "Does it speak to you?"

"Not with words. It's more like it communicates with feelings instead, but they're far more complex than what you'd expect from such a simple creature."

Xalt craned his neck back to take in the semi-circular part of the ring of fire visible from the bridge. "It does not seem like something simple to me."

Esprë giggled again. "It is only what it is, nothing else. It is pure fire. It lives to burn. What could be simpler than that?"

Xalt watched the ring burn. "It sounds . . . tempting."

"I know what you mean," said Esprë. "There are many days I wish my life was a simple as that of the elemental that drives this ship, but it has problems too."

"Like what?"

"The people who made this airship tore the elemental from its home and bound it to the *Phoenix* by magical means. Before that, it burned only for the sake of burning. Now it burns to go home."

Xalt considered that for a moment. "Should we not release it?"

Esprë shuddered at the thought. "Don't you remember what happened with the other ship?" The image of the *Keeper's Claw* exploding into a ball of fire hungry enough to consume a dragon flashed through her mind.

"We could abandon the ship and set it free. You've said before how hard the elemental has tried to crash the *Phoenix*. We could help it succeed."

"What would happen then?"

"The elemental would be freed."

"Then what?"

Xalt stopped and absently tapped the finger on his maimed hand to his head. "I don't know. What happened to the other elemental?"

"It died," said Esprë. "As powerful as it was, it couldn't find a way back home. It devoured the dragon then burned out forever."

"Can fire die?"

"Just like putting out a candle. One moment it's there, and the next it's nothing but a memory."

"Do you want to die?"

Esprë's breath caught in her chest. "Sometimes," she said. "Mostly not."

"Why?"

"There's nothing simpler than being dead."

"I see."

The two stood there in silence for a moment. Te'oma and Monja tended the roasting tribex, and the smell of the cooking meat made Esprë's stomach rumble. It would be ready soon, and she felt famished.

Out at the bow, Esprë saw Kandler, Sallah, and Burch talking. They glanced back at her from time to time, but she could not make out their words over the roar of the burning ring of fire.

"Then why do you continue to live?" Xalt said.

A sudden urge to slap the warforged surged in Esprë's heart, but she put it aside. He was so young, and just as she had said, innocent.

"It's complicated," she said. "I may wish that I had the simple life of an elemental, but I do not. I am who I am, and I have to learn to deal with that—no matter how horrible it may be."

"Is it so horrible to be you?" The warforged put a hand on the girl's shoulder.

She refused to look at him, keeping her eyes pointed straight ahead. She saw Kandler and the others leave the bow and start toward the roast. She hoped that Sallah or Monja would come up and relieve her soon, as much so she could get away from Xalt's questions as so she could fill her belly.

"It's not easy," she said, "not as easy as I would like, but it's my life, and I'm not going to throw it away."

"I understand." Xalt's tone said that perhaps he didn't.

Esprë turned and offered the warforged a weak smile. "It's not just stubbornness that keeps me going," she said, "although that's part of it. I've thought more than once about tossing myself over the ship's railing. In fact, when we crashed outside of Fort Bones, it was no accident. I flew the *Phoenix* straight into the ground. I wanted us to die."

"Perhaps it would have solved your problems."

Esprë snorted softly at that. "No. It would just have ended them."

Xalt's head bobbed. "I see."

This time Esprë believed he did.

The warforged gestured toward the roasting tribex. "I think your life is about to become more complicated."

Kandler and Sallah broke off from the others, leaving Burch with Monja and Te'oma to start carving the succulent tribex.

"Yours too, I'm afraid," Esprë said to Xalt.

"We need to talk with you," Kandler said as he and Sallah climbed onto the bridge.

When they'd been standing out on the bow and even next to the others roasting the tribex, they'd seemed much smaller. From atop the bridge, Esprë had stood far taller than any of them. As they stood next to her, though, she couldn't help but think how small she still was compared to them.

Of course, Esprina had been shorter than either Kandler or Sallah, and she'd been an adult too. Humans grew taller than elves. It was nothing to be ashamed of, but it still made her feel like a child.

"What is it?" she asked, keeping her voice even.

"Sallah here has made it clear to me that I haven't been taking you much into account when making decisions for you. According to her and Burch—and probably everyone else on this ship who's yet to weigh in with me—I need to start treating you more like an adult."

Sprites danced in Esprë's stomach. She'd longed for Kandler to give her more respect for years, but she'd given up on it happening years ago. She'd figured she'd outlast him one way or the others, as was often the case with elves when they dealt with humans.

One time, when Esprina and Kandler had a spat, Esprina eventually gave in to Kandler's demands. When Esprë had asked her why, her mother had said, "When it comes to bickering over such petty matters, life is far too short—especially for him."

With everything that had been happening, though, Esprë had once again started to entertain ideas of Kandler treating her as an equal. While she wasn't sure he was ready for it quite yet, the fact that he'd even been talking to someone else about it sent a thrill through her.

Then she turned suspicious. Why would Kandler want to start doing something like this right now? She'd hoped to be able to push her case once they'd survived whatever lay ahead of them. For now, though, she'd been happy to let Kandler make the decisions.

"Oh no," she said as she realized what he was after. "No. You can't do that to me."

"Yes, he can," said Sallah. "He needs to. This is larger than him."

"It's larger than any of us," said Esprë. "Too large."

Kandler put an arm on Esprë's shoulder. She could tell he wanted to pick her up and hold her, but he'd kept himself from doing so. That would be what an adult would do for a child. If they were to be equals, they'd have to start treating each other as such.

"It has to be your choice, Esprë," Kandler said. "This is your life we're talking about. You should have a say in how you want to live it. You know what the stakes are."

Esprë grimaced. "Do I want to live on the run for as long as I can, always looking over my shoulder, never sure when someone is going to kidnap me again or just slay me where I stand? Or would it be better to sail an airship straight into the collective maw of the most dangerous collection of creatures in the world?"

"That is an excellent summary," said Xalt.

CHAPTER

30

Esprë giggled at the warforged's deadpan praise at such a tense moment. She cut herself off an instant later, but not before she caught Kandler smirking at her just a bit too. Sallah, on the other hand, just looked annoyed.

"I wish to impress upon you how serious this is," Sallah said, leaning toward the young elf.

"You don't think I understand that?" Esprë wondered if the knight had meant to be insulting.

"I don't think Kandler has been as clear with you about it as he could. If you decide to sail to Argonnessen, you will surely be killed."

Behind Sallah, Kandler shook his head and pursed his lips, "No."

Esprë suppressed the giggle tickling at her mouth. Sallah wasn't so successful.

"Does he think I can't see him?" Sallah said with half a smile.

"I have to put up with antics like that all the time," Esprë said.

Sallah's face turned serious again. "This is why I suspect

you may not understand how mortally serious this all is."

The lady knight straightened up and pointed off to the southeast. "That way lies Argonnessen," she said. "That way lies death."

She turned toward the northwest. "In that direction lies Thrane. There we would have the whole of the Knights of the Silver Flame to act as your bodyguard. Jaela Daran, the Keeper of the Flame, will protect you and keep you from harm."

Kandler tapped Sallah on the shoulder. "May I be allowed the opportunity to present my point of view?"

He spoke as politely as Esprë had ever heard him, and this worried her. Kandler wasn't much for manners. When he became polite, she knew something was horribly wrong.

"I must add one thing first," Sallah said.

The lady knight got down on one knee before the girl. As she did, she drew her sword and held it up before herself. The silvery flames flickered before her, and Esprë could see the light from the blade reflected in Sallah's emerald eyes.

"No matter what your decision, Esprë, I pledge myself to your cause. I will not abandon you. Our fates will be intertwined. I say this so you know that I do not take your choice here lightly. I place my life in your hands, and I can only pray that you will choose what is clearly the correct path." Sallah stood up then and resheathed her sword. "Look into your heart, Esprë. You will see the Flame burning there, and it will light your way."

Sallah snapped a quick salute to the girl then stepped aside, gesturing for Kandler to move up. He took one step forward and put his hands on Esprë's arms. Then he thought better of it and sat down before her. In this position, Kandler had to look up at Esprë, and she found she liked it. She wanted to reach out and tousle his hair. The several days' worth of beard he wore on his face ruined the illusion of him being a child though—that, and the few gray hairs she could see on his head from this unfamiliar angle.

Kandler folded his hands in his lap and spoke. He kept his words clear and distinct and his tone even and reasonable. Esprë saw no drama in his presentation, just the facts as he saw them.

"I've been to Thrane," he said. "They have good people there and bad. If the Knights of the Silver Flame say they will protect you, they will do their best. But they will fail."

Sallah started to interrupt, but Kandler, Esprë, and even Xalt cut her off with unforgiving glares.

"Thrane cannot hide you from the world. One way or another, Vol has been able to follow your movements. Majeeda did it too. Others—like the dragons or the Undying Court—will figure out a way. I've infiltrated Flamekeep myself."

Sallah gasped at this news, but Kandler ignored her and pressed on.

"I trust that the Church of the Silver Flame will not give you up to its foes. It will do whatever it must to protect you, including go to war. If the church teaches its members anything, it's to value their vows. I can see this breaking down in two different ways, though, and neither is pleasant. In the first, the people who want you dead send assassin after assassin to kill you until they succeed. They will have an inexhaustible supply of murderers willing to risk anything for the reward offered for your head."

Esprë put a hand to her throat.

"The second, sadly, is much worse. Some nation may decide that the assassins aren't working or won't work or are too damn subtle or whatever. It'll opt for the direct approach instead. They'll send an army to Thrane for you. It'll be war."

"You really think they'd go to war over me?"

Kandler frowned. "Over what you represent. Remember, the Treaty of Thronehold was only signed two years ago. Some nations didn't want to sign it. They'll take any excuse they can find to start the conflict up again. The reemergence of the Mark of Death, that's going to be enough for them, especially if they find it in the custody of one of their foes."

Esprë felt her legs start to wobble. To think that something like the Last War—which had taken her mother's life—could start up again over her made her think that perhaps she'd been too hasty with Xalt. Throwing herself over the gunwale didn't seem like such a bad idea after all.

"I know, Esprë," Kandler said softly. "This isn't fair. No one should have to shoulder something like this. No one should be expected to have to make these kinds of decisions, especially not you."

Esprë wiped at her eyes. She hadn't felt any tears there yet, but she wanted to make sure. "What—and what if we go to Argonnessen?" she asked, her voice raw and low.

"I won't lie to you," Kandler said, his face grim and drawn. "Sallah's right. It's probably death for all of us. Tactically, we don't stand a chance against a continent full of dragons. Killing Nithkorrh, well, you saw how hard that was, and we got lucky. We can't count on our luck to hold out for that long."

"But it won't mean war," Esprë said. "We'd be the only ones to die."

Kandler nodded. "You never know. I've never been to Argonnessen. No one on the ship has, not even Burch."

"I thought he'd been everywhere!" Esprë said with a false grin.

It had been a long-running joke in Mardakine that there wasn't a place in Khorvaire where Burch didn't know someone. Of course, they weren't talking about Khorvaire any longer.

"You would counsel your daughter to enter the darkness rather than face the light?" Sallah said.

Xalt spoke up. "To sacrifice herself so that others may live?"

Kandler craned back his neck and gave the knight a weak smile. "Didn't think I had it in me?"

Sallah gazed down at Kandler, and Esprë saw her love for the man shine in her face. The lady knight had done such a good job of suppressing that affection since she had declared her intentions to leave the *Phoenix* that Esprë had begun to wonder if it had ever existed at all.

"I always knew," Sallah said. "I just didn't understand." She reached down and placed a gentle hand on Kandler's shoulder, and he reached up and covered it with his own.

"Well," Esprë said, bringing the eyes of the others back to her.

She saw the soft curls at the edges of their mouths now, and somehow she knew that everything would be all right—at least between Kandler and Sallah.

"It seems the decision has already been made," the young elf said. An enormous relief washed over her. The horrible choice that they'd placed before her had been removed, or so she thought.

Kandler grimaced. "Sorry, Esprë, but it's still your call. I just laid out the facts as I see them. Whether Sallah agrees with me or not, this isn't something we're putting to a vote. There's only one voice that matters here, and it's yours."

Esprë frowned. "That doesn't seem fair."

"It's not. It's not fair that any of this has happened to you—to any of us."

"That's not the point, is it?"

"You can only do what you can do," Kandler said. "The question is: What would you like to do?"

"How very cryptic of you," Sallah said. "You'd make a fine priest of the Flame, I think."

"I couldn't handle the vows of celibacy," he said.

Sallah looked confused. "There aren't any vows of celibacy," she said as if the very thought were alien to her. "How do you think my parents had me?"

"I don't know," Kandler said, smiling at Esprë, knowing that Sallah couldn't see his face. "I've heard some religions going on and on about virgin births."

Sallah smacked the justicar in the back of the head.

"Hey!" he said with a mischievous grin.

"Excuse me," Esprë said before the two could grab each other and started rolling around on the bridge. "I have a decision to announce here."

Kandler and Sallah fell silent and looked up at her with expectant eyes. Esprë noticed that the chatter around the roast tribex had ceased too. Everyone on the ship waited to hear her speak.

When it finally came to it, Esprë could hardly the name of their location out. Her lips seemed to freeze together, but soon they thawed and she spoke her mind.

"Argonnessen," she said. "We're going to Argonnessen."

CHAPTER

31

I t seems like they've been gone forever," Esprë said. She chewed on her lower lip as she stared out over the port railing of the bridge. "Should it take so long?"

"Supplying a ship isn't like popping into the market for a quick bite," Monja said, perched next to her on the gunwale. "It's going to be a long journey, across the sea. The water alone will be too heavy for them to carry. They'll have to hire a wagon."

Esprë hated the way the halfling sat on the railing. She always felt that the little shaman would go tumbling off to the ground. True, they were only a couple dozen feet in the air—just high enough to keep the ring of fire from burning the grass below—but such a fall would still hurt and could even kill. If she hadn't been standing at the wheel, she would have reached over and plucked Monja from the gunwale, but she knew if she let go of the controls the airship would probably buck the halfling off before Esprë could reach her.

"I wish we could have just sailed the ship to Pitchwall." Esprë slumped against the wheel.

"Airships are great for travel, but they attract too much

attention," said Monja. "We need less of that right now. Remember how smoothly everything went in Aerie?"

"Burch said there are only a few hundred people in Pitchwall. How dangerous can they be?"

"If they're either afraid or greedy? Very. Humans are notorious for thinking about their skins and their purses far too much. Best to avoid it altogether, I say."

Esprë sighed. The others had all agreed with Monja, and hours ago Kandler, Burch, Te'oma, and Sallah had set out for the little village of Pitchwall on their own. That left Esprë with Xalt and Monja, lolling about in the floating airship as the craft hovered behind series of low hills that separated her from Pitchwall and the ocean beyond.

"I thought Q'barra was full of monsters," Esprë said.

"It was," said Xalt who stood next to Esprë, "but after the Last War began, a Cyran duke came here to found his own nation, a place separate from the battles that ravaged the rest of the continent."

Esprë and Monja stared at the warforged. The young elf thought the warforged would have smiled if he'd been able to move his mouth in that way. Instead, he cocked his head at them and said, "History lessons were part of my training. My instructors thought it would motivate the warforged to fight better if we had an idea of the reasons why we fought. They meant to help us put the battlefield into context."

"Did it work?" Monja said.

"No. Just the opposite. Once I understood what had caused the war, it seemed more senseless than ever. That's when they decided to make me an artificer and trained me to repair my fellow warforged." As he spoke, Xalt's hand wandered up to his thick, severed finger, which he wore on a lanyard around his neck.

"What else do you know about Q'barra?" Esprë asked, eager to help the warforged get his mind off his injury.

"Many of the same thunder lizards that roam the Talenta Plains live here too, alongside the largest lizardfolk civilization on the continent. They often attack the settlers from the Five Nations who come here, most of which are the roughest sorts of refugees who band together only as long as it takes to repel each raid."

"Why are we here again?" Monja asked.

Esprë stared out into the distance. A few lines of smoke curling from far beyond the hills in the distance marked the direction of the town. "Where are they?" she said.

❦

"Do you have any idea where we are?" Sallah asked.

Kandler ignored her and snapped the reins again. The team of three horses drawing the wagon surged forward, pulling the vehicle's wide-tracked wheels along the narrow path that was only barely drier than the surrounding wetlands.

"We're not stuck in the swamp yet," he said. "That's all I care about." He twisted his head around to look for Burch. "Did we lose them yet?"

Crouched atop barrels of water and other supplies they'd procured from that shady merchant in Pitchwall, the shifter sat scanning the sky. It had been a long time since Kandler had felt like washing his hands after cutting a deal with someone, but Sliford's oily handshake had made that happen.

"They're three of them up there still," Burch said. "They're hanging back a bit."

"Just waiting for the right moment," Te'oma said.

She'd morphed into a copy of Burch right now. In the village, she'd resumed the look of Shawda again. Now that they were in for a fight, though, she seemed to have duplicated Burch to throw their attackers off a bit.

Seeing the two Burches next to each other had rattled Sallah at first, who'd said a quick prayer to the Silver Flame when she'd first noticed. Burch, on the other hand, didn't seem to mind at all. In fact, he'd taken to calling the changeling "Lady Burch."

Kandler didn't care. He'd known Burch long enough that Te'oma couldn't fool him for an instant. Her voice, her stance, even her eyes, were all wrong—at least to someone looking for his best friend.

"They're moving up," Burch said. He held his voice even as he raised his crossbow and took aim at the sky.

Kandler wanted to keep his eyes on the road ahead—such as it was—but he decided to trust the horses for a moment and peek back at the sky. Three winged thunder lizards hung there above them, their white-scaled skins hard to pick out against the clouds in the sky.

They reminded Kandler of the glidewings they'd ridden from the Wandering Inn to Fort Bones, but Burch—who'd called them soarwings—had said they were even larger. Without any means of comparison at this distance, Kandler could only trust his friend's judgment. The fact that each of them looked to be carrying a lizardman lent the claim credence.

"Duck!" Te'oma cried. The changeling flung herself from the wagon as its wheels squelched through the muddy terrain. Her bloodwings burst open before she hit the ground, and an instant later they started to carry her into the sky.

Kandler saw none of that though. The sudden appearance of a feathered spear right next to him jarred his concentration. It embedded itself deep into the wooden plant on which Kandler sat. A half foot to the right, and it would have run him through. He snapped the reins again—harder.

❦

"Uh-oh," said Monja. The halfling twisted about on the gunwale and stood upon it, staring out toward where the village of Pitchwall was supposed to be.

"What?" said Esprë. "What's that supposed to mean?"

The halfling raised a tiny finger and pointed up at the sky to the east. Following the gesture with her eyes, Esprë's spotted three shapes moving in the sky above the hills.

"They look like birds," Xalt said.

Monja scowled as she leaped down to the bridge's deck. "Those are soarwings, and they have riders. This can only mean trouble."

"Maybe they are escorting the others back to the ship," Xalt said in a more than normally helpful tone.

"Or chasing them," said Esprë. "Are they coming this way?"

The sharp-eyed Monja nodded. "And they're armed. I just saw one throw a spear."

"They must have spotted us by now," said Xalt. "The ring of fire can be seen for miles from the air."

"That'll make them even more desperate to finish their job before we can stop them," Monja said. "Get this boat moving!" she shouted at Esprë. "We'll be too late!"

CHAPTER

32

The wagon tipped hard to the left as Kandler wrenched the reins, forcing the horses to weave back and forth harder than even the twisting the path ahead demanded. If those three bandits were going to keep taking cheap shots at them, he refused to sit still and make it easy for them.

Burch's crossbow twanged just as they came out of the turn, and the shifter cursed. "Wide and high," he said back to Kandler. "You're not making this easy on me."

"You're the better aim," the justicar said. "You can handle it."

"Your faith is inspiring."

Burch ratcheted his crossbow back and slammed another bolt home. "When we're about to hit a smooth patch, let me know."

"How about a smooth-*er* patch?" Kandler didn't see anything like level ground ahead, much less smooth.

"It'll have to do."

"I feel so useless," Sallah said. The lady knight pulled her sword half out of its sheath.

"Put it away!" Kandler said. "It only gives them something to aim at."

With a determined set to her chin, Sallah brought the blade free, and it burst into flames. "That doesn't sound so useless to me," she said.

She turned in her seat and stood on her knees, then she waved the burning sword at the soarwings as they dove nearer. The lizardmen atop the beasts had decided that they needed to get closer for a good throw. They couldn't have too many more of those spears up there with them, Kandler told himself. From now on, they'd have to make each attack count.

"Get down!" Kandler said to Sallah.

He tried to reach out and grab her with his free hand, but she just shoved his attempt aside. Then the wagon reached another turn in the road, and he needed both hands on the reins again.

"That's great," Burch said. "Nothing like bait to bring them closer."

"Who's hunting whom here?" Kandler asked.

"I'll let you know when this is over."

The crossbow twanged again, and a horrible cry pierced the sky. Kandler glanced up and spotted a lizardman tumbling through the air, the soarwing above him now riderless.

"One down, two to go," Burch said.

"Where's Te'oma?" Kandler said.

"Run off again," said Sallah. "As always. She's not much for a fight."

"She did save Monja," Burch pointed out.

"How convenient that it took her away from the battle with the Stillborn."

"Did you see the crest on that creature's sash?" Burch said, pointing a clawed finger at the falling lizardman as he smashed into the swamp with a horrible smack. "It showed a boar's head on a blue field."

"Just like the one over Sliford's door," Kandler said. "Should have guessed."

"We paid handsomely for our goods," Sallah said, aghast. "How dare he?"

"If it works, he gets his stuff back, plus he gets to keep our gold," Burch said. "Plus anything else we might have, like that pretty sword of yours. Even if he just sold the news about us to those lizardmen, it's a good deal for him."

"Damn," Kandler said. "You just can't trust a slimy merchant in a hotbed of iniquity anymore."

"Are you mocking me?" Sallah asked.

"Never mock a lady with a burning sword."

A spear thumped into the wagon behind Kandler, and Burch yelped. The justicar heard the sound of dripping fluids, but he couldn't turn to look at that moment.

"Burch!" he shouted. "You all right?"

"Those thin-tailed bastards busted open that cask of Brelish brandy!" the shifter said with a growl. "For that, they're going to pay!"

❦

Trapped in the wagon, Te'oma had felt like a bound chicken waiting for the axe to fall. Here, up in the air, she was safe and free—or so it seemed. So far, the lizardmen had ignored her for the laden wagon bouncing along the swamp road at top speed.

It only made sense. They were after the goods and the gold. If one of the travelers got away, they cared little. They could always track her down and kill her later at their leisure. The swamps, after all, were their home.

Te'oma considered soaring straight up at the flying lizards, but she knew that the great creatures would tear her apart. Even from this distance she could see that their long, sharp claws could shred her wings with a single swipe, leaving her to fall to her doom.

Instead, she let a thermal updraft from the swamp push her higher in the air. She flew in a long spiral of tight circles that brought her up, up, up, toward the sun as it poked out through a break in the clouds.

Should she do something to help the others? Perhaps just getting herself out of harm's way was enough for now. Maybe she could go to the airship and rally the others to the wagon's defense.

Then she saw the *Phoenix* moving toward her—toward the two remaining soarwings and their riders. The airship's ring of fire blazed bright and strong, even in the direct sunlight. Te'oma wondered what the lizardmen would make of that sight.

She kept climbing higher and higher into the sheltering sky.

*   ❦

"What do I do?" Esprë said as she brought the ship to bear on the two soarwings. She, Xalt, and Monja had cheered when Burch's bolt had knocked one of the lizardmen from the sky, but that joy had not lasted long.

"Ram them!" Monja said.

"That's insane!" Esprë glanced around for Xalt to give her some moral support on this issue, but he had disappeared.

"Do you have a better idea?" the halfling asked. "I don't think your dragonmark will work on them from here."

Esprë stared at Monja for a moment, then set her jaw and reached out with her mind to push the airship forward at top speed. "All right," she said. "They'll never know what hit them."

"You missed!" Sallah said to Burch after the shifter's crossbow twanged again.

Kandler gritted his teeth as they charged over a low hill and down the other side. The horses were getting winded. He didn't know how much more they could take of this.

The more tired the horses got, the more likely they would make a mistake. At this speed, if one of them stumbled and fell, it might take the whole wagon with it. While the supplies were replaceable, Kandler didn't relish the thought of having to go back into Pitchwall and go through this all over again.

Also, they'd been relying on the gold that Sallah and other Knights of the Silver Flame had brought with them on their quest. Kandler didn't know just how much of it was left, but he knew it couldn't last forever.

"Think what you want," Burch said. "Not every attack is meant to kill—not directly."

"You're hoping to knock them from the air with the whizzing sound the bolts make as they pass right by?"

"Something like that."

Kandler spotted a clearing up ahead. It seemed like as good a place as any to make a stand. He couldn't just drive the wagon straight up on to the airship. They'd have to put an end to the race sooner or later, and he preferred to do so on his own terms.

"I'm pulling in," Kandler shouted. "Dive under the wagon to take cover. Make them come to us!"

"I'd like that," Sallah said, still brandishing her sword at the two soarwings circling in the sky. "I'm tired of playing this game on their terms."

Then a spear appeared in the back of one of the horses, stabbing straight through, and the beast went down.

CHAPTER

33

Hard to starboard!" Xalt called from the airship's bow.
The two long-necked soarwings had split up and dove further down as Esprë came at them. She couldn't see them
under the tip of the bow, so the warforged had run ahead to
serve as her eyes.

She coaxed the ship into a tight circle that peeled off
down and to the right. As she did, one of the soarwings spun
into view, and she aimed straight for it.

The deck pitched sharply under her feet, and she
gripped the wheel tighter to keep from flipping forward on
to the main deck below. She heard Monja yowl in protest
as she lost her footing, but when she glanced toward the
halfling, she saw that the shaman had been forethoughtful
enough to grab one of the leather straps on the bridge's
console before she'd fallen.

"There's no way I'm going to be able to hit that thing,"
Esprë said.

As if to prove her point, the soarwing flung itself out
of the airship's path and rolled off to the port. Esprë tried
to follow it, but it zoomed away underneath her, and she

lost track of it again.

"Where'd it go?" she asked, scanning the sky. A dull panic gripped her as she thought of the soarwing swooping in from some unknown angle and plucking her from the bridge.

❦

Te'oma spun in an almost lazy circle and watched the attack unfold below her. It seemed like some distant image in a scrying pool, something that was happening far away and that could not possibly have any effect upon her. It would be so easy to just keep riding that thermal until it took her far from the reach of the lizardmen, the people on the ground, the ones on the airship, and even from Vol herself.

But to do that would be to admit defeat, to acknowledge that the Lich Queen had beaten her. While the changeling knew she had no hope of standing directly against such a powerful figure, she was still determined to do what she could to become a thorn in the horrible monster's bony side—metaphorically, at least. To do that, she needed to keep Esprë alive but out of Vol's reach for as long as she could.

The fact that this might help redeem Te'oma for all the ills she'd done in her life had not escaped her, but since the gods had never seemed to care for her, she didn't care about them. Who would the redemption be for? Her? The spirit of her dead daughter?

Sometimes Te'oma wondered if her daughter watched over her from beyond the grave. If so, did she wish her well or ill? The changeling had never been much of a mother, and she wouldn't be surprised if the girl had grown up hating her.

Despite that, Te'oma had always loved her daughter, even if she hadn't known how to raise her. She'd known that giving her up had been wrong, and in her lowest moments she'd considered going back for her.

Once she'd gone so far as to track the girl down. She'd met her in the street, posing as a doddering old woman who'd confused the girl for her own daughter. She'd not even known her name, but she'd recognized the people who had taken her in.

As they walked down the street, they'd each put their arms around her and laughed with her in such a loving way. Te'oma's heart had nearly burst with jealousy at the sight. She'd tried to summon up some gratitude for the fact that they'd taken in this stranger's infant and raised her to be healthy and happy, but the bitterness at everything she'd missed—of her own accord, which only made it worse—drowned all that out.

As the elderly woman, Te'oma had stumbled into the girl's path, and the kind child had reached out to lend her a hand. When they'd touched, the feel of the girl's hand on her own had nearly reduced Te'oma to tears. She'd been grateful that she'd chosen to use a form in which such strange and sudden displays of emotion wouldn't seem so out of place.

That girl was long dead now, and Vol—who had promised to bring her back—had destroyed her body and any chance for her to return.

At first, Te'oma had wanted to avenge herself on the Lich Queen, who'd used her so callously as little more than a weapon to be aimed at her foes. Later, she realized that Vol might never have been able to revive Te'oma's daughter. Even if the changeling had brought Esprë back to Illmarrow, there would be no way that Te'oma could have forced the ancient, long-dead elf to live up to her part of the deal. Vol may have stuck to the bargain, but she just as likely might have not.

Te'oma had let her emotions control her, and Vol had played her for the fool. The Lich Queen had told Te'oma of the destruction of her daughter's body in a fit of pique. There was no way of knowing if that was true either. Vol could easily try to contact her again soon and offer her another chance at saving her little girl.

Perhaps she'd even been trying. In her grief, Te'oma had severed her telepathic link with the Lich Queen, determined that she would never have use for it again. If Vol had only meant to scare her by lying about the fate of the girl's body, then her plans had backfired on her—at least as far as Te'oma was concerned.

With that act, Vol had murdered the changeling's daughter, as surely had the angry mob that had stoned the girl to death. This time, though, she'd killed off Te'oma's last hope for the girl as well. There would be no bringing that back.

If Te'oma couldn't do anything to save her own daughter, at least she could help save someone else's. Despite herself, the changeling had come to care about Esprë. She was aware that the young elf hated her, and she didn't blame her for it. She only knew that she had to do whatever she could to make right all the wrong she'd done to the girl, even if that meant following her into the jaws of certain death.

If that meant following Esprë and her friends to the ends of Eberron, then so be it.

Te'oma couldn't stomach the idea of returning to Khorvaire anyhow. If she flew off now, where would she go? What would she do?

She desperately needed some kind of purpose to fill the void her daughter's death had left in her. This one seemed as good as any.

With that thought burning in her brain, Te'oma folded her wings against her body and let gravity pull her into an accelerating dive toward one of the soarwings sliding through the air below her.

The soarwing appeared off to the port again, closer this time. Esprë could see the green-scaled rider now, his long, thin tongue slipping out of his mouth and flapping in the wind. He pulled back his lips to bare his rows of sharp, white teeth as he glared at her with his baleful, yellow eyes.

Esprë froze. The rider's reptilian form reminded her so much of the half-dragon Ibrido that she feared that the villain had somehow come back to life and chased them across the desert, the mountains, and the plains to finally finish them off here, before they could even leave Khorvaire behind in their quest to confront his distant masters. She watched as he brought back his arm to hurl a feathered spear at her, and she had no doubt that it was destined to pierce her heart.

Then the lizardman squealed in surprise as the soarwing under him swerved toward the airship. A crossbow bolt sailed through the air, just missing the creature and causing it to duck in the direction of the *Phoenix*.

The movement shocked Esprë into action. She roared at the fire elemental in her mind, and the ship lurched toward the soarwing.

The ring of fire caught one of the thunder lizard's wings and crisped it in an instant. The beast screeched in mortal pain as it tried to flap away from the airship on its single remaining wing.

Thrown from his mount, the lizardman spun off into the sky and disappeared beyond the port rail. The soarwing, though, flopped toward the deck and landed hard on its wooden surface to the sound of breaking bones. It did not move again.

"Where's the other one?" Esprë yelled. "Where is it?"

Xalt scanned the sky but saw just as little as Esprë. Then

he flung his head over the bow. A moment later, he sprang back up. "Down there!" he said. "Down and to port!"

Grateful to have some direction to head in—any direction at all—Esprë pushed the airship in that direction. As she did, Monja let loose of her leather strap and flung herself to the bridge's rear gunwale.

"He's going after the wagon," Monja said, straining to be heard over the roar of the ring of fire. "He looks like he's going to— Spirits! He killed one of their horses. I think they're going to crash!"

Esprë's heart sank, but she pushed out with her mind harder, striving to shove the performance of the airship's elemental to new heights. Just as the wagon hove into view beneath the twisting and turning *Phoenix*, something dropped past the airship's deck at top speed, heading right for the wagon below.

Then Esprë realized that the falling object wasn't some-thing but some*one*. "Te'oma!" she shouted, fearful of what the treacherous changeling might do. "Te'oma!"

CHAPTER

34

The horses screamed as their companion lost his footing and sagged in the harness. They fought hard to remain
on their hooves, but gravity and momentum worked against
them.

Kandler cursed and hauled back on the reins as hard as
he could. "Hold on!" he shouted.

The wagon went up on two wheels and threatened to tip
right over, but Kandler pulled on the reins and wrestled the
surviving horses away from the direction in which their dead
fellow had fallen. The beasts bellowed in protest at the way
he forced them to twist and turn, but he ignored the noise
and forced them to come to a thundering halt and pull the
wagon back onto all four wheels.

It was everything Kandler could do to keep his seat.
Behind him, he heard Burch growling as the barrels and
casks in the back of the wagon threatened to crush him under
their rolling bulk. Sallah grunted as she held on to the wagon
with her free hand, refusing to drop her sacred blade.

Then the wagon hit a bump, probably just the roots to
some long decaying tree, the trunk of which had long rotted

away into the swamp. The wheels came to such an abrupt halt that Sallah lost her grip and catapulted forward, past the horses and onto the marshy ground beyond.

"No!" Kandler shouted. He flung out an arm to grab her as she went by, but his fingers failed to find purchase on her armor. She hit the ground hard and did not get up.

Kandler dropped the reins and leaped from the wagon. As his feet hit the ground, he heard a horrifying screech from above. He flung his head back and saw a soarwing coming straight down at him as he raced for Sallah. The lizardman rider on its back hissed triumphantly and brought back its arm to hurl its last spear through the justicar's heart.

As Kandler reached Sallah, he saw that she still lived. The fall had knocked the air from her lungs, though, and she had yet to catch her breath. He fell to his knees next to her and drew his sword, unwilling to let the long-beaked soarwing have either of them without a fight.

The justicar glanced at the wagon, but he could not see Burch under the pile of supplies that had crushed forward against the front of the wagon's bed. The two horses stood there, terrified, and probably would have stampeded off again if they hadn't had their companion's corpse weighing down their harnesses.

The soarwing screeched again, closer now, and Kandler's heart started to pound. Should he cower over Sallah, protecting her with his body, or should he stand and fight?

He leaped to his feet and held his sword over his head, directly between himself and the soarwing. He stood straight over Sallah, ready to hurl himself between her and danger of any sort.

Then he spotted something coming straight at the soarwing, right out of the sky. At first he wondered if it could be the second soarwing, which he'd somehow lost track of. It moved too fast, though, and it was too small.

Perhaps it was the rider from the other soarwing. It could have tumbled from the back of the creature, just like the one Burch had shot before. Had the shifter taken out another rider with a last, desperate shot before he'd disappeared under a pile of supplies? Kandler couldn't be sure.

Then something struck the ground behind Kandler with a hard, wet sound. He snapped his neck around to see a green-scaled body bounce up from the road beyond him, spraying bits of mud and blood as it arced into the air and came down again.

The soarwing screeched a third time, and when Kandler looked back at it, the creature was reaching for him with its claws. He readied his sword for a desperate swing, hoping to at least be able to take the monstrous lizard with him. If he could manage that, then maybe Sallah and Burch would survive, especially if they could find Esprë, Monja, and Xalt, wherever they were now.

He spotted the telltale ring of fire from the airship just then, but the soarwing's ivory-colored shape eclipsed it before he could do more than focus on the orange blaze. He grasped the hilt of the fangblade in both hands and prepared to swing at the onrushing talons slicing through the air at him.

Kandler knew that the trick to such a defense was to wait until the last possible instant to strike. Swing the sword too soon and you wasted your chance, leaving yourself even more vulnerable to the raptor. Swing too late, and you might never get your chance at all.

The fact that the soarwing was the largest flying predator Kandler had ever seen—outside of a dragon—meant the beast had eaten a lot of other creatures before this. Many of them had probably been snatched up in an attack just like this. Kandler promised himself not to be taken the same way.

Even if the soarwing grabbed him, Kandler hoped to slash the thing to ribbons. Its long, white neck practically begged for the fangblade's edge, and he meant to make the two meet, whether he survived the encounter or not.

Then the thing zooming up behind the soarwing slammed into its back. Kandler heard a loud crack, as of bone on bone. The lizardman riding the beast was knocked from his perch on the soarwing's back, and the creature spun forward, head over tail, stunned.

The ground shook when the soarwing smacked into it, just beyond Sallah. It tumbled along from the point of impact like a monstrous ball of sinew and scales until it crashed to a halt in a boggy patch of ground so wet and treacherous that it seemed to start pulling the beast down as soon as it fell in.

Kandler spun about as he watched the soarwing smash into the earth, watching its demise in stunned silence. The fangblade hung loose in his hands as he gaped at the thing. Its wings had to have been forty feet across. He'd probably have swung too early at it just because his brain wouldn't have been able to believe it had been that large.

For a moment, Kandler wondered if the soarwing represented some ancient, distant relative of the dragons like Nithkorrh. Although the dragons had far greater smarts on their side, when it came to sheer, brute force in the sky the fruit didn't seem to have fallen far from that fearsome tree.

Kandler heard a horrible, gurgling noise behind him. He turned to see Te'oma standing over the fallen lizardman, whose legs had been shattered in the fall. Before he could say a word to stop her, she took her obsidian dagger and slit open the cold-blooded creature's throat. His struggles ceased.

Kandler gave the changeling a grim nod. He never liked

to see someone killed like that, but he bore no doubts that the lizardman would have done the same to each and every one of them given half the chance.

"Thanks," he said. He surprised himself by how much he meant it.

The changeling shrugged as if she'd done nothing more than slap down a stinging insect. She bent down and wiped her blade on the lizardman's sash then sheathed it.

Kandler reached down and helped Sallah to her feet. The lady knight flushed with shame at not having been able to defend herself at the end.

"I should have been the one over you," she said.

"Play your cards right, and maybe you'll get a chance later," Kandler said with a grin.

"I'm not hurt," Burch said as he extricated himself from the mess of supplies strewn about the back of the wagon. "If anyone cares, that is."

A bit of blood trickled down from the shifter's scalp, but he didn't appear to notice it. He grinned at the others as he wiped the red from his face. "Looks like I missed a good scrap. Everyone still breathing?"

As if in answer, the roar of the airship grew louder. Kandler craned back his neck to look up at the *Phoenix* and had to step back out of the way as a rope ladder fell down where he had been.

Xalt's head poked out over the gunwale. "Are you hurt?"

"No," Kandler shouted as he reached for the ladder and started climbing toward the airship's deck. Sallah followed close behind him. "How about up there? Where's Esprë?"

"She has the wheel," the warforged said.

"And Monja?" Burch asked, shading his eyes as he peered up at the *Phoenix*.

"She's fine."

"What happened to the third flyer?"

"The soarwing you forced toward the ring of fire? It's here on the deck behind me, half-cooked." The warforged glanced back over his shoulder. "I believe Monja is already cleaning the corpse. She said something about not wanting to waste a single bit of food before a long ocean voyage."

"Fantastic," Burch said, flashing a toothy grin. "I hear those things taste like stirges."

CHAPTER

35

Kandler breathed in deep the scent of the open sea. From here, the sun still set over Khorvaire, but he knew that this would be the last such dusk he'd enjoy with that piece of land framed in it for some time. The sun's dying rays lit up the sky like glowing lava, liming the clouds in pinks, purples, and reds. In the distance, he spied a flock of what looked like seagulls working their way along the shore, and he wondered for a moment if they were soarwings instead.

It had been years since Kandler had seen the ocean, and he found that he had missed it more than he'd known. He couldn't hear the vacillating roar of the pounding surf over the crackling of the *Phoenix*'s ring of fire, but he watched a pod of dolphins playing in the waves and let his mind carry him back to more peaceful times when he could have enjoyed a simple day on a beach.

Growing up in Sharn, the largest city in Breland, he'd spent many a day on the shores of the Dagger River or wandering along the edge of the Hilt. On more than one occasion, his parents had brought the whole family out to Zilspar to visit family. From there they'd made ventures to the ocean proper, and Kandler had fallen in love with it. The smells always conjured thoughts of travel and adventure in his mind, and he credited those trips with inspiring the wanderlust that had caused him to join up with the Citadel as a young man.

As a Brelish agent, he'd traveled throughout much of Khorvaire. He'd seen the Lake of Fire in the Demon Wastes. He'd visited with the Old Woman of the Swamp who stared into the Pond of Shadows in the distant Shadow Marches. He'd walked through the Court of King Kaius in Karrnath, and met more diplomats and mercenaries than he could count.

Since marrying Esprina, though, he'd given up much of that. They'd only been together for a short time before the Day of Mourning—far too short—and after that he'd dedicated himself to taking care of Esprë. Bereft of her mother, she'd required much of his attention, and their bond had grown to the point that he considered her to be far more than merely a daughter by marriage.

After the end of the Last War, he'd helped found Mardakine as a means of plumbing the depths of the Mournland. He'd hoped to discover what had killed his beloved wife along with so many other souls. For whatever reason—responsibilities to Esprë, to everyone else in Mardakine—he'd never made much progress.

While he understood that he couldn't have expected to unlock the secrets of the Mournland, his failure to do so still disappointed him. His head knew that even if he'd spent every waking moment scouring that horrible, wasted place, he probably wouldn't have had any better luck. His heart, though, bore the guilt of not having given every moment of his life to solving that particular riddle.

He heard the footsteps behind him, soft and familiar, and he waited for her to speak. She opened her mouth and began to say something, then flung her arms around his waist instead. He turned around and embraced her as well.

"What's that for?" he said to Esprë.

The young elf smiled up at him. "I just wanted to say thanks."

"No need," he said, tousling her hair.

"You don't even know what I'm thanking you for." She grinned up at him, and his heart melted. When happy, she reminded him so much of her mother.

"It doesn't matter," he said. "You don't need to say a thing. I already know."

"I still want to say it," she said. "For my sake, not yours."

"In that case, don't let me get in your way."

He laughed, and it came light and easy. Now that they were finally on their way across the ocean, he felt as if a millstone had been lifted from his neck. The decision had been made, and there would be no turning back. They would face their fate together.

No danger lurking behind them could do more than pale before the danger they had chosen to confront.

"Thank you," Esprë said, "for saving my life."

"Back there?" Kandler gave her a confused look. "I didn't do anything more than keep a wagon from crashing. You should be thanking Burch—and Te'oma, I suppose."

"I already did." Esprë frowned. "Thanking Te'oma wasn't easy."

"I don't suspect it was. One good deed doesn't make up for everything else."

"She did help Burch kill Nithkorrh too." Esprë shrugged as if to say how sad it was that there wasn't anything they could do about it.

"I thought you came here to thank me," said Kandler. "Sounds like I've been pretty useless."

Esprë smiled and gave him another hug. "I think you've

done a few amazing things since we left Mardakine too."

"Thanks," he said, letting gentle sarcasm drip from his tongue.

"No, thank *you*." She hesitated for a moment. "For everything. For taking me in after my mother died."

"You're my stepdaughter." Kandler couldn't conceive of having done otherwise for her.

"Yes, but that's not always enough, is it? Don't you know all those stories about wicked stepfathers?"

"That's stepmothers."

"Well, I don't have one of them, so I can't speak to that. I just know you came through for me at a time when you had to be suffering a lot too."

Kandler grimaced. "Don't worry about that," he said in a rough voice. "Helping you out got me through he worst of it. You were there for me just as much."

"And—and thank you for coming after me. You didn't have to do that."

Kandler stepped back and held Esprë out at arms' length. "Are you mad? I'd never let anyone run off with you like that."

"I . . . I know." Esprë refused to meet Kandler's eyes. "When Te'oma first took me, though—when she was posing as my aunt—I wondered if you'd bother to come after me to say good-bye. I know I've been a horrible burden on you—"

"That's *not* true—"

"Let me finish. Please."

Kandler took a deep breath, then nodded. He wanted to see where it was she planned to take this conversation, even if he didn't like its direction.

"You married my mother, not me. You've been a fine father to me, the first real one I've known."

"When I asked your mother to marry me, I knew you two came as a package deal. That didn't stop me."

"The best part of that package is missing now." She held up her hands to cut off Kandler before he could protest. "I know. It's silly, but it's how I felt."

Esprë turned and looked back down the deck at the fire over which Monja, Burch, and Te'oma were roasting the soarwing. Sallah had the wheel, and Xalt stood on the bridge with her to keep her company and to help with the navigation.

"When I figured out who Te'oma really was—or wasn't, I suppose—I resigned myself to my fate. I didn't dare hope that you'd come after me. The last I'd seen of Mardakine, it had been going up in flames, and I had no idea if you'd been killed or not. I figured I'd have to start doing things on my own.

"That didn't work so well. I never would have survived if you hadn't come after me. I'd have been stuck in that tower with Majeeda forever—or at least until she contacted my father and arranged to accompany me back to Aerenal. Then I'd have ended up in the hands of the Undying Court, or the Stillborn, or worse."

"You underestimate yourself. You always did."

"Sure," Esprë said with a weak smile. "I might have managed to get away on my own, I suppose, but they would have just tracked me down again. Even with you, how many times did Te'oma alone snatch me in those first few days?"

Kandler smirked. "I think I lost track. She's a tenacious one."

"Right up until Ibrido broke her neck, at least."

"She held on right through that too. A lot of people would have given up and died."

Esprë shrugged. "The point is that I would have never made it through all this without you. I just wanted to thank you for that."

"You should thank the others too," Kandler said, trying

hard to not sound ungrateful. "They had just as much to do with it as I did."

"Don't fool yourself," Esprë said. "Without you, they'd all be dead."

"Even Burch?"

The girl grinned. "Maybe not Burch."

Esprë wrapped her arms around Kandler and pulled him into a long hug. "I love you, Kandler," she said, her voice little more than a whisper.

"I love you too."

CHAPTER

36

Lightning cracked the sky so close that it left an after-image like a tree trunk in Kandler's eyes. The thunder sounded more like an explosion than the distant rumbles that had echoed around the *Phoenix* for most of the day, ever since the storm had swallowed them up.

The hair on the back of Kandler's neck stood on end, despite the rain lashing him. Although he stood straight under the airship's ring of fire, which vaporized any rain that fell near it, he could not avoid getting wet. The wind brought the water down almost horizontally, spattering against the justicar's front as he stared out past the ship's bow.

Xalt said something to Kandler, but the justicar's ears still rang from the lightning strike that had barely missed the ship.

"What?" Kandler said, squinting at the warforged standing next to him.

"Smells like a forge doused with a bucket of rusty water," Xalt said as he sniffed at the air. He wiped the rain from the surfaces of his obsidian eyes. "The lightning does, I mean. It's as if it burned the air."

Kandler nodded as his hearing returned. The hiss of the rain evaporating as it passed too close to the ring of fire let him know he hadn't been deafened forever.

He glanced back and saw Sallah at the wheel. He waved at the lady knight, but she ignored the gesture. Standing there on the bridge had to be miserable, but she had not complained or asked anyone else to relieve her during her shift at the airship's controls. He wondered if the Silver Flame was all she needed to keep herself warm.

"Burch, Monja, and Esprë are still below?" Xalt asked.

"Until the storm lets up," said Kandler. "We're not all as durable as you when it comes to the weather."

"Then why are you up here?"

Kandler grimaced. "I thought I heard something."

"What?"

"If I knew that, I wouldn't be up here."

"What did it sound like?"

Kandler stared at the warforged for a moment. "Wings. It sounded like beating wings."

"I heard that too. Do you think it could be dragons?"

"Possibly. We should be close to Argonnessen by now."

"What do you think they want?"

Kandler ran a hand over his face. "I don't know."

Xalt pointed over Kandler's shoulder with his one-fingered hand. "That's unusual."

The justicar turned and saw what the warforged meant. Something out in the depths of the black, roiling clouds glowed soft and reddish. It flared brighter for a moment then disappeared.

"That didn't look like lightning to me," Kandler said, his voice barely loud enough to pierce the blustery wind.

Xalt shook his head. The water sluiced off the warforged's hard outer surface.

Then something large smacked into the bottom of the airship, hard.

Kandler fell to his hands and knees. As he landed on the deck, he heard Esprë scream. The board between them muffled the sound, but he knew it was her.

He pounded on the slick wood beneath him. A quick series of knocks answered—yet another of the signals that he and Burch had worked out between themselves over the years. Everything seemed all right in the ship's hold, at least for now.

Kandler scrambled over to the gunwale, Xalt right behind him, and thrust his head over the railing. "What was that?" he asked.

"It wasn't lightning," Xalt said.

Kandler ignored the warforged and scanned the dark sky below. Despite the light from the ring of fire, he couldn't tell how high up they were. The swirling material below seemed like clouds rather than the sea's black waves, but he couldn't be sure.

"Whatever it was, it wanted to get our attention," Kandler said.

"It did that," Burch said as he slinked up behind the others.

"You left Esprë down below?"

The shifter jerked a thumb over his shoulder. "She's up on the bridge with Monja and Sallah."

Kandler glanced back and spied the trio standing there at the aft of the ship. Esprë gave the justicar a quick wave before ducking behind the console, out of the wind and away from the terrors of the night. It took everything he had not to race over to comfort her.

Lightning crashed all around the ship, slashing down in different places. None of the strikes came as close as the one that had nearly deafened Kandler. Instead of blinding him, they cast fogged illumination into bright pockets in the sky, although only for a split-second each.

"Did you see that?" Xalt asked.

Kandler raised an eyebrow at the warforged. Xalt pointed a finger straight up.

At first, all Kandler saw was the ring of fire arcing over them like a hungry, orange rainbow. Its light made it hard to see too far beyond it.

"What am I looking for?" Kandler asked. He peered at the restraining arc that held the ring of fire in place, inspecting it for widening cracks.

"Wait."

Rain ran down Kandler's face and into his eyes. As he blinked it away, lightning flashed overhead, and he saw it — a long, wide, winged shape silhouetted against the clouds in the brief instant of light.

Kandler wiped the rain from his eyes. "What's it doing there?"

"Not much yet," said Xalt.

Kandler stared up into the darkness a while longer. When the lightning flashed again, the silhouette no long hung over the ship.

The justicar glanced back at the bridge and saw Esprë peering over the console at him. The thought that the dragons might come to them now and destroy the airship without even accosting them, like predators cruising the skies for their next meal, infuriated him. He refused to let this happen.

Kandler hadn't come all this way just to let some flying, scaled monster knock him out of the sky. He headed for the bow. When he reached the ship's stem, he grabbed the gunwale with both hands then threw back his head and shouted at the creature stalking them.

"I know you're out there! We're coming to your home.

Even if you knock us from the sky, I'll swim the rest of the way to your lair, and I'll shove my sword right through your front damned doors!"

Kandler fell silent for a moment. He'd hoped that the dragon—if that's what it had been—would show itself. Nothing—only the raging storm and the hiss of rain dying on the ring of fire.

"Come out, you coward!" he shouted. "Show yourself so I can tear off your wings like the gnat you are!"

"What do you hope to accomplish?" Xalt said.

The warforged's interruption startled Kandler, and he stepped back from the rail.

"I figure we can either wait for the bastards to try to kill us, or we can shame them into leaving us alone."

"Do dragons feel shame?"

Kandler grinned. "I'm not sure, but I know I don't—at least when it comes to this."

Xalt stared at Kandler with his unblinking obsidian eyes. Then he tossed back his head and shouted, "Come out, you coward!"

Kandler joined right in. As far as he could tell, the dragon never came back.

CHAPTER

37

"B oss," Burch said, popping his head in through the open hatch. "Got dragons dead ahead."

Kandler leaped out of the hammock in the hold in which he'd been trying to sleep. He'd not had much success. As they grew closer to Argonnessen, the idea of closing his eyes, even for a moment, seemed insane. Now, with the call to action finally being sounded, he breathed a sigh of relief.

The justicar clambered up onto the main deck and trotted after the shifter, who led him straight to the bow.

"Xalt spotted it a few minutes ago," Burch said, pointing off toward the southeastern horizon. "Took me a while to figure out what they are."

Kandler shaded his eyes and spied what the shifter meant for him to see instantly. Two winged shapes spiraled about in the cloudless sky. From their silhouettes, they seemed to be dragons, but from such a distance Kandler couldn't be sure.

"Positive?" Kandler asked.

"About three quarters," Burch said. "Either way, it's trouble. If they're not dragons, they're still something we're going to have to deal with. They're right in our path."

"Can't we just go around them?"

"It's a big sky," Sallah said, as she strolled up the deck behind them. "Trying to avoid them would add dozens of miles to our trip."

Kandler met her eyes. She'd kept her distance from him ever since the *Phoenix* had left Khorvaire behind. He couldn't help but think she blamed him for the fact that they were out here crossing the Dragonreach. He doubted she gave Esprë much credit for having her own mind.

He would have talked with her about it, but he'd wanted to do so privately. She'd always managed to find herself other company, though, and she'd pointedly refused to acknowledge his hints that he'd prefer to speak with her alone.

"I didn't think you were that eager to reach Argonnessen," he said to her.

She grimaced. "We are doomed to die on this fool's quest. Where it happens does not matter much."

"I never thought you to be so casual about your death."

Sallah shrugged. "Death by one dragon's talons is just as good as another."

"It's all in the timing," Burch said. "I prefer to put it off as long as possible."

"Think there's any chance they haven't spotted us?" Kandler asked the shifter.

Burch pointedly looked up at the ring of fire that encircled the airship. "Doubt it."

"The *Phoenix* is a wonderful craft," Xalt said as he joined them, "but she is not subtle."

Kandler stared off at the dragons. They already seemed to be coming closer. Sometimes they flew toward the airship, sometimes not, but they never went farther away. They didn't seem to be in any hurry to reach the *Phoenix*, but

Kandler supposed they had all the time in the world.

"You're wondering if we can take them," Sallah said, astonishment tainting her voice. "You're insane."

Kandler had to admit that the thought had crossed his mind—but not to her. Not now, at least.

"We need to speak with them somehow. We can't assume every dragon we meet is a threat."

Monja snorted. "What else can they be? Creatures that large, old, and cruel can crush the bunch of us and barely notice. They're born threats."

"That makes all of this utterly hopeless, doesn't it?" asked Sallah. Kandler hoped that he didn't hear a note of sour triumph in her voice.

"Does anyone here really think we have a chance of beating them, much less surviving this trip?" Te'oma said. "If we're going to die, I vote for getting it over in a relatively painless way."

"I don't recall anyone asking for a vote on the matter," Sallah said.

"This is a dictatorship," Kandler said, "not a democracy—and none of you is in charge."

"And you are?" asked Te'oma.

Kandler shook his head. "Esprë's the one in charge here," he said. "It's her fate were all wrapped up in. We should be taking her orders from here."

"I agree," said Sallah. The others nodded as well.

"So," Kandler asked, "where is she?"

As one, the justicar and the others turned around to see Esprë, who stood alone at the wheel. She smiled at them and waved when she saw them, and they each gave her a half-hearted wave in return.

After a tense moment, Kandler strode off toward his stepdaughter. The others fell into line behind him, and soon all of them gathered on the bridge around the girl.

"What do you say?" Kandler asked Esprë. "Do we try to go around them or just head straight in?"

The girl stroked her chin for a moment. Kandler could see that, despite the horrible danger they might soon be in, she enjoyed this: the attention, the power, the fact that people not only asked her questions but hung waiting for the answers. Then something terrible dawned on her, and she pointed off toward the dragons.

"I don't think it's our choice anymore," she said. "Look."

Kandler turned about to do just that, and he saw that the dragons had gotten much larger. Worse yet, they had given up on the pretense that they hadn't yet seen the airship. They were headed straight for her.

The creatures closed with the *Phoenix* with terrifying speed. Kandler supposed that if they and the airship raced toward each other it would add their speeds together, a dizzying prospect for sure. He could hardly imagine what might happen to either the airship or the dragons if they collided at such speeds. That was enough, though, for him to start formulating a plan for pulling off just that if need be.

As the dragons drew closer, they moved from beneath the shadow of a cloud. A brilliant beam of sunlight glinted off their steely scales and splashed across their widespread wings, transforming them from darkened silhouettes into crimson-painted monsters of the mightiest kind.

Each beat of their wings brought them closer and revealed them to be larger and larger. At first, Kandler had thought they couldn't be larger than Nithkorrh. As they neared, though, he saw that they were two different sizes, and the bigger one dwarfed the black dragon they'd fought over the Ironroot Mountains.

Kandler's jaw dropped as he realized just how humongous these creatures were. His mind boggled at the thought of them being any bigger than they already seemed, but they kept coming, growing more and more gigantic by the moment. All thoughts of ramming the dragons with the ship scurried away now, replaced by a fear that the creatures might be able to tear *Phoenix* apart with their bare claws—or perhaps rip her from the sky like an eagle might snatch a sparrow.

"Got a plan, boss?" Burch said. The shifter spoke in an awed tone, never taking his eyes from the oncoming creatures.

"Sallah? Monja?" Kandler said. "You still in good with your gods?"

Both of them nodded, then cleared their throats and said softly, "Yes."

"Then you'd better get praying. It's the only hope we have."

"I thought you didn't care for the gods," Sallah said.

Burch grunted. "Long shot's better than no shot at all."

"The gods don't care for me," Kandler said, "but the rest of you might have a chance." He glanced at the knight and the shaman. "Save your prayers for Esprë—and for yourselves if you have any left over."

Kandler turned to Burch. "You don't happen to have any of those shockbolts left, do you?"

The shifter grimaced. "I played out that hand long ago. This one, with these two, this is a whole new game."

Kandler stopped then, stunned. Ibrido stood right behind Esprë. Then he snarled. "That's not going to save you."

"What?" the half-dragon said in Te'oma's voice. "Do you have a better idea?"

Before Kandler could respond, the sound of two ear-splitting howls drowned out the roar of the airship's ring of fire as if it was no louder than a babbling brook. They grew louder and higher as they approached, and then they passed overhead, marked by a pair of massive shadows that seemed to blot out the sky. Just as fast, they faded away, the noises dropping lower and fainter as they zoomed by.

Kandler barely got his head up in time to see the underbelly of the pair of dragons jetting across the sky overhead. The wind of their passage almost knocked him from his feet. It lifted Monja clean off her toes. If not for the leather strap that she'd grabbed on the console, she might have been swept straight over the aft railing.

The justicar flung himself at the aft rail and caught it, watching the dragons go. They touched wingtips briefly for a moment, then separated and curled about in opposite directions to come up behind the ship, surpassing her speed and then matching it.

"Get her below," Kandler said to Burch, pushing the shifter toward Esprë. "Now."

CHAPTER

38

The shifter didn't waste a word to argue. He wrapped an arm around the young elf's waist, then vaulted both of them over the console to land on the main deck below. The ship started to pitch, but Sallah darted forward and grabbed the wheel, bringing the *Phoenix* back under control.

As the airship stabilized, Burch and Esprë disappeared through the hatch, into the darkness of the airship's hold. With his stepdaughter as safe as she could be, Kandler turned his attention back to the dragons. The two of them growled at each other for a moment in their arcane tongue. When they were done, the smaller of the two dove forward, straight for the *Phoenix*.

To Kandler, it looked like the dragon might be launching an attack. The justicar looked for the telltale inhalation that such creatures employed before loosing their caustic breath at a hapless foe, but it never came, nor did the dragon extend its claws.

At the last moment, the dragon beat its wings once, and it scudded right over the top of the bridge and through the ring of fire. As it went, Kandler noticed it seemed smaller and paler.

The dragon seemed ready to slam right into the ship's main deck, and Kandler's stomach tied itself in knots as he wondered if it meant to go after Burch and Esprë. If the dragon wanted to, it could probably rip right through the wooden planks before anyone could do anything about it. Kandler drew his fangblade and hoped that if anything could slice through a dragon's armor it would be a sword forged from a dragon's tooth.

Then, just as the dragon alit on the deck, its back to the observers on the bridge, it changed. It morphed from the fearsome monster it had been into a tall, thin person with short hair the color of blood. It—or he, as the creature now seemed to be—wore a shirt and trousers of perfect black, cut in a style that Kandler had never seen, ancient and timeless at the same time.

The new arrival turned toward the bridge and acknowledged Kandler and the others with a brief wave. He had a long, sharp face, an aquiline nose, and high, pointed ears. The only flaw—if it could be called that—in his preternatural beauty was a scattering of reddish freckles that stretched across both of his high, sharp cheekbones and his nose.

In another face, these might have humanized the bearer. Instead, they made him seem even more alien in the way they set off his unblinking, crimson-colored eyes. His sharp smile, in which every tooth seemed a fang, completed the image in a horrifying way.

"Welcome to the Dragonreach," the man said, his voice—which bore no kindness, only disdain—was higher than Kandler would have guessed. "This is the gateway to the path that leads to Argonnessen, and we have been charged with protecting it. State your business in this part of the world, or we will help you along into the next."

"We . . ." Kandler's voice faltered. As he gazed at the man who stared up at him expectantly, he couldn't help but think about the dragon soaring through the sky just off the *Phoenix*'s stern.

"We're on our way to establish a trade relationship between Argonnessen and Thrane," Sallah said.

The man scoffed. "We have lived for untold millennia without needing anything from the younger races. Your goods are not wanted here."

"What of Seren?" Te'oma said, her voice far more like Ibrido's now. "The people who live on the isle that rests in your land's long shadow may not be so satisfied with their lot."

The man smirked. "Well said, cousin, but don't think your mixed blood will carry you far with me or the barbarians who take so much pride in the way they supposedly guard our gates. Many dragons see such as you as aberrations, insults to our blood that should be laid to rest before they can spread."

"We wish only to travel to Seren," Kandler said, trying to avoid any confrontation with their guest. "We mean you no disrespect."

The man stood there silent for a long moment, the wind flapping at his clothes. "Very well," he said. "We will escort you there. You will not proceed any farther, nor will you deviate from the path on which we lead you, or we will burn you from the sky."

With that, the man turned and walked toward the starboard gunwale. He climbed up on to it and balanced there for a moment in the rushing wind. Then he leaped over the side of the airship and disappeared.

A moment later, the smaller dragon rose above the ship's starboard railing, rising fast on swift-beating wings. He moved out toward the front of the *Phoenix* and matched the airship's speed right there.

"Follow that dragon," Kandler said to Sallah. "I'll be right back."

"Aye," the lady knight said with a nervous wink.

Kandler sauntered down from the bridge and made his way to the hatch. With a quick glance to the rear, he noticed that the dragon behind the airship could not see the hatchway from here. The bridge blocked its way.

"These dragons seem much friendlier than the last one we met," Kandler said as he slipped below the deck.

Esprë rushed forward and threw herself into Kandler's arms. He could feel her shivering there for a moment. Then she pushed herself away.

"Don't do that again," she said. "I can handle this myself." She held her arms tight around her and scowled at him, her anger warring with relief.

"Good for you," Kandler said softly. "I don't think I can."

"I know I can't," said Burch. "Two dragons flapping around us over the middle of the Dragonreach? I'm just happy to still be sucking air instead of water—or fire.

"What's the plan now?" Esprë said.

Kandler wanted to reach out and hug her, but she clearly didn't want that right now. Instead, he rubbed his chin and said, "I told them we were heading to Seren to set up a trade agreement, and they seemed to buy it—or not care enough about it to object. They're escorting us there now. You two should probably stay down here until we get there, just to avoid any more trouble."

"Sold," Burch said. He leaped into the nearest hammock and stretched out his long, furry legs.

"But . . ." Esprë started.

Kandler didn't cut her off. He waited for her to continue. When she didn't, he prompted her. "But what?"

"But shouldn't you have asked me first?"

"You weren't there."

"Because you had Burch take me down here."

"True enough," Kandler nodded. He put a hand on her shoulder. "I'm sorry, Esprë. I'm used to treating you like a child still, and I'll have to work to get over that. I can tell you one thing though."

"What's that?" she said, her lower lip poking out in a suspicious pout.

"I'm never going to stop trying to keep you safe, no matter how old you get."

Esprë tried to snarl at this, but she ended up grinning instead. "All right," she said, putting her arm around Kandler's waist. "Just next time try to give me a bit of warning, eh?"

"Sure." Kandler leaned down and kissed her on the top of the head.

"Ahoy, below!" Monja said as she stuck her head down through the hatch.

"What is it?" said Kandler. He noticed Burch slide right down out of his hammock, ready for action.

"Land ho." The halfling grinned. Then her head disappeared.

Kandler started up the ladder. Before he crawled out the hatch, he turned and said, "I'll be back as soon as I can. Stay put here." He looked at Esprë. "Please."

"All right," she said with a wistful frown.

Up top, Kandler followed Monja out to the bow. Te'oma and Xalt stood there shading their eyes and peering out into the distance.

"Right there," Xalt said, pointing toward the horizon straight ahead of them. "You can just see it."

Kandler squinted, trying to ignore the red dragon flapping along ahead of the airship, and followed the direction of Xalt's finger until he spotted it: land. They'd spend a long time out over the waves with nothing to see on any side but water, sky, and clouds. Despite the company they'd brought with them, the justicar felt like jumping with joy at the sight of the tops of the high mountains ahead, stabbing just out of the waves.

"Welcome to Seren Island," Te'oma said. "Let's hope it's not the last place we ever see."

CHAPTER

39

Kandler led the others back to the bridge where Sallah stood at the wheel. He saw sweat breaking out on her brow.

"The fire elemental doesn't want to go this way," she said. She never took her eyes from the horizon in front of her, right where the mountains grew taller by the second.

"Can you point out that straying from the wake of that dragon in front of us will probably result in the ship's destruction?" Xalt said.

"It wants to be destroyed," Monja said in a far too chipper tone. "Remember?"

"Destroyed is one thing," Te'oma said. "Being devoured by a pair of angry dragons is a whole new kind of awful."

"Just keep the ship on course," Kandler said, placing a hand on the lady knight's arm. "I know you can do it."

"Would you say you have faith in me?" Sallah said, a small smile on her lips.

Kandler grunted. "I don't have faith in much more than my family and friends. I have faith in you."

Sallah's smile widened, but she didn't say a word. She adjusted her grasp on the airship's wheel, and her shoulders relaxed.

Kandler patted her on the back then stared out past the dragon high above their bow. There on the horizon, the mountains had grown larger and strung out wider across the edge of the sea. In the area closest to the airship, Kandler saw a strip of white sand. This wrapped around the island as far as he could see in either direction.

As they scudded through the sky, a bay appeared in the island, a sheltered natural harbor from which a clearing ran back from the beach. In the clearing stood a handful of low huts made of some kind of grass or bamboo that had turned silver in the harsh rays of the sun.

The lead dragon came in toward the huts hard and fast. Kandler looked at Sallah, who shrugged at him. With a dragon before and behind, she had little choice but to follow along.

For a moment, Kandler wondered if this might be some sort of trap. Then he realized how pointless it would be for the dragons to try to trap someone they could just as easily incinerate. The creatures might have something other than a simple death in mind for the people aboard the *Phoenix*, but whatever their fate was to be, he would have to be patient.

The dragon to the rear put on a burst of speed and zoomed past the airship. It flew on ahead and reached the tiny hamlet on the beach long before the airship and the dragon still escorting her would arrive.

Kandler suppressed an urge to attack the dragons. The soldier in him wanted to get the hostilities out in the open and dealt with as soon as possible. Had he not been entirely sure that this would result in instant doom for everyone else aboard the *Phoenix*, he might have given it a try.

Sallah urged the airship along and brought her to a halt over the beach. The dragon that had raced before them kept flying away, not even looking back. When Kandler glanced behind the *Phoenix*, the dragon that had been to her aft was no longer there.

"We must be here," he said.

Kandler moved to the port rail and looked down at the land below. A trio of dragon-headed longboats sat on the shore, right in the safest part of the harbor's gentle arc. They had been painted silver long ago, although the colors had worn badly below their waterlines. Sets of long oars lay stashed in each boat. None of them bore sails.

Beyond the huts stood a wooden palisade. A carved dragon's head topped each of the tall poles, bristling with teeth and spikes. Each shone in a different color, some glinting metallic, others not.

Human-sized skeletons, strung together with strips of leather hung from several of the poles, especially the ones nearest the gate, which stood closed. The hot sun had long since bleached the bones as white as Te'oma's skin. The skulls bore holes and missing teeth, and the arms and legs were broken in many places.

There were no people on the beach, and the village beyond seemed empty as well.

"Should we just drop in on them?" Burch asked.

Kandler jumped at the shifter's voice then turned on him, mad. "I thought I told you to stay below." As he spoke, he glared at Esprë too, who stood behind the shifter.

Burch grinned. "We're here, aren't we? Let's get to it."

"The place is empty, but there's no sign of battle," Kandler said as Sallah strode up. Past her, he saw Monja take the wheel. The halfling waved at him with a grin.

Although the path ahead lay filled with treachery and horrors, Kandler could see that the others were just as ready to move on as he. Spending nearly two weeks cooped on the *Phoenix* together had not been easy. There were few private spaces on the ship, and with the stress everyone was under they each had struggled to keep their tempers in check—everyone except Xalt, who didn't seem to have one.

"Doesn't that seem like a trap?" Sallah said.

"Of course it's a trap," Burch said. "We just have to walk into it to see what kind it is."

"I'm coming with you," Esprë said.

Kandler grimaced. "No." When she started to protest, he added. "No arguing this one."

Esprë clamped her lips shut and glared at Kandler. It surprised him that she had folded so easily, but perhaps this was part of the new maturity she wanted so desperately to display. In any case, he wasn't about to argue with her about agreeing with him, no matter how much she might resent it.

Kandler pointed at Burch and Sallah. "You two are with me. Monja has the wheel. Xalt, you watch over Esprë."

He looked to the changeling and hesitated. He didn't want to trust her, but he didn't have much choice. She could be too useful to ignore. Besides, if she'd meant to betray them, she could have done so long before now—or so he hoped.

"I want you for air support. If we're in trouble, you take to the skies and give us cover. There's an extra crossbow and plenty of bolts in the hold. Use them."

Te'oma turned on her heel and went for the hold without a word.

"I'll go first, then Sallah," Kandler said to Burch and Sallah. "Burch, you cover us until we're on the sand, then follow fast. Got it?'

They both nodded.

Kandler strode for starboard gunwale and dropped a rope ladder over the side. A moment later, he clambered down it and dropped the last few feet to the hot, white sand.

The crashing of the surf behind him pounded in his ears, as did the strong, salty scent of the sea air. Walking along the dry sand reminded him of tramping through the ashes that had once filled the crater in which he had helped found Mardakine. While he'd hated the ashes, though, he had to fight the urge to throw himself down on the beach and embrace it.

The sun seemed hotter here in the thick, steamy air. Years living in the shadow of the Mournland had robbed his complexion of much of its color. The weeks aboard the *Phoenix* had bronzed his skin, protecting him now from the sun's strong southern rays.

Strange, unseen creatures called in the distance, either welcoming the newcomers or warning them away. Bright, colorful birds—splashes of primary colors in a sunbleached land—flitted through the fronds of the tall, thin, branchless trees that lined the beach's edge then disappeared in the thick tangle of a jungle beyond. A family of indigo-shelled crabs scattered at his arrival and scuttled away in a serpentine line.

A vermillion lizard darted out at them from its hiding hole in the sand, moving along on a dozen tentacles rather than legs. Before it could snatch one of the crabs up and make off with its meal, though, it spotted Kandler. The lizard stared at him for a moment with its bulging, green eyes then scampered off to the safety of the jungle instead.

Kandler raised his face toward the sky for a moment and basked in the sun. The breeze swirled about, cooling him and carrying the scent of roasting meat and exotic spices from past the palisades.

Up in the airship, the altitude had separated him from the surface world, insulating him. Here, setting foot on this strange, new beach, felt like stepping down on to another world—one bursting with life.

Sallah landed next to him. She made to draw her sword, but he put his hand on hers to stop her.

"If we wanted a fight, I'd have had Monja put the ship right over the town. We could have dropped down behind the palisades and killed everyone that came our way."

"Why didn't we do that?" Sallah asked.

"It's rude," Kandler said with a wry smile.

Looking up at the palisades that towered over the inland edge of the beach, though, Kandler wondered if he'd made a mistake. The bravado he'd shown Sallah had been designed to allay her nerves, although he suspected it had just irritated her instead. Still, he wasn't ready to plunge into the heart of an unknown village without so much as a hello.

Perhaps he could have sent Te'oma out to scout the area from the air, but that might have invited the dragons back. Also, he preferred to not show the natives their full hand until they had to.

Burch landed behind the other two. "So," he said, "who's going over the wall first?" Kandler could tell his old friend truly enjoyed this. Burch was never so alive as he was just before a fight.

Sallah frowned at the shifter, but before she could respond, a loud thumping of war drums emanated from the other side of the palisades.

"I think they're coming to us instead," said Kandler. He put his hand on Sallah's hilt again, to keep her from drawing her sword.

"Don't you think we should stand ready to defend ourselves?" she asked.

"That'll just make them think we're enemies."

"We're not?"

"Not yet."

"Those drums are setting my teeth on edge."

"They're supposed to make you nervous, goad you into doing something rash."

"Well, they're working."

CHAPTER

40

The drums stopped, and Sallah shouted into the eerie silence. Her face flushed as she realized how far her voice had carried. Kandler reached out and held her hand, this time for comfort. She did not pull away. The gate to the palisade lifted up half a foot and began to swing open. Sallah gripped Kandler's fingers tighter, and his other hand went to his sword.

"You never hold *my* hand any more," Burch said.

Kandler ignored him as he and the others stared at the opening gate. It spread in the center, about six feet wide. As it did, it exposed a single figure standing there.

The figure stood covered in a many-colored shroud made of stitched-together dragon scales that covered it from head to toe. It stayed there for a moment, framed between the two sides of the gate, just long enough for Kandler to wonder if this could be a statue or perhaps another corpse.

Then it strode out across the open sand between the palisades and the three strangers, the shroud rustling like metallic leaves as it moved with its wearer. Kandler gave

Sallah's hand a squeeze and then let go, knowing she'd understand. They needed to have their hands free.

"Hold your ground," Kandler said as the figure grew nearer. "Don't do anything to alarm it."

"It?" Burch said. "What about us?"

The figure came to a stop about a dozen feet from Kandler and the others. He wondered how whoever was inside the shroud could see through it. Or was the figure blind? Did it somehow not need its eyes?

Then the figure said something Kandler could not understand. The voice sounded low and harsh—angry almost—but feminine.

"That was Draconic," he said softly, never taking his eyes off the woman in the shroud. "Burch?"

"Mine's rusty," the shifter said. "It sounded like she said, 'You're not welcome here.'"

"I don't speak the language at all, and I understood that," said Sallah.

"There had to be more to it than that," Kandler said.

"That last bit sounded like, 'Which of you is of the dragon?'"

"What in Khyber is that supposed to mean?"

"She saw the dragons escort us here. Maybe that's what she means."

"I don't think so," said Burch.

"Does anyone on the airship speak Draconic?" Sallah said.

Kandler shrugged. "Ask her to repeat that," he told Burch.

"Two weeks aboard a ship with a crew, and you don't know any of them well enough to ask what languages they speak?" said Sallah.

"It didn't come up," Kandler said as Burch said something to the shrouded woman in her strange, twisting tongue.

The woman snarled something this time, angrier than ever. It sounded like she spat on the ground inside her shroud. With that movement, the gate in the palisades grew wider still, and a small army of men and women marched out.

The Seren warriors were short and stocky, with tar-black hair and skin that had been burnished a deep, rich brown. Their eyes were narrow slits cut into their faces, exposing only pit-black pupils. Many of them wore bits of bone or dragon scales pierced through their noses or their lips. Each of them bore a wicked weapon—a spear, axe, or club—fashioned from bone, wood, or even large bits of what looked like shells that had once served as homes to mon-strous creatures.

Each of the warriors wore a skirt made of silver-bleached grass but nothing else. They had painted bands of silver across their faces and over their eyes that gave them an inhuman look.

The Seren surrounded Kandler, Burch, and Sallah. They spoke not a single word but moved into place with the surety of a well-trained unit, their bare feet almost silent on the sand.

"They're barbarians," Sallah said, wrinkling her nose.

One of the Seren women jabbed at Sallah with a spear tipped with the tooth of a gigantic shark. The other warriors started chattering among themselves, rattling their weapons against each other.

"Better smile when you say that," said Burch. He flashed the warriors a sincere grin and held up his empty hands to show them that he meant them no harm.

"They're as sophisticated as they come around here," Kandler said, "and we need their help."

He wondered when Xalt or Te'oma might decide to loose a bolt into the crowd. They had to be getting nervous aboard the ship, which meant he had to make something good happen here fast.

The woman in the shroud shrieked something and flung her arms into the air, exposing hands as brown as those of any of the other Seren. The others fell silent and brought their weapons back in front of them. Kandler could tell that they wanted to attack, to kill him and the others where they stood. Only the word of the shrouded woman kept them back.

The woman said something to Burch again. The shifter scratched his chin and responded. He chose each word with care, and he stumbled over a few pronunciations, but the head inside the shroud bobbed in understanding.

After a few tense exchanges, the woman stopped speaking.

"What's the story?" Kandler asked Burch.

"This is the Gref tribe, guardians of this particular stretch of beach. They serve the dragon who founded this village for them: a silver beast by the name Greffykor."

"The ones who brought us here were red," said Sallah.

"The dragons put the Seren in charge of protecting Argonnessen from the rest of the world. Since the island lies straight between their home and Aerenal and Khorvaire, most traffic toward Argonnessen passes around the island of Seren."

"But the Seren can't patrol the skies," Kandler said.

"So the dragons help them out there. Most of the time, the dragons just blast people out of the sky. Other times, they bring them down to whichever village they figure's the best fit."

"So why are we here?" asked Sallah, staring at the angry eyes surrounding them.

"Seems the Gref have a fine reputation for killing most of the people they come across. I'd guess the dragons wanted us dead but didn't feel like dirtying their claws on us."

"Doesn't look like the Gref are so picky," said Kandler.

Burch spoke with the shrouded woman again. She replied forcefully.

"She says that the Prophecy said that circle of fire would bring the favored of the dragons to them."

A horrible thought struck Kandler. He hesitated to voice it, but eventually he spat it out. "Are you sure she doesn't mean 'dragonmarked'?"

"Ah!" said Burch, his yellow eyes lighting up. "That's it!"

The shifter's face fell even quicker than it had brightened. "They want Esprë."

Kandler glanced up at the airship. "All right," he said. "On my mark, draw your swords, and let's do this. If we spill some blood quick that might frighten the others enough for us to make it on to the ship."

"And once we get there?"

"Did I ever give you the impression I was doing more than making this up as I went along?"

"No!"

Kandler recognized Xalt's voice instantly. He looked up just in time to see a flash of blond hair, then his stepdaughter landed next to him. The warforged still stood on the deck, reaching out his empty hands that had missed grabbing the girl and keeping her safe aboard the airship.

The islanders leaped back—all of them but the woman in the shroud. Then they closed in again, tighter than ever. Esprë's sudden appearance had startled them for an instant, but now they were shamefaced and mad.

"Go!" Kandler said.

Burch slung his crossbow off his shoulder and into his waiting hands with a single, practiced shrug. Sallah's sword appeared in her hand, just as the fangblade did in Kandler's. The three of them put their backs to each other to cover all angles, leaving enough room between each of them to form a protective pocket in which Esprë could stand.

Kandler lashed out with his sword and sliced the heads off a pair of spears that had reached in too close for his liking. They tumbled to the soft sand and embedded themselves there point-down.

Sallah's holy blade burst into silvery flames, and she brandished it at the Seren nearest her. They leaped back out of her reach and gaped in awe at her weapon.

Burch leveled his crossbow at the shrouded woman's head. Kandler wondered how well a bolt would do against tightly arranged dragon scales like those, but he figured now was as good a time as any to find out.

"No!" Esprë screeched. She pushed between Kandler and Sallah and thrust herself in front of the shrouded woman.

Esprë said something to the woman in Draconic.

CHAPTER

41

"Stop!" Esprë said to the woman in Draconic. "Just tell me what you want!"

The Seren warriors froze. All eyes turned to the woman in the dragon-scale shroud. She hesitated for the barest of moments then raised her hands to signal a halt to the hostilities.

The warriors each took a step backward. This put them out of the reach of the invaders' swords, although Burch's crossbow could still take down any of them with a single pull of the trigger.

"Your mother taught you Draconic," Kandler said behind her. His voice betrayed how impressed he was. In other circumstances, Esprë would have smiled.

"Good job," Burch said gruffly, "but don't think Kandler's not still going to spank you when we get back on the airship."

"If we survive that long," Sallah said. The lady knight began muttering some sort of prayer under her breath.

Esprë ignored all three of them and focused on the woman in the shroud.

"Our founder told us to await the bearer of the dragon-mark," the shrouded woman said.

"Founder?" Esprë glanced at the faces of the islanders and spotted nothing but humans among them. "How long have you been here?"

"For over four thousand years our people have protected this part of the shore and helped to keep invaders like yourself away from the land of the dragons beyond."

"Four thousand years?" Esprë couldn't believe the number. That was a long time, even in elf terms. "How could your founder tell you about dragonmarks? He must have— Did he inscribe his prophecy to you on a scroll?"

"Greffykor lives still high atop the Wyrmsperch Mountains. He bequeathed to me this part of the Prophecy only two weeks ago, and we have been alert for the bearer of a dragonmark ever since."

"What if we do not have this dragonmark—or are unwilling to show it to you?"

"Then we kill you."

Esprë wondered what it would be like to be part of a tribe that murdered any strangers who happened to cross its path. It sounded horrible. "You kill anyone who does not have a dragonmark?" she asked.

"Yes. So Greffykor demands."

A chill coursed through Esprë's guts. "Who is this Greffykor?"

"A dragon of the purest silver and the most inquisitive of minds. He has dedicated his life to the study of the Prophecy, and we are blessed to rank among his servants."

Esprë felt like she wanted to stop breathing. "So the dragonmark shows that the stranger is favored by your dragon?"

"Today, when Greffykor has decreed it so, it is so."

"What about our lady knight here? She has a sword that

burns with a silver flame. Our warrior here bears a blade made from a dragon's fang."

"These are the finest of omens. They cause Greffykor's faithful to search even harder for evidence of the fulfillment of the Prophecy. Without them, we may have slain you already."

"You may have tried."

"Produce the dragonmark now, or we will bring the full force of our people upon you."

Esprë looked to Kandler. He shrugged at her. "I have no idea what you've been talking about," he said, "but if you want to start showing off that dragonmark of yours, go right ahead." He hefted his sword in his hand. "If you'd rather keep it private, I'd be happy to help cut our way out of here instead."

"What would you do?" she asked.

Kandler smiled. "I don't want to influence your decision."

"That's a first."

"What do you think you should do?" Kandler said.

Esprë stood there, stunned. For the first time, her stepfather seemed to be treating her like an adult. She reached out and gave him a quick hug.

"Go get 'em," he whispered to her as she broke away from him once again.

Esprë wrinkled her brow at him, a strange, wry smile on her face. Then she reached behind herself to pull the collar of her shirt down, exposing her back to the islanders who stood waiting for her decision.

As one, they gasped.

CHAPTER

42

Kandler had to suppress every paternal urge in his body to keep himself from grabbing Esprë and hauling her back on to the *Phoenix*. He stood with his sword ready, prepared to slash out at the first islander who made a dangerous move toward the girl. He didn't think he and the others stood a chance of surviving a battle with so many—especially if the dragons that had brought them there returned—but he'd take down as many of them with him as he could. Centuries from now, the survivors would talk of the trio of warriors who nearly wiped them all out.

Kandler ran through a plan of action in his head. He figured he could kill three of them before they could reach Esprë, perhaps five with the fangblade. He'd never used a blade so sharp and deadly before, and he marveled at the way it could slice through just about anything. With none of the islanders sporting any armor thicker than a thatch of grass, the sword would make quick work of them.

Then the shrouded woman raised her arms and said

something in Draconic. The other islanders lowered their weapons.

Some of them seemed relieved, but the turn of events clearly disappointed most of them. They'd gotten their blood boiling and the lack of a battle left them frustrated. Kandler wondered if they had much else to do here on the island other than get into fights, heal from the last fight, and prepare for the next one. Still, they did as the woman in the shroud had ordered and gave up on the battle.

That didn't mean they'd welcome the intruders with open arms. Kandler read hostility and suspicion in every face—except that of the woman under the shroud.

Then the woman lifted the front of the shroud over her head, draping it over her shoulders. Unlike most of the others in the tribe, her hair bore streaks of gray, and her face showed fine lines around her mouth and eyes that showed that she often smiled. Still, she was not smiling now.

"My name is Zanga," the woman said. Her voice was low and rough but sweet, a pleasant counterpart to her exotic accent. "Welcome to Seren. We are the Gref."

"You speak—?" Kandler could not believe his ears. "You can understand us?"

"In my youth, I spent time in Port Krez."

Burch grunted at that. "You don't look much like a pirate."

"It's been a long life." She smiled. "For such reasons, my people do not trust strangers. You will not be permitted inside the palisades."

"We don't wish to stay long," Esprë said. "We probably wouldn't have come at all if not for the dragons."

"Where are you bound?" asked Zanga.

Esprë looked back at Kandler. He sheathed his sword

and stepped forward, meeting Zanga's studious gaze.

"We're on our way to Argonnessen," he said.

"Of course," said Zanga. "My people can take you to Totem Beach. That is where we worship at the feet of the great idols."

"Who do you worship?" asked Sallah, carefully nonchalant.

Zanga glanced at the silver flame embroidered on Sallah's tabard. Blood and dirt stained the slashed and torn garment, which now barely covered the lady knight's breastplate, but Sallah had refused to abandon it.

"The dragons, of course."

Kandler saw Sallah bite her tongue. Her first instinct when faced with such beliefs would be to spread the faith of the Silver Flame, but she managed to avoid any hint of proselytizing. For that, the justicar gave thanks.

"We'll want to go a bit farther inland," Burch said.

Zanga's brow creased with concern. "How far?" she asked.

"Did you recognize the mark on Esprë's back?" Kandler said.

He didn't want to talk about any long-range plans with Zanga, not right now. If her people could bring them to Totem Beach, perhaps that would be enough.

"Of course. It is a dragonmark."

"Could you tell which one?"

Kandler heard Esprë's breath catch in her chest. If the Seren had recognized the Mark of Death, he needed to know what that meant to them—including why they had not killed the girl on the spot.

Zanga shook her head. "We do not see many of the marks of favor on Seren. We have little need for them. We enjoy the direct attention of the dragons instead."

"Then why did you demand to see it?"

"How'd you know she had one?" Burch asked the islander.

Zanga flashed a serene smile. "I didn't. We only knew that Greffykor bade us watch for one among the invaders who sometimes find our shores."

"That's the silver dragon who founded Gref," Esprë said to Kandler and the others. "He studies the Prophecy."

"Did the Prophecy tell him to look for you?"

Esprë shrugged. "It seems so."

Kandler stared at the islanders all around them, then back at Zanga. "I think I'd like to meet this dragon."

"Greffykor said you would," Zanga said. "Once more, his wisdom is proven."

The shrouded woman turned to say something in Draconic to the other islanders, and a cry of joy went up among them. It pleased Kandler to see them smiling. They seemed far less dangerous.

"So," Kandler said, "can you tell us how to reach this Greffykor?"

"No," Zanga said, beaming with excitement. "It is a dangerous journey through unfamiliar territory. There are no roads. It must be approached by air."

Burch pointed a finger toward the airship overhead. "I think we got that angle covered."

"I know," Zanga said, her eyes wide and her smile growing larger. "That's what makes this all so wonderful."

"How's that?" Kandler asked. The woman's glee confused him. He wondered if they might not have been better off getting into the fight. At least with swords drawn he knew what to expect.

"Because I will take you there myself."

Zanga said this not as a request or an order, but as a matter of fact, as if she had chosen to comment on the particular shade of blue in the sky.

"Fantastic!" said Esprë. As the words left her mouth, though, she spied the sour look on Kandler's face and winced. "That's not a good thing?"

Kandler forced a smile onto his lips. "It's a very gracious offer," he said, "especially from someone we just met, but I would guess that Zanga's people need her here far more than we would."

The shrouded woman laughed. "You do not know much about Seren life," she said. "Most days the biggest challenge put before me is to divine the weather. Sometimes I need to prepare a poultice or set a broken bone, but all are well here now. Unlike in Khorvaire, we have few sicknesses here. We live by the sea, and by the grace of the dragons it and the jungle provide all that we need. For what we want, we sometimes go to war against our neighbors, but at the moment we are at peace."

"Sounds nice," Burch said, eyeing the long, sandy beach and the tropical trees that lined it. "When this is all over, I might think about shacking up in one of those huts."

"Still," Kandler said to Zanga, "Burch here is an excellent navigator. If you just point him in the right direction, I'm sure we'll be able to find the way."

Zanga frowned. "Without a Shroud of Scales aboard, the first dragon that sees you will knock your little airship from the sky."

Kandler grimaced. "Perhaps we could borrow the shroud from you for the trip. I wouldn't want to—" He could tell from the look on Zanga's face that this path led nowhere.

"A Shroud of Scales is more than the garment," she said. "It is the person inside of it. Without me, my shroud is just a set of scales." She gave Kandler a shrewd look. "You cannot fool the dragons. They see everything."

That was just what Kandler feared most.

"Very well," he said, surrendering. "I would be delighted."

CHAPTER

43

The sun hung low in the western sky, out over the open waters of the Dragonreach as the *Phoenix* scudded along the Seren shoreline. As they rounded the southwestern tip of the island, a breathtaking mountain range hove into the eastern horizon. The rays of the setting sun painted the white-rock mountains a breathtaking panoply of reds, oranges, and purples.

"Beautiful, isn't it?" Sallah said as she joined Kandler where he'd been standing alone at the airship's bow. The breeze ruffled her curly, red hair, teasing it out in long spirals behind her as she faced into the wind.

Kandler nodded. "In most cases, I'd be thrilled about the sunset for an entirely different reason."

"So we could approach this dragon under cover of night?" She looked back at the ring of fire encircling the airship. "This may be a wonderful way to travel, but we won't be sneaking up on anyone."

Kandler smiled at her and brushed a stray strand of hair from her face. "I'm glad you found me," he said.

"There aren't many places to lose someone on a ship this size."

"I meant in Mardakine."

Sallah stared out at the mountains. "I know what you meant."

Kandler let the comment lie for a moment, then said. "I wanted to thank you for coming along with us."

"I told Esprë I would honor her decision. I am true to my word."

"You didn't have to do that. You could have gone back to Thrane empty handed, or you could have tried to kidnap her and stolen her away to Flamekeep."

Sallah gasped. "You know, I hadn't thought of that." She saw Kandler's stunned look and smiled. "I'm only joking—of course I thought of that."

Despite himself, the thought of Sallah considering going to any means to accomplish her goals impressed Kandler—although not as much as the fact that she'd chosen the high road instead.

"I'm a Knight of the Silver Flame. I've been trained since birth to become the best of my Order, and I have never failed in my missions."

"How many missions have you had?" Kandler couldn't resist the urge to needle the woman a bit. She rewarded his efforts with a sly smile.

"That's not the point."

"Then what is?"

"That this was the first mission given to me by Jaela Daran directly from the Flame itself, and you presented me with two options: kidnap an innocent girl and succeed or travel with her instead and watch her die."

Sallah grew quiet. She bowed her head and closed her eyes. "I had my orders, and I defied them."

"Why did you do it?"

Sallah sighed and stared out at the darkest part of the sky. There in the east, the stars had begun to come out, and Kandler could see traces of the Ring of Siberys there. He could see seven of the moons already, and the night was still young.

"Being a Knight of the Silver Flame is about far more than just following orders," Sallah said. "We serve as a shining example of what is right in the world. We inspire others to reach for the heights we have attained and maintain. We follow a higher moral code so that we may become closer to the Flame's purity with both our actions and our words. Kidnapping an innocent child doesn't fit with that, no matter what the excuse."

Kandler gazed at the woman. She seemed more beautiful than ever. "You might want to tell that to Te'oma," he said.

"She wouldn't make much of a knight." Sallah gave Kandler a half smile and moved closer to him. "I've learned a great deal on this trip."

"About what?"

"The world. Myself."

"Any of it good?"

"I learned what I like in a man."

Kandler smiled into the darkness. "The Order must not have left you a lot of time for men."

"Not much," she said, moving closer to him.

"You think if you had the chance to see even more of the world that you might change your mind?"

"About the world?"

Kandler leaned in and kissed Sallah. Her warm, soft lips bore unspoken promises that he knew would have to go unfulfilled for now.

"No," she whispered into his ear. "I don't think I would."

"I thought you didn't want to have much to do with me."

"That would have made life easier I'm sure. I'm not here on this airship because of you. Esprë is my main concern.

Just because I haven't convinced her to come with me to
Thrane yet doesn't mean I never will."

"Hope means a lot to you."

"I prefer to call it faith. The Speaker of the Flame sent
me here for a reason. I may not yet entirely fathom what
it is—or which way my path lies—but I have faith that it
will work out for the best if I remain strong and pure and
dedicated to my beliefs."

"The best for you, or the best for your Order?" Kandler
thought of the other knights they'd lost along the way:
Gweir, Levritt, Brendis—even Sallah's father, Deothen.
Had dying been the best thing for them?

"They are one and the same thing. I have dedicated my
life to the Silver Flame. It is my cause, and anything that
advances it—even my own death, should that be called for—is
in my interests."

Kandler rubbed his chin. "So where do I fit into all of
that?"

"Wherever you would like." Sallah's smile turned coy.

"Are Knights of the Silver Flame allowed to marry outside of the Order?"

"You're getting a little ahead of yourself, I think."

"Humor me."

"All right," she said. "I'm living proof of such mar-
riages. My mother grew up on a farm outside Flamekeep.
She served as the innkeeper in her father's inn until she
met my father."

"Did your mother convert to the faith?"

"What makes you think that she wasn't an adherent of
the Church?"

"Most innkeepers I know are agnostic."

"Fair enough." Sallah paused. "No, she never did. It was
what drove them apart."

"They ended their marriage?"

"The Church doesn't permit such things. A matrimonial vow is until death. They chose to live separate but faithful lives."

"That must have been hard on you."

Sallah lowered her eyes. "We all have our burdens to bear."

"Am I to be your salve?"

Sallah raised her chin and gazed at him. "I'd like that."

Kandler took her in his arms, and they kissed again. When they parted, he said. "Why tell me all this now? Right before we're about to go meet with a dragon?"

"If we survive this, I want for us to be together. I thought you should know that."

"You don't think we'll survive this." He peered deep into her eyes.

She did not flinch. "No, and I couldn't stand the idea of dying without telling you how I feel."

"I'm glad you did," Kandler said.

"Truly?"

"I've been standing here at the bow for the past few hours, trying to figure out just how I could find a way to tell you the same thing."

The justicar took the lady knight in his arms.

"Land ho!" Monja called from the bridge.

Sallah and Kandler broke apart. "She must have been a pirate in a previous life," said Kandler.

"Do you believe in such things? Multiple lives?"

Kandler grinned as he walked back down the deck of the airship with her, hand in hand. "No more than I believe in anything else."

As they approached the bridge, Kandler turned his head to port to see what Monja was pointing at. Off in the distance, he spotted a series of floating lights. In the darkness, he would have thought they were a little more than a tightly clustered constellation of stars. When he looked at them closely, though, he saw that they moved.

He turned back to call out to Zanga, who stood on the bridge between Monja and Esprë. "Is that where we're going?" he asked.

The shrouded woman nodded. "That is the observatory of Greffykor."

"Observatory?" said Burch, who'd been helping Te'oma cook up a hot meal over the firepit on the main deck. "What do dragons observe?"

"Everything!" Zanga said.

"Then I guess he'll know we're on our way," the shifter said, "and I hope he has something better to eat than this. I'm getting tired of leftover soarwing."

CHAPTER

44

Kandler felt strangely numb as the *Phoenix* approached the observatory. The idea of meeting with a dragon and perhaps learning more about what he might be able to do to save Esprë thrilled him. At the same time, he feared that the dragon might slaughter them all. The two notions canceled each other out and left him with nothing.

As the ship drew closer, the observatory stood out like a silver spike stabbing from the top of the mountains. The light of the moons shimmered on its glittering surface, and a series of large glowing balls swirled about the place for a moment then froze in place. These luminescent spheres seemed to be made of crystal wrapped in bands of silver. Runes had been cut all the way through these straps of metal, and the light shone through them, spelling out mystic words Kandler knew he would never comprehend.

"There are thirteen spheres," Zanga said from her perch on the edge of the bridge, "one for each of the moons. These have three bands of metal crossing them, one along each axis."

"What are the runes?" Esprë said.

They'd gotten close enough that Kandler thought he could almost recognize some of them. Beyond them, the tower loomed larger than ever. It stood at least a hundred feet above the tallest of the mountain peaks, and frost and ice crusted its smooth-carved walls. Kandler wondered how cold it would feel inside, far from the airship's warming ring of fire.

"Each band has thirteen runes. Those on the first stand for the thirteen moons again. Those on the second represent the thirteen planes of existence. On the third, they depict the thirteen dragonmarks."

Kandler's gut flipped. "I thought there were only twelve dragonmarks." He hoped Zanga could not hear the deception in his voice.

"You forget the Mark of Death," Zanga said.

The justicar gave his stepdaughter's shoulder a squeeze and stared up at the tremendous structure. It swept up from the mountains as if part of the toothy peaks and then lanced far out above them. This close, the walls seemed to have been made from gigantic columns of rock drilled from some distant quarry and then dropped here atop the mountain, their inward-sweeping tops tipped toward each other until they almost touched.

The gaps between the columns seemed to have been mortared with pure silver. Spaces showed in these long lines, forming tall, thin windows that glowed with a bluish light. The top of the tower seemed to be open to the air, although it was impossible to tell from the low angle of their approach. The light emanating from the top could have come from a raging bonfire, although it shared the same hue as the illumination that spilled out through the sides of the tower, particularly through the solitary arched entrance.

This gaped like a toothed maw about a quarter of the way down from the tower's top. A long, stone platform jutted out from the arch, resembling a wide, flat tongue. Monja, who had the airship's wheel, aimed the craft straight for it.

"Where is the dragon?" Xalt asked. The warforged strained his neck to see through the tower's entrance. He had stuck close to Esprë since they'd left Seren behind. The thought that the girl had such a protector at her side at all times relieved Kandler. It freed him up to think about more than just standing between her and danger.

"He waits for us inside," Zanga said. She dropped her shroud over the front of herself again, disappearing underneath it.

"Have you ever been here before?" Sallah asked.

"Once. Right after my mentor passed the shroud to me. It was . . . sublime. I will not spoil the experience with more words. Soon enough, you will share in it yourself."

Burch emerged from the ship's hold with a double armful of crossbows, plus four quivers full of bolts, and some thin rope of elven make. He set them down on the deck with care, and arranged them in a row. Kandler counted four standard crossbows—plus a smaller one that looked like it would be a good fit for Monja—as well as two coils of rope.

When the shifter noticed the others watching him, he winked at them. "Can't be too careful," he said.

"Those toys cannot harm Greffykor," Zanga said. "Your bolts will bounce off his scales."

"Who said I'd aim for his scales?" Burch said, needling the shrouded woman. "Anyhow, these aren't for your armored god in there."

"Then who?"

"Like I said, you can't be too careful."

Burch picked up the small crossbow and one of the larger ones. He laid the first at Monja's feet, along with a quiver of bolts. He gave the second to Xalt, who murmured his thanks as he checked the weapon's action. Then the shifter handed one coil of rope to Kandler and kept the other for himself.

Burch vaulted back down to the deck and slung his own crossbow and a stuffed quiver over his shoulder. Then he picked up the other one and glanced around, confused.

"What happened to Te'oma?" he asked.

Kandler scanned the ship but saw no sign of the changeling. He cursed softly for not having kept a closer eye on her. Then he peered over at Zanga to see how she would react. Her shroud made her impossible to read.

"I am worried," Zanga said, her light tone belying her words. "Not for Greffykor's safety, but for your friend's."

"Will this anger the dragon?" Esprë asked.

The shroud rustled as Zanga shook her head. "I am sure he foresaw this as well. We could not surprise such a student of the Prophecy as this."

"Let's hope you're right," Kandler said as they neared the landing platform.

The *Phoenix* slowed as she approached the platform. It had been built to accommodate dragons, not airships, and it showed no mooring lines or gangplanks.

"Just slip in over the platform," Kandler told Monja. "We'll take a ladder down."

The halfling smiled. "I'll try not to set the place on fire."

Kandler patted her on the back. "We'll be back as soon as we can."

He strode over to the starboard rail and unfurled a rope ladder over it. Then he slipped down it to the platform below.

The long expanse of stone seemed as solid as the mountain peak over which it hung. Kandler put his hand on his sword but did not draw it. He reminded himself that he was here to talk, even if they were meeting with a dragon.

Sallah came down after Kandler, then Esprë, Xalt, and

Zanga. With a quick wave to Monja, who had to keep her hand on the ship's wheel, Burch brought up the rear. Each of them—with the exception of Burch and Zanga—shivered in the cold. Away from the airship's ring of fire, the chill of the heights began to work its way into their bones.

"Shouldn't we knock?" Sallah said as she crept toward the brightly lit opening.

From here, Kandler could see one large room inside the tower. It seemed to occupy the entire floor—which sprawled as far across as an open field—and the ceiling was too high above to see through the arched entry. A wide hole gaped in the far side of the floor, no railing around it.

Strange apparatuses, most of which stood taller than a human, lined the walls of the room, some atop carved tables or ornate cabinets large enough to hide a wagon inside. Kandler couldn't guess as to their purposes, but he could see that they had been built for a dragon to use. Even if he knew what to do with the things, he wasn't sure he could get them to activate or move.

Some were made of gleaming metals of every color. Others had been formed from polished woods that curled in such intricate and delicate shapes that it seemed they might still be living. Tinted glass, shaped like cubes, cylinders, or bells covered many of the pieces, and although Kandler could see through the material he doubted that even one of Burch's explosive shockbolts—which had all been used up long ago—would have cracked them.

In one glass-fronted cabinet stood a miniature city, complete with walls and towers built from tiny bricks. It reminded Kandler of a section of Sharn, the Brelish metropolis he'd once called home. When he peered closer at it, he saw that it crawled with pinkish, finger-sized worms rather than people, inching along blindly through their land and lives.

Lightning flashed along the edges of a blue-metal cone

that rose into a bronze cloud that shimmering and shifted with the raw energy that coursed along its surface. Sparks rising from it floated through the air to the devices on either side of it. These sucked the glowing specks into coils and nets of translucent tubing through which they pulsed with a staccato beat.

Sparkling steam spun leafy green wheels and billowed from a pair of glassy chimneys set in the far wall. Shapes twisted in the artificial clouds as they spilled forth, forming full-color visions of fantastic, winged creatures with scaly skins and stretched bat-wings. As the images fell and faded, the pulsating gas cascaded down and flowed out across the floor, lending a diffuse glow to the polished stone there, as it edged its way toward the landing platform.

As Kandler and the others walked closer to the entrance, he had to shade his eyes against the intense light. It seemed like every corner of the place glowed of its own accord, making the place brighter now, even at night, than during the height of day.

The light became more intense as a gigantic crystal ball hove into view near the north wall to their left as they came in through the open portal. The massive crystal, which stood taller than a house—or even a fortress, seemed to glow with an inner light. A mixture of strange images swam within its depths. Some of these seemed to pull Kandler in, while others made him want to flee.

When Kandler reached the tower's threshold, he stopped. The others filed up next to him and stood alongside him at the edge. The justicar wouldn't have been surprised to find that every one of them had stopped breathing, stunned into breathlessness.

"Shall we?" Zanga said, her face seeming to glow nearly as much as the crystal globe. With that, she strode into the room.

Kandler waited for a moment. When nothing happened, he breathed a sigh of relief. Then he took Esprë in one hand and Sallah in the other and crossed into the dragon's tower. Burch and Xalt came in right behind them.

Kandler pulled back his head and looked straight up to see the night sky above. The top of the tower lay open to the cold night beyond. The light from the tower nearly drowned out the sight of the stars hanging there in the cold distance.

"Maybe he's not home?" Esprë said, hope rising in her voice.

Then a titanic shape moved from behind the crystal ball and shuffled toward the empty middle of the room on long-taloned feet. It held its wings close to its body to keep them out of the way. Its silvery scales clinked together as it moved, sounding something like the chimes of an entire army of chain-mailed soldiers marching off to war.

"Call me Greffykor," the dragon said, in a voice that seemed to rumble right through Kandler's chest, so that he felt it more than he heard it. It peeled back its armored lips, revealing uncountable rows of long, sharp teeth spread in an approximation of a smile. "Enter my home."

CHAPTER

45

Zanga screamed, and before he could think about it, Kandler drew his sword. Sallah did the same, and Burch and Xalt unlimbered their crossbows with practiced moves. Of those who had made the trip to Seren on the *Phoenix*, only Esprë held no weapon in her hands. Of course, Kandler reminded himself, she didn't need one.

The Shroud of Scales fell to Zanga's knees and she continued to keen. The dragon did not move more than to let its terrible excuse for a smile close around its vicious teeth.

"Check on her," Kandler said to Esprë. "See if she's hurt."

The girl reached out for the woman, but before her hand even touched the shroud, Zanga threw back her head and sat on her haunches. "Do not fear for me," the woman said under the shroud. "I was overcome with delight, and I fell to my knees to beg my lord for his mercy and understanding."

"Rise, faithful one," the dragon said. His gray eyes took in the intruders all at once. "Come in further and speak."

Kandler fought an urge to fall on his knees himself. He'd never been in the presence of a creature so . . . regal.

He couldn't think of a better word for it. By its sheer physique the dragon seemed to demand worship or at least awe. He understood, in that moment, how the Seren had come to revere such beasts.

"O great Greffykor," Zanga said as she leaped to her feet. "I have brought to you the one you sought, as well as her traveling companions. They come to you in the greatest of need and beg for you to bestow your wisdom upon them."

"Tell me which one it is."

The dragon stared at each of the newcomers in turn. When Greffykor's eyes fell on Kandler, he had a strong desire to turn and flee from the tower. Perhaps if he could reach the landing in time, he might be able to hurl himself from its edge before the dragon caught up to him—but he doubted it.

Esprë stepped forward before Zanga could speak. "Hello," she said. Her voice did not tremble, nor did her knees shake, but Kandler could tell from the set of her shoulders that she was a fragile piece of crystal ready to shatter at the slightest touch. Despite that, she had not shirked her responsibilities here, and he could not have been prouder of her for that.

"Come forward," Greffykor said.

The dragon shifted his weight onto his rear feet, and Esprë froze. She took a deep breath and walked toward the creature, ready as she would ever be for whatever might be coming next.

Kandler had never been entirely sure of the wisdom of coming to Argonnessen. It had just seemed like the best choice out of a handful of horrible alternatives. Now, here, standing in a dragon's tower while Esprë walked toward the creature, every doubt he had resurfaced.

He hefted the fangblade in his hand again. He wanted to call out to the dragon, to remind him to be careful with the girl, to threaten him if he did anything to hurt her. The justicar knew, though, that the dragon would only laugh at such hollow words.

Still, Kandler wanted Esprë to know he stood behind her, no matter what danger she might face. He followed her, his footsteps echoing hers as they moved toward the dragon through the large, empty chamber.

As he walked, Kandler realized that another set of footsteps shadowed his. He glanced back to see Sallah marching behind him, the metal of her armored boots clanking hard and cold against the thick, stone floor. Her eyes shone with love and fear, and he mouthed his thanks to her.

Back near the great entrance to the tower, Burch and Xalt had spread out in opposite directions perpendicular to Esprë's path. Each of them had their crossbows trained on the dragon, ready to loose their bolts at the first provocation. Between them, Zanga glanced back and forth at them and giggled at their foolhardiness.

When Kandler looked forward again, Esprë had stopped walking and turned to talk with him. She focused her bright blue eyes on him, and the determination he saw there reminded him so much of her mother.

"I have to do this on my own," she said.

Kandler opened his mouth to protest but then shut it instead. He leaned forward and planted a soft kiss on her forehead, then stood back and smiled at her.

"Go get him," he said.

Esprë smiled at him, a tear welling in one eye, then turned back to the dragon. She strode up to the creature, more confident this time, and presented herself.

"I am Esprë of Mardakine," she said, "daughter of Esprina and Kandler. I bear the Mark of Death."

Behind Kandler, Zanga screamed again. This time, the sound came not from joy but astonishment.

"So the Prophecy foretold," Greffykor said. "Ask your questions of me."

Esprë paused, and Kandler feared she might break down with the dragon's full attention focused on her. When she spoke, though, her voice was proud and strong.

"How can I avoid my fate?"

The dragon spoke without hesitating, as if he had anticipated the question and formulated an answer long before Esprë spoke.

"Fate cannot be avoided, only fulfilled."

"Then what is my fate?"

"That has not yet been written."

Esprë pouted for a moment. "What does the Prophecy say about my fate?"

"You are doomed."

"How?"

"That is unclear. Your thread in the great tapestry ends soon."

"How soon?"

Kandler could hear the tremble enter Esprë's voice.

"Soon."

He rushed forward when he saw her knees start to buckle, but she managed to right herself before he reached her. She waved him off without even turning to see him.

"How?"

"That is unclear. It involves grief and pain."

"Is there anything I can do about it?"

"No."

Esprë's shoulders started shuddering then, and Kandler knew she had started to cry. He wanted to reach out and comfort her, but he knew that she wouldn't want that right now. First, she needed to finish this conversation.

When she spoke again, her voice was raw and low. "Is—is there anything you can do about it?"

The dragon remained silent. He stayed as still as a statue as he stared at the girl with his unblinking eyes.

"Is there anything you can do about it?" Esprë repeated.

"Ask me to kill you."

Kandler's heart sank.

"Wh-what?" said Esprë.

"Ask me to kill you."

"Why?" she asked, her surprise already turning to frustration.

"As a favor."

"A favor?" Her frustration had started to become rage.

"I will not cause you to suffer."

Esprë gagged. It took her a moment before she could continue.

"Is that the only way? To prevent me from suffering?"

The dragon inclined its head but did not speak.

"I . . ." said Esprë.

"Stay as long as you like. Inform me when you reach your decision. My tower is impervious to scrying. No one will find you here."

With that, the dragon turned and prowled back to the giant crystal. It did not look back.

Esprë walked back to Kandler. He gathered her up in a comforting hug.

"I heard everything," he said. "That dragon doesn't know a thing."

"I think Zanga and her people would disagree with you."

"Prophecies are a fraud," Kandler said. "They're just a collection of ancient words cast so broad that they could catch any victim in their net."

Esprë pushed herself away from Kandler and craned her neck back to look at the crystal ball and all the strange, dragon-sized mechanisms in the room. "You can stand in a place like this and tell me Prophecy has no meaning?"

"Not to you or me," Kandler said. "Humans are short-timers. We don't think in terms of the grand sweep of history. Each of us is just a stitch on the 'great tapestry' that dragon went on about. We're beneath their notice."

Esprë smiled as she wiped her face. "But I'm an elf."

"You're a young elf, and your thread has been woven mostly with humans. I think someone with eyes as large as Greffykor can make a mistake about such things."

Kandler felt Sallah's hand on his back as he spoke. She didn't say a word, just squeezed his shoulder in solidarity, but it meant the world to him. He smiled at Esprë.

"Do you really mean that?" the girl said.

Kandler gave her a wry half-smile. "Honestly, I don't know. All this stuff is over my head. All I know is that we have to make the best decisions we can with what we have. Worrying about things like fate can only help make bad predictions about us come true."

Esprë began to respond, but the smile that had been forming on her lips melted away into a look of sheer terror as she gazed over Kandler's shoulder.

The justicar whirled about toward the entrance, and there—framed in the entrance of Greffykor's tower—stood a gigantic red dragon, its wings unfurled.

CHAPTER

46

Te'oma shivered in the chill night air as she perched atop one of the inward curving tips atop the pylons that formed Greffykor's tower. She thought that she might look like a mighty bird of prey if she hadn't been shuddering so hard. She wrapped her wings around her even tighter when a freezing blast of wind blew through her. Part of her hoped it might knock her from the tower and put an end to the cold.

As the *Phoenix* had flown south, the changeling had enjoyed the growing warmth of the weather. She'd taken many flights of her own throughout those days, basking in the stronger rays of the sun. Her bloodwings tired more quickly than she did, and she always had to return to the airship before they gave out, but she relished the opportunity to stretch them for long periods of time, free from the fear that someone below might spot her.

Like most changelings, Te'oma shunned the spotlight— at least when wearing her own skin. Many people didn't care for members of her race, and so she often wore the guise of one of them. She'd pretended to be so many different kinds of people over the years that she sometimes wondered if she might somehow forget what she looked like herself.

These past couple weeks, though, in the company of Esprë and her family (such as it was) and friends, Te'oma had been able to truly relax for the first time in as long as she could remember. The fact that Vol had destroyed her dead daughter's body in what seemed a fit of pique had horrified Te'oma at first. She'd wanted to do nothing but mourn the long-dead girl again. Instead, fate had forced her to put those emotions aside while she helped Kandler and the others save Esprë from sharing her daughter's fate.

Once the *Phoenix* had left Khorvaire behind, though, few distractions had surfaced, and Te'oma had been forced to deal with her grief once more. Mostly she had kept away from the others, preferring to mourn privately. She doubted that any of them would have been able to understand. They had no reason to empathize with her at all, much less pity her.

Only Burch had reached out to Te'oma. Although he had kept her at arm's length—as any wary hunter like him would—he had checked in on her regularly and made sure that she kept herself feed and rested. She'd been unable to tell him how much she'd appreciated even such small gestures.

Still, she'd been unable to get Esprë out of her mind. She'd known when she struck the deal to help kidnap the girl that she'd agreed to participate in an act of horrible evil against an innocent child. The parallels with her own daughter's fate had not escaped her.

Yet she'd done it all the same.

The changeling peered down past the tips of the pylons into the brightly lit chamber below. She saw Kandler, Esprë, Sallah, and Xalt approach the silver dragon. They looked like insects next to the massive beast.

As the dragon moved to speak with them, it glanced

upward. Its gaze seemed to pierce Te'oma's brain, and she felt petrified, unable to move—to even breathe—until the majestic monster turned its attention away.

Te'oma had hoped to scout out the area without the dragon or the others interfering with her. She'd considered telling Kandler, or even Burch, but she hadn't wanted to deal with the inevitable bickering and mistrust. Instead, she'd taken off on her own initiative to discover what she could. All she'd learned so far was how little of a chance any of them had against such a creature.

Then she spotted a pair of silhouettes framed against the blood-red western horizon. The sun had set, and the last traces of daylight would be gone entirely within minutes, but she saw the edges of the forms of these two creatures clearly in those final moments.

Dragons.

Te'oma stood up on the tip of one of the tower's pylons and stretched out her stiff arms and frozen wings, flexing blood back into them. Then she looked down and let the attraction of the terrible distance to the ground pull her from her perch. Her wings caught the wind, and she aimed herself straight for the bridge of the *Phoenix*, where Monja stood staring at the entrance into the observatory, unaware of either Te'oma or the dragons soaring in behind her.

"We have to get out of here," Te'oma said as she landed on the bridge, just feet from Monja's side.

The halfling screamed in surprise. She spun about, grabbing for the knife hanging from her belt. As she did, her hands left the airship's wheel.

The *Phoenix* bucked, hard. To Te'oma, it felt like the ship had run aground. The force of the ship's movement slammed her to the deck. An instant later, she found herself hanging in the air above it as the ship dropped lower instead.

Te'oma closed her eyes and braced for the *Phoenix* to leap

up and slam into her again as her wings held her hovering in the air. When nothing happened, she peeled them open them a moment later.

Monja lay hanging over the airship's wheel like a dirty shirt. She had her hands wrapped around the wheel's spars and was struggling into a more dignified position. As she did, she turned around and fumed at the changeling.

"Don't you ever do that again!" the halfling snarled.

Te'oma ignored the tiny shaman's wrath. "What happened there?" she said, scared enough to forget about the dragons for the moment.

"You've flown this ship," Monja said. "You know how ornery the elemental in that fiery ring is. Well, it sensed what happened to the *Keeper's Claw* when the elemental in it blew up and destroyed that dragon. Now it's linked dragons with enough destructive power to free it."

"But it was Burch's shockbolt that did that."

"There's no reasoning with it. That's what it thinks, and now that it's this close to a dragon's home again, it's aching for a chance to bust loose."

Panic entered Monja's heart. "We need to get this ship out of here," she said. "There's a pair of dragons coming this way right now!"

The changeling pointed off into the sky, but where there had been colors before now held only darkness. The thought that Monja might not believe her struck her like a brick.

"Probably some kind of family reunion," the halfling said, or maybe Greffykor's invited a couple of friends over for dinner—with a ship full of idiots on the menu."

"We have to get the airship out of here," Te'oma said. "If the dragons destroy her, we'll never be able to leave."

Monja shook her head. "Not a chance," she said. "I'm not abandoning the others—especially not to a trio of dragons."

"If we get away, we can come back later to pick them up."

"If any of them survive."

"They'll be killed with or without us. Why compound the error?"

Monja winked at the changeling. "You talk a good game, lady, but I'm not in the mood to play it. We're staying put and taking our chances with the others."

"But—"

Before Te'oma could complete her thought, a gust of wind blasted past her. It seemed like it might be strong enough to blow out the ring of fire like a lonely candle. The changeling glanced up as she cringed against the bridge's console, and she saw a flash of something red and scaly block out the stars.

The dragon went past them before Te'oma could even think about screaming. It landed square on the platform, right between the airship and the entrance into the observatory. It ignored the airship entirely and moved straight through the portal and into the gigantic room beyond.

"We're just insects to it," Te'oma said, awestruck. "It could have torn us apart, but we're not worth the bother."

"I wouldn't say that," a voice said from behind Te'oma and Monja.

The two turned around. On the bridge just a few feet from them, stood the tall, slender, red-haired man they'd met over the ocean. He showed his inhuman teeth to them and stood there as comfortably as if he'd been on this trip with them the entire time.

"If Mother hadn't the slightest concern about you and your flying toy here, I don't think she would have bothered to ask me to watch over you."

CHAPTER

47

"Move!" Kandler said as soon as he saw the dragon. "Scatter! Force it to choose a target!"

He grabbed Esprë by the arm and half-led, half-dragged her toward the hole. Burch dashed past them, anticipating where Kandler wanted to go.

Sallah and Xalt went in the opposite direction, toward the crystal ball Greffykor had been studying before. As she looked back over her shoulder, Kandler saw in her eyes that she'd rather have gone with him, even if only to make a final stand against this new foe, but she did as he asked instead. He only hoped it turned out to be the right thing.

He knew they had no way to harm the dragon. Their only hope was to hide from it. Perhaps in a place as large as the observatory—built on a scale to accommodate the largest sorts of dragons—there might be some spaces tight enough that a dragon could not fit in them.

Even if they could find a hole in which to hide, Kandler wondered how long they might be able to hold out that way. Could they live like rats within the walls, scurrying out to steal what food and water they could find whenever the dragons disappeared or bedded down for the night?

Did dragons sleep? Kandler had heard tales of them resting on lavish beds made of fortunes in invaluable gems and precious metals, dormant for months, years, even decades, but he had no way of knowing if they were true—or if they applied to every dragon he might meet.

In any case, he only knew one thing: He had to get Esprë away from this new dragon and fast.

The red dragon folded its wings against its back and crept through the open portal. As it did, Greffykor said something to it in Draconic.

Zanga stood in the center of the room, between the two dragons, covered in her scaled shroud, which shimmered with its varied colors. She raised her arms in supplication to the red dragon.

"Welcome, O Great One," she said to the creature. Her voice rang out loud and proud. "I speak in the repulsive tongue of our guests so that they may understand your holy intent. Permit me to be the conduit through which you may make your will be known."

Greffykor interrupted before the intruding dragon could respond. "I speak in the tongue of my guests to show my disrespect for those of my kind who would disregard our traditions and arrive in my observatory unannounced. You may leave at once."

The red dragon growled something. Zanga translated its words.

"The dragon-god known as Frekkainta greets Greffykor. She does not feel compelled to meet with traitors against the race of dragons or to treat them with respect. She has traveled many miles to come here to exterminate the lesser peoples and to take Greffykor prisoner for his crimes."

Greffykor snarled. "You stray beyond your authority. I

do not answer to you, nor shall my guests, who abide here under my protection."

Kandler and Esprë reached the hole, and he saw that Burch had already lashed one end of his rope to a bit of strange machinery jutting from a nearby wall. The shifter tossed the other end of the coil over the edge of the hole, and it played out smooth and straight until it slapped into the floor, which seemed a score of yards below.

The dragons hadn't turned to look at them. In fact, they had locked eyes with each other as if they both were sizing a foe up for a monstrous battle—or a meal. Kandler wondered if even the fortified walls of this amazing observatory would be able to withstand a brawl between two such terrifying beasts. He suspected the whole place could crumble around them without them giving much notice.

"Go with Burch," Kandler said. He gave Esprë a quick hug with his free arm, then a kiss on the top of her head. He brandished his fangblade before him. "I'll cover your escape."

"But—"

Burch cut off the girl's protest by wrapping his arm around her waist and leaping into the hole. Kandler knew the shifter would let the thin, strong rope pay out from around his free arm, slowing their descent to a safe but zippy speed.

The red dragon's gaze flicked toward Sallah and Xalt then back across to face toward Kandler. Her head did not move, but Kandler swore he could hear the creature's massive orbs swiveling in her head.

The justicar froze in the focus of the bright yellow eyes. He wondered if he might fit inside one of their pupils, they were so large. He had to remind himself to keep breathing. Then he realized he'd stopped out of fear that the creature might hear him.

He didn't want to do anything to offend the dragon. He could see now why the Seren worshipped the dragons as gods. He'd never been much for religion, but Frekkainta was the closest thing to a deity he'd ever encountered.

The dragon's eyes told Kandler everything he needed to know about her. She cared nothing for him. He meant less than an insect, despite the stinger he held in his hand. She could crush him flat or incinerate him in the space of a single blink of her massive eyes. He lived or died only at her whim.

Then Frekkainta turned her attention back to Greffykor, and Kandler found he could breathe freely again. He reached for the rope and knelt at the edge of the hole. Below, he heard Burch and Esprë touch down on the lower floor.

The red dragon growled something horrible. Zanga began to translate as the creature snarled out her intent at Greffykor.

"If the vermin present here do not show themselves immediately, Frekkainta will kill everyone in the observatory and then destroy the building itself. The traitor Greffykor will comply with her wishes or be subdued and crucified as a traitor. We have but moments to—"

Zanga stopped. "Everyone?" She stared up at Frekkainta, her face a mixture of confusion and awe. "But, my lady, I am the Shroud of Scales of the Tribe of Gref. I lead my people in the worship of your kind and your host in this observatory. Surely I—"

Frekkainta cut off Zanga with a cold-blooded snarl that Kandler didn't need translated.

"But—"

The crimson dragon bowed its head until its nose nearly touched the Seren shaman. Kandler held his breath as he waited to see what would happen next.

A gout of fire spouted from the dragon's nostrils and

licked along the front of the shroud that Zanga wore. The woman shrieked and fell to her knees, the flames continuing to cascade down her back.

The fire stopped, leaving twin curls of thick smoke curling from each of the red dragon's blackened nostrils. Zanga kept screaming until Greffykor reached out and tapped her on her shoulder with a careful, silver talon. She stopped so fast then that the effort sent her into an uncontrollable fit of coughing.

Greffykor cocked his head at Frekkainta, a scolding look in his eyes. As a child, Kandler had seen that look in his father's eyes when the man had caught him playing with an innocent inchworm he'd found crawling across the front step of their home in Sharn. He'd stepped away from the harmless creature and let it go on its way.

Frekkainta, on the other hand, had no intention of letting Zanga go free. She growled something at the shaman, and Zanga staggered to her feet, the shroud falling from her tear-stained face. Smoke rose from her singed hair and reddened skin.

"No," Zanga rasped. "Don't kill me last—don't kill me at all! I—" She swallowed hard. "I know— One of the people who arrived on the airship bears a dragonmark, a sign of blessing. I can tell you who it is."

Kandler shivered. The Shroud of Scales was about to sell Esprë out, and he didn't see what he could do about it. He considered charging Zanga and cutting her down before she could speak, but he knew that the dragon could flick him away with a single talon instead. He wished he had a bow—or that Burch was there.

The justicar knew, though, that he had no other choices. He would have to sacrifice himself. It might not ensure that Esprë would live, but it would buy her a few much-needed moments.

Thoughts of Esprina filled Kandler's head. Then Sallah's face entered his mind as well, sharing space with Esprë's mother, never crowding her out. Whatever time the justicar could bargain for would help Sallah too.

Kandler shifted his grip on his fangblade and prepared to charge.

CHAPTER

48

The redheaded man grinned at Te'oma, and his mouth parted wider than humanly possible. The changeling doubted that even she could have pulled off such a trick.

What frightened her most was that the dragon-man didn't seem to be trying. Pulling and twisting himself into different shapes didn't strain him at all. Only a creature of horrible power could do such things so effortlessly.

"Welcome to the *Phoenix*," Monja said, keeping her hands lightly on the wheel. "We're pleased to have you as our guest again."

The dragon-man snorted. "I doubt that," he said, "but for the sake of amusement, let's pretend it is." He stared directly at Te'oma as he spoke.

The changeling willed a smile on to her face. "Let's."

"If it's no bother, what business brings you here?" Monja asked. Te'oma could tell that the halfling was taking great care to keep her voice and her attitude proper and light.

The changeling marveled that the tiny shaman could keep her cool so well in the face of such horrible danger. After all, the redheaded man could transform into a dragon in an instant and murder them where they stood. She was sure that he wouldn't suffer a single pang of regret for doing so, no more than she would for crushing a stinging bug.

The dragon-man looked at them, his eyes wide and unblinking as he studied them up close. He seemed to be able to see right through their skin and peer into their bones.

"Of course," he said. "It's only natural for thinking creatures to want to know why they must die."

Te'oma gasped despite herself, but the dragon-man ignored it. In fact, he gave no evidence he had even heard her outburst.

"It has to do with the Prophecy," Monja said, prompting the dragon.

"Of course. The Prophecy dictates all our actions. It guides our thoughts. Only by the greatest struggle can we maintain the illusion of free will and exert our own desires upon it."

"How is that?" Monja asked. "If the Prophecy is infallible, can it not predict every moment with complete accuracy?"

The dragon-man glared at the halfling for a moment to assess whether or not she was mocking him. Te'oma wasn't sure she knew the answer to that question either. However, the dragon seemed to conclude that such a tiny creature wouldn't dare toy so carelessly with its own life, and he spoke to answer her question.

"The Prophecy models reality—or reality models the Prophecy. It is impossible to tell. Either is so complex as to be unknowable. Even such as we cannot comprehend it in all its glory."

"Like blind hunters feeling the different parts of the thunder lizard," Monja said.

The dragon-man spat out a mirthless laugh. "It is a poor metaphor for a poor mind, but not without some truth."

"So why are you here?" It surprised Te'oma to realize the voice asking the question was hers.

The dragon-man's eyes swiveled to meet her gaze. "Great things happen here and now, and we of the Chamber wish to influence the events."

"How?"

"The bearer of the dragonmark among your number must die."

Te'oma shivered at this. She'd not come so far to let anyone kill Esprë so easily. There had to be some way that she could spirit the girl away to safety.

Instinct told her to find Esprë right away. Her cunning, though, kept her rooted to the spot. It would not do to rush into a battle between two—or three—dragons. Better to arm herself first with the only weapon that would be any good against such creatures: information.

"Is your mother part of the Chamber too?" Monja asked.

The dragon-man's eyes widened and turned a blazing yellow. "She does not concern herself with such things. She knows only that she must kill the bearer of the dragonmark. The Prophecy makes it clear that this will happen."

"And who interprets the Prophecy for your mother?"

The dragon-man's smile spread wide enough to show several rows of wicked teeth.

Te'oma stifled a gasp. The dragon-man had twisted the Prophecy to his own unfathomable ends. If she could get away from the ship, she might be able to use that to her advantage.

The changeling fingered the knife at her belt, but she knew that the dragon-man would slay her before she could clear the blade from its sheath. Perhaps his mind wouldn't be protected quite so well though. If she could reach out with her psionic powers before the creature could muster his defenses, she might have a chance to stun him. Then he would be at her mercy.

Te'oma's breath caught in her chest as the dragon-man transfixed her with his stare. At that moment, she knew that he understood what she meant to do. Still, he hadn't done anything to stop her.

Desperate, Te'oma focused the power of her mind into a mental whip and lashed out at the dragon-man with it. She hoped to feel it curl around his mind, draw tight, and then squeeze it until it split. Instead, her efforts struck a mental wall that might as well have been built from iron.

The dragon-man's expression did not change. If anything, he looked bored at Te'oma's feeble attempt to do him harm.

The changeling drew back her mental resources again, forming them into a sharp-edged wedge this time, hoping to stab it through the dragon-man's defenses. Before she could strike, though, she felt the dragon-man's wall lurch forward and smash her down.

Te'oma's knees buckled as her mind gave way. She fell to the deck, unable to feel the wood beneath her as her mental protections crumbled beneath the dragon-man's crushing attack. The world became dark and began to spin.

"Stop!" Monja's voice seemed to be calling out from a distant tower. "She is no threat to you. Killing a harmless creature is cruel."

Te'oma felt the pressure in her mind ease up, and she realized she'd stopped breathing. She forced air back into her lungs with a cough that felt like it might tear out her throat. Her eyes watered, and her head wobbled on the end of her neck.

When Te'oma's vision finally cleared, she sat back on

her haunches and glanced up at the dragon-man. He stared down at her, his face as expressionless as a mask.

"Go," he said. "If you wish. Mother won't listen to you. She won't even talk to you. She considers your kind a lower form of life."

"My kind?"

"Non-dragons."

Te'oma shivered and turned away. She spied the top of the rope ladder still hanging over the gunwale, and she scrambled toward it. She knew that moving fast would make no difference. If the dragon-man wanted to kill her, she would be dead before she reached the rail.

Despite that, she lurched for the ladder and let herself fall over the railing. She slid down the ropes fast enough to leave burns on her hands, but she didn't feel them. Her feet slammed into the landing platform, and her knees buckled. As she pushed herself to her feet, she smelled brimstone from where the red dragon had passed just moments before.

Te'oma glanced up at the airship and breathed a silent prayer of thanks that she could not see the ship's bridge from here. She didn't think she could bear the dragon-man's penetrating gaze, not so soon after he'd nearly smashed her mind flat.

She turned toward the observatory. For a moment, she considered spreading her bloodwings and flapping up toward the top of the place again, but the thought of drawing any attention to herself made her shiver. Far better, she thought, to creep into the place like a cockroach, hoping that no one of any import—no dragons—would notice her.

CHAPTER

49

S tay here," Burch said as he dropped Esprë gently on the floor. "Something's wrong."

"Kandler's not following us," the girl said. She grabbed at the shifter's arm before he could scurry back up the rope. "Don't leave me here."

Esprë peered around at the darkest corners of the dimly lit room in which Burch had deposited her. Strange machinery hung throughout the room, from both the walls and the ceiling. Much of it seemed like interlocking rings of steel that bore etchings and demarcations, measurements of something that the shifter couldn't understand. Then he recognized them.

"Those markings, they're just like the ones on the spheres outside," he said.

Esprë's grip on his arm loosened. "Maybe they control the spheres," she said. "That way the dragon can simulate the positioning of the planets, the planes, and the dragonmarks."

Burch gave out a low whistle. "All the better to figure out parts of their damned Prophecy." He patted Esprë on the head and said, "Hide."

With that, he started hauling himself back up the rope—toward the dragons and his friend.

As he climbed, he used only his arms, knowing that pushing on the rope with his legs would only slow him down. Hand over hand, he pulled himself up, wondering if he could reach the next level in time to do any good—or whether or not his efforts would matter at all. Maybe he was just racing toward his death.

He felt a pang of regret at leaving Esprë by herself in the chamber below, but he knew she'd be all right. If a dragon found her, she'd be just as dead with him as without him—or at least that's what he told himself.

When he reached the edge, he heard Zanga talking and the dragons snarling at each other in their terrible tongue. He knew only snatches of the language, enough to offend a dragon in its own language but not enough to know which way the conversation had turned. The tone of Frekkainta's growls, though, said all he needed to hear.

Burch popped his head over the edge of the hole and spotted Zanga standing between the two dragons. She'd thrown back her shimmering Shroud of Scales and stood weeping at the red dragon's taloned feet. As the shifter crept over the lip and unlimbered his crossbow, Zanga said something about selling out Esprë in exchange for her life.

Burch pointed his weapon at the Seren shaman and took careful aim, looking for the right angle through which he could bury a bolt in the woman's head. Before he could pull the trigger, though, Kandler lowered his head and charged straight at her.

Burch hurled himself forward too, although at an angle that would take him behind the red dragon. If he could put enough space between his path and Kandler's, he might be able to find a clean angle at the Shroud of Scales again. He just hoped he could manage it before one of the dragons killed his friend instead. With luck, he'd be able to do it before the dragons bothered to take notice of either himself or Kandler, and they could find someplace to hide before either of them got killed.

As he scuttled to his left, though, Burch couldn't see a good angle at all. Any bolt he loosed stood just as good a chance of bouncing off a dragon's scales as it did of hitting Zanga. Worse yet, the best angles he could find skated so close to Kandler's back that they put the justicar in more danger than the Seren.

Then Zanga caught Kandler's movement out of the corner of her eye. She turned to look at the onrushing man, his lethal fangblade held high. She opened her mouth to scream, and Burch knew that any hope for killing her quietly and slipping away had been lost.

The shifter stopped and planted his feet. He found his angle. It passed right between Kandler's left arm and his neck. The bolt would fly true, but if the justicar moved even an inch in the wrong direction he'd end up with the shaft in his chest or neck instead.

Burch summoned up his most commanding voice, the one he'd used on the battlefield during the Last War. He hadn't employed it often. He preferred to work from cover, alone, when he could, but it had proven enough to herd soldiers into battle and to face nearly certain death.

"Down!" the shifter bellowed.

As the words left his lips, he counted off three heartbeats.

On the first, his shout reached the ears of everyone in the room. Zanga's eyes flew wide. The crest atop the red dragon's head twitched, and the silver dragon's gaze flicked in the shifter's direction.

Kandler kept running.

On the second beat, Zanga turned to look in Burch's direction. As she did, her shroud fell away from head, gathering around her shoulders and framing her neck. Burch's finger tightened on his crossbow's trigger.

Something that seemed like a smile curled the corners of the silver dragon's lips. Amusement glinted in the creature's eyes.

The red dragon's nostrils wrinkled back as if she had smelled something repulsive and rotting. The one eye of hers that Burch could see swiveled toward Kandler, but her monstrous skull did not move an inch.

Kandler raised his sword higher and bent forward as he ran even harder toward his goal. It seemed that he would let nothing come between him and killing Zanga—not dragons and not even a shout from a friend.

On the third beat, Burch pulled his crossbow's trigger.

As the bolt whizzed through the air, Kandler left his feet and dived forward, thrusting his sword before him. The justicar would fall short of his goal, but Burch's desperate shout had gotten through to him just in the nick of time.

The bolt skimmed right past Kandler's left ear, nicking away a lock of hair from the side of his head as it went. A moment earlier, and it would have buried itself next to his shoulder blade and perhaps punctured his lung. Instead, it proceeded unimpeded toward its target.

Zanga's eyes grew even wider as she saw Kandler dive to the ground. She never saw the bolt itself. It traveled too fast and presented too small a profile for her to spot it until it slipped under her upraised chin and through her throat.

Only the bolt's feathers kept it from passing completely through her. They caught on her larynx and crushed it as the bolt's tip stabbed out through the back of Zanga's neck.

Burch didn't bother to reload his crossbow before slinging it across his back. He knew it wouldn't do any good against the dragon. Even if he managed to find a soft spot amid the red beast's scales, it would be little more than a bee's sting against such a creature.

Kandler skidded along the floor on his chest. Before he could even come to a stop, Zanga collapsed before the red dragon, her treacherous words caught in her throat, blocked by the wooden shaft that now lodged there.

Burch reached behind him for the rope that led to the safety of the chamber below—however temporary that might be. He could not wrench his eyes away from his friend, though, whom he saw skitter to a halt in the shadow of the two dragons.

Kandler did not scramble to his feet. He pressed his fists down on the stone floor before him—one of them still wrapped around the hilt of his fangblade—and pushed himself up on to his knees. As he did, the red dragon turned toward the justicar, her nostrils flaring, smoke curling from their edges.

Burch's mouth went dry. He knew that the dragon could swallow Kandler whole. In less time than it would take him to slam another bolt into his crossbow, his best friend could be gone.

The crimson creature growled, ruffling Kandler's hair in her fetid breath. Even from where he stood, Burch could smell brimstone billowing from the beast's mouth. The scent made his eyes water.

Kandler staggered to his feet and brandished his blade before him. Burch smiled. Even faced with certain death, the justicar refused to beg for mercy.

"I have the dragonmark," Kandler said, his voice raspy. "The others are worthless to you. Kill me, and let them go free."

CHAPTER

50

The red dragon snorted at Kandler. The justicar felt her sulfur-scented breath envelop him, burning his eyes. He fought the urge to cough, instead clearing his throat with a low grunt.

The dragon snarled, and Kandler wondered if his knees would give out on him. Instead, he wiped his eyes with his off hand and met the creature's gaze. He weighed his fangblade in the other hand and wondered if he could leap high enough to drive it into one of the beast's great, yellow eyes.

"He is my guest," Greffykor said, "as are his companions. They are under my protection."

The red dragon rumbled out a hoarse, bleating noise. Kandler realized she meant it to be a laugh.

"You may be a queen in your own land," Greffykor said, "but this is my domain. Mine alone. You hold no sway here."

The red dragon rumbled again. As she did, she raised herself up on her rear haunches and spread her wings until they blotted out the bit of sky that Kandler had been able to see through the tower's top. She arched back her neck and bared her teeth, preparing to strike.

Greffykor bent his own neck forward and down, showing deference to the larger beast. As he did, the crimson creature's spiked tail came whipping around on the side opposite Kandler and smacked into the silver dragon's face.

Kandler jumped back at Greffykor's head lurched toward him. Hot blood from the silver dragon's slashed face splattered along the floor and across the justicar's legs.

Greffykor flinched as the blow struck him, causing him to close his eyes. When he opened them, he saw Kandler standing right there before him, his fangblade held high in his fist.

The silver dragon grunted at the justicar, and Kandler felt the creature's frigid breath wash over him. Then Greffykor straightened himself up and glared at the red dragon.

"You have made your point," the silver dragon said.

Kandler cursed himself for not taking the opportunity to strike at the red dragon when he'd had the chance. Now, with the thing looming over him like a building, he had no hope of harming it. He would have to bide his time and keep looking for the right chance to attack.

The red dragon turned its attention to him again and growled.

"She wants proof," Greffykor said in a brittle tone.

Kandler gaped at the silver dragon. "Of what?"

"Your dragonmark. She wants to see it."

Kandler grimaced. "Tell her she can pry it off my hairy ass."

The red dragon drew back her lips, and her long, sinuous tongue flickered out from between her rows of terrifying teeth.

"She can understand your language," Greffykor said. "She refuses to sully her mouth with it."

Kandler pursed his lips. If he could get the creature

angry enough that she would incinerate him with her burning breath, she would never know if he really had a dragonmark or not, but to do that, he would have to get her closer.

"All right," Kandler said, tugging at the collar of his shirt. "She'll need to come closer to see it."

He slipped his hand with the fangblade in it behind his back. He hoped the red dragon would see it as some form of deference to her.

The monstrous creature folded her wings back against her body and lowered herself onto all four legs once more. Kandler's arm tensed behind him until it felt as taut as a loaded catapult. He ached to unleash it, to let it whip around and bury his deadly blade into the dragon queen's flesh, but he forced himself to wait.

The red dragon squinted down at Kandler, and he realized that each of her eyes stood as tall as Esprë. They seemed like such large targets that he didn't see how he could avoid them, much less miss them, but they still hovered just out of his reach.

"It's not very large," Kandler said as he tugged at the edge of his shirt, pulling it down past his collarbone. "You'll have to get closer."

He tried to keep his voice even, dull, even flat. He just needed the dragon queen to get a few more feet closer. If he tried to leap for her now, he might slice her across the end of her nose, but he wanted to plunge his blade into her eye. Half blinding her would trigger the kind of rage he needed to inspire in her. Nothing less would do.

The red dragon's head stopped moving downward. Her tongue lashed out toward Kandler's face. Only his combat-trained reflexes prevented her from flicking out an eye.

The silver dragon opened his mouth. "For a human, you are a terrible liar."

Kandler whipped his sword around in a vicious arc. It caught nothing but air.

The red dragon sat back on her haunches and rumbled at him again.

Then she threw back her head and roared.

Fire erupted from the dragon queen's snout and billowed up to the tower's open top like fireworks exploding into the sky. Kandler backpedaled, nearly stumbling as he went, keeping his sword before him like some sort of talisman that could ward off such all-powerful evil, even though he knew it would be exactly that useless.

A cry of triumph went up from behind the dragon. Kandler peered past the creature and spied Sallah and Xalt racing away from the creature's rear as fast as their legs would carry them. Sallah's fists were empty, but Xalt tried to cover their retreat with a crossbow aimed at the dragon.

The dragon queen thrashed her tail, slamming it to the left and right, howling in pain as she did. Even with the thing moving so fast, Kandler could see something was wrong. The end of the massive tail bent at an odd angle, dangling downward.

When the tail swished in his direction again, Kandler saw that the tip of it had almost been chopped off. There, stabbing out of the top of the tail, hung the culprit: a bright-bladed sword that blazed with a silver light.

Kandler halted for a moment. If Sallah had managed to harm the dragon, then maybe he could hope to as well. As he adjusted his grip on his fangblade, he watched the dragon queen pound her tail on the floor, trying to dislodge it.

Greffykor turned to the justicar and spotted him standing there, just before the hole that led down to the lower level. The silver dragon shook his snout at Kandler and gestured him away with a quick sweep of one claw.

Kandler understood. The dragon queen hadn't been

hurt—not really. To it, Sallah's sword felt no worse than a thorn in a lion's paw.

The observatory's floor shook with the force of the dragon queen's throes, but Kandler saw that these came not from a creature that was wounded but angered. The red dragon's outburst was little more than a tantrum thrown by a beast used to getting its way in all things—instantly.

Greffykor growled something at the dragon queen, and the red dragon froze. She glared at the silver dragon with hate-filled eyes then swung her tail around to her right, the side closest to Kandler.

He could see now that she could not reach the end of her own tail—at least not without undergoing some back-bending contortions. The blazing sword sat there in her tail, crackling away but not burning her scales a bit. A rivulet of blood trickled down from the wound, but it clearly seemed more of a nuisance than a threat.

The dragon queen snarled at Greffykor. Keeping his head low, the silver dragon crept toward the crimson tail, the talons on one of its hands extended toward the offending piece of burning metal. Greffykor snatched the blade free from the dragon queen's flesh with one sharp move, and the red dragon howled in pain and relief.

Kandler reached for the rope that down the hole, and he began to lower himself down it. As his eyes became level with the floor, though, he stopped and watched.

The dragon queen growled at Greffykor, and the silver dragon nodded in response. "Of course," he said, "you are both gracious and wise in your mercy. I do not wish for you to have to trouble with destroying my home to find these vermin. I will roust them out for you and present them to you as my gift."

CHAPTER

51

Kandler wrapped the rope around one leg and then slid down it fast enough to make the fabric in his pants grow hot. As he hit the floor of the chamber below, he spotted Burch and Esprë peering out from behind one of the gigantic sets of rings that cluttered the chamber from floor to ceiling.

"Hide!" Kandler said as he sprinted toward them. He had no idea how long it would take Greffykor to come around looking for them, but he had no intention of leaving any of them standing out where the creature could see them.

Esprë started for Kandler, her arms held wide, fear and joy warring on her face. Burch grabbed her by the arm and pulled her back behind a cabinet that looked large enough to hide an entire wagon inside it. She started to protest but gave up when she saw Kandler coming straight for them.

Kandler didn't hear the dragon come into the room behind him so much as he felt it. The beating of the creature's wings made barely a sound, but it displaced so much air as it descended into the gigantic chamber that the justicar could feel the increase of pressure in his ears.

He charged forward, convinced for a moment that the creature might land on top of him and crush the life from him. Burch and Esprë disappeared behind the cabinet in front of him in the blink of an eye.

Kandler hoped that the dragon might not have seen the pair in the dimness, so he peeled off to the right instead of joining the others. He spied one of the massive, demarcated rings hanging in the air before him, nearly but not quite touching the floor. As he passed it, he reached out and grabbed it, swinging himself behind it.

The ring moved as Kandler's hand touched it, and the formerly dim chamber leaped to life. The runes carved into the metallic rings began to glow with the light of dying embers. Each ring glowed with a slightly different hue, ranging from reddish to bluish and every color in between.

Kandler released the ring in his hand and stepped back. It had started to hum beneath his fingers as he held it, and he had heard a single note ringing in his ears. It had wavered and warbled in some kind of pattern, so regular that it seemed like it might be trying to communicate something to him—or to a creature with a larger mind.

The justicar stared at his tingling hand for a moment and decided not to touch any of the rings again.

Then he heard the dragon snort.

"Such devices are not meant for your kind," the silvery creature said. "The Prophecy is too much for you. Even a dragon can only conceive of a fractional aspect of the whole. For you to attempt to do so would cause your brains to leak from your ears."

Kandler took a half-step back from the ring in front of him, but he kept it between himself and the dragon.

"You need to turn the girl over to me," Greffykor said. "I will present her to the queen. With luck and a bit of well-placed flattery, she may then deign to leave the rest of us alone."

"No," Kandler said.

"She is doomed in any case. The Prophecy has foretold this. I could not see the means of her death, but now I see why. She dies here, tonight."

"And your observatory is impervious to scrying."

"Even from my own eyes." Greffykor nodded.

Kandler hefted his fangblade and tapped it against the ring in front of him. The metallic circle spun a few inches then came to a stop.

"You can stop her," Kandler said, his voice dripping with disgust. "This is your home. How can you let this 'queen' of yours barge in here and order you about?"

Greffykor snorted. "You are amusing. You think to shame me into confronting my guests over your welfare."

"From my experience, dragons have no shame."

"Not the way that humans think of it." Greffykor closed his tooth-lined maw, then opened it again. "The queen is more powerful than you could imagine. She could murder me here in my own home and suffer no consequences for her actions."

"Is she your queen?"

"No, but that doesn't matter. In her land, her word is law."

"And here?"

"Out here on our frontier, I am a law unto myself."

"Which means nothing."

"It means most dragons respect my work and my solitude. If anyone else were to attack me, I could call on others to come to my aid."

"But not against this queen."

"Not without the ear of another queen or king, but I am my own dragon, and I do not fall under anyone's wing."

Kandler grimaced. He didn't see a good way out of this. He could only hope that Burch and Esprë were doing something to save themselves while he kept Greffykor occupied.

"We are your guests. Doesn't that mean anything?"

Greffykor shook his head, his silvery crest waving above him as he moved.

"If I do not deliver the girl soon, the queen will kill me and tear down my tower with her bare claws."

Kandler stared at the dragon and then at their surroundings. The tower seemed invulnerable to him, as eternal as a mountain, as did Greffykor, but he decided to take the dragon at his word. The queen, it seemed, did not make idle threats—and Kandler had seen what a dragon could do to a mountain.

In frustration, the justicar slashed at the steel circle in front of him. The blow clanged off the ring's surface, and the strange letters on it glowed brighter. Near where the blade had notched the circle, the runes shone blindingly bright.

Greffykor hissed. "You do not know what magics you tamper with here."

"I don't care," Kandler said. "I just want my daughter left alone."

"You might as well ask for the moons to stop spinning through the sky."

"If that's what it takes."

Somewhere above, a woman screamed.

Kandler recognized Sallah's voice, even raised as it was. He started to dash forward, around the ring between him and the rope that led to the upper level, but Greffykor stepped into his way.

That single step was like a house falling into Kandler's path. He stopped cold.

"Let me by," the justicar snarled.

Greffykor flicked a single talon forward. It caught Kandler in the chest and sent him flying back past the ring. He landed in a heap where the floor met the wall behind him.

Kandler heard another scream. This time it came from Esprë.

The justicar felt like a horse had dropped onto his chest. He couldn't get to his feet. He couldn't even breathe. His vision tunneled hard. All he could see was the vicious end of Greffykor's snout bared at him.

Then Esprë was at his side, holding him and trying to shake some life into him. He followed his first instinct and tried to push her away.

"No," he said. "I won't let her have you."

Esprë gasped in relief. "You're alive."

"At my pleasure," Greffykor said. "You will come with me now, or I will kill him."

Burch appeared between Kandler and the dragon, his crossbow leveled at the creature. "Try it, and I'll put out your eye."

"I will not harm the elf," Greffykor said.

"It's not you I'm worried about," Kandler said between gasps. His breathing had started to ease, but every time he drew a gulp of air into his lungs he wondered if it might be the last he would taste.

"I will intercede with the queen on the—"

Burch's crossbow twanged. The bolt in it slammed into the dragon's right eye and ricocheted off the transparent eyelid that protected it.

Kandler drew a breath to curse, but before he could the dragon beat him to it.

Greffykor recoiled and slapped a claw over his bruised eye. He sat back on his haunches and howled in pain.

Kandler shoved himself to his feet, using his sword—

which he still gripped in his hand—as a cane. "Run!" he said to Esprë, although it came out more as a hiss than a shout. "Run!"

The girl turned her wide and determined eyes on him.

"No," she said.

CHAPTER

52

Sallah stood over the dragon queen's crimson tail, her sword held high in both hands. She'd reversed her grip on the hilt and pointed the tip straight down so that she could stab into the dragon's flesh with every ounce of her weight.

She glanced at Xalt, who'd suggested this mad plan. At first she'd thought him insane. Attacking a dragon as large and powerful as the queen was tantamount to begging to be murdered.

"No one lives forever," the warforged had said in his sanguine way.

She'd had to kiss him on the cheek for that. He'd stared at her in stunned silence afterward, and although she could not read his stolid face, she'd decided to interpret his bare expression as a smile.

Now, though, the plan—if it could be called that—seemed madder than ever. The Church of the Silver Flame had sent her on a mission to recover a young elf from the edges of the Mournland, not battle dragons in far-off lands where the light of the flame had yet to reach.

She'd lost her friends and her father in the course of following their quest, though, and to back away from that now, to admit defeat, would only dishonor their memories. If she were to fail, she knew that she could do no less than die in the process, just as they had.

Sallah could barely believe that she and Xalt had been able to sneak over here behind the dragon queen. She suspected that the crimson creature knew that they were there but had long since decided that they were insignificant enough to ignore. If so, she would soon regret that choice.

The knight glanced back over her shoulder and saw Te'oma come sliding down the rope ladder leading down from the *Phoenix*, more falling than climbing. She wondered what could have happened to cause the changeling to leave the airship so quickly, but she didn't have time to ponder it. She had to strike now, before the red dragon noticed Te'oma approaching.

Sallah gritted her teeth tight and brought her blade down as hard as she could. The tip of the sword glanced off of the dragon's blood-red scales, and stabbed into the stone floor, jarring the knight's arms.

The dragon froze at the strange sensation and sound near her tail.

"Do it again," Xalt whispered. "Now!"

Without another thought, Sallah reversed her grip on her blade, and it burst into silvery flames along its length. With a desperate prayer to the Silver Flame, she slammed the blade down once more, this time hammering the dragon's tail with the edge of her sword rather than its point.

The blazing blade sliced through the red scales and kept going through the far softer flesh beneath—until it cut into the bone under that. Sallah yanked on the sword, hoping to get in one more blow before the dragon could turn on her, but the force of her strike had embedded the blade in the bone. Straining with all her might, she still could not draw it forth.

Xalt grabbed the lady knight by the collar of her armor and hauled her away. Her fingers—still a bit numb from her first, failed attack—slipped from her weapon's hilt.

Before Sallah could protest, the dragon's tail rose up and sliced through the air. The bottom of it just nicked the knight's shoulder. Without the warforged's support, the impact would have sent her sprawling. Instead, the spaulder covering her right shoulder tore away from the rest of her armor and went spinning off to clatter against the far wall.

Sallah gritted her teeth and suppressed a scream as Xalt hauled her toward the gigantic crystal at which they'd found Greffykor working when they'd first entered the observatory. "We may find shelter there," the warforged said.

The knight could barely hope for that to be so, but true to her training she murmured a prayer to the Silver Flame to deliver herself and her fellows from the evil that the dragon queen represented. She knew that if she fell, her mission—given to her by the Speaker of the Flame herself—would fail. No one would take up where she left off and bring Esprë to Flamekeep.

As long as the Flame burns, there is hope, Sallah recited in her head. Her father had spoken these words to her countless times. She still remembered the first time she heard them clearly, though, and understood what they meant.

Her family had followed Deothen, her father, on yet another one of his seemingly endless series of quests. She had only been six years old at the time, and her mother had been younger than Sallah was now. They'd had the same mane of long, red hair, and Sallah remembered being so proud when people would remark how much alike they looked. She'd thought of her mother as the most beautiful woman in the world, and being linked to that made her smile.

On their way from Flamekeep to Arthawn Keep—a Thranite holding on the border with both Breland and Cyre—they'd fallen prey to an ambush at the hands of the Azure Bandits. The Cyran government had given this notorious group of killers a letter of marques, absolving them from responsibility for any crimes they might commit—as long as they were committed against Cyre's foes in the Last War.

The bandits' strike against the Thranite caravan had been doomed from the start, although they couldn't have known it at the time. As leader of the caravan, Deothen had ordered the wagons and their accompanying cavalry to be disguised as an apolitical wagon train of merchants traveling through Thrane.

He had, of course, been hoping the Azure Bandits would attack. When they took the bait, Deothen led the charge against the bandits. He and the other knights stripped off their disguises and rushed into action, their polished armor and shining blades glinting in the sun.

Sallah remembered thinking that she wanted nothing more at that moment than to be a knight, to follow in her father's footsteps. The battle lasted mere minutes. In the end, the Knights of the Silver Flame crushed their foes.

Sallah's mother lay dead.

An errant arrow had skittered past the knights and entered the woman's unarmored chest as she'd wrapped her arms around Sallah to protect her with her own body. Had she not done so, the arrow might have taken Sallah's life instead. Many times in the following years, she would wish that it had.

Right then, though, she had no other thoughts than to mourn her mother, to hold her red-haired head in her tiny lap as the woman coughed her life's blood up from her lungs.

As long as the Flame burns, there is hope. Deothen had said these words to Sallah as he pulled her from her mother's corpse, and he'd repeated them to her time and again since. She was sure those would have been his dying words to her if she'd been able to hear them instead of fighting for her own life in Construct.

These words had echoed in her head as she'd considered parting ways with Kandler and Esprë and heading back to Thrane. Frustrated as she'd been, she'd threatened to leave, but Kandler had called her bluff—even when she hadn't known it was a bluff herself.

The man amazed her. He understood her so well, and they'd only known each other for such a short time. It almost seemed as if fate—or the Flame—had pushed them together.

That wasn't the reason she'd changed her mind and decided to come with them to Argonnessen. Her love for the justicar might be growing by the day, but to Sallah, her duty to the Flame would always come first.

As long as Esprë still lived, there would be hope that she would accompany Sallah back to Thrane. The knight clung to that notion with every bit of her faith. It had brought her here to this observatory, and it had forced her forth to take a stab at a dragon's tail.

Now, it seemed, it might put out the light that burned within her own soul.

As Xalt dragged Sallah toward the gigantic crystal, she felt the floor behind them shake. The impact of something the size of a small mountain behind her nearly knocked the knight from her feet. She stumbled forward, reaching out for the crystal, wishing she still had her sword in her hand, knowing it would do her no good.

A claw as wide as Sallah was tall slashed across her back, laying open her armor and slicing into the flesh beneath.

The blow slammed her forward, and she slid under the transparent base that held the massive crystal in its place. She scrambled forward on her hands and knees, praying that the dragon would not hit her again.

Sallah didn't think she could take another blow like the last. It would kill her for sure. A part of her prayed for that to happen, to put an end to her struggles, which seemed to have gone on for so long. To fall in battle in the service of the Silver Flame would ensure that her own light would join with it in the afterlife.

The Flame still burned.

Sallah stopped scrambling when she ran into the observatory's outer wall, against which the towering crystal sat. As she considered her next move, Xalt pulled her to her feet and turned her around.

Looking through the crystal, she could see something that had to be the dragon queen. It seemed far tinier than could be possible, though, and it took her a moment to realize that the shape of the crystal distorted the creature's size.

The dragon leaned forward and snarled, almost putting the end of her snout against the crystal. Her image swelled until its bloated face filled the entire crystal, and Sallah's breath caught in her chest as she waited for the monstrosity to swallow her alive.

But the crystal still stood between her and the dragon. The spaces around the crystal were too small for the dragon to fit through, she could tell. When she noticed this, she started to laugh.

The laughter arose not from humor but relief, but the dragon didn't take it that way. The creature sat back on her haunches—shrinking again as she did—and bellowed at the lady knight and her warforged companion.

"Perhaps angering it wasn't such a good idea," Xalt said.

"She would have killed Kandler," she said. "It's too late for recriminations."

"Or, perhaps, for anything else."

Sallah had never heard such terror in the unflappable warforged's voice before. She looked up at the crystal and saw the dragon's head seem to explode inside it as the creature thrust her snout forward.

Then fire seemed to engulf the entire world.

Sallah screamed, and the effort burned her lungs.

CHAPTER

53

W hat do you mean no?" Kandler said. He couldn't believe he had heard the word come from Esprë's mouth.

"Just what I said." The set of the young elf's jaw reminded Kandler of her mother at that instant. "I'm not going to run any more, not if it means letting everyone I care about get killed."

Kandler glanced up at the silver dragon looming over him. The creature sat there on his haunches, rubbing his injured eye with a long-taloned claw. Burch's bolt hadn't done any real harm to the dragon, just annoyed it.

The justicar grabbed his daughter by the shoulders. "You can't throw your life away. Every one of us is ready to die for you."

"Which is exactly the problem," said Esprë. "I don't want any of you to do that."

Kandler gaped at the girl as he stared defiantly at him. "You're in shock," he said. "I'm half in shock myself."

"No," Esprë said, and Kandler found himself starting to hate the word. "I'm not. I'm seeing things clearly for the first time." She reached up and held Kandler by the chin. "You need to let me go."

Kandler felt like his guts might melt out of him. He grabbed her hand and held it tight. "After all we've done to take care of you, there's no way I'm going to let you throw your life away."

The justicar heard the shifting of the dragon's massive bulk behind him. The fact that the creature had yet to turn him into a bloody paste was good, but it also meant that Greffykor had decided to watch this argument with Esprë to see who might win. If Kandler failed, the dragon would have no need to kill him.

Which, of course, was Esprë's point.

"Do you think you're old enough to make this kind of decision?" Kandler asked.

Esprë's eyes flared. "It's time to quit using that argument against me," she said. "I'm older than you."

"But still not full grown." Kandler pointedly looked down at the girl. He knew he was grasping at ghosts here, but it was all he had left. "When your mother and I got married, I swore to her—"

" 'That I would always protect you.' I know. I've heard it a million times, but answer me this, Kandler. When did you think that duty would end?"

"Never!" The word surprised Kandler as it leaped from his lips, but he knew it to be the truth.

He'd thought that he would act as aging father to Esprë constant childhood until the day someone slid him into his grave. The idea that she might somehow mature then leave him had failed to enter his mind.

Esprë steamed at Kandler. As she did, he could feel the dragon move behind him. No matter how silently the creature shifted about, he displaced the air around him so much that the justicar could feel it caress his bare neck.

"It ends now," Esprë said. "I don't care about the dragon-mark any more. I never really did. I didn't want this damned thing on my back, and it seems like there's only one way for this torture my life has become to end."

"I'm not letting you give up on me."

"I'm not running from my fate," Esprë said, a wry grin twisting her lips. "I'm embracing it. From the moment that dragonmark appeared on my skin, I was doomed. At least this way I get to choose the how and the why.

"I don't want to be killed like a trapped rat," she said. "I want to go out there on my own two feet and tell that bitch of a dragon just what I think of her."

Kandler nodded as he tried to collect himself. "I understand how you feel," he said. "I really do. There's something noble in what you'd like to do."

"But what?"

"But this is no time for nobility."

Esprë laughed. "It's the perfect time."

"I'm not going to let you do this," Kandler said.

Esprë peered up at the justicar, tears welling in her eyes. "Don't make me do it," she said.

It took Kandler a moment to understand what the girl meant. Then he glanced down at her hands and saw them glowing black.

Kandler felt his heart stop, just for an instant. "Don't," he said in a soft voice.

Esprë blinked away the tears, and the blackness grew until Kandler could see it running up and down her arms too. He told himself that she would never hurt him, but he'd never seen her like this before.

"Think about this," the justicar said. "You'd kill me to save my life? You're letting your emotions rule you. Use your head."

"I—I won't kill you," Esprë said. "I just want stop you from stopping me. Just let me by. Greffykor will take me to the queen, and this will be all over."

Kandler looked back over his shoulder at the dragon looming over him. The creature stopped rubbing his eyes and gave him what he probably thought was an understanding smile. The dragon's breath smelled like ancient ice.

As Kandler brought his head back around, his gaze flicked toward Burch. The shifter had reloaded his crossbow, and he stood with the weapon aimed at Greffykor's teeth.

Kandler opened his mouth to say, "No," one more time. He'd keep repeating it to Esprë for as long as it took to sink in.

No matter how hardheaded she insisted on being about it, he would never allow her to sacrifice herself for him. That was the role of the parent, not the child.

Before he could explain all this, though, Sallah screamed in the chamber above.

"We don't have time to argue about this now," Kandler told Esprë.

The girl reached out to put a hand on Kandler, but seeing the black glow still on her fingers he pulled his arm away. "If you leave to help her, I'll surrender myself to Greffykor," she said.

Kandler hesitated. He couldn't let Esprë give herself up to the silver dragon. To do so would be certain death for her, but he couldn't just wait and listen while the red dragon made Sallah the first victim of a murderous rampage.

Something rumbled in Greffykor's chest, and it sounded like the thunder of an approaching storm. "You should listen to the girl," he said.

Kandler spun on the dragon. "You're just worried about your damned observatory." He raised his sword to strike. He refused to give Esprë up without a fight.

Burch's crossbow twanged, and a bolt whizzed past Kandler's shoulder. The dragon raised its snout, and the bolt glanced off his teeth. Then the creature pursed his lips and blew.

A blast of arctic air burst between the dragon's teeth. Kandler dodged to the side to avoid it, and it passed straight over his head in a white cone of wind.

The air above the justicar froze. Snowflakes crystallized out of nowhere and cascaded down onto his face. The dragon's breath missed him, though, and the snowflakes melted as they touched down on his skin.

Kandler rolled to his feet and glanced behind him. He saw that he hadn't been the dragon's target after all.

A frost-rimed Burch knelt on the floor, curled around his knees, his empty crossbow on the floor beside him. The frozen weapon had broken when it struck the hard, stone floor, its bow snapped in half.

At first, Kandler thought his friend might be dead. Then he heard the chattering of the shifter's teeth and saw him shivering as his body fought the dreadful cold.

Kandler took a half step back and prepared to launch himself at the dragon. It was a hopeless fight, he knew, but he hoped that he might be able to at least give the beast some sort of scar to remember him by.

Then something icy seized the justicar's sword arm. He yelped in surprise, and that emotion turned to horror as he saw Esprë's slim fingers there on his forearm, her hands glowing black.

Kandler tried to pull away from the girl, but his limbs refused to respond. The power of Esprë's dragonmark had paralyzed him. There was nothing he could do now but wait for his daughter to end his life.

From somewhere above, Kandler heard Sallah scream again.

CHAPTER

54

Te'oma peeked around the edge of the doorway leading into the observatory and saw Sallah and Xalt standing behind the red dragon. In the air, the creature had seemed large enough to swallow the sun. Here, squatting inside a building—even one so massive as this—she seemed even bigger, as if the walls bent away from her to avoid her touch.

When Sallah raised her sword to strike at the dragon, the changeling considered shouting out a warning to the queen. She knew it would be a betrayal of those she had accompanied here, but there was little love lost between her and Sallah or Xalt. To alert the queen to the danger would put the dragon in her debt.

Te'oma doubted, though, that the dragon would see it that way. She'd probably kill the changeling right after she finished incinerating the warforged and the knight. The best that Te'oma could hope for from such a betrayal would be a quicker death.

She had to admit, though, that this was not the only reason she opted to let the lady knight strike. Te'oma wanted nothing more than to see these dragons hurt—killed if possible—and if she couldn't muster the courage to attack them again herself, she at least wouldn't stand in anyone else's way.

Te'oma winced when Sallah's first blow glanced off the dragon's scales. Then she cheered silently when the lady knight's blade cut deep into the dragon queen's tail—although she slipped back behind the edge of the portal and out of the creature's sight, just in case.

As the changeling waited for the furor inside to die down, she felt like a fly on an open table. She knew that the dragon-man aboard the *Phoenix* with Monja could kill her in an instant. She lived only at the creature's whim. Fortunately, he seemed happy to ignore her for now, if only because Monja would be happily chatting his ears off.

Te'oma peeked back into the observatory in time to see Kandler—off to the right—disappearing down the hole in the floor. To the left, Xalt dragged Sallah away from the angry dragon and toward the monstrous crystal that towered against the chamber's wall.

The changeling didn't see Esprë anywhere, nor Burch. She assumed the young elf was in the shifter's capable hands, and she guessed that was where Kandler was headed too. For a moment, she considered following the justicar down the hole, to wherever it might lead, but she couldn't bring herself to risk the dragon queen spotting her.

Te'oma cursed herself. Then she cursed the Lich Queen, Tan Du, Ibrido, Majeeda, and Nithkorrh to boot. She wanted to curse her long-dead daughter, but she couldn't bring herself to do it. She cursed the girl's father instead.

He'd been so slick and sweet, the kind of male that she'd dreamed about her whole life. For one, he'd been a changeling, which meant he knew what her life had been like. She hadn't met too many of her own kind at that point, and few of them had been kind enough to spare her more than a few words, probably out of fear that their true identities might be exposed to those who lived around them.

Mondaro, though, he'd swept her into his arms and given her the first hint of love she'd ever tasted. For months, nothing could separate them. They'd taken the city of Sharn and made it their own, using their shapeshifting powers to sneak into the finest restaurants and stay in the best inns, all without ever spilling a copper from their pockets.

They'd even talked of marriage, of settling down and starting up legitimate careers, perhaps as actors in one of the local troupes. For the first time that Te'oma could remember, she'd felt happy.

Then she'd gotten pregnant.

The night she told Mondaro, he sat there in shock, unable to digest the news. The next morning when she awoke, she could not find him. She would never see him again.

Te'oma considered getting rid of the baby. She knew of an apothecary that would sell her the potion to make that happen, but she couldn't bring herself to visit his shop. She carried her little girl to term and cradled her in her arms.

Every time she looked at her daughter, though, she couldn't help but think of the girl's father. This drove her deeper and deeper into despair, and soon she couldn't bear the sight of her child's blank, cherubic face. She left her with those she thought could care for her, then she left Sharn far behind.

Te'oma had never regretted anything in her life more than that.

That is, until she agreed to find the bearer of the Mark of Death.

More than anything else, now, Te'oma needed to make up for what she'd done to Esprë. The fact that it would put a thumb in the Lich Queen's empty eye socket only added to the changeling's determination. She saw no other way to redeem herself—in the judgment of both herself and her daughter, whom she felt watching over her from beyond.

She could not let the dragons have the girl.

Te'oma stepped into the observatory just as the dragon queen took a swipe at Sallah that almost put an end to the lady knight's quest. The changeling forced herself to ignore the woman and the warforged who pulled her to temporary safety behind the massive crystal. The two had attacked the dragon as a diversion away from the girl, and Te'oma meant to take as much advantage of that as she could.

She slunk toward the hole and peered down into it. The silver dragon blasted Burch with its icy breath, then Esprë reached out and attacked Kandler with the powers granted by her dragonmark.

Te'oma stifled a gasp. She'd never dreamed that the girl would be pressed far enough into a corner to lash out at her stepfather.

"Go," the dragon said to Esprë. "I will watch over them."

Esprë knelt down next to Kandler and felt his neck for a pulse. Then she slumped over him, and Te'oma heard her muffled sobs.

"You do not have long," Greffykor said. "I will watch over them. They will not interfere."

"You must promise me you will keep them safe," the girl said. As she spoke, she moved over and stroked Burch's mane. The half-frozen shifter stopped shivering for a moment.

"That is Frekkainta's choice, not mine. I will not harm them."

Esprë stood up and wiped her face with her sleeves. "Then that will have to be enough."

The girl walked over to the rope and began to climb. She ascended faster than Te'oma would have thought she could have managed, but the girl's heart had to be pumping fast enough that she must have felt as if she were flying up the rope.

Te'oma admired the girl's resolve. Despite everything that had happened to her, she had set herself on a course from which she refused to be swayed, and she would do anything—even attack Kandler—to make sure she achieved her goal.

Te'oma felt only the tiniest pang of regret that she would have to derail those plans.

As Esprë reached the top of the hole, the changeling reached down and offered her a hand up. Despite the fact that her arms had to feel like wet noodles at that point, the girl ignored Te'oma's hand and pulled herself up to the floor above her.

"I should have known I'd find you here," Esprë said. "Every time something horrible happens, you're right by my side."

"How kind of you to eliminate your protectors." Te'oma smiled at the girl, showing her perfectly even rows of teeth. "Now you have no way to keep me from spiriting you away from here."

Esprë groaned. "We're not going to go through all that again, are we? I thought you'd given up on trying to kidnap me."

Te'oma put on a pained look. "I think of this as saving you."

"I don't want to be saved. I'm through being saved."

Te'oma smirked. "I don't recall offering you a choice."

"I've already made it."

The changeling looked down and saw the black glow suffusing the young elf's hands.

CHAPTER

55

Sallah hated screaming, but she couldn't help herself. She'd thought that Deothen had long ago hammered the urge out of her during her childhood training drills. Having a dragon queen breathe fire down at her seemed to have subverted all that though.

The lady knight took a deep breath, as if to scream once more, but this time Xalt slapped a steely hand across her mouth. He held it there until the urge to scream passed from her, and she pulled his fingers away.

The dragon put an eye up to the other side of the crystal, which magnified it until it seemed the yellowish orb had to stand at least twenty feet tall. It growled as it did, although Sallah couldn't tell if the dragon meant to say something in Draconic or just wished to growl in frustration at the way the crystal blocked most of the effects of her flames.

While the jet of fire from the dragon's mouth hadn't been powerful enough to reach all the way around the crystal, much of the heat from it had. Sallah felt rivulets of sweat slipping down the inside of her armor, soaking her from head to toe and plastering her red curls against her neck and forehead.

"I will run to the left," Xalt said. "When it follows me, you run for the doorway."

"You'll be killed."

Xalt nodded toward the dragon's monstrous eye. "That seems inevitable. This way, at least, one of us might have a chance."

Sallah considered this for a moment, then made to bolt to the left. The warforged's arms shot out and stopped her. "Let me do this," he said.

"I can't let someone else die in my stead."

"I might not die. I'm not flesh and blood like you. The fire might not affect me as much."

"Do you believe that?"

The warforged stared at her with his unblinking obsidian eyes. "Not really."

Sallah reached over and kissed Xalt on the cheek. Despite the fact that his face was made of metal and wood instead of skin, it felt warm and smelled something like wet copper.

"You're sweet," she said, "but we're getting out of this together or not at all."

The crystal before them shuddered as the dragon queen slammed one of her mighty wings into it.

This time, Xalt screamed.

❦

Monja wished nothing more than to fly the *Phoenix* straight into the observatory. She couldn't tell for sure if the airship would fit through the gigantic doorway at the end of the landing platform, but that didn't matter so much to her. She wanted to crash the craft into the observatory and destroy her, unleashing the rebellious elemental trapped in the ship's ring of fire.

With luck, such an explosion would bring the observatory tumbling down. She knew it might kill every one of her friends—and perhaps herself—but if it killed the dragons too it would be worth it.

Unfortunately, the dragon-man refused to leave her alone. She knew that he could kill her in an instant. If he wanted to, he could murder her and be off the ship before her corpse even smacked into the deck.

"Go ahead," he said to her. "Try it."

Monja stared at the dragon-man. His eyes burned like lava.

"You never know," he said as he turned to gaze at the observatory. "It might work. You might kill her. You might save them all."

Monja bit her lower lip. "You just want an excuse to kill me."

The dragon-man's lips peeled apart, showing his several rows of pointed teeth. "What makes you think I need one?"

Monja's hands felt sweaty on the airship's wheel. "You want me to kill your mother?"

The dragon-man pursed his lips and kept staring straight ahead at the observatory. "I've waited a long time to become king."

"How long?"

"Your people were still living in tents instead of burrows."

Monja's brow creased. "We do live in tents."

The dragon-man arched an eyebrow. "See? The Prophecy isn't infallible after all."

"You would let me kill your mother."

The dragon-man looked down at the shaman. "I would probably stop you."

"You don't sound too sure of yourself."

Monja could feel the elemental in the airship's ring of

fire straining at her will. The creature had no doubts about what should be done. If it could have spoken, it would have begged her to chance it, to aim the ship at the observatory's doorway and smash her into the place, to leave this world in a glorious blaze.

"No matter what you do, I win," the dragon-man said. "If you stay here, it does me no harm, and my mother will be pleased that I obeyed her orders. If you attack the observatory and fail, you will convince her that those from beyond the borders of our fair isle are unbalanced. That kind of paranoia I am sure I can exploit to my benefit."

"And if I do not fail?"

"Then I become king."

Monja waited for the dragon-man to continue talking, but he did not. Somewhere inside the observatory, Sallah screamed.

"Is this not what you want?" The palms of Monja's hands began to itch.

"Mine is a long life, and I have many tomorrows before me."

The dragon-man looked back at the halfling. "If I were to blink, your life would escape me entirely. Time is my friend." He turned back to gaze at the observatory. "It is not yours."

Monja felt the ship inch forward, right toward the open doorway. The *Phoenix* moved without the halfling willing her to, but Monja knew that the elemental within still obeyed her. The shaman wanted to charge the airship straight into the place and lay about with her until everything came tumbling down, but she knew she couldn't.

She had to trust her friends. She had to give them a chance.

She had come along with Kandler, Esprë, Burch and the others to help—to heal them when they needed it and to fly the airship. As a shaman, the need to aid others ran thick in her blood, but she had to admit that she would have come along just so she could keep flying the airship.

Monja had spent much of her life soaring through the air on the back of one glidewing or another. Since childhood, she'd taken to the sky whenever she could find one of the winged lizards ready to give her a ride.

Soaring above the waving grasses of the Talenta Plains gave the halfling the kind of perspective she could find nowhere else. In the air, she could leave her earthbound problems—which were mostly other people's problems—behind and revel in the vibrancy of life.

Flying the airship didn't feel the same.

A glidewing flew in concert with the winds. It rode the updrafts and downdrafts and currents and eddies of the sky. It danced with nature.

The airship represented power. She did not respect the weather but defied it. Nothing stood in the way of the *Phoenix*.

Monja recognized the irony that a fiery elemental—the quintessence of a natural force—powered the airship. Trapped in the rune-crusted restraining arcs, the ring of fire had been harnessed to allow the craft to own the skies. Up here in the air, it could challenge anything—even a dragon.

To have all that power in her hands intoxicated Monja. She took every spare shift at the helm that she could cadge from the others. Even though she had to stand on the middle spars to be able to see over the bridge's console, she spent almost all of her moments behind the wheel with a gleeful grin on her face.

To have all that power now, it seemed a shame not to use it. Monja felt the *Phoenix* edge forward again, and she reined the airship in hard.

From somewhere in the tower, she heard a strange bellow. It could only be the sound of a warforged's scream.

"Are you a coward?" the dragon-man asked.

Wondering what her father would think of her, Monja felt sick. What would he do in such a situation? Would he tolerate the dragon-man's taunting? Or would he make the vicious creature pay?

As lathon of the tribes of the Talenta Plains, Halpum knew all about war. He had fought bitter struggles in his youth to prevent other ambitious laths from destroying their tribe or bringing it to heel, but in his elder years, he had shunned the horrors of the battlefield for the comforts of the campfire.

It had been he who had represented all of the Talenta tribes at the peace talks that brought an end to the Last War. He had brought his fractious peoples together not through strength of arms but force of will. He had used that same skill with others to help forge the peace that now held over most of Khorvaire, ever since the signing of the Treaty of Thronehold.

He was no coward. Nor was his daughter.

Monja smiled as she wiped her hands on her shirt and then readjusted them on the airship's wheel. Despite removing her fingers from the controls for a moment, the fire elemental had not moved the ship an inch. It knew who held sway over it—at least now that she held sway over herself.

"I am content as I am," Monja said, the words flowing from her like wind under wings.

The dragon-man scowled.

CHAPTER

56

Kandler felt his heart stop.

Until that moment, he'd been able to hear his blood pounding through his veins. Despite the fact that he could not move, that Esprë had paralyzed him with her deadly powers, his heart had hammered away in his chest, faster than ever.

When he saw his daughter reach for the rope and begin the long climb back up to where the dragon queen rampaged, his heart halted in mid-beat. To have come all this way and fought so hard to save the girl, he couldn't bear to watch her charge off to sacrifice herself on his behalf.

"No," Kandler rasped, bringing his arms to his chest. The thrill he felt at being able to move again, even so weakly, paled at the pain he felt spreading across his tightening ribs. It felt like someone had sat on his sternum, meaning to crush the life from him.

The justicar wanted to say more, to call out to Esprë, to ask her—beg her—to stop, but he couldn't suck enough air into his lungs to do more than whisper, "No."

Esprë didn't hear him. If she did, she didn't look back.

He knew she couldn't be that cold-blooded to him, not after all the years they'd lived together as father and daughter. He suspected that she feared she might lose her resolve if she turned around and saw him lying there on the floor, dying. If that was true, then his only hope right now was to get her to do just that.

"Esprë." He tried to shout the words, but they came out as barely more than a whisper. He tried again, but with results no better.

Clutching his chest, he rolled over and spotted Burch. The effort took everything he had. When he tried to say the shifter's name, nothing came out.

Burch lay there before him, curled in a ball, his eyes clenched shut. Frost tipped the shifter's dark mane and furry arms, and he shivered as if someone had turned his insides to ice.

Kandler reached out and slapped Burch's arm. The shifter's yellow eyes popped open. They burned with determination.

Despite the cold that gripped him, Burch unfolded himself and rolled onto his back. Kandler saw the shifter's eyes light up when he spotted Esprë climbing the rope.

"Esp-prë!" Burch growled.

Kandler fell back and stared up at the girl. His vision had been closing in on him since his heart had stopped, and now it seemed that he gazed up at her through a long dark tunnel. She was the only light at the end of it.

She'd gotten almost halfway to the upper floor by now, but she'd stopped climbing now. Her shoulders shook, and Kandler feared that she might lose her grip and come crashing down on the unforgiving stone. He tried to call out to her once more, but he couldn't find the breath.

"Save them," Esprë said, her voice raw. She did not look back down. "Don't let them die."

Then she started climbing upward again.

Greffykor nodded at the girl's words. Then he chanted a few phrases in his native tongue. As he did, one of his claws began to glow.

The silver dragon reached out with a talon on that claw and tapped Kandler in the chest just as his world went dark. It felt like the tip of that talon might stab right through the justicar's ribs. Instead, the glow flowed from the talon into Kandler's form.

His heart started beating again. It felt weak at first, but within three beats it pounded as strong as ever. He opened his eyes and saw that Esprë had nearly made it to the upper floor.

He tried to leap to his feet, but his arms and legs would not work the way they needed to. He felt as powerless as a newborn child.

"Esprë!" he called out. The word felt strange on his tongue, but he tried it again. "Esprë!"

The girl did not stop.

Kandler flung his head to the side to see Greffykor leaning over Burch, his claw glowing once more. The dragon touched a silvery talon to the shifter's shoulder, and the color that fled from his claw enveloped Burch's form.

Where the glow touched, the frost covering the shifter melted away, leaving him soaked through. Soon, Burch stopped shivering, and his mouth twisted into a snarl.

"Don't do it!" Burch shouted after the young elf.

Kandler's stomach flipped when he saw the girl hesitate near the top of the rope. "Esprë!" he called. "Come back!"

Then he noticed the black glow spreading over the girl's hands as she reached for the lip of the upper floor.

At first, Kandler couldn't understand what she might be doing. Had she changed her mind about sacrificing herself to the dragon queen on behalf of the others? Would she try to kill the creature instead?

Then Te'oma's white oval of a face appeared leering down over Esprë's shoulder.

"No!" Kandler said.

He flipped over on to his belly and pushed himself to his knees. He spotted his fangblade on the floor in front of him and snatched it up in an unsteady fist.

The feel of the hilt in his hand gave Kandler hope. He was not a diplomat but a fighter. He solved problems not with his head but the edge of his sword. With a blade like this in his hands, anything could be possible.

The justicar didn't think about how tired he was or how much the effort to get back up hurt or about the dragon standing next to him. He focused on Esprë and her alone. He had to get up there and stop her. He had to save her somehow, whether that meant finding a way to abscond with her on the airship or just killing every damn dragon that crossed his path.

Kandler staggered to his feet and looked up to see what had happed to Esprë. The silver dragon towered there before him like a moon blocking out part of the sky.

"Get out of my way," Kandler said.

"I will not kill you," Greffykor said, "but you will not interfere. The girl has made her decision—the right decision—and you cannot stop her."

Kandler brought his sword over his head and slashed out at the dragon. Greffykor plucked back its claw but not fast enough. The fangblade hacked off one of the dragon's talons, which clattered on the floor like a dropped dagger.

Unperturbed, the dragon stood up on its hind legs, stretched its wings, and buffeted the air with them. The resultant wind knocked Kandler from his feet. He managed to keep hold of his blade, but only by sheer determination.

The dragon slunk back down onto its haunches and regarded the two intruders. His silvery eyes shone like mirrors in the light cast by the glowing runes set into the various rings that hung about the cavernous chamber.

Defiant, Kandler struggled to his feet once more, this time using his sword as a crutch to help keep himself standing tall. Locking his legs into a warrior's stance, he hefted the sword once more and prepared to charge. He meant to save Esprë now or die trying.

The justicar felt a taloned hand on his shoulder, and he spun about to find Burch standing behind him, a forlorn look on his face.

"Give it up, boss," Burch said. "She's gone."

Kandler gasped at what he could only see as an act of betrayal by his best friend. He shrugged the shifter's hand off his shoulder and brandished his sword between them.

"No," he said. "No one's going to stop me. Not even you."

"What about her?" Burch asked, pointing upward.

Kandler craned his neck back and saw nothing. Esprë wasn't there at the lip of the hole anymore, and neither was Te'oma. It took him a moment to spy what else was gone.

The rope.

"We're stuck down here," Burch said.

Kandler cast his gaze around the room, scanning the walls for some kind of opening—anything at all. There had to be another way to the upper floor: a set of stairs, a series of rungs carved into the tower's wall, a flying platform—anything.

"Your cause is hopeless," Greffykor said.

Maybe he could climb from one rotating ring to the next, Kandler thought. He sheathed his sword and leaped for the nearest one. He caught it halfway up its side, but as it took his weight it spun in midair—suspended in no way that the justicar could discern—so that he hung from its lowest possible point.

Kandler dropped back to the ground and bellowed in

rage. "This can't happen," he said. "I won't let it!"

"The choice is no longer yours," Greffykor said. "Perhaps it never was."

Kandler turned to Burch.

"Only one way out of here, boss," the shifter said. "Besides dying, that is."

Hope started to spark in Kandler's heart, but the look his friend gave him snuffed it out. Burch pointed over Kandler's shoulder at the dragon. "We got to hitch a ride."

Kandler scowled. He wondered for a moment if they could kill the dragon and then climb to the upper floor on the creature's corpse. He knew it was nothing more than a desperate fantasy though.

"All right," he said in a beaten voice, tinged with desperation. "What will it take for you to fly us up there?"

To Kandler's surprise, the dragon did not laugh at the question.

"Put down your weapons," Greffykor said, "and I will carry you up to where you wish to go."

Kandler hefted the fangblade in his hand for a moment. Without the blade, he didn't have a prayer of hurting the dragon queen, but the blade would do him no good down here.

He dumped the fangblade onto the floor. Burch's crossbow and knife clattered there next to it.

"Very well," Kandler said, feeling as naked as he ever had in his life. "Let's go."

CHAPTER

57

Te'oma backpedaled, dodging just out of Esprë's lethal reach. The changeling felt the chill air left behind in the wake of the girl's fingers as they brushed by her.

"Almost, dear." Te'oma clucked her tongue. "Though I'm afraid, as always, that you don't have that killer instinct."

Esprë snarled as she pulled herself up over the lip of the hole. "Get a little bit closer, and maybe you'll find out."

"What makes you so determined to kill me before you kill yourself?" Te'oma asked. "What difference will my fate make to you when you're dead?"

"It'll help me enjoy my last moments," the girl said. As she spoke, she reached back behind her and began to haul up the rope.

Te'oma smiled. The girl had grown a great deal in the past few weeks. Even with everything going on around her, she still kept cool enough to realize that she needed to cover her escape from Kandler and Burch. She looked very much like the girl the changeling had kidnapped in Mardakine, but she acted far more worldly.

Te'oma took some small amount of pride in knowing she

had helped make that happen. It helped to balance out the shame she felt for the same deeds.

"Do you really plan to end your life," Te'oma said, "or is this just a ploy to get close enough to kill the dragon queen?"

Esprë smirked at the changeling. She'd never looked so adult since Te'oma had known her. Something about her eyes had changed. If not older, they shone with a hard-won wisdom that had been thrust upon her by the turns her life had taken.

Te'oma imagined that the girl could never have dreamed of finding herself here in Argonnessen dealing with dragons who wanted her dead. She'd probably hoped to live for years in Mardakine with Kandler, only leaving once she'd buried him. Perhaps then she'd have made her way back to Aerenal, hoping to connect with her long-lost father.

The changeling wondered how Ledenstrae would have treated the girl if she'd never developed the dragonmark. Would he have refused to recognize her claim on him, or would he have put aside any bitterness toward her mother and taken his prodigal daughter in?

Such questions were pointless, of course. It hadn't worked out that way, and pondering such possibilities only distracted from how things really were.

Esprë seemed to have abandoned any such illusions—along with any hope for a future.

"Do you think I would have a chance?" Esprë asked. "I thought you were smarter than that."

"I used to think so too," said Te'oma. "The years keep proving me wrong."

Esprë tossed the rope to one side of the hole.

"Come with me," the changeling said. "We can escape this."

"How?" Esprë said, glancing over Te'oma's shoulder at where the dragon queen continued to knock against the gigantic crystal on the far side of the chamber.

"The airship—"

"Too slow."

"My bloodwings—"

"Not strong enough to carry us both—and too slow."

"We can hide. We can—"

"From that?" Esprë pointed at the dragon queen as the creature belched another gout of fire from its snout. "From the hundreds just like her?"

Te'oma frowned. "She'll kill us all anyhow. Your sacrifice will mean nothing."

"Then either way I'll die. At least this way I get to choose how. I get to stand there before her on my own two feet and ask for it."

"That's what you want?" Te'oma couldn't believe it. This girl had fought so hard to live.

"If I can just spit in her eye, I'll be happy."

Then Te'oma remembered how the girl had crashed the *Phoenix* straight into the Talenta Plains. Even then Esprë had been ready to die rather than surrender her life to forces beyond her control. She'd nearly killed them both in the process—and had expected to succeed.

"I can't let you do this," Te'oma said.

"You don't have anything to say about it."

Te'oma gathered her resolve deep in her mind and then lashed out with a mental blast that would have dropped a charging minotaur.

Esprë grunted and fell to one knee. The girl had been prepared for the changeling to try something like this, though, and she had her mental defenses in place.

Te'oma cursed. She'd hoped to take the girl out with a single, crushing blow. She didn't have the time to dance around the observatory with her. Sooner or later the dragon queen would get tired of trying to kill Xalt and Sallah—or would succeed—and then she'd spot Esprë. Once that happened, their dance would come to a crashing end.

Of course, the girl knew that. All she really had to do was shout at the dragon to bring doom down on her head—and Te'oma's too.

Te'oma took a deep breath through her nostrils and lanced out with her mind at a specific part of the girl's brain.

Esprë clutched her head in pain then opened her mouth to scream. Te'oma winced in anticipation, but nothing came out. The girl's lips curled in frustration, but try as she might she could not speak a single word nor utter even a feeble grunt.

Te'oma charged Esprë then. She knew that if she gave the girl a chance to think, she'd come up with some other way to get the dragon's attention, even if that meant going over and kicking the queen in her red, scaly rump.

Esprë had to present herself to the dragon though. Just getting killed wouldn't do anyone a bit of good. She needed to show the dragon her mark and explain that killing her would be enough to fulfill the dragon's needs. After that, bothering to chase down the others would only be a waste of the dragon's time.

As Te'oma came at the girl, Esprë raised her arms to defend herself. Her hands still glowed black.

Unlike a wizard or a priest, the girl didn't need her voice to activate her power. She had no incantations to recite or petitions to pray. She only needed to summon up her powers with her own will.

Te'oma drew her black-bladed knife and brandished it before her. Esprë's eyes grew wide as she watched the changeling handle the blade. Then, just as Te'oma advanced on her, the girl smiled.

Esprë came at Te'oma with her glowing-black hands spread wide. Instead of putting her arms up in front of her, she made no attempt to protect herself or to avoid the blade.

Surprised, Te'oma pulled her knife back. The girl had called her bluff. Esprë knew that the changeling wanted to save her, not kill her. To stab her with the knife would work against that goal.

Esprë smiled, and the black glow arced between her outstretched hands. Te'oma had never seen it do that before. It seemed the girl's powers were growing still.

Perhaps Kandler had been wrong not to take the girl into hiding. If they had tried that, they might have been able to delay the inevitable long enough for all of Esprë's horrible powers to reach maturity. Then she might have stood a real chance against the dragons or any others who would have wished to harm her.

Still, to then have to live her life forever on the run, only able to keep people away by killing them, that wasn't what Esprë wanted, but wouldn't that be better than being dead?

Apparently not, from the girl's point of view.

Esprë swiped at Te'oma again, and the changeling ducked out of the way. The glow on the girl's hands seemed to whisper with the muted accusations of the souls of those she had already killed. Her voice may not have worked, but her powers strove to speak for her.

Te'oma reached deep into the darkest pockets of her mind, struggling to summon up enough power to stab once more into Esprë's brain. She figured she'd only get one more chance at taking the girl out before everything went to hell.

When learning to hone her mental powers, Te'oma had spent many hours—days, even—meditating, practicing at concentrating. Whereas some students of the mind liked to cloister themselves in silent abbeys or dank dungeons, she preferred to work at her art in the midst of chaos. She went to the main square of whatever town she was in at dawn and stayed there until dusk, forcing herself to tune out any distractions that came her way.

In the wealthier cities, she'd put an empty hat in front of her to collect change from those passersby who thought her a sad veteran of the Last War. In such efforts, she rarely sat alone.

The trick, she had found, was to be able to ignore everything about yourself but the threats. Discerning a true threat when concentrating on something else wasn't easy, and Te'oma had taken many a boot in the rib before she managed to master the skill. Eventually, though, she'd come to know instinctually the difference between a threat, a bluff, and the bluster of life.

All that training paid off now when Esprë came at Te'oma. Instead of stepping out of the way—or just turning tail to run—the changeling knew what the girl was after. She wanted not to kill but to die.

Esprë raised her arms, her hands strained into the shape of claws, and charged straight at Te'oma. The changeling knew that if she let the girl by she'd keep running past her until she could tap on the dragon queen's tail.

Te'oma reached out and grabbed Esprë's glowing arms by the wrists instead.

Esprë screamed in frustration at the changeling, although no sound came from her mouth. Then she flexed her arms and started to bring her hands together.

The girl's anger at the changeling had pushed her over the edge. Her use of her dragonmark was no longer an idle threat. If Esprë managed to touch Te'oma with one of her hands, the changeling would die.

"Don't," Te'oma whispered. "You don't really want to kill me." She hoped she could convince the girl to believe in the lie.

Esprë snarled voicelessly at the changeling.

Holding Esprë like this, Te'oma couldn't help but think of all the horrible things she'd done in her life. The worst—surpassed only, possibly, by abandoning her own daughter—had been to turn this innocent child into a murderer.

When Te'oma had first entered Esprë's life, the girl's powers had already started to kill, but without Esprë's knowledge or control. When the girl had discovered what had happened, she'd been mortified.

Since then, Esprë had been pushed into trying to kill others over and over again. Each time, she'd approached the task with some reluctance—or so Te'oma had told herself, perhaps to assuage her own conscience.

Now, though, the girl held nothing back. She wanted to kill the changeling before she died.

Te'oma's vision blurred, and for a moment she feared that the girl had managed to use her dragonmark's powers against her after all. Then she blinked away the tears that had formed in her eyes.

"You don't have to do this," Te'oma said, her voice raw and pained. "You don't."

The girl pulled herself backward and crumpled toward the ground. Surprised, Te'oma kept her grasp on the girl's wrists and toppled over on top of her. It wasn't until she started to fall forward that the changeling realized her mistake. If she and the girl fell to the floor together, she'd be at the girl's mercy.

Te'oma released Esprë's wrists and tried to pluck her

hands away. The girl's left hand shot out, though, and caught the changeling around the shoulder.

As the black glow began to flow from Esprë into Te'oma, the girl mouthed a single word at the panicked changeling. "Die!"

Te'oma gathered everything she had left in her mind and formed it into a black-bladed knife. "There's no other way," she said. "I'll do whatever it takes."

With but a single, desperate thought, she flung the blade at Esprë's brain.

Everything turned black.

CHAPTER

58

The dragon queen smashed the horned crests that ran along the top of her head into the crystal again. She had already forced a half-dozen spiderweb-patterned sets of cracks into the opposite surface of the crystal in the same way. This time, though, Sallah heard something larger give, and she looked up to see that a good chunk of the crystal had caved away. The shard toppled from the top of the crystal and shattered on the stone floor near the crimson dragon's feet.

"We can't hide back here much longer," Xalt said. He had stopped screaming, but his voice still held a histrionic edge.

"We don't have anywhere else to go!" Sallah said. She peered around the crystal and spotted Esprë and Te'oma talking near the hole.

The knight's heart sank. If Esprë had come up from the lower level by herself—without Kandler or Burch—then something horrible had to be wrong. Te'oma had disappeared before they'd reached the observatory. What could she be doing with the girl now?

Although Burch had vouched for Te'oma, Sallah shared Kandler's distrust of the changeling. If not for her, they would be safe in Flamekeep now, with Esprë in the caring hands of the Voice of the Flame.

The dragon smashed into the crystal. Once more, a piece that could have crushed Sallah dead cascaded to the floor.

Xalt screamed.

Sallah turned on him and snarled. "When did you lose your nerve?"

Xalt froze. "Is this not the right way to act in such a situation? I was taking my cues from you."

If Sallah had thought for a moment that the warforged was mocking her, she'd have considered separating his head from his shoulders and then toting around his skull as a warning to others who might be tempted to try it. As it was, she knew he meant her no disrespect. The dragon had rattled her, and she'd let it show.

She hadn't acted so cowardly in the battle with Nithkorrh, but she hadn't faced the great beast directly in that fight. Now, come face to snout with an enraged dragon the size of a cathedral, she'd given in to fear and taken to cowering behind cover like some common mercenary. If her father could see her now, he would turn away from her and hang his head in shame, she knew.

This had to end.

The dragon queen smacked her head into the crystal again, and another boulder-sized piece of it came away. The beast roared in triumph, so loud that Sallah wondered if her ears might bleed. Only half of the crystal remained now. It would disappear entirely with just a few more blows.

Sallah peeked around the crystal again and saw Esprë and Te'oma wrestling with each other. The girl's hands glowed in a telltale shade of black.

The knight turned back and grabbed Xalt by the shoulder.

She pointed behind him. "I need you to run as fast as you can in that direction."

"Of course," Xalt said. "I will lead the way."

Sallah started to say something, but yet another crystal-cracking strike from the dragon cut her off.

"Go!" she yelled at the warforged. She spun him about and slapped him on the back. "Go!"

Xalt took off as ordered and did not look back. Sallah spun on her heel and chased around the other side of the crystal instead.

The dragon queen reared up for another attack and froze in mid-strike. Her head snapped to her right, her eyes following Xalt's progress as he dashed away, oblivious to the fact that Sallah had not followed him.

Then she roared and started after him.

For a creature so large and powerful, the dragon queen moved with surprising grace. She lowered her head to the ground and prowled forward, every stride of her gigantic legs pulling her forward faster than the warforged could run. She would be on him before he could find another place to hide.

The dragon queen's tongue slithered across her slavering lips as she closed in on the hapless Xalt.

As the dragon turned, Sallah raced around behind her. There, still stuck in the dragon's tail, hung the knight's blazing sword. Black-baked blood caked the blade, and the tip of it had been broken off at the point where it had stuck out of the dragon's scales. The hilt still jabbed up out of the dragon queen's flesh, though, and Sallah charged straight for it.

While the dragon moved fast, it took a moment for her tail to catch up, and Sallah leaped atop the end of it. This part of the tail was nearly severed from the rest. The dragon's thrashing attempts to dislodge the sword had only made matters worse, and Sallah doubted the creature could even feel her back here on the deadened flesh.

Somewhere up ahead, Xalt screamed again. Sallah hated that she hadn't been able to explain her plan to the warforged. He probably thought that she'd abandoned him for her own gain, perhaps plotting to slink away while the dragon queen tore him to pieces.

It added up to just one more reason why she could not fail.

Sallah pulled herself up the dragging tail, hand over hand, until she could reach her sword's gleaming hilt. As she went, she looked up the vermillion crest that ran up the dragon queen's back, right from the tip of her tail to where it split at the base of her neck and thrust along either side of the crown of her skull. It felt like looking up a mountain.

Just as she put her hand out for what was left of her sword, the dragon came to a halt and reared up on her haunches. The sudden movement threatened to throw the knight from her seat. She knew, though, that the change meant that the dragon meant to strike. If the knight did not act soon, the beast would destroy Xalt with a single, crushing blow.

Sallah snapped out her hand and closed it around her sword's hilt. As she did, she let her body fall backward. The weight of her armored form pried the weapon free.

As the blazing sword left the dragon's tail, it cut through the flesh there again. The dragon queen stiffened, then threw back her head and howled.

Sallah let her momentum roll her off the dragon's tail and somersaulted to her feet. She stood there, her broken sword in hand, still defiantly blazing away, and shouted out a prayer.

"Silver Flame, guide my way!" she cried as the dragon turned to face her.

The dragon queen's head spun about on her sinuous

neck first, her gaze darting back and forth until it landed on Sallah and her sword-shard. The creature's eyes narrowed, the reptilian slits in the great yellow orbs constricting until they seemed like vertical lines.

The dragon's tail cocked back, and Sallah tensed, ready to move. When the tail whipped around, she leaped into the air. The dragon queen, though, had anticipated this, and the tail came up and knocked the woman's legs from beneath her.

The blow sent Sallah clanging to the floor. Despite that, she kept her grip on her sword.

By the time Sallah had scrambled back to her feet, the dragon queen had spun her entire body around, bringing the whole of her fearsome visage to bear on the knight.

Sallah felt a tremor pass through her body, but she suppressed it. If these were to be her last moments in this world, she refused to spend them afraid. She held her broken sword before her, interposing its silvery light between herself and the dragon.

The flickering blaze echoed in Sallah's own soul and set it afire. She felt the heat of it burn in her eyes in her determination to deport herself as she had always been meant to be: a Knight of the Silver Flame.

"Come, queen of dragons," Sallah said. "Let us bring this to an end."

The monstrous creature peered down at the knight as if she'd come across some curious insect crawling across her path, something that bore closer inspection before she crushed it. A low growl escaped from her mouth. It sounded like rolling thunder.

Sallah assumed a warrior's stance. From here, she could not reach the dragon's snout or neck. The creature had been hurt once already, and the wound had made it cautious.

Sallah considered charging the beast, her sword held

high. One look at the dragon's maw told her all she needed to know about how well that would succeed. The creature could swallow her whole then use her blade to pick her teeth.

"Wait!" a voice said behind her.

Sallah snapped her head around to see Esprë walking up behind her, an unfamiliar look painted on her face.

The moment Sallah took her eyes from the dragon queen's, she knew she had made a mistake. She heard the rush of air as the creature's head darted forward. She had time to say a single word before the slab-like snout smashed into her in an attempt to snuff out her light forever.

"Run!" Sallah said to Esprë.

The instant before the dragon's attack knocked her senseless, though, she recognized the look in the young elf's eyes. She would do anything but run.

CHAPTER

59

Kandler hadn't felt so helpless since the Day of Mourning. Trapped in a dragon's clutches as the silver creature took to the air with both him and Burch in its clutches, he knew he had no power at all.

He lived and breathed only at Greffykor's whim. If the dragon wished, it could crush him between its talons before he could scream for it to stop. Kandler told himself not to do anything to make the dragon angry.

The worst part, though, was knowing that he would probably have to do just that. If Greffykor insisted on keeping the justicar from saving Esprë, then he would have no choice.

Kandler wished that the dragon hadn't made him give up his sword. Trying to kill a dragon—or even hurt it—with his bare hands would be like trying to cart away a mountain without even a shovel. The fangblade could cut through dragon scales the way nothing else would, but now it lay on a floor at least twenty yards below, although it might as well have been a world away.

When Kandler reached the upper floor, he scanned

the room for Esprë. He found her—in the worst possible situation.

Against the far wall, the dragon queen had trapped a terrified Xalt. The only reason the dragon hadn't yet turned the warforged into a pile of ash was because Sallah stood on her tail, wrenching the remnants of her broken blade out of the creature's tail. Esprë came stalking up behind the lady knight, getting closer to the dragon queen with every step.

Kandler tried to shout out a warning to her, but Greffykor squeezed his chest hard the moment he took a large breath. His yell came out only as the barest wheeze.

"We will watch this happen," the silver dragon said. "We will not interfere."

Kandler looked to Burch and saw the shifter struggling against the dragon's grip too. He had as much success as the justicar did at prying loose those silvery talons: none. They seemed to be made of polished steel rather than flesh, and they gave not one inch despite Kandler's most desperate efforts to make them move.

The dragon queen knocked Sallah flat, and Kandler tried to shout again, this time in dismay. Greffykor stifled him once more.

"If you do not cease your struggles, I will kill you," Greffykor said. "This is far too important for you to disrupt."

Esprë stood over Sallah's fallen form, between the lady knight and the dragon. "Leaver her alone!" she shouted. "I'm the one you want!"

The dragon queen paused and considered the young elf's words. Then she opened her mouth and arched her neck back as she prepared to strike.

"Wait!" Esprë said. "I wish to make a bargain with you."

The dragon ignored her. Kandler could see that the

creature would just slay the girl on the spot.

"I am the one with the dragonmark!" Esprë shouted. "I bear the Mark of Death!"

The dragon queen's eyes flew wide, and her mouth snapped shut. She regarded the girl in suspicion. She turned one eye toward Esprë and squinted at her as if she were an unusual—rare, even—cut of meat.

The dragon queen snarled something at the girl. Her voice was low and calm, despite the way her nostrils flared and tossed off rising plumes of smoke.

"She requires proof," Greffykor said, translating for everyone else in the room.

Esprë spun about and spied Kandler and Burch in the silver dragon's clutches. As she did, the creature relaxed his grip on them. Kandler still had no hope of breaking free, but at least now he could breathe freely.

"Esprë!" Kandler said. "Get out of here!"

The girl lowered her head and shook it. Kandler couldn't remember seeing her so serious, so sad, since word of her mother's death.

"Good-bye, Father," she said to him. Then she turned her back on him and Burch and faced the dragon.

"I will surrender to you," Esprë said, "if you swear to leave here afterward and let Greffykor and his other guests be."

The dragon made a halting, coughing sound that Kandler could only guess was meant to be a laugh. Then it snarled at the girl.

As the dragon spoke, Kandler spotted Xalt creeping around behind the dragon. The warforged seemed to be looking for a means of attacking the dragon or—barring that—charging out and running off with Esprë.

Before he could make a move, though, the dragon queen's tail lashed out and caught him in the chest, knocking him flat against the tower's far wall. It stayed there then, pinning Xalt against the wall. The cut Sallah had made in the dragon's tail started to bleed once again, and some of the crimson liquid trickled over Xalt's legs, but the dragon queen ignored it.

"Frekkainta is curious to know why she shouldn't just kill you all," Greffykor said. "Permit me to answer that."

The silver dragon held up Kandler and Burch to illustrate the point he planned to make. "These people are my guests, and they have no means of harming you. If you insist upon trying to jail me and kill them, I will fight you tooth and claw. You may defeat me, but I will make you pay for your victory."

"And," said Esprë, "once you do what you came here for—to find the dragonmark and destroy it—it would be a waste of your time to bother with the rest of us. Why would my friends and family be worth even your notice?"

The dragon queen murmured something in a tone of grudging assent.

"Also," Esprë said, "if you do not swear to let the others go free, I will kill you. I have learned many things about my dragonmark over the past few weeks, and I believe I can work it to stop your heart cold in your chest."

The dragon queen regarded Esprë with a stony eye.

Kandler renewed his struggles to free himself from Greffykor's grasp. The moment he moved, though, the dragon tightened its grip enough that the justicar could barely breathe once more.

"Esprë!" Kandler shouted. "No!"

The dragon queen nodded at the girl and growled softly at her.

Greffykor cleared his throat and said, "The dragon queen finds your terms adequate and agrees to them—provided you do bear a dragonmark."

Esprë grunted. Then she turned about and tore open her shirt to her navel. Maintaining her modesty, she pushed the fabric back, exposing the skin between her shoulder blades to the dragon's eyes.

The dragon queen reached forward with a taloned claw and tugged the shirt back just an inch farther. As she did, Kandler noticed the girl shaking like a sail tacking toward the wind. He wondered if she might collapse before the dragon could see what it wanted to find. He hoped so.

The dragon queen growled something soft. As she did, Esprë raised her bright blue eyes and stared straight at Kandler. A tear rolled out of her reddened lids.

The justicar strained and pulled at Greffykor's talons. "Let go of me, damn it! Let me go!"

In the dragon's other hand, Burch struggled and fought like a wild animal. His teeth and claws could not get past Greffykor's silvered scales. He might as well have been trying to chew on a suit of armor. The shifter howled in frustration and desperation, but Greffykor grip altered not one bit.

Kandler cast about everywhere for help. He refused to just let this happen.

The dragon queen still had Xalt trapped under her bleeding tail. The warforged tried to reach for the open wound, but his arms were not long enough by at least a yard.

Sallah lay sprawled on the ground, her broken sword fallen from her curled fingers. She might just be unconscious, but Kandler feared she could just as easily be dead.

In a break between Burch's howls, Kandler heard the crackle of the *Phoenix*'s ring of fire as she hovered moored over the landing platform outside.

"Monja!" Kandler shouted. "Monja!"

Burch took up the call too. "Monja!" the two friends

shouted in unison, their voices already run hoarse.

The halfling didn't respond, and the airship didn't move. Kandler wondered if the little shaman might also be dead, but that didn't matter to him now. All he cared about was stopping the dragon queen from killing his daughter.

Where, he asked himself, was Te'oma? He'd written the changeling off long ago, but her affection for Esprë was clear. He couldn't believe that she'd just stand by and watch the girl sacrifice herself—unless, of course, she was already dead too.

The blood-colored dragon stooped low over the girl and turned her snout so that she could focus a single eye on the dragonmark between Esprë's shoulders. She grunted, and noxious, black smoke billowed from her nostrils.

Turn around, Esprë, Kandler thought

Then the dragon queen sat back on her haunches again and spread her lips wide. This exposed all her rows of sharp, vicious teeth, most of which were long enough that they could have been used to fashion a fangblade like the one Kandler had been forced to leave behind.

Kandler shuddered in horror.

"The dragon queen finds the girl's offer acceptable," Greffykor said. Not a trace of emotion tainted the silver dragon's voice.

"Remember me," Esprë said. Then she turned to face the dragon queen and accept her fate.

The crimson dragon huffed in a great gulp of air and held it inside her for a moment.

"NOOOO!" Kandler shouted.

The dragon queen's snout snapped forward, and a jet of fire gouted from between her teeth. The blinding orange flames swallowed Esprë whole, and the girl screamed. The sound lasted only an instant before it was cut short.

The dragon continued to drench the girl in fire.

Esprë—who now seemed nothing more than a blackened silhouette framed in the incinerating blaze—fell to her knees for a heartbeat and then collapsed on the stone floor, flames engulfing her on every side.

Kandler kept screaming until his voice gave out, but the dragon did not stop. She poured fire from her gullet onto the girl for what seemed like forever, until nothing remained but ashes and tiny fragments of bone.

When the dragon queen finally stopped, the stone floor glowed bright red in a circle centered on what little was left of Esprë. Wisps of smoke trailed up from the tiny pile of remains, reaching up through the observatory to the stars watching down from the open sky above.

Then the dragon queen took another deep breath and blew the last bits of ash away. In an instant the floor cooled and cracked where Esprë had last stood, and nothing remained of her but those last few tendrils of smoke still wafting into the night sky.

CHAPTER

60

Kandler felt like his heart might burst. He slouched forward in Greffykor's iron grip and buried his face in his hands.

He allowed himself only an instant of grief at that moment, then wiped his face and stretched back up tall. He would weep for his daughter later. First, he wanted to memorize her murderer's face, so he would know her later when he found her and punished her for her deeds.

The dragon queen snarled at Greffykor, then spread her wings and leaped into the air. Instead of passing over Kandler and Burch and their silvery captor, she zoomed straight up toward the tower's open top, disappearing into the night sky. She left only the horrible scent of Esprë's execution behind.

Greffykor leaned forward and deposited Kandler and Burch on the floor before him. The justicar raced over to where Sallah lay on the floor.

Freed from the dragon queen's tail, Xalt had already reached the knight's side, but he had not touched her yet. "She is still breathing," the warforged said, "although not well."

Kandler nodded his thanks to Xalt as he knelt and put his arms under the woman's shoulders. "Take her legs," he said. "With her armor on, she's too heavy for me to carry alone."

"Perhaps we should remove it."

"We don't have the time. We need to get her to Monja right now."

Xalt put his hands under Sallah's legs and nodded. The two lifted the knight together and began to carry her toward the doorway.

"I am so sorry for—"

"Not now," Kandler said, choking up as he spoke. "It's too late for Esprë, but maybe not Sallah."

Greffykor swept out of the way as Kandler and Xalt trotted Sallah out of his home. The silver dragon watched them every moment, seemingly oblivious to the murderous looks Kandler shot his way. As Kandler and the others left, Greffykor turned to examine his destroyed crystal, a mournful look on his reptilian face.

Burch met them at the tall, open archway. "Monja brought the airship down closer," he said as he guided them into the chill night air.

Outside on the landing platform, Kandler saw the *Phoenix* hovering to the right. Her deck hung level with the platform now, and Monja waved to them tentatively from where she stood on the wheel.

Burch leaped from the platform to the airship and grabbed the gangplank. He thrust it over the gunwale, and as soon as it touched down Kandler and Xalt bore the unconscious Sallah onto the main deck.

Before Kandler could turn around to tell Burch to take the wheel, the shifter had already done so. Monja leaped down from the bridge and dashed over to inspect the knight.

"What in the names of the spirits happened in there?" the shaman said as she bent over the knight.

"You didn't see the red dragon?" Kandler asked.

Monja peeled open Sallah's eyelids. "Of course, I had her son out here to keep me company." She felt her neck for a pulse. "He took off as soon as he saw her fly out of the top of the tower."

Kandler grimaced. He wanted to blame the halfling for not doing something, but what could she have done? None of the others had been able to stop the dragon queen either. Even trying would have probably cost Monja her life too.

He realized he should probably have been grateful that so many of them had survived their meeting with the dragon queen. He just couldn't manage to muster that feeling up.

"Can you help her?" Kandler asked.

"Give me some room," Monja said.

As Kandler stepped back, the halfling spread her arms wide and looked up toward the sky. She chanted a heartfelt prayer to her people's spirits, and a warm, golden glow flowed around her arms. She reached forward and laid her hands on either side of Sallah's forehead.

The pleasant glow flowed off of Monja's hands and surrounded Sallah instead. As Kandler watched, the woman's breathing grew steadier, and the creases of pain in her brow smoothed down.

As Monja sat back to examine her work, Kandler knelt down next to Sallah and took her hand in his. After a moment, her emerald eyes fluttered open, and she smiled up at him.

"Did we do it?" Sallah asked.

Kandler swept the woman up in his arms and clutched her to his chest. Gratitude that she would be all right washed over him then, and sobs wracked his body.

"Oh, no," Sallah said softly as she began to weep with him. "Oh, no."

Monja glanced at Burch with a questioning look, and he gave her a grim nod. She covered her mouth with her hands, stifling an exclamation of grief. The shifter knelt down and reached out for her, and she buried her face in his shoulder.

Xalt stood watching over the others. "Never before in my life," he said, "have I wished I could cry."

After a moment, Greffykor lumbered out of his observatory, framed against the light spilling out through the archway. Kandler loosened his grasp on Sallah and kissed her on her full lips, light and tenderly. Then, arm in arm, they got to their feet.

"What is it?" Kandler said. "Come to tell us that the dragon queen has changed her mind?"

For an instant, he hoped she had. He felt like the one thing he wanted at the moment would be to die trying to pull the dragon's eyes from her head with his bare hands.

Greffykor's snout swung from side to side. The dragon didn't say a word. Kandler thought the creature's shame in failing to stand up to the dragon queen might have silenced him.

Then a small shape detached itself from the dragon's silhouette and ran toward the ship.

CHAPTER

61

As the figure approached, Kandler froze in Sallah's arms. Then he grabbed her hand and pulled her along with him as he rushed down the gangplank. The others raced along behind them.

There on the edge of the wide, flat landing platform— her bright-eyed face lit in warm tones by the airship's ring of fire—stood Esprë.

Kandler and Sallah pulled up just shy of the girl and stared at her. With the tears he'd cried for her still wet on his face, he couldn't believe his eyes. He reached out with an unsure hand to touch her.

"Are you . . . ?"

He'd just seen her incinerated. She couldn't be real. Perhaps her ghost had come back to haunt him for his failure to protect her. He knew he deserved no less torment than that.

When his fingers reached her face, though, he felt no chill spirit but warm flesh. At his touch, she grinned and leaped into his arms.

Kandler reveled in the moment, refusing to let her go.

He kissed her cheek and felt her giggle with laughter and relief, and he joined her. He shamelessly wept fat tears of joy.

"How?" he said eventually, letting her go enough that he could look her in the face.

Esprë shook her head, still groggy. "I don't know. The last thing I remember was fighting with Te'oma. Then I woke up in one of the cabinets near the doorway. I had to knock for Greffykor to let me out."

The girl looked around at the others staring at her. "What happened to the dragon queen?" she asked.

Kandler gasped. He knew.

He held Esprë tight and told her how Te'oma had taken her place.

The girl nearly collapsed in his arms.

"How?" Esprë said, stunned. "Why?"

"She told me once she had a lot to make up for," Burch said, calling from his spot at the wheel.

"She said that to me too," said Xalt. "I thought she meant to apologize for stabbing me when we were in Construct."

"By the light of the Flame," Sallah said. "She redeemed herself."

"May the spirits bless her," Monja said before she headed back for the bridge, "wherever her soul may now rest."

While Te'oma might have won Kandler's respect and undying gratitude with her death, he could not suppress how he felt about the results. "The dragon queen thinks you're dead."

Esprë grinned and hugged Kandler with all her might. "Does this mean it's all over?" she said, her voice filled with wonder.

"I am afraid not," Greffykor said.

All eyes turned toward the dragon, who had loomed silently over the joyful reunion until now. Burch trotted up to stand beside Kandler, a loaded crossbow in his hands. The justicar flexed his empty hands, remembering that his fangblade still lay where he had cast it aside in the lower level of the observatory.

"I plan to take my daughter and fly out of here," Kandler said. "You're not going to stop me."

"No," Esprë said, standing away from him. "I will."

Kandler narrowed his eyes at his daughter. "Explain."

"The dragon queen thinks I'm dead. She will probably spread word of that far and wide." The girl looked to Greffykor for confirmation, which she received.

"That's just what we want," Kandler said.

"It won't last," said Esprë. "How did the Lich Queen know where to find me? Or the Keeper of the Flame?"

Sallah frowned. "The emergence of your dragonmark alerted those who keep their fingers on the pulse of the world."

"Would they be fooled by what they'll see as a rumor of my death?"

"Got a point," Burch said ruefully.

"So we go back to the original plan," Kandler said. "We confront the bastards behind this brewing conflict and put an end to it."

Monja cleared her throat then blushed as the others turned to look at her. "Well," she said, "that was never all that much of a plan, was it?"

Kandler bristled at the comment, mostly because he could not deny it. "Did anyone have a better idea?" he asked.

"Not at the time," Xalt said, "but I think Esprë does now."

Kandler's heart sank as he looked to the girl. "You seem older," he said. He wasn't sure who'd changed, though, him or her.

"I hear coming back from the dead can do that to you." She offered him a weak smile, and he clung to it.

"Tell me," he said.

Esprë frowned, and Kandler braced himself.

"I have to stay here," she said. "Forever."

Kandler's knees wobbled. Sallah put her arm around him, and he leaned on her a bit.

"Of course," said Xalt. "You'll be safe here."

Monja stared up at the top of the tower. "Won't the people who found Esprë before just find her here?"

Greffykor shook his head. "My observatory is invisible to magical detection. As long as Esprë stays here with me, no one will be able to find her."

"The dragon queen knew where we were because she followed us," said Sallah.

Esprë craned her neck back and looked up at the silver dragon. "Is that an invitation?"

"I offered before to keep you here," Greffykor said. "You may stay as long as you wish. My home will be your own."

Kandler grumbled. "How is this going to work? Where will she sleep? How are you going to feed her? What if other dragons come to visit?"

Esprë cut Kandler off with a hand laid across his lips.

"Greffykor is a powerful sorcerer. He can care for me here."

"Why?" Kandler said, eyeing the dragon. "Why would you do that for her?"

"It would give me a chance to study her dragonmark," Greffykor said. "It is an unparalleled chance to research the effects of such a mark on the Prophecy. Perhaps I might even be able to determine if it is, in fact, the Mark of Death."

"It's not?" said Kandler. Hope warred with outrage in his head. "Then what's all this been about? You can't tell me we've gone through all this because of some sort of mystical case of mistaken identity."

"The Voice of the Silver Flame herself sent me to Mardakine to find the Mark of Death," said Sallah. "I do not believe that she would make such a mistake."

"Did she say 'the Mark of Death'?" Monja asked. "Those exact words?"

"I—"

"I remember Deothen saying you came looking for a 'lost mark,' " said Burch.

"Only one mark has ever been lost," Sallah said, struggling to keep her tone even.

"That you know of," said Xalt.

Sallah opened her mouth to respond, but Greffykor cut her off. The dragon snorted puffs of icy air from his snout. "There are other dragonmarks beside the true marks. Sometimes these aberrations resemble the true marks. There is something unusual about the mark on this girl, but I am no expert on such matters. Whether or not it is the Mark of Death is not important. No one has seen that dragonmark for centuries, and most of those souls have long since passed on. While the memories of dragons are long, they are not always without fault. It may be impossible to tell for sure."

"If it's not the Mark of Death, then Esprë can come—"

"If it is the Mark of Death, nothing changes, boss," Burch said. "Even if it's not, it's still something everybody wants, and nothing changes again."

Kandler closed his mouth. "Why do you always have to be right?" he asked.

"Force of habit."

"I'll be safe here," Esprë said. "I can study sorcery under Greffykor. We can research my dragonmark together and learn how to harness every bit of its powers."

"It may only be a century or two before we learn enough to set you free," Greffykor said. "The time will pass swiftly."

"I'll be lucky to live another forty years," Kandler said softly.

The dragon stiffened then gave Kandler a woeful look. "I can barely imagine a life so short. Other than elves and dwarves, you people seemed doomed from your hatching."

"I'll miss you," Esprë said, reaching out and caressing her stepfather's unshaven cheek.

Kandler refused to mourn losing the girl in front of her. "It's all right, Esprë," he said, his voice brimming with affection. "We both knew I'd end up leaving you sooner or later. I just always hoped for much, much later."

He leaned down and kissed Esprë on the cheek then used his thumb to wipe away the single tear that rolled down her face. He smiled at her as his heart shattered inside him.

"Your mother would be so proud of you," he said.

CHAPTER

62

As dawn rose over the Dragonreach, Kandler stood on the bridge of the *Phoenix*, staring toward the rising sun behind them as it chased the night away. The wind ruffled his hair and curled around him like an old friend that wanted to carry him away to show him all the new things it had discovered since he'd been gone.

Burch and Monja were sleeping in the hold. They'd been up for most of the night, letting the spent Kandler and the battered Sallah get some much-needed rest. Xalt had orchestrated the switch between shifts when he noticed Monja falling asleep on top of the wheel.

"You did the right thing," Sallah said, curling an arm around him, keeping her other hand on the airship's wheel.

With Esprë and Te'oma gone, only she and Monja were left as decent pilots. Kandler or Burch could handle the airship in a pinch, but they were rank amateurs when compared to the skill the two ladies showed with the *Phoenix*.

Xalt had no aptitude for flying the airship at all. The one time he tried, the craft bucked so hard that Monja had almost been sent flying off the ship to drown in the surf far below. The others never let him near the wheel again.

"I know," Kandler said. "At least I think I do. Who can tell for sure?"

"Do you regret it already?"

"I regretted it the moment I agreed to it. I just didn't see any other way."

Sallah stared out at the fading stars toward which the airship ran. "Time will grant you the perspective you need."

"How do you know that?"

"I have my faith. It serves me well. You were not the only one to lose a loved one on this quest."

"Was that what it was?" Kandler asked. "It seemed more like a chase to me." He kissed her on the cheek. "I'm sorry about your father."

"So am I. At least I know his troubles are over and that he has found rest in a better place." She gave him a sidelong glance then pecked him on the lips. "Perhaps you could say the same of Esprë."

Kandler nodded silently as he held the woman in his arms and tried to enjoy the moment. It would be at least two weeks before they would see the coast of Khorvaire. There was no need to bring up any burning issues now. It would be better to let them lie, to savor what he had right then instead.

He just couldn't do it.

"She's not quite as unreachable as your father, though," he said, testing the waters.

"True enough," Sallah said. "I don't know how wise it would be for you to arrange a visit with her soon though. The less contact you have with her, the safer she'll be."

"Good point," Kandler said. "That's not exactly what I meant though."

Sallah pursed her lips. "Speak plainly then. Please."

Kandler took a step back from the knight. "I need to— What do you plan to tell your superiors back in Flamekeep?"

Sallah lowered her eyes. "I wondered when you might consider that question. Do you not trust me?"

Kandler searched for a hint of anger in her voice but found none. "I do. I would put my life in your hands, but this is Esprë's life we're talking about, and keeping her location—or even the fact that she still lives—a secret means you would have to lie to your superiors in your order."

Sallah grimaced. "Perhaps even to Jaela Daran herself."

"Can you bring yourself to do that?"

"Do you expect me to?"

"Yes."

"Why?"

The question stunned Kandler. "To keep Esprë alive. To save her from all the bastards out there who would like to use her for their own ends."

"Do you think the Church of the Silver Flame is not to be trusted?"

Kandler groaned. "Do you really want to get into this with me?"

"Yes," Sallah said. "I am a Knight of the Silver Flame. There is nothing in my life that is more important than the Flame itself. I'd like to know how you feel about it."

"I don't care much for gods or churches of any kind," Kandler said. "I don't think the Silver Flame is evil, but it's made up of men and women with lots of different agendas. It doesn't take much for me to think of a way how one of your church elders might decide that going to Argonnessen to take Esprë back to Flamekeep would be the right thing to do."

Kandler stopped and stared at the knight. "You considered that yourself, didn't you?"

Sallah met the justicar's gaze. "Of course I did. That was the mission I was given."

"Why didn't you go through with it?"

Sallah frowned. "It seems that I am a rotten knight."

Kandler softened his stance. "That's not—"

"I failed to complete a mission of the utmost importance, not because I couldn't have done so but because I chose not to. Some would say that such actions are tantamount to treason."

"Who would say that?"

"My father, for one."

"You're saying your father would have hurt Esprë."

"Not directly, but to him, orders were orders, and the law was the law. In his mind, his duty was always clear. He never let anything stand between him and getting his job done. Esprë's welfare would have paled in comparison to that."

"You're not your father."

"That's all too clear, I think." Sallah looked off toward the darkness again, her lips a tight, straight line.

Kandler wanted to wrap his arms around her then and tell her everything would be all right. She could give up being a knight and go away with him to somewhere—anywhere—else. They could put all this behind them and forget about it, or at least try.

He knew it would never work. Sallah loved the Silver Flame. Her vocation, her calling to become a knight, defined her. To ask her to abandon that would be to ask her to abandon herself.

"You're a great knight," Kandler said, moving closer to her.

"I don't see how you can say that," she said. He had to strain to hear her words over the crackling of the ring of fire.

"You're my kind of knight. You take your beliefs seriously, and you respect your orders, but they do not bind you. You follow your own heart, and you do what you think is right—not what others say is right."

He reached out and caressed her cheek, turning her chin so that she would look at him with those sparkling emerald eyes.

"A knight serves good over all else, right? That's just what you do."

Sallah reached up and took his hand, then leaned in and nuzzled against his neck. He held her close.

"I would never do anything to hurt Esprë," she said in a whisper. "I won't tell a soul where she is or what happened to her."

"I know," Kandler said. "I just needed to hear you say it."

Toward midday, Burch and Monja emerged from the hold and prepared a simple meal for the others. They brought the food up onto the bridge so they could all dine together. Even Xalt, who could not eat, joined them.

"Our stores going to hold out?" Kandler asked the shifter.

Burch nodded. "I wasn't too sure about it when we got to Argonnessen, but we're a few mouths shy going back. We should be fine."

With the reminder of the fates of Esprë and Te'oma, a silence fell over the meal. After a while, Xalt spoke up.

"So," the agitated warforged said, "what is the plan from here?"

When Kandler noticed everyone looking at him, he managed a wry smile. "I don't know. I never planned on surviving this long."

"I need to return to Thrane," Sallah said, looking like something bitter had found its way into her mouth. "I must report in."

Burch nodded. "I don't know about you, boss, but I don't see much point in going back to Mardakine."

Kandler rubbed his chin. "Not to stay there, for sure. I might want to collect some of the things we left behind and make a few proper good-byes."

"We did leave in a hurry." The shifter turned toward Monja. "Back to the plains for you? Seems like that would be our first stop."

The halfling smiled, her teeth shining white in her sun-browned face. "No hurries for me. Old Wodager will hold that shaman spot a few years more, I'm sure."

Monja held her face up toward the sun and grinned, her eyes sparkling.

"Xalt?" Kandler asked.

"Yes?" The warforged started a bit, surprised that someone would direct the conversation toward him.

"We could always drop you somewhere outside Construct."

Xalt gave the justicar a look so blank that Kandler could no longer stifle a chuckle. "Don't you worry," he said to the warforged. "You're a good and faithful friend. You have a spot by our side for as long as you want it—if you want it."

"Of course I do," Xalt said. As he spoke, he absently reached for his severed finger, which still hung from a lanyard around his neck.

"We can have the healers in Flamekeep help you with that," Sallah said.

The warforged's stolid face brightened. "Would they do that?"

"Not for just anybody," the lady knight said, "but once they hear the tale of how you lost it while saving several knights from an ignoble death, I'm sure I can prevail upon them to restore your hand to you in perfect health."

Xalt cradled the finger in his hand and stared at it with his unblinking obsidian eyes. "Thank you," he said. "I would like that very much."

"How about you?" Monja asked. "What do you plan to do with yourselves now?"

At first, Kandler didn't realize she was talking to Burch and him. When he did, he glanced at the shifter, who shrugged at him.

"What do you say?" Burch asked. "We've been spies, soldiers, and justicars. We spent two years in Mardakine, which has to be the longest I've been in one place since I was chewing on my mother's ankles."

"You're ready to move on?"

"Where to?"

Kandler craned his neck back and gazed up at the ring of fire burning and crackling within its restraining arcs. He reached out and put a hand on Sallah's.

"A quick visit to the Wandering Inn, then up over the Mournland to Mardakine. From there, on to Flamekeep—at least for a while."

Sallah's eyes glinted at that.

Burch's grin showed all his sharp, pointed teeth. "And from there?"

"Wherever the whims of the *Phoenix* take us."

While the others laughed in agreement, Kandler held up his index finger. "Before we do all that, though, there's one little stop we need to make first."

CHAPTER

63

Duro cursed his fate. To be caught by a pack of stinking elves was one thing, but the bastards hadn't deigned to grant him a hero's death. Instead of killing him and putting his head on a pike outside their foul fort's gates—where he could have spent many more months scaring cowards who came too close—they'd beaten him senseless and tossed him in this awful cell, where he'd spent the past few weeks.

His captors had interrogated him here atop the tower for days on end, torturing him with devices both painful and cruel. He had refused to break for them under any sort of punishment. All that they had learned from him had been a series of new curses he'd concocted on the spot.

When the interrogators pushed him past his limits, they left him alone to heal for a few days. As soon as he had seemed ready, they came at him again, striving to break down his irony resolve.

This last time, though, they'd given up on him. The morning after the torturers left, the fort's commander came to announce that his execution would be in three days' time.

"Why three days?" Duro asked.

The commander looked down on him. "Think on your doom for three days. Perhaps it will loosen your tongue. If not, we will waste no more time with you."

The evening before he was to be executed for his crimes, Duro peered out one of the barred windows in his high cell and watched the sun set for what he believed would be the last time. Having spent much of his life without seeing a sunset, he cherished each one he witnessed, a spectacular example of the beauty and wonder of the world in which he lived. It also served to remind him that Eberron was a large world and that he had only seen a small fraction of it. As the sun sank to the horizon, he wondered what lands it would warm next.

Most nights, Duro vowed that he would one day explore those distant locales, and the sense of possible and inevitable adventure always gave him vivid dreams. Tonight, though, watching the sunset saddened him instead. He knew he would never see another.

As Duro sat there on his cell's floor—fashioned from wood rather than stone—his forehead resting on his arms, he heard the crackling of a large fire. He wondered if the elves had decided to get an early start on the bonfire meant to kill him or if they'd just built such a blaze to celebrate the eve of his death.

He refused to get up and peer through the window to find out. The damned noise kept getting louder and louder, though, which made it hard for Duro to ignore it. He pushed his head farther into his arms until his biceps covered his ears, and that seemed to work.

Then something clanged against the window above him.

"Get back!" someone yelled. "Get away from the window!"

Duro scrambled away from the window and put his back

to the door. Staring at the window, he saw the grappling hook attached to the bars. It dangled there with its hooks wrapped around a pair of the bars.

"Go!" someone shouted. With a mighty crack, the entire window yanked away at the end of the hook, along with a good chunk of the cell's outer wall.

Duro stood up and shaded his eyes with his hand. He saw a ring of fire crackling away from him into the dusk, then backing up and heading straight for him again. He watched it open-mouthed, too stunned to consider fleeing or—given that he had no way to flee—calling for help.

Then the ring narrowed and turned into a vertical line.

Down in the fort below, Duro heard an alarm. Soldiers shouted, and bells rang out in the gathering darkness.

The *Phoenix* drew close enough that Duro could make out four figures standing at the gunwale. From their silhouettes, he knew them. Kandler, Burch, Sallah, and Xalt.

The dwarf whooped with joy and ran toward the splinter-edged hole that had once been his cell wall. As he did, a gangplank stabbed out from the airship. The end of it slid toward him and came to a rest on the edge of the cell's floor.

"Move it!" Burch shouted. As the shifter spoke, a ball of flaming pitch went sailing over the airship's bow. "They'll find the range soon!"

Duro charged straight up the gangplank, willing himself to not look down. If he had, he knew the hundred foot drop would have made him woozy, and this was no place to lose your footing.

When the dwarf reached the airship's deck, Kandler and Sallah grabbed him and dragged him the last few feet. As the pair deposited him on the deck, Xalt shouted, "He's aboard!"

Duro glimpsed Monja standing at—or rather on—the ship's wheel. The ship took off so fast that Duro tumbled to the deck. Had Kandler not been there to steady him, he might have gone cartwheeling out over the rail.

The dwarf sat there awestruck on the airship's deck as the *Phoenix* raced off in the direction of the dying glow of the setting sun. "Gods above and below," he said. "I'd given up hope. I'd have laid odds I had a better chance with the executioner than you lot did in Argonnessen."

"Surprised?" Burch said with a toothy grin.

"That's a paltry word," Duro said.

"Did you think we would leave you behind?" asked Xalt. The warforged's curiosity seemed genuine.

Duro laughed. "The thought crossed my mind."

Sallah put out a hand and helped the dwarf to his feet. "Honorable people don't leave friends behind," she said.

"So I've been with you the past few weeks then? I hadn't noticed." The lack of bitterness in Duro's voice surprised even himself. He was too happy to be free to consider recriminations.

Kandler clapped the dwarf on the back and joined him in a celebratory roar. "Like rivers to the sea," the justicar said. "We might run our separate courses for a while, but we always meet again in the end."

Glossary

Aerenal: An island nation off the southeastern coast of Khorvaire. Aerenal is known as the homeland of the elves.

Aerie: A fort in eastern Valenar near the border of Q'barra.

Argonnessen: A large continent to the southeast of Eberron, said to be the home of dragons.

Arthawn Keep: A battered keep situated in the southeastern part of Thrane, where the nation's borders meet with those of Breland and the Mournland.

Bastard: A warforged lieutenant of the Lord of Blades and commander of Construct.

Blade Desert: A barren landscape at the western foot of the Endworld and Ironroot Mountains that form the eastern border of the Talenta Plains.

Blood of Vol: Those who worship the Blood of Vol refuse to bow to the power of death. Drawn from the traditions of an ancient line of elven necromancers, the Blood of Vol seeks to abolish death. They revere vampires and other undead creatures as champions in this struggle. This tradition is especially strong in the nation of Karrnath, and while it is not inherently evil, there are subsects—notably the infamous Order of the Emerald Claw—that have turned the battle against death into a struggle to dominate the living. As a result, throughout most of the Five Nations the common image of a follower of the Blood is that of a crazed necromancer leading an army of zombies as part of some mad scheme. The Church of the Silver Flame takes a particularly hard stand against followers of the Blood, and knights of the Flame may assume the worst when dealing with acolytes of Vol.

bloodwing: A fibrous, living symbiont, possessed of its own intelligence, which can sometimes bond to another creature. When dormant, the bloodwing's fibrous body shrinks to a very small size, but when aroused, the creature expands to large batlike wings, enabling its host the power of flight.

Breland: The largest of the original Five Nations of Galifar, Breland is a center of heavy industry. The current ruler of Breland is King Boranel ir'Wyrnarn.

Brendis: A young Knight of the Silver Flame.

Burch: A shifter and deputy justicar of Mardakine.

Captain of Bones: Commander of Fort Bones, currently Berre Stonefist.

changeling: Members of the changeling race possess a limited ability to change face and form, allowing a changeling to disguise itself as a member of another race or to impersonate an individual. Changelings are said to be the offspring of humans and doppelgangers. They are relatively few in number and have no lands or culture of their own but are scattered across Khorvaire.

cold fire: Magical flame that produces no heat and does not burn. Cold fire is used to provide light in most cities of Khorvaire.

Construct: A mobile city of the warforged in the Mournland.

Council of Cardinals: Along with the Keeper of the Flame, the ruling council of the Church of the Silver Flame.

Cyre: One of the original Five Nations of Galifar, known for its fine arts and crafts. The governor of Cyre was traditionally raised to the throne of Galifar, but in 894 YK, Kaius of Karrnath, Wroann of Breland, and Thalin of Thrane rebelled against Mishann of Cyre. During the war, Cyre lost significant amounts of territory to elf and goblin mercenaries, creating the nations of Valenar and Darguun. In 994 YK, Cyre was devastated by a disaster of unknown origin that transformed the nation into a hostile wasteland populated by deadly monsters. Breland offered sanctuary to the survivors of the Mourning, and most of the Cyran refugees have taken advantage of this amnesty.

Dagger River: One of the largest rivers in Khorvaire, the Dagger runs south through Breland and into the Thunder Sea.

Darumnakt, Duro: A dwarf of Clan Drakyager of the Mror Holds, leader of the patrols through Mount Darumkrak.

Day of Mourning, the: A disaster that occurred on Olarune 20, 994 YK. The origin and precise nature of the Mourning are unknown. On Ollarune 20, gray mists spread across Cyre, and anything caught within the mists was transformed or destroyed. See the Mournland.

Deothen: A senior Knight of the Silver Flame.

Dolurrh: The plane of the dead. When mortals die, their spirits are said to travel to Dolurrh and then slowly fade away, passing to whatever final fate awaits the dead.

dragonmark: 1) A mystical mark that appears on the surface of the skin and grants mystical powers to its bearer. 2) A slang term for the bearer of a dragonmark.

Dragonmarked Houses: One of the thirteen families whose bloodlines carry the potential to manifest a dragonmark. Many of the dragonmarked houses existed before the kingdom of Galifar, and they have used their mystical powers to gain considerable political and economic influence.

Dragonreach: The open sea that stretches between Khorvaire and Argonnessen.

Drakyager: A clan of dwarves who once lived under Mount Darumkrak in the Mror Holds.

Durviska: A dwarf settlement built into the northern wall of the Goradra Gap. The word means "overlook" in Dwarven.

Eberron: 1) The world. 2) A mythical dragon said to have formed the world from her body in primordial times and to have given birth to natural life. Also known as "The Dragon Between."

Emerald Claw, Order of: A knightly order founded in Karrnath to serve the interests of the nation. Vol has since subverted it to her cause, twisting it into a secret terrorist organization outlawed in Karrnath.

Endworld Mountains: A large chain of mountains that separates the southeastern Talenta Plains from the land of Q'barra.

Esprë: Kandler's elven step-daughter.

Esprina: Kandler's elven wife, now deceased.

everbright lantern: A lantern infused with cold fire, creating a permanent light source. These items are used to provide illumination in most of the cities and larger communities of Khorvaire. An everbright lantern usually has a shutter allowing the light to be sealed off when darkness is desirable.

Five Nations: The five provinces of the Kingdom of Galifar: Aundair, Breland, Cyre, Karrnath, and Thrane.

Flamekeep: The capital of Thrane.

Flying Leap: A dwarf tavern located in Durviska, noted for its airship pier and its stunning views of the Goradra Gap, over which it hangs.

'forged: A slang term for the warforged.

Fort Bones: A Karrnathi outpost that guards the border between Karrnath and the Talenta Plains. It is manned primarily by human and dwarf mercenaries, bolstered by a large force of almost one hundred Karrnathi skeletons.

Frekkainta: A red dragon who rules over a portion of Argonnessen.

Frostmantle: A dwarf city in the Mror Holds, located below the southern end of Mirror Lake.

glidewing: A large, birdlike reptile with a long, toothy beak, a thin headcrest, sharp talons, and small claws at the joints of its leathery wings. It is often used as a mount by Talenta Plains halflings. (A pterosaur.)

Goradra Gap: The largest and deepest canyon in all of Khorvaire, situated in the Ironroot Mountains of the Mror Holds. It's said that the bottom of the canyon reaches directly into Khyber itself.

Great Barrier: A chain of mountains that stretches across the northwestern shore of Argonnessen, overlooking Totem Beach. These separate Argonnessen from Seren and the Dragonreach beyond.

Gref: A village on the western shore of Seren Island. The people here worship Greffykor, and their Shroud of Scales is called Zanga.

Greffykor: A silver dragon who lives and works in an observatory that towers over the southwestern end of the Great Barrier.

Gweir: A young Knight of the Silver Flame.

Halpum: Lathon (high chief) of one of the largest nomadic tribes of the Talenta Plains halflings.

House Cannith: The Dragonmarked House that carries the Mark of Making. The artificers and magewrights of House Cannith are responsible for most of the magical innovations of the past millennia. The house made tremendous profits during the Last War through sales of arms and armor, including warforged soldiers.

Ibrido: A lieutenant of the Captain of Bones.

Ikar the Black: The leader of a band of outlaws who often venture into the Mournland in search of treasure and artifacts.

Illmarrow Castle: Home of Vol on the island of Farlnen.

Ironroot Mountains: The large mountain chain that makes up the western border of the Mror Holds.

Jaela Daran: The young Keeper of the Flame, head of the Church of the Silver Flame.

justicar: An official chosen to enforce the law and keep the peace. Justicars have little legal authority beyond their local jurisdiction.

Kaius III: King of Karrnath.

Kandler: Justicar of Mardakine.

Karaktrok, Medd: A slow-witted dwarf of Clan Drakyager of the Mror Holds, who works under Duro Darumnakt.

Karrnath: One of the original Five Nations of Galifar. Karrnath is a cold, grim land whose people are renowned for their martial prowess. The current ruler of Karrnath is King Kaius ir'Wyrnarn III.

Keeper of the Flame, the: The head of the Church of the Silver Flame.

Keeper's Claw: A Karrnathi airship currently stationed at Fort Bones.

Khorvaire: One of the continents of Eberron, home of the Five Nations of Galifar as well as many other regions.

Khyber: 1) The underworld. 2) A mythical dragon, also known as "The Dragon Below." After killing Siberys, Khyber was imprisoned by Eberron and transformed into the underworld. Khyber is said to have given birth to a host of demons and other unnatural creatures. See *Eberron, Siberys*.

Krezent: An ancient ruin in the Talenta Plains. It is home to a tribe of benevolent yuan-ti who revere the Silver Flame.

Last War, The: This conflict began in 894 YK with the death of King Jarot ir'Wyrnarn, the last king of Galifar. Following Jarot's death, three of his five children refused to follow the ancient traditions of succession, and the kingdom split. The war lasted over a hundred years, and it took the utter destruction of Cyre to bring the other nations to the negotiating table. No one has admitted defeat, but no one wants to risk being the next victim of the Mourning. The chronicles are calling the conflict "the Last War," hoping that the bloodshed might have finally slaked humanity's thirst for battle. Only time will tell if this hope is in vain.

lath: The tribal chief among Talenta Plains halflings.

lathon: The "chief of chiefs," i.e., a leader of several tribes among the Talenta Plains halflings.

Ledenstrae: An elf from Aerenal. Esprë's father.

Levritt: A young Knight of the Silver Flame.

lightning rail: A means of transportation by which a coach propelled by an air elemental travels along a rail system of conductor stones, which hold the craft aloft.

Lord of Blades: A warforged leader reputed to be gathering a substantial following of other warforged somewhere in the Mournland.

Lost Mark: Common term for the Mark of Death.

Majeeda: An ancient elf wizard.

Mardakine: A small settlement on the border between Breland and the Mournland.

Mondaro: A changeling lover of Te'oma who fathered her child.

Monja: Halfling shaman of the Talenta Plains, daughter of Lathon Halpum.

Mount Darumkrak: A large peak in the Ironroot Mountains.

Mournland, The: A common name for the wasteland left behind in the wake of *the Mourning*. A wall of dead-gray mist surrounds the borders of the land that once was Cyre. Behind this mist, the land has been transformed into something dark and twisted. Most creatures that weren't killed were transformed into horrific monsters. Stories speak of storms of blood, corpses that do not decompose, ghostly soldiers fighting endless battles, and far worse things.

Mror Holds: A nation of dwarves and gnomes located in the Ironroot Mountains.

Mrothdalt, Krangel: A dwarf of Clan Nroth who runs the Flying Leap.

Nithkorrh: A black dragon.

Norra: A resident of Mardakine and friend of Kandler. She often watches Esprë when Kandler is out.

Olladra: One of the Sovereign Host, goddess of feast and fortune, bringer of luck and joy.

Phoenix: The name given to the airship that once belonged to Majeeda.

Pitchwall: A small settlement on the southwestern shore of Q'barra.

Port Krez: The capital city of the island of Krag, the seat of the Cloudreavers of the Lhazaar Principalities.

Puakel: Karrnathi soldier at Fort Bones.

Pylas Talaear: A city located on the northwestern shore of Aerenal. Most of the shipping traffic that comes from Khorvaire to Aerenal puts in here.

Q'barra: A young nation hidden within the jungles of southeastern Khorvaire.

Sallah: A Knight of the Silver Flame.

Seren Island: A barrier island off the northwest coast of Aerenal. The people who live here worship the nearby dragons as gods and are known as the Seren.

Shae Cairdal: The capital and largest city of Aerenal.

Sharn: Also known as the City of Towers, Sharn is the largest city in Khorvaire.

Shawda: The mother of Norra, Esprë's best friend in Mardakine. Also the last person to die mysteriously before Te'oma and Tan Du kidnapped Esprë.

shifter: A humanoid race said to be descended from humans and lycanthropes. Shifters have a feral, bestial appearance and can briefly call on their lycanthropic heritage to draw animalistic characteristics to the fore. While they are most comfortable in natural environs, shifters can be found in most of the major cities of Khorvaire.

shockbolt: Magical crossbow bolts that explode on contact.

Shroud of Scales: A magic shroud composed of dragon scales. Also, a Seren shaman who wears such a shroud.

Siberys: 1) The ring of stones that circle the world. 2) A mythical dragon, also called "The Dragon Above." Siberys is said to have been destroyed by Khyber. Some believe that the ring of Siberys is the source of all magic.

Silver Flame, the: A powerful spiritual force dedicated to cleaning evil influences from the world. Over the last five hundred years, a powerful church has been established around the Silver Flame.

soarwing: Large, flying lizards.

Sovereign: 1) A silver coin depicting a current or recent monarch. A sovereign is worth ten crowns. 2) One of the deities of the Sovereign Host.

Sovereign Host, the: A pantheistic religion with a strong following across Khorvaire.

stirge: A tiny, batwinged monster with a long proboscis, through which it feeds on the blood of living creatures.

Taer Shantara: A fort in Valenar.

Taer Valaestas: The capital and largest city of Valenar.

Talenta Plains: A vast stretch of grassland to the east of Khorvaire, the Talenta Plains are home to a proud halfling culture. The people of the Talenta Plains live a nomadic lifestyle that has remained more or less unchanged for thousands of years, though over the centuries a number of tribes have left the grasslands to settle in the Five Nations. A wide variety of large reptiles are found in the Talenta Plains, and the halfling warriors are known for their fearsome clawfoot mounts.

Tan Du: A vampire.

Te'oma: A changeling.

Thrane: One of the original Five Nations of Galifar, Thrane is the seat of power for the Church of the Silver Flame. During the Last War, the people of Thrane chose to give the church power above that of the throne. Queen Diani ir'Wynarn serves as a figurehead, but true power rests in the hands of the Church, which is governed by the council of cardinals and Jaela Daeran, the young Keeper of the Flame.

threehorn: A large herbivorous lizard of the Talenta Plains. (A triceratops.)

Thunder Sea: The large sea separating Khorvaire from the continent of Xen'drik.

Totem Beach: A long stretch of sandy beach along Argonnessen's northwestern shore. The Seren sail here to pay homage to their dragon-gods.

Treaty of Thronehold: The treaty that ended the Last War.

tribex: A large breed of wild animal that resembles a bison. These bear a trio of ribbed and edged horns that sweep back from the top of its head. Tribexes can vary in color, but they are usually dark brown on top and light brown on the bottom, separated by a strip of sky blue.

Undying Court: The council of deathless elders that advises and empowers the rulers of Aerenal.

Valenar: A realm of southeastern Khorvaire populated primarily by elves who came to Khorvaire to fight in the Last War and later founded their own nation.

Vol: The Lich Queen, founder of the Blood of Vol.

Wandering Inn: A traveling fair run by House Ghallanda that moves throughout the Talenta Plains. It provides a place for rest and trade for the tribes and other travelers that range far from Gatherhold.

warforged: A race of humanoid constructs crafted from wood, leather, metal, and stone, and given life and sentience through magic. The warforged were created by House Cannith, which sought to produce tireless, expendable soldiers capable of adapting to any tactical situation. Cannith developed a wide range of military automatons, but the spark of true sentience eluded them until 965 YK, when *Aaren d'Cannith* perfected the first of the modern warforged. A warforged soldier is roughly the same shape as an adult male human, though typically slightly taller and heavier. There are many different styles of warforged, each crafted for a specific military function: heavily-armored infantry troops, faster scouts and skirmishers, and many more. While warforged are brought into existence with the knowledge required to fulfill their function, they have the capacity to learn, and with the war coming to a close, many are searching their souls: and questioning whether they have souls: and wondering what place they might have in a world at peace.

Wodager: The halfling shaman who trained Monja.

Xalt: A warforged artificer.

yuan-ti: One of the minor races of Eberron, yuan-ti are descended from humans who mingled their bloodlines with serpentine creatures.

Zanga: The Shroud of Scales who watches over the village of Gref on the island of Seren.

Zilspar: A Brelish town that lies to the east of Sharn, near the shore of the Thunder Sea.